Kathryn started her working life as a retail pharmacist but soon realised trying to decipher doctors' handwriting wasn't for her. In 2011, backed by her family, she left the world of pharmaceutical science to begin life as a self-employed writer.

She lives with two teenage boys and a husband who asks every Valentine's Day whether he has to bother buying a card again this year (yes, he does) so the romance in her life is all in her head.

@KathrynFreeman1
@kathrynfreeman
kathrynfreeman.co.uk

The New Guy

Kathryn Freeman

One More Chapter
a division of HarperCollins*Publishers*
The News Building
1 London Bridge Street
London SE1 9GF

www.harpercollins.co.uk

This paperback edition 2020

First published in Great Britain in ebook format by
HarperCollins*Publishers* 2020

A catalogue record for this book
is available from the British Library

ISBN: 978-0-00-836582-0

Set in Birka by Palimpsest Book Production Ltd, Falkirk
Stirlingshire

Printed and bound in Great Britain by
CPI Group (UK) Ltd, Croydon CR0 4YY

PART ONE

A Chance Meeting

Chapter 1

Sitting alone at the bar in her local pub wasn't how she wanted to spend the evening. Only a few hours ago, Sam had been with her family in Cornwall, saying goodbye to her grandad. And by saying goodbye she meant watching, tears streaming down her face, as his coffin slid behind a heavy velvet curtain.

She wanted to be back in Cornwall now, celebrating his life with her slowly-turning-hippy parents, her beautiful, slightly crazy sisters and her raucous but salt of the earth brothers. Drinking too much and laughing too loud, because when you'd lost the head of the family, the linchpin, the man they'd all turned to for advice at some point in their lives, what else was there to do?

Full of misery, she downed the rest of her glass. She could at least drink. And while she was drinking, the dark, brooding guy who'd eased onto the stool to her right was a welcome distraction. Catching the barman's eye, she smiled and signalled for another glass of champagne.

'I'm celebrating.' Sam turned to find brooding guy's dark brown eyes looking at her; wary, a little irritated. Surprisingly magnetic. When she realised he wasn't going to say anything, she laughed. Sober Sam would have been embarrassed, but two glasses of fizz had given her a buzz. 'Celebrating isn't the right word, but Grumps would appreciate the sentiment.'

Brooding guy kept his eyes fixed on hers. *Come on*, she willed him. *I've given you a neat opening.*

He turned his attention back to the half-drunk pint in front of him. 'Enjoy.'

Enjoy? Had she lost her touch? She wasn't a woman whom men tripped over themselves to talk to; her hair was too red, skin too pale, eyes abnormally large and her mouth too big. All on top of a body that might have the height of a model but had the size of someone who enjoyed her food. Still, she was a woman most people, male or female, responded to. Charisma, her parents called it, but they were hardly unbiased. She preferred empathetic. Sensitive and perceptive worked, too. Actually no, scratch that last one. Perceptive implied an ability to assess, to judge a person's character. History confirmed she was lousy at that.

'Not interested in who Grumps is?' Again, sober Sam wouldn't have pushed, but tipsy Sam was determined to prove she still had the knack of getting others to talk.

They guy's eyes flicked back to her and he gave her a dark look, annoyance radiating off him. 'A weird dwarf?'

She blinked, then burst out laughing. 'Grumpy, Snow White, I see where you're coming from.'

He gave her a brief, false smile – if she read it correctly, it said *bugger off and leave me alone.* Then he hunched back over his pint.

With a sigh, Sam took a gulp from her freshly filled champagne. It tasted sour now, the bubbles too joyful. Against her will her mind circled back to the last week, and the sorrow of sitting uselessly by her grandad's side as she watched him bravely lose his battle against cancer.

Oh, sod it. She wasn't going to wallow. 'Grumps was my grandad.' She didn't care if the guy next to her didn't want to listen. She was going to talk. 'He died a few days ago and it's gutting to think I won't get to talk to him again. We cremated him this morning.' Shamefully she realised she hadn't even changed from her funeral suit. Too desperate to escape the four walls of her flat. 'I want to be drowning my sorrows with my family right now, but I had to come back.' She shrugged, aware of his dark eyes on her. 'Work, you know? So here I am, drinking to celebrate his life, because it's what he'd have wanted. I seem to be doing a lousy job of it though.' Her voice wobbled and she paused to take a breath. No more tears. 'I know you're dying to ask but are too shy, so I'll tell you. When I was little I couldn't say Gramps, which was what my brothers and sisters called him. I'd say Grumps. I kept the nickname because I loved the irony. He was the least grumpy man I've ever met. And I've met a few.' Her eyes flicked towards him.

He glowered. 'What?'

She smiled sweetly. 'Nothing.'

He grunted and turned away again, swivelling the pint glass round and round in his hands. Elegant, she realised with surprise. She'd expected hands that fitted his face. Hard, blunt. Not that he wasn't good-looking, but his attraction was more that of the boxer than the artist. A nose that she'd like to bet had been broken and not set properly. A square, stubborn jaw. Very short brown hair, cut in a way that was more about practicality than style. Deep, dark eyes that were the focus of his face. Lips that could have been described as sensitive but seemed permanently turned down in a scowl.

'So, what's your story?'

Another glare from his expressive eyes. 'No story.'

'Come on, give me something. Doesn't even have to be the truth. Just talk to me for a while. Take my mind off losing my grandad.'

'Jeeze,' he muttered. 'No offence but piss off and find someone else. Talking isn't my thing.'

Though the words were harsh, alcohol had dulled her sensitivity. Besides, his expression was more resigned than angry. Noticing his eyes still on her, she made an exaggerated scan of the pub. 'Shame, I can't see anyone else sitting by themselves. You'll have to do. And anyway, talking is good for the soul. You'd be amazed how therapeutic it can be, even if it's with a stranger.' When she once again failed to get a reply, she waved a hand towards his face. 'Do you box? Your nose looks kind of crooked.'

Other than an almost imperceptible shake of the head, which could have been an answer, but could equally have signalled that he thought she was nuts, he remained silent.

'It's still a good nose,' she added. 'I was just making conversation. You said talking wasn't your thing, so I thought you'd find it easier if I asked questions and you answered them.'

'Frigging unbelievable.' He shook his head more forcefully this time, but there was no heat to his words.

'So, do you? Box, I mean?'

'No.'

'How did you break it, then?'

He exhaled, the sound bursting with frustration. 'Lady, you don't need to be in a ring to fight.'

'Ah, got it. Somebody punched you. What had you done?' The sharp look he gave her was loaded with warning. 'Okay, touchy subject.' She indicated his now empty pint. 'Let me buy you a drink while I think of another question.' Signalling again to the barman, she fought to hide her smile. She was actually starting to enjoy this game, teasing snippets of conversation from a moody, attractive stranger.

It wasn't how he'd wanted to spend his evening. The pub was okay, if you liked the posh gastropub type. Ryan was more of a traditionalist, but the beer was good. Bloody expensive, but good. Guess he'd have to get used to London prices now he'd moved here. Just as he'd have to get used to the shithole of a flat he'd come to the pub to escape from.

It wasn't all doom and gloom, mind. Some fancy lady was now buying him a pint. Not bad-looking either, he thought as he watched her giving her order to the barman. He was a fan of big blue eyes and high cheekbones, wasn't sure about pale skin and red hair but it looked good on her. He even dug her sexy wide mouth, though she could do with keeping it shut more. She was clearly one of those chatty, life-is-full-of-rainbows-and-unicorns types. The ones who believed all the world's problems could be solved by people being nice to each other. They really did his head in. Life was hard and people were gits. Accept it and get on with it.

Who the hell drank champagne in a pub anyway – and to celebrate the life of a man called *Grumps*?

Still, he wasn't going to turn down a free pint at these prices, no matter who bought it.

'Thanks,' he said when the warm, slightly too frothy pint was put in front of him. As she'd bought it for him, he could at least be civil. 'Cheers.' He nodded to the full glass of champagne she was being handed by the barman. 'Still celebrating?'

Her eyes, already too big for her face, widened a fraction before she twigged. 'I think I'm more drowning my sorrows now. Do you have a grandad you're close to?'

'No.'

'That's a shame.' Undeterred by his monosyllabic answer, she gave him a bright smile. 'Grandads are really special. When all the world is rushing, they always have time for you.'

Slowly her cheery smile faded. Bizarrely, Ryan found he missed it. Sure, she irritated him. He'd come to the pub to escape his shitty four walls. Not to become embroiled in polite conversation – something he was pathetically poor at. But now she'd gone quiet, her spark dimmed, and he had this weird compulsion to see it back again. 'You want to talk about him?' Her eyes widened. Christ, they were amazing. He'd never seen the like. Blue pools big enough to dive into. Now her smile was back, her eyes sort of ... shone, he guessed, was the word.

'You mean that? You'd seriously listen if I told you all the Grumps anecdotes burning through my brain right now?'

Shit, maybe this was a bad idea. Then again, it wasn't like his other options – staring at his pint, or at his crappy four walls – were thrilling alternatives. 'Two. I'll listen to two stories.'

Her smile racked up another watt, those eyes sucking him further in. 'Ten.'

He blanched. 'Give me a break. Four.'

She held out her hand. 'Let's shake on five.'

Before he knew what was happening, he was holding her hand. Okay, he was shaking it, but the jolt of unexpected desire that shot through him at the contact made it feel just as intimate. The way her eyes darkened and her smile froze told him she'd experienced it too.

He dragged his hand away, aware that suddenly everything between them felt different. For the first time that night he noticed what she was wearing: a fancy dark suit – had she come straight from the funeral? Noticed too the subtle, yet he'd like to bet stupidly expensive, perfume she wore. And the hint of cleavage revealed by her white silk blouse. No longer was she a random stranger sitting on a bar stool. Now she was a warm, vibrant, sexy woman. All those ditzy rainbows and unicorns aside.

Clearing his throat, he nodded at her to start. 'You've got ten minutes.'

'What? We didn't agree a time limit.'

He smirked, glad to feel his control returning. 'So, I play dirty.' He glanced at his watch. 'Nine minutes, thirty seconds.'

She looked like she didn't know whether to laugh or throttle him. Then she took a sip of her drink, rolled those ginormous eyes and began to talk.

Did he listen to a word she was saying? Nah, of course he didn't. He'd asked because she'd looked like she wanted to talk, not because he was interested in some dead old guy he'd never met. With a ridiculous nickname. Although while he wasn't listening to the words, he did enjoy the sound of her voice. Almost as much as he enjoyed watching her talk. The expressive face, the self-mocking laughter, the seemingly random movement of her hands which appeared to 'talk' almost as much as she did. Yeah, watching her was as good a way as any to spend the evening.

Except maybe *touching* her.

He lunged for his forgotten pint and took a deep swig. Did he have the guts to chat her up? It wasn't his usual MO. Not being good with words, he tended to wait for women to come on to him, though it meant he attracted a certain type. Classy, champagne-swigging ladies were a serious upgrade.

Chapter 2

Sam was on a roll. Halfway through her fourth anecdote about her grandad and the words were flying, her misery temporarily forgotten. Somehow this taciturn stranger had realised exactly what she'd needed. Sam knew the guy wasn't listening, but it didn't matter. Only that he was pretending to be interested, so she didn't look like a total nutter, sitting here talking to herself.

'Three more minutes.' His gruff voice sliced through her flow.

'You're actually timing me?'

'A deal's a deal.'

She wanted to argue, press her point that she'd not agreed to a time limit, but it would cut into the precious minutes. 'Fine. Last one. Grumps was the one who told me I could do whatever I put my mind to. He's the reason I took a business degree.'

His eyes swept her face, assessing her. 'He is, huh? Well, good old Grumps.'

Amusement glittered in the dark eyes that stared back at her, and the flutter she'd felt when he'd clasped her hand returned with a vengeance, sending a rush of desire surging through her. Raw, primal, it was unlike anything she'd felt before. She was used to the slow burn. A building attraction that morphed into desire over time, once she'd got to know someone. Friends to lovers. And then to enemies, she remembered bitterly, before shaking away the thought.

She'd never be friends with this stranger. He was too dour, too surly, but heaven help her, she fancied him. Clearly champagne had lowered her threshold for finding men attractive. Either that or her libido, after being thoroughly decimated eighteen months ago, was starting to pull itself together.

The guy continued to stare, his amusement fading. 'I don't care what degree you did.'

'Right, okay. Of course you don't.' The heat from his eyes was making her skin prick.

'Don't care what your name is, either,' he added roughly.

'Fine.' The dismissive tone was at odds with the intense expression on his face. She started to turn away, confused by his mixed messages and her acute reaction to him, when he cleared his throat, his lips curving in a half smile.

'All I care about is whether your bedroom is less of a shithole than mine.'

Shocked, she almost fell off the stool. As her heart bounced against her ribs, she grabbed hold of the bar. 'Pardon?'

His mouth opened, as if he was about to reply, then slammed shut again. God, what was wrong with her that, despite his crude statement, she wanted to feel those lips on her skin?

Suddenly he grabbed at his beer and swallowed the rest down in one, long, gulp. 'Forget it. It's been fun, Champagne Lady, but I'm off.'

'That's it?' Disappointment crashed through her, making her blurt the next words without thinking. 'What about my bedroom?'

His cheeks reddened. 'Dumb move.' He shifted off the stool, his movements tight and jerky. 'Blame the beer.'

She could blame the champagne for what she was about to say, but Sam knew that would be a lie. The alcohol only made it easier to be brave. 'So, you're not interested in how my bedroom stacks on the shithole scale?'

His eyes flashed. 'Piss off.'

He snatched at the brown leather jacket draped over the back of the stool. Sam had a brief sense of height and bulk – hard, muscular bulk – before he turned and headed for the exit.

She should leave it at that. He was embarrassed and she'd compounded it by making it appear like she was teasing him, when actually she'd been trying to come on to him. Looks like they were both useless when it came to the art of propositioning.

Yet her eyes wouldn't stray from his broad shoulders as he cut his way through the now heaving pub.

What would Grumps have said? *Life is for living, Sam. One day you'll wake up and be as old as me.*

Making a snap decision she jumped down from the stool. One night. It's all she wanted. A night when she could remember what it felt like to be a sexually attractive woman.

'Wait!'

She caught up with him as he was about to cross the road outside the pub. Her breath caught as he halted and slowly turned to face her. He'd shrugged on his jacket and jammed his hands into the pockets, a scowl still on his face. At five foot ten, it wasn't often Sam came across men who made her feel small. Not that this guy was excessively tall – she'd put him at six-two, maybe three. Yet the shoulders that strained against the leather of the jacket, the broken nose and the whole brooding thing he had going on, gave him a dangerous vibe. He looked big and mean. Intimidating. A bull, facing down the matador.

'What?'

Maybe this was a bad idea. Inviting this guy to her place was pure insanity. *But he pretended to listen while you talked about your grandad.*

'You planning on saying anything?'

He quirked a brow and she was relieved to see he seemed more irritated than angry now.

'Sorry.' She waved her hands about uselessly. 'I think somehow I've offended you and I wanted you to know that it wasn't my intention.'

'You haven't.' His eyes drifted over her shoulder, the muscle in his jaw twitching.

'Then why did you run away?'

'Jesus.' He inhaled slowly, then let it out in a hiss. 'I tried a clumsy come-on, you shot me down. No big deal.'

'I didn't.' When no reply came, she elaborated. 'I said pardon, not no.'

'Right.' The muscle jumped again. 'And is pardon code for yes now?'

'Pardon means—'

'I know what it means.' He drew in another sharp breath. 'You surely didn't need me to repeat what I'd just said. It was fucking embarrassing enough the first time.'

'You're right, I didn't.' It was her turn for the deep breath. Come on, Sam, this isn't hard. Take the jump. Live a little. 'I said it to cover my surprise. Given longer to think, what I'd have actually asked is: do you want to come back with me because you hate your place? Or because you want me?'

The simmering anger faded. 'Look, lady, I want to go back with you because you're hot.' He shrugged those impressive shoulders. 'I mean, you talk too much, so we won't be heading down the aisle, but you're seriously hot. The chance to get away from my shithole for a while is a bonus.'

His words incited a zing of excitement. 'You're not my type, either. Too quiet and you don't smile enough. But I find myself strangely attracted to you.'

'Yeah? Does that mean we're heading to yours?' When she nodded, he started to laugh. 'Well, lead the way, Champagne Lady.'

Ryan couldn't believe his luck. One minute he'd been going back to his dump with his tail between his legs, dragging his battered ego behind him. Next, he was walking down the road with an elegant lady, about to get laid. Not that his godawful chat-up line deserved such an outcome but hey, he wasn't about to complain. Either Champagne Lady was desperate – hard to imagine, looking like she did – or she fancied lowering her standards for the night. Lucky him.

Of course, there was a third option.

He glanced sideways at her. She was walking in a straight line, wasn't she? A moment later, as if to prove how biased his judgement was, she stumbled. He shot out a hand and grabbed at her arm.

'Thanks.' She darted him an embarrassed smile and pointed to her sexy high shoes. 'I don't usually go to the pub in a black suit. I should have changed. At least put on some flat shoes. No woman in their right mind decides to get drunk while wearing heels.'

Damn it. He lurched to a stop, which, as he was still clutching her arm, brought her to a halt too. 'Tell me you're not drunk.'

She nibbled on her bottom lip, sending bolts of lust surging through him. 'Umm, I'm not drunk?'

The wide-eyed look she gave him was cute, a mix of mischief and innocence, and he cursed under his breath. 'Look, you've been drinking so I need to know this isn't going to come back and bite me on the arse later.' He held her by the shoulders, staring down at her. 'Do you know what you're doing?'

'I thought we were going back to my place to screw like bunnies.' Her mouth curved in a sexy smile. 'That's a sentence I didn't think I'd ever say.'

Not unfocused, he decided. Her eyes were sexy as hell, but not unfocused. Still, his conscience pushed him. 'You're not going to wake up tomorrow morning with a bucketload of regrets? Cursing me for taking advantage?'

'I'm going to curse you for ruining the mood if you carry on like this.' She wasn't just getting annoyed now, he noted with alarm, she was becoming agitated.

Way to go, Ryan Black. First man in history to talk himself out of getting laid. His hands still on her shoulders, he looked past the eyes that had held him transfixed, and down to the rapid rise and fall of her chest. The enticing curve of her cleavage, peeping out of the V of her blouse. No way was he going to blow this. No bloody way. Dipping his head – with her heels on, he didn't have too far to bend – he kissed her.

She gasped, but he swallowed whatever she was going to say as he pressed his mouth more firmly, teasing her lips open with his tongue so he could dive into the heat of her. He groaned as he got his first taste. Champagne. And those bloody rainbows. Far sweeter than he'd thought, yet even more intoxicating. Desire ripped through him and he dropped a hand to her back, then lower, to the curve of her buttocks, pressing her against the part of him that ached and throbbed.

Mind fogged with lust, he continued to drive them both crazy right there, on the pavement, until a shrill wolf whistle and the unsubtle cry of 'get a room' broke his stride just enough for sanity to return. Breathing heavily, he eased back. 'How's your mood now?' he asked hoarsely.

Her lips, swollen from his kisses, broke into a grin. 'Back on track.'

'Good. Let's get to your place before I balls this up again.'

Dimly he noticed they were headed to the posh end of town. The opposite direction to the way he'd come. He'd had to get on a tube for a few stops in order to find a pub he was reasonably confident he wouldn't get stabbed in. Just when he was about to ask how much further – her heels looked hell to walk in – she turned off the high street and into a smart side road where a cluster of elegant Georgian town-houses surrounded a small green.

She halted outside the second house. 'I'm, umm, in this one.'

'Nice.'

'Yes.' He knew her nerves had reappeared when she wouldn't look him in the eye. 'You're not like an axe murderer or anything, are you?'

He made a play of opening his jacket and looking in the inside pocket. 'No axe today.'

Her smile looked strained. 'Sorry, you can probably tell, I'm not used to doing this.'

'Sex?'

It got the smile he'd hoped for. 'Sex I can manage. It's bringing a guy I don't know back to mine that's giving me the heebie-jeebies.'

Yet again, he felt the evening slipping away from him. 'If it helps, I'm no expert at this either.'

'You're not?'

He wasn't sure whether to be pleased or insulted at her obvious surprise. 'You couldn't tell from my smooth pick-up line?' Because he didn't want to dwell on that again, he added, 'We can always go back to mine, instead.' Though he shuddered at the thought.

'The shithole?'

'Yeah. Bed's comfy.' He'd made sure of it. Renting a furnished dive was bad enough. He wasn't going to sleep on a mattress that rats had partied on.

'No, we're good here.'

She shifted from foot to foot and he knew, despite her words, she was still debating. He reached into his jeans pocket and drew out his wallet. 'Would it help if I told you my name and address? Showed you some ID?'

'No.' She pushed his hand away, all that shiny red hair bouncing around her shoulders as she shook her head. 'I kind of like that we don't know each other.'

'You got a sex-with-a-stranger kink going on?' He didn't mind that. Didn't mind it at all.

'I don't think so. More *recovering from a shitty breakup and not ready to date but I miss sex.*'

Reassured, he clasped her hand. 'Then let's get you laid.'

She laughed softly. 'Not exactly Mr Romantic, are you?'

He watched as she opened the heavy black door and stepped into the hallway. 'Thought you wanted a one-night stand?'

She glanced up at him beneath her lashes. 'I do.'

Placing his hands beneath her buttocks he lifted her and marched them to the nearest wall. There he pushed her against it, settling his hips between her legs. His arousal against her core. 'Then who needs romance?' He asked roughly, before plundering her mouth.

Her legs – he had a flash of bunched skirt and long, shapely leg – wrapped around him, sending further jolts of heat through him. As he continued to kiss her, he pushed the jacket off her shoulders and started to undo the buttons of her blouse. Christ, if he wasn't careful, he wouldn't even get to her bedroom. Panting like a dog on heat, he drew back and let her legs slide slowly back to the ground. 'What floor are you on?'

'Third.' At least she looked and sounded as turned on as he did.

'Okay then.' Three flights of stairs. Nothing to a man who worked out like he did, yet right now it felt like he had to climb Everest.

But then he looked at her flushed cheeks, her glittering blue eyes. The rise and fall of a pair of glorious lace-covered breasts, now partly exposed by his wandering hands. Climbing Everest was a small price to pay for spending the night with this woman.

Chapter 3

The nerves that had been successfully wiped out by his kiss returned as Sam opened the front door to her flat. She was being rash, sure, but women did this all the time. She just had to trust her instinct.

Her stomach fluttered as the nerves bedded in. There'd been a time when she wouldn't have hesitated. A time when she'd known for sure she could judge a man's character.

'You okay?'

She turned to find her guest filling the doorway, his expression showing a hint of concern. Downstairs they'd been about to rip each other's clothes off. Now she was considering putting on the brakes, even though she'd already made the decision to let him in.

She sighed, hanging her jacket on the peg in the hallway. She didn't want it to be like this, all cautious and fearful. She wanted passion. A wild night when she could forget everything. And if the kiss downstairs was anything to go by, the pair of them had so much sexual chemistry, passion was as good as guaranteed. Providing she could get past these jitters.

He shifted on his feet. 'Look, maybe this was a bad idea.'

Oh no. She wasn't letting go of her plan that easily. She didn't do wussing out. Straightening her shoulders, she tugged his hand, pulling him inside. Then shut the door behind him with a deliberate shove.

The action caused him to raise an eyebrow. 'Or maybe it's not.'

'It's not.' She focused not on what she didn't know about him, but what she did. He'd made sure she wasn't drunk. He'd offered to show her his ID. Even now, he was giving her an out. They weren't the actions of a man she needed to be afraid of. 'Just tell me what we do now.' As the words played back to her, she started to laugh. 'I mean, I know we need to get naked at some point, but do you want a drink first?'

His mouth quirked. 'I thought we'd done that at the pub.'

'Yes, we have, sorry. I told you, I don't usually do this sort of thing. I'm not sure of the rules.'

'Don't apologise.' He cupped her face in a surprisingly gentle gesture. 'This is just you and me, Champagne Lady. There are no rules.'

She watched as his mouth lowered towards hers; sensuous lips, surrounded by very male stubble. Her heart kicked up a gear. What was it about him that had made her act so out of character tonight? Or was it the circumstances, more than the man? Would she have invited any half-decent-looking guy back with her tonight? Those lips touched hers and she moaned as a dozen fireworks exploded, shooting heat through her blood.

No. It was *this* man she wanted tonight. Before he reduced her to a puddle of hormones again, she pushed on his chest, and wow, that was one hell of a wall of muscle. 'We should head for the bedroom.'

'If you like.' His expression said he didn't care where it happened, as long as it did.

And now the fluttering in her stomach was excitement, not nerves.

She started to lead the way when she came to an abrupt halt. 'Can you carry me?' At his puzzled look, she laughed, a teeny bit self-conscious. '"The hot stranger carried her to the bedroom."' She bit into her lip, aware she was making a fool of herself yet also uncaring, because she wasn't going to see him again. The beauty of sex with a stranger. 'Sounds better than "They walked to the bedroom".'

He let out a low laugh and it looked good on him. Softened the edges of his rather blunt masculinity. 'Are you writing a dirty book?'

'Only in my head.'

Suddenly her feet were lifted off the floor, but rather than being swept into his arms, as she'd envisioned, she was thrown over his shoulder in a fireman's lift. The absurdity of it got to her and she started to giggle, thumping on his back as he walked down the hallway, opening the door to the bathroom and the storage cupboard before he found one with a bed in it. 'This one yours?'

'Yes!' she squeaked as he threw her – okay, it wasn't hard, but still, he *threw* her – onto the bed. Blowing her hair out of her eyes, she stared up at him. 'Not quite what I'd imagined.'

'No? Your book doesn't feature hunky firemen?'

It was because he said it with a straight face, she realised. Most men grinned when they used humour, but with this guy, it took a moment to realise he was joking.

But then he was climbing onto the bed, leaning over her, staring into her eyes, and all humour fled. His amusement might be hard to read but his arousal, his need, burned so bright she felt the searing intensity of it all the way to her toes. 'This is the part where we get naked.'

'Right.' She swallowed, her stomach performing a series of frantic somersaults. 'You first.'

'Oh no. Ladies first.' Lying alongside her, resting his weight on his left arm, he used his right to slowly undo the remaining buttons on her blouse. 'Nice.'

Not the most eloquent compliment she'd ever had, but it was the look of wonder on his face that made it seem better than any flowery phrase he could have given her.

Wordlessly he slipped his hand behind her and flicked open the snap of her bra, tugging it off. 'Very nice.'

She smiled, stopping him as he began to undo her skirt. 'My turn.' Her hands trembled slightly as she undid the buttons of his shirt.

'Nervous?' She shook her head. 'Good.'

Excitement licked at her insides as she revealed the muscled expanse of his chest; the dusting of dark hair that covered his pecs, trailing erotically down past his navel and into the waistband of his jeans. Thrilled, she ran her hands across the ridges and planes of his stomach, feeling a throb of exquisite arousal as he let out a guttural groan.

'You're nicely packaged,' she whispered.

He let out a strangled-sounding laugh. 'Thanks.'

'Go on, do that again.'

'What?'

'Laugh. You're really sexy when you laugh.'

He hissed in a breath as her fingers reached for the button of his jeans. 'I'm sexy and nicely packaged,' he repeated hoarsely. 'You must be drunker than I thought.' With that his hand clamped over hers. 'My turn again.'

Ryan didn't know how much longer he could keep it together. For a man who couldn't remember the last time he'd had sex – and yeah, how humiliating was that? – having this sexy redhead in bed with him, her stupendous breasts now revealed, was almost too much. If she'd opened his fly, it could have been game over.

Summoning all his wavering control, he focused back on her. Off came the little black skirt, the natty white underwear and the sexy stockings that seemed to be able to hold themselves up all on their own. She had curves, he thought with satisfaction, and a pair of legs that were every bit as good as he'd imagined. He opened his mouth to say 'nice' again, then clamped it shut. He'd like to bet that word didn't feature in any erotic book she had going on in her head.

Instead of talking he bent to kiss her calf, trailing his lips up to her hips, across the gentle curve of her stomach and then to those magnificent breasts.

When he'd had the satisfaction of turning her into a writhing, moaning, sexy-as-hell mess, he hastily shrugged off the rest of his clothes and settled over her. They both groaned at the contact of naked skin on naked skin, but as he reached to touch her breast again, he froze. 'Hang on a minute.'

Condom. Damn and blast, did he have one in his wallet still? Leaping off the bed, he lunged for his jeans and started frantically searching through his wallet.

'Everything okay?' She was propped up on her elbows, looking over at him like a flame-haired temptress.

'Yeah. Just, you know, protection.' Smooth, Black. Really frigging smooth.

'Ah. I guess that's sexual fling 101.'

He knew it was meant as a joke, yet it made him feel stupid. How come he'd not thought of this until now? Just as his heart, and his libido, was in danger of sinking, he found a foil packet hidden behind the rarely used credit card. He almost blurted, 'Eureka' but stopped himself.

'Sorry.' He sorted himself out before easing back onto the bed, worried he might have totally ruined the moment.

'Don't be. At least you remembered.' She grinned up at him. 'Are we good to mate like bunnies now?'

There was a moment, a heartbeat, as he stared into her dancing eyes, that he felt a connection. Something beyond the sexual attraction. She was amused, not annoyed. Kind, not snippy. It made him regret there would only be tonight.

Then he shook the thought away. The last thing he needed was another complication in his life. Besides, she'd made it quite clear he wasn't her type.

Still, he took a moment to brush the hair from her face. To

gaze steadily into her eyes and give her a gentle, teasing kiss before thrusting into her.

Chest heaving, Ryan flopped back onto the bed. Christ, that wasn't just sex. It was an out-of-body experience.

'Holy shit.'

With the few remaining vestiges of strength he had left, he turned towards her. 'Yeah. Ditto.'

'We didn't do too badly, for a pair of inexperienced one-night standers.'

He nodded, shifting his gaze up to the ceiling. She's too chatty, he reminded himself, though he was kind of getting used to chatty.

The boundaries were very clear, though. Reluctantly he swung his legs off the bed. 'Guess I should get going.'

'You don't have to.'

He stilled, looking over his shoulder at her. 'Thought it was a one-time thing.'

Her hand clutched the sheet, pulling it up to hide her breasts. Her red hair was a messy riot, her cheeks flushed. She looked both sex goddess and innocent. 'One night, I think we said.' Her mouth curved into a sexy smile, notching up the siren.

With a shrug, as if he was cool either way, as if his body wasn't already firing bolts of arousal back through his system, and his mind not already full of all the things he still wanted to do with her, Ryan shifted back into the bed. 'Sure.' He coughed to clear the hoarseness from his throat. 'I can go with that.'

As dawn filtered through the shutters, he picked up the clothes he'd discarded round her bedroom and threw them on. A glance over to the bed confirmed she was still asleep. Ignoring the tug of disappointment, he picked up his jacket and crept out of the room. Better this way.

Last night he'd noticed nothing but her. This morning, as he walked back down the hallway, he checked out the place. Smart, upmarket. Much like she was. He'd like to bet rats didn't party in her swanky kitchen or hang out on her vivid red velvet sofa, peeing on all the multicoloured cushions. Clearly, he hadn't been wrong about the rainbow thing she had going on.

Whoever the hell she was, she had a lot more money than he did. It made him glad he'd escaped before she woke up. He'd like to bet she'd have a tonne of regrets – along with a humdinger of a headache – when she finally surfaced.

PART TWO

The New Guy

Chapter 4

As the sun shone through her curtains, Sam winced. Her mouth felt like sandpaper, her head like men with sharp tools were banging away inside it, trying to get out.

Serves her right for drinking so much. As for that saying about not getting a hangover from champagne, she could officially declare it bogus.

The events from last night began to trickle through her consciousness and she sat up with a start, frantically looking round the room. Relief washed through her as she noticed his clothes had gone. There would be no awkward morning conversation to taint the memory of what, she had to admit, had been a night of stupendous sex.

With a wistful sigh, she dropped her head back against the pillow. Would she do it again? Doubtful. Yet despite that, last night had been exactly what she'd needed. A few hours when the sadness of saying goodbye to her grandad, and the worries that seemed to be her constant companion these days, had been numbed by alcohol. And then obliterated by wild, fabulously hot sex with a total stranger.

Her eyes drifted to the bedside clock and she shrieked,

then put her hand to her head as the men began banging with their tools even harder.

Three-quarters of an hour later she strolled into the foyer of Privacy Solutions. Five years ago it had been an idea conjured up by two bright-eyed undergraduates. Two years ago, the company had launched the Privacy app, a software solution that enabled users to identify websites storing information on them. It had catapulted them into the headlines, catching the imagination of the media and leading to sales that had outperformed their wildest predictions. It had meant moving the headquarters from a living room to the space it now occupied – the ground floor of a recently renovated old warehouse. Now the company employed fifteen full-time employees, several more contractors, and had an annual turnover of more than two million pounds.

But that was all in the past. Threats of a rival app, a superior app, meant things were about to get cut-throat.

'Sam.' Becky, marketing director and Sam's best friend from school, ran over, burying her in a giant bear hug. 'I'm so sorry about Grumps. How are you doing? How was the funeral? How's your mum coping?'

Sam laughed as she tried to extricate herself. 'I'll tell you when you stop firing questions at me.' Becky was one of life's good people. Her hard shell – electric blue hair, pierced nose, leather skirt and heavy Doc Marten boots – hid a heart that was soft and surprisingly easy to bruise.

Becky took Sam's hand and dragged her into a meeting room, pushing her unceremoniously onto a chair. 'Talk to me.'

Because she knew Becky was asking out of genuine concern – she was almost part of the family – Sam patiently answered all the questions before asking a critical one of her own. 'This new software developer that's joining us. You're sure about him?'

Becky rolled eyes that were heavily defined with black eyeliner. 'Too late now. He's starting in' – she glanced at the large man's watch on her wrist – 'forty minutes.'

'But he interviewed okay? I know he must have, or you wouldn't have hired him, but reassure me the man doesn't have two heads.' It was the first recruitment Sam hadn't handled personally, and it felt uncomfortable.

'One head. Kind of good-looking too, if you like your man on the macho side.'

'Which I don't.' Her ex had been classically handsome. Considering what a shit he'd turned out to be though, maybe it was time to change type.

'Me neither, but some women go for it.' Becky liked them lean, artistic and tortured. Men she could try and fix, like the bartender-come-wannabe-drummer she was currently dating. 'Aside from being macho and unimpressed that I was interviewing him instead of you, he was fine. He didn't smile much, actually scratch that, he didn't smile at all, but Hank had warned me he was a bit on the dour side.' Hank was Becky's brother, and he also happened to be the man who'd suggested the guy to them.

'Remind me again how he lost his job? He was fired for what, exactly?'

'Officially for refusing to toe the company line. Unofficially,

Hank said he point-blank refused to work on the next project they assigned him.'

'Because?' Becky loved to tease. To draw out a story. Probably because she knew it drove Sam crazy.

Becky grinned. '*Because* he believed it was morally wrong. It was some sort of gambling app. According to Hank, he went apeshit, said he didn't agree with the concept and he wasn't having anything to do with it.'

Sam winced. Not that she didn't admire the guy's stance, but there were better, more constructive ways to say no than going apeshit. 'Well, I hope your Hank's right about him being a genius, because he sounds like a handful to work with.'

'Chill. He's on a three-month probation, so we can kick him out if he's a nightmare. Hank did say he's the best he's ever worked with though, and considering Hank always told me he thought *he* was the best, that's saying something.'

They needed the best, Sam thought grimly. For eighteen months, the development team had been working on an update to the Privacy app and getting nowhere. Now it was crunch time. Sam couldn't be sure, but best guess was they had three months to get the modified app out before their rival hit the markets. And by rival, read bitter enemy. And by crunch time, read if they failed, the company was finished, investors lost their money. Everyone lost their jobs.

The heartburn that had begun a month ago flared again, leaving a sharp, burning pain in her chest. Automatically she reached for the antacids in her bag. As she chewed on one, both of their phones buzzed with an identical message.

Becky got to hers first. 'Well, look at that. Our new employee may lack people skills, but you can't fault his timekeeping. That's Kerry to say he's arrived and is sitting in reception.'

Kerry was their sweet, slightly ditzy office manager. She'd been with them eighteen months and what she lacked in common sense, she made up for in her sunny, happy-to-do-anything-asked-of-her nature. Of course, her predecessor had been very accommodating too. In fact, she'd bent over backwards to help, literally. As Sam could testify.

Grimly she shook the unhelpful thought away. 'Great. Let's go and meet him.'

As they stood, Becky gave her a stern look. 'Don't think I haven't noticed you've turned into a Rennies addict. You need to decrease your stress levels.'

Sam gave her what she hoped was a bright smile. 'Worry not. That's exactly what Ryan Black is here to do.'

They walked together towards the reception, a funky space with modern black leather sofas, steel desk and original brickwork. As her eyes glanced towards the man sitting down, Sam careered to a halt, her stress levels going through the roof. This had to be some sort of joke. The guy slouched on the sofa, wearing dark-blue jeans, a familiar brown leather jacket and even more familiar scowl, couldn't be the guy she'd just hired.

Could he?

'That's ...' Adrenaline, mixed with dread, had turned her voice scratchy so she tried again. '*That's* Ryan Black?'

Becky looked at her oddly. 'Yes. Why, do you know him?'

I know the sounds he makes when he's having sex. The expression on his face when he comes. Shit, shit, shit. 'I might have had a one-night stand last night with a guy I met in the bar. And he might have looked exactly like the guy sitting over there.'

Becky's heavy black eyebrows shot into her blue hairline. 'Holy shit. There's so much I need to ask you right now.'

'Later.' Sam's heart was beating so erratically, she thought she might faint. 'For now, you need to focus on telling me how to play this. Pretend I can't remember any of it? Laugh it off, like I often hire men I've had sleazy one-night stands with?' Hysteria threatened as she felt a totally inappropriate desire to laugh. For the love of God, how was she supposed to look him in the eye, to command his respect, knowing he'd seen her naked only a few hours ago. And knowing *she'd* picked *him* up.

She wasn't meant to see this guy ever again. Yet by some cruel twist of fate here he was, sitting large as life in the Privacy Solutions foyer.

Ryan Black chose that moment to look up. And catch her eye.

For fuck's sake. Ryan blinked and sat bolt upright. No, he hadn't dozed off into some weird fantasy land. Drunk girl from the bar *was* walking towards him. Taking in a deep breath, he ignored the queasy feeling in his stomach and told himself it wasn't as bad as it seemed. Sure, it was never ideal to work in the same company as a woman you'd had a drunken one-night stand with but hey, they'd had a good time. At least he had. Hell, she'd asked him to stay for more when he'd been about to leave, so she can't have hated it. Regretted it, probably, but that was on her. He'd been very careful to make sure it had been her choice.

As the shock receded and his brain started to function, he consoled himself with the thought that she might not even work for Privacy Solutions – and yeah, that wasn't a company name he was going to be shouting out very often. She might just be visiting her odd, blue-haired friend. Becky, the marketing director who stood in for her boss when the man couldn't be arsed turning up. Ryan was looking forward to meeting this Sam Huxton bloke and finding out if he really was as much of a tosser as he expected him to be. In Ryan's experience, small tech company bosses were shiny-suited upstarts who thought they could make a quick buck by starting a company and selling it on. Usually by using their trust fund, or their mate's trust fund.

As the unlikely pair walked towards him – one with red hair, one with blue: if they stood with the dizzy blonde who'd introduced herself as office manager, they'd have a flag going on – Ryan rose to his feet. It wasn't manners. More a determination to use his height to send a message. *We slept together. So what.*

Champagne Lady seemed calm and collected as she stopped in front of him but when she held her hand out to him it trembled slightly. Good. 'You must be Ryan Black.' Her lips formed a small, wry smile. 'I feel like we've met before.'

As he gave her hand a brief shake, he cursed that he was as attracted to her now as he had been last night. That wide mouth, the red hair, those magnificent blue eyes. And that's without factoring in the mind-blowing curves he knew lay beneath the cream trousers and soft pink jumper she wore. 'If we had, I'd remember.' He stared right back at her, pleased with his equally enigmatic reply. Words weren't his thing. Give him numbers, code, and he was frigging eloquent. Make him talk, or write, and he felt dumb as shit.

'Yes. I imagine a meeting between us would be memorable.' She drew in a breath. 'Welcome to Privacy Solutions. I'm Sam Huxton.'

WTF? He felt his legs give way and he took an involuntary step back, bumping his calf against the chair. 'You're Sam Huxton,' he repeated dumbly, his mind deciding to really crap on the moment by replaying an image from last night. Her naked, on her bed. Him leaning over her, sliding into her.

'I am.'

It hadn't been a question, but he was grateful for her reply, even if it did confirm his fears, because it gave him another two seconds to try and unscramble his messy, wayward, frozen head. 'And you didn't turn up to the interview because ...' Belatedly, stupidly, he remembered exactly why not.

'I had a family emergency.' Her eyes flickered away from his and he knew she was remembering telling him all about dear old Grumps. 'But you met Becky, our marketing director.'

'Yeah.' He nodded to the blue-haired goth, wondering if she felt the tension – both sexual and otherwise – that was pinging between him and Sam ... fuck, between him and the *CEO* ... like a pinball on acid.

'Right, I'll leave you both to it,' Becky said with a smirk, and Ryan couldn't be sure if it was because she knew what had gone down between him and Sam, or if she was just very good at reading minds.

As soon as she was out of earshot, all the angst, the shock, the mortification of having slept with his boss – his frigging *boss* – exploded inside him. 'Look, Champagne Lady—'

'Sam.'

Why did she look and sound so cool when he was a melting pot of jumbled emotions? 'Sam,' he said tightly, the word feeling like a sharp stone on his tongue. For Christ's sake, why hadn't he asked her name yesterday? 'I can see why you want to brush last night under the carpet. Trust me, in hindsight it wasn't my finest hour, either.' *He'd had sex with the boss woman.* His mind was stuck on the words. How did he move forward from this? Bad enough when he'd thought she was a co-worker, but oh no, Champagne Lady wasn't just that. She owned the company he'd signed a contract to work for.

Godammit, she *owned* him, because he couldn't walk out. He needed the job, and the money, too badly. Who else was going to take on a guy who'd been fired from his last company?

'We're both adults.' Her smile was polite and professional. Nothing like the sexy, teasing one she'd directed his way most of yesterday evening. 'We can put last night behind us and move on.'

It irked him that she was handling this way better than he was. He wanted to be the detached one. The one able to coolly dismiss the previous evening, as if it had hardly registered as an event at all.

Not the one who couldn't stop thinking about every blasted second of it.

Not the one who wanted nothing more right now than to drag her out of this squeaky-clean office, mess up her tidy hair, yank off her neat jumper and do very dirty things to her.

'Fine.' He leant forward, eyes blazing into hers. 'But know this. I remember every single moment. How you look naked. How your eyes glazed over when I thrust into you. And I know you do, too.' With that he took a deliberate step back and shoved his hands in his pockets. 'How about you show me where I'll be working?'

Chapter 5

Sam blinked, hating the arousal she felt at the memories Ryan's words evoked. But he wasn't the only one who could play at mind games. Screwing up her courage, she took a step forward so that once again they were eye to eye. Heaving chest to heaving chest.

'You're right. I remember exactly what went on last night, too.' She tried to curl her lips into a smirk. 'Think on that, when I'm doing your performance review.' As a satisfying flush crept up his neck she stepped back, like he had, and pasted a sickly-sweet smile on her face. 'I'm going to hand you back to Kerry now. I'm sure she'll be delighted to give you a quick tour of the place and show you to your workstation. I'll catch up with you later.' *When I've finished my more important tasks*.

He must have read her subtext, because the flush on his face deepened. And God, this bitch wasn't her, but she didn't know how else to deal with him. Why hadn't he taken her lead and chosen the civilised, professional way out; ignore, ignore, ignore? Why had he not only acknowledged the elephant in the room, but shoved it right under her nose?

Leaving him fuming – he obviously hadn't mastered the art of hiding his feelings – she strode sharply over to Kerry. 'Would you do me a favour and show the new guy round? I'm swamped after being off last week.' It wasn't a lie, though usually she was the one who did the tour, combining it with an introductory pep talk on the philosophy of the company. That would have to come later, when she didn't feel the need to knee him in the balls. And then kiss him. Heavens above, why did she still want to do that?

'No problem, Sam.' Kerry glanced over to Ryan and giggled. 'No problem *at all*.'

'Kerry.' She wanted to warn her off, but what could she say? He's great in bed, but seems a total prick out of it? Or worse, and perhaps even closer to the truth: I might not want him, but I can't stand the thought of him with anyone else just yet?

'What?'

Sam sighed. 'Nothing. Just, be careful.'

Kerry burst out laughing. 'Don't you worry about me. Look, don't touch, right? I'm not daft enough to come on to a guy from work.' She waggled her eyebrows. 'Even someone as tasty as him.'

And that, Sam thought despairingly, just about said it all. For the millionth time since she'd seen Ryan Black sitting in the foyer, she cursed her champagne-addled hormones.

Still feeling dazed, Sam walked slowly back to her desk. Usually when she was in the office her mind buzzed, but now it was stuck on last night. Please God it was nothing that a strong coffee wouldn't fix.

She'd barely stepped into her office, mug in hand, when Becky hurtled in behind her and shut the door. 'Spill.'

Sam glanced down. 'The coffee?'

Becky hissed. 'I want details. For eighteen months, I've been telling you to put Douchebag Damien behind you and get out there again, but you've been *oh no, I hate men, I'm never doing that again, I'm perfectly happy being single.*' In what Sam presumed was supposed to be an imitation of her, Becky swished back her non-existent hair and pouted. 'And now I hear that you did the dirty with a guy and didn't even find out his name.'

Sam winced. The stupid thing was, if fate had been kinder, if Ryan Black had been confined to a naughty memory, only to be replayed when she needed a dose of feeling like a woman and not a CEO, she'd have felt liberated by her decision. Not flattened by it. 'Kind of badass, huh?'

Becky's eyes widened. Then she burst out laughing. 'Is this the new you then?'

'Of course, because it's worked out so well for me, don't you think?' Letting out a pained groan, Sam buried her face in her hands. 'Oh God, I'm not sure I can do this.' Lifting her head up, she eyed Becky hopefully. 'How about we get rid of him and find someone else?' Becky wasn't just marketing director, she was also their nominated HR person.

'Sure, boss, as long as you don't mind if it takes more time than we can afford, because not only will we have to find a brilliant software developer with the right skillset to achieve in a few months what our previous guy couldn't do in eighteen, he or she will have to work their notice. Not everyone is available straight away like Black.'

'Because he got *fired.*'

'True, but it wasn't for reasons that concern us.' Becky sighed. 'Look, it's your call, but you're the one who told me how desperately we need to get the modifications to the app done and launched before *they* do.'

'I know.' Sam straightened up, took in a breath and had a quick slug of coffee. 'Okay, I can do this. It was one dumb night. I'm not going to let it interfere with the chance of keeping this company ahead of the game. It's not like either of us want a repeat.'

Becky studied her with narrowed eyes. 'You're sure about that? There must have been something about the guy that got through the solid concrete wall you usually put up to ward off men.'

The dark eyes, brooding expression, big, hulking presence? Was she really that shallow? 'Whatever it was, daylight and a hangover have successfully obliterated it.' And she was a total liar. She'd still felt a pulse of arousal when he'd shaken her hand. Her stomach had still dipped when he'd crudely reminded her what they'd done together.

'I don't know.' Becky looked like she didn't believe her. 'He's not my type, but even I can see he's got something. And the only drink I've had is raspberry tea.'

'I'll never understand how you can swallow that stuff.' When Becky just looked at her, Sam knew she wasn't going to be let off the hook that easily. 'Look, I'll admit he's attractive, and last night, after the week I'd had, his sullen,

I-don't-give-a-shit attitude was just what I needed.' He'd also been considerate, she remembered. Chivalrous almost, in the way he'd taken care of her. Very different to the man she'd just faced. 'Trust me when I say: the only thing I want from him now is the bit between his ears. So, if he really is the genius software developer your brother claims, I'll happily fix a smile on my face and be a good boss.' The company was her priority right now and everything else, including her pride, would have to take a running jump.

'Understood.' Becky turned to walk out. Just before she opened the door, she glanced over her shoulder. 'Do me a favour and satisfy my curiosity. The part between his legs. How good was he at using it, exactly?'

Sam spluttered out a laugh. 'You've got to be kidding me.' When Becky raised her eyebrows and gave her a cheeky grin, Sam gave in. 'Put it this way, if he's as good with the part between his ears, we'll be okay.'

Ryan dumped his rucksack onto his new desk and gave the blonde – Kerry – a half-hearted smile. 'Thanks.'

She smiled brightly. 'No problem. Hopefully you've got everything you need. If there's anything we've forgotten though, just shout. I mean, not literally, obviously, but you can call me, or, you know, just walk around the corner.' She mimed walking with her fingers, clearly not aware he could actually understand English. Then she pointed the twenty or so yards over to where she sat. The same place she'd also pointed out to him five minutes ago.

'Got it.'

'Okay then.' She smiled again. It was like her face couldn't do anything else. 'Well, I'll let you know when Sam's free to see you.'

But she didn't move; just stood there, shifting from foot to foot, staring at him. 'Was there something else?'

Her smile slipped a little, possibly because he'd let his irritation show in his voice. 'Oh, no, it's all good.' She gave him a daft little wave. 'Well, have a good day. I hope you enjoy working for Privacy Solutions. The people here are so lovely. It's like a family, you know?'

Good God. Next she was going to tell him they all met up for Sunday lunch and had sing-songs round the piano.

Because he didn't have a clue how to reply to her, he muttered another thanks, relieved when she finally took the hint and walked away.

Sighing deeply, he slumped onto his chair and took a minute, a very vital minute, to rub a hand over his face and curse. What the hell had he got himself into? A boss he'd somehow managed to sleep with, and a firm the staff thought was like a family. For a man who didn't mix well, who liked to keep himself to himself, it felt like he'd landed in purgatory.

Taking a few deep breaths, he forced himself to sit up straight. There was no point getting all narked about things. He had a job, didn't he? Well, as long as Huxton didn't throw him out. She could hardly do that because of what he'd done *before* he officially started though. Could she?

Crap, this is why one-night stands were a stupid frigging idea. Now she had him by the balls and he had no choice but to suck it up.

He spent the rest of the morning and most of the afternoon trying to get a feel for the size of the problem he'd been tasked with fixing. Well, he and some junior programmer called Alice who kept asking him if he needed anything. If Huxton only employed people who had smiling as their default face, he was going to be kicked out by the end of the day.

Suddenly the smell of something expensive and elegant wafted up his nostrils.

'I'm free to see you now.'

He turned round with a start. 'Should I tug my forelock?'

Sam gave him a cool smile. 'Only if you want to.'

You need the blasted job. Giving her a sharp nod, he stood, glad that he could at least look down on her physically, even if in every other area she held all the cards.

He followed her to her office, keeping his eyes firmly on the back of her head, and not where they wanted to drift. No doubt she'd seek a reason to boot him out as soon as possible. He was damned if he was going to make it easy for her.

Her office was small and unassuming. It backed onto the original brickwork, the other three walls being made of glass; the bottom part frosted, the top clear. More of a meeting room, he sensed, from the lack of anything personal in it. She pointed to a chair and he dropped into it, feeling a creeping sense of dread as she slowly walked round her shiny modern desk to sit opposite him.

'Are you firing me?' he blurted into the oppressive silence, then cursed himself for sounding so desperate.

'Have you given me cause to?' she shot back.

He hissed in a breath at her sharpness. 'I've not had a

chance to read your rules. Do they prohibit sleeping with the boss, before you knew she was the boss?'

Those huge blue eyes flashed at him. 'Your contract with us started this morning. I suggest you read it carefully. If you stick to the terms of the agreement, and perform as we'd expect, I won't have a reason to fire you.'

Sarky responses bombarded his brain. *You can already vouch for my performance.* Painfully he swallowed them down, along with his pride. 'Understood.'

'Good.' She did something weird then. She smiled at him. Not one of the cute, tipsy smiles from last night; this was strained, as if it was a real effort. But it was a vast improvement on the snottily polite stuff she'd thrown at him earlier. 'I'd like to officially welcome you to Privacy Solutions, Ryan.' His name sounded odd on her tongue. As if she was speaking to a friend, which he knew he'd never be, not by any definition of the word. 'As you've probably already seen, we're a small company but we have high ambitions and a big heart. Our philosophy is one team, one mission, one heart.'

Not the time to snigger, but seriously, one frigging heart?

'Problem?'

'Nope.' Those eyes held his and he found it hard to ignore their quiet demand. 'Look, it's just a bit happy, clappy, skipping with daisy chains for me. I'm more: rely on nobody, nobody lets you down.'

'That's rather sad, don't you think?' Her wide mouth curved. 'Though the image of you skipping with daisy chains is certainly an interesting one.'

'Yeah?' Frustratingly, her smile still did things to him. 'I don't make a habit of it.'

For a brief moment some of the warmth from last night drifted between them, along with the pulsing attraction. But then she looked away and pasted that professional look back on her face. 'The Privacy Solutions mission is to be the go-to company for your online privacy concerns. We were the first to show you who's storing information on you. Now we want to be the first to go further and let you see not only the who, but the what. Who has your data, and what data they have.' She met his gaze head on. 'If you don't think that's something you can do, I need to know now.'

He didn't flinch. She might have him by his balls, but his ego was alive and kicking. 'You want me to do that in, what, six months?' he hazarded, remembering the blue-haired goth had told him at the interview timelines were tight. Six months was definitely that.

'Three.'

Panic slithered through him, coiling round his insides. Three was his probation period. The glint in her eyes told him she knew it too, and he could almost feel her grip on his balls tightening. 'Fine.' He stared her down. 'You want me to achieve in three months what your last software developer failed to sort in eighteen.'

'Yes.'

Translation. He had three months to achieve the impossible, or he was out on his ear. He forced his mouth into a cocky smile. 'Piece of cake.'

'Good.' She leant back in her chair, a picture of cool sophistication. He hated that he still found her unbelievably sexy. Hated that despite the grip she had on his balls, the power she wielded over him, he'd like nothing better tonight than a repeat performance. 'I admire confidence, as long it's backed by results.'

'And I'm up for a challenge, as long as I'm not being shafted.'

He'd never know what her comeback would have been because at that moment there was a cursory knock on the door and a tall blond guy wearing a foul citrus-green shirt strode in. 'Darling, you're back.' He stopped short when he noticed she had company. 'Oh, my bad. I didn't realise you were giving our new boy a grilling.'

Every single one of Ryan's heckles rose – *new* he could handle but *our boy*, and *grilling*, like he was some sort of wayward kid they'd taken in off the streets? She must sense his irritation, too, because those freaky eyes of hers looked like were laughing at him.

Camp lime-green guy was either oblivious or in on the joke. 'You must be the software whizz-kid Becky's been warning me about.' He gave Ryan a careful study before sticking out his hand. 'Lucas Baker.'

'Ryan Black.' Expecting something limp and clammy, Ryan was surprised to find his hand gripped in a firm, confident handshake.

'Lucas is our design director,' Sam added and yes, that half-smile was still on her lips as she watched him quickly extract his hand.

'Pleased to meet you, Ryan Black. You need me for anything' – the look Lucas gave him from his glittering blue eyes was loaded with innuendo – 'anything at all, just shout.'

Ryan willed himself to hold his gaze and not to flush. He was pretty certain the guy was messing with him, but it didn't stop him feeling acutely uncomfortable. Or exhaling with relief when Lucas turned his eyes back on Sam.

'Should I pop back later, sweet cheeks?'

And yeah, there was definitely a joke going on between the pair of them. Sam was clearly trying hard not to laugh.

Ryan shot to his feet. Stuff this shit. He wasn't going to sit around being the butt of their jokes. 'No need. We're done.' Giving them both a stiff nod, he headed smartly for the door. Call him paranoid, but he was pretty certain he could hear laughter before they shut the door.

Chapter 6

Sam rolled her eyes at Lucas as he gracefully slid into the chair opposite her.

'Sweet cheeks?'

He grinned unapologetically. 'I wanted to see how he'd react.'

Lucas was handsome, openly gay and a total flirt. He was also fiercely loyal, an astute judge of character and the best app designer Sam had ever come across. 'And?'

'Fair play, he looked more annoyed than horrified. He didn't back down from the Baker stare, either.' His eyes lit up. 'Maybe that hunk of manhood swings my way.'

Sam opened her mouth to tell him otherwise, then thought better of it. Bad enough Becky knew her embarrassing secret. If Lucas got an inkling she'd slept with that *hunk of manhood*, she'd never hear the end of it. 'I don't care which way he swings, as long as he can do what we hired him for.' She rubbed at her forehead, trying to ease the thumping headache. That would teach her to drink on a school night. 'Did you waltz in here just to cop a look at the new guy, or was there something else you wanted?'

Lucas tipped back his head and laughed. 'The first, obviously. But as I'm here, remember we've got a meeting at 3pm to get the scrumptious Mr Black up to speed with where we are with the Privacy 2 app.'

'I hadn't forgotten.'

He grinned, dramatically uncrossing his legs. 'Then my work here is done.'

As he strolled out, thankfully closing the door behind him, Sam sank back against her chair. Torture, that's how this day felt. Discovering she'd employed the man she'd supposedly had anonymous sex with last night, on top of a backlog of work, thanks to her few days away. All served with a humdinger of a hangover. Yep, today officially sucked. And she still had a meeting to get through. With her not so anonymous one-night stand.

Her eyes fluttered closed as she recalled the look on his face when he'd asked if she was going to fire him. Desperate. He'd covered it quickly enough, but that glimpse of vulnerability had shown her that despite how unbalanced she felt, she was actually the one in control, the one with all the power. The realisation wasn't pleasant. It felt even less pleasant when she imagined how she'd feel if it had been the other way round. If she'd found herself working for a guy she'd unwittingly slept with.

It brought a new level of shame to her earlier comment about his performance review. Sure he'd been crass, but she'd managed to out-crass him.

Now it was up to her to put them back on the right footing and treat him like she would any new employee. It meant wiping all memories of last night from her mind, including the reasons she'd found him attractive.

Piece of cake. And no, she didn't have an image in her head of him saying those exact words a moment ago. His full lips curving in that sexy half-smile, half-smirk.

Ryan Black was the only one in the meeting room. Sam slowed as she neared it, watching him through the glass wall. He was leaning forward, those big shoulders slightly hunched as he looked down at his phone. Ordinary hair. And a crooked nose. Not much to go gaga about really.

Just then he looked up. As his dark gaze snared hers, her stomach flipped over and she swallowed to try and quell the jitters.

'First one here, I see.' A statement of the bleeding obvious. Clearly her wit had deserted her.

There was that more-smirk-than-smile again. 'Didn't want to get in trouble with the boss.'

Her heart was beating far too fast for someone trying to convince herself he held zero interest for her. 'Good idea. I hear she's a real tyrant.'

They shared a look of quiet amusement which immediately took Sam back to last night, and the way they'd seemed to click, even though they were so totally different.

Memories she needed to wipe out.

His gaze lingered on hers before darkening as it dropped to her mouth. 'Shit, Champagne Lady. How the hell did this happen?'

Her heart bumped against her ribs. 'I'm not sure.' Where

had her real voice gone, and what was this breathy replacement? 'In hindsight, maybe I should have checked your ID, after all.'

'You think?' Shaking his head, he cursed before aiming those eloquent dark eyes back in her direction. 'I can't scrub it from my databank. I want to, but I can't.'

The intensity of his gaze made her legs tremble and as heat pooled between them, she sank gratefully into the nearest chair. What the hell she could say to *that?*

'Sorry we're late.' She'd never been more grateful to hear Lucas's voice. 'Becks insisted on grabbing me a mochaccino.'

'As if.' Becky's eyes bounced between her and Ryan, widening as they landed back on hers.

Lucas also paused for a moment before, thank God, expounding on where they could find the best mochaccino. As he continued to talk, Becky slipped onto the chair next to her. A few seconds later, she pushed a note pad towards her. Sam quickly glanced at the words.

Sexual tension is bouncing off the walls. Should we leave??

Horrified, Sam wrote back in big, shouty capitals: *DON'T YOU BLOODY DARE.*

'Oh dear, am I late?' Alice, the junior programmer, bounded in, blonde hair bouncing in her ponytail. She'd joined them straight out of university, nearly nine months ago now. Sam had liked her attitude at the interview: confident, not afraid to ask questions. Keen to learn. 'Totally my fault. There was me, so focused on the code I was working on I forgot to check the time.' She laughed, rolling her eyes and looking her age. Twenty-two. 'I guess only Ryan would understand how much those sneaky codes can suck you in.'

Ryan's face, as Alice sat down beside him, was a picture; the tight smile, the small shake of the head. Yep, he was definitely wondering how on earth he was going to work with her. The man would be useless at poker.

'No problem, Alice. We hadn't started.' Sam nodded over to Lucas. 'Lucas suggested we have this meeting to give Ryan some background to the Privacy 2 app. What we're trying to achieve, what we've agreed so far and where we're at.' She forced herself to look at Ryan. 'Feel free to barrage us with questions as we go through.'

He nodded once, which she guessed was all the thanks they were going to get.

'I'll start by talking through the aim of the Privacy app in general, and then Becky will go through the modifications the market is looking for, and Lucas will share where we've got to on the design for the mark 2. Finally, Alice will discuss some of the technical issues she and your predecessor have come up against.'

Silence. She was used to chat, to animated meetings, but Ryan's quiet, sullen presence had clearly rubbed off on everyone. As her eyes skimmed over him, she wondered if he was looking at her as the CEO. Or the woman he'd had sex with multiple times last night.

Don't think about it, don't think about it. Hastily she reached for her water and took a few sips. 'Okey-dokey, so, the Privacy app.'

Ryan watched Sam, but he didn't listen. Not because he didn't care, but because he'd already read up on the mark 2 app this morning. He might have slept with his boss, but he wasn't totally unprofessional.

Reluctantly – she was far too easy to look at – he dragged his eyes away.

'Anything you need clarification on so far?'

At her cool tone, he snapped his head up. 'You and some bloke came up with the whole Privacy app idea. He developed it, you marketed it. Purpose was to show punters which firms held data on them. Now you want to take it to the next level, but you and he had a bust-up and the guy you employed after him was a dud, so that's where I come in.'

Surprise shot across her face and he inwardly high-fived himself. If she was trying to catch him out, she'd have to do better than that. He'd researched not just the app, but the company. He might not know why her business partner – Damien Lynch – had left, but he sure as hell knew it hadn't been as simple as she'd painted it, a disagreement on the future direction of the company. Yeah, right. He *disagreed* with their cheesy company motto: one team, one ... something, one frigging heart. Didn't mean he was going to waltz out and set up a rival company just to piss her off.

'Thank you for the ... interesting summary.' The way she said it, so controlled, so collected, both annoyed and impressed him. With one final assessing look in his direction, she swung those big eyes towards her blue-haired mate. 'Becky, please can you remind us, and enlighten Ryan, about what the market is hoping for with the mark 2 version?'

'Sure, boss.'

Ryan saw the look that passed between the pair of them.

He'd bet his first pay packet that Sam had told her friend all about last night. Prickles of discomfort travelled down his back at the thought of them having a laugh at his expense. *His chat-up line was awful, something about wanting to know if my bedroom was as much of a dive as his was. Oh, and did I tell you, he struggled to find a condom?*

The prickles turned into an angry flush. Damn it, he needed to focus on the meeting. Last night hadn't happened. That's how she was playing it, and he needed to learn the same game.

'Basically, what the research is saying is that users love what the app can do, and they're excited about the possibility of it being able to do more. Like show them not only which companies hold personal data on them but what information is being held. They also want a simpler registration process with fewer inputs.' Becky shifted her gaze to him. 'That's why Lucas has been working on a much more streamlined design for the mark 2. But I'll leave him to talk about that.'

Ryan shifted on his chair, belatedly realising he'd missed something vital in what Becky had been saying. 'Wait. What do you mean, fewer inputs?'

Becky heaved out a sigh. 'If you'd been listening, you'd know. Users don't want the hassle of putting all the information in about the various social media sites they use. They just want to put in the basics; name, address, date of birth, email.'

He sat up bolt upright. 'You're seriously going to tell me you guys are trying to get this mark 2 app to do what it did before, and more, but with less input?'

Becky looked at Lucas, and then at Sam, who both nodded. 'Yes. That's what the market wants.'

He started to laugh. 'Yeah, right. I bet they want spray that makes them invisible and chocolate with no calories. Doesn't mean they're going to get it.'

Becky's eyes flashed at him. 'We need to respond to market needs, or they'll go elsewhere.'

'You mean to this rival you're all so worried about.'

'You should be worried about it too,' Sam cut in. 'Unless you've got another job lined up already?' She gave him one of those cutting looks she was so good at. All calm and in charge, blue eyes as cool as an Icelandic lake.

'Okay, point taken.' He took a moment to breathe. To remind himself this was just a business meeting. So what if they were taking the piss out of him behind his back. Wasn't like he hadn't experienced that before. 'My point still stands. No way can all this be done. Not by me, not by another software developer. Not by your rival.'

'Sebastian said it could.' Sam arched an eyebrow. 'He was the man you replaced.'

'Sebastian clearly enjoyed blowing smoke up your arse.'

'Sebastian was a friend.' Seems it was Lucas's turn to give Ryan the evil eye. 'And he was a very fine software developer who saw what was needed and was keen to help. A real *team player*.'

Ryan tried to ignore the dig. Since being a teenager, he'd become used to being the outsider. The one people didn't like. He'd learnt to develop a tough skin. 'So keen he left?'

Yep, they were all looking daggers at him now. Even smiley-face Alice.

Sam cleared her throat. 'Sebastian didn't choose to go. I asked him if he was able to complete the upgrade within the next few months. He said he wasn't and agreed to leave so we could find someone who could.' She raised her eyes to his. 'I understood you were that person.'

He might not be great with words, or manners and nice-ties, but Ryan knew software, particularly app development. He knew what was possible and what was not. And he knew he was bloody good at his job. 'I can make your app for you in three months. What I can't do is the impossible. Doesn't matter how brilliant you are, you can't programme an app to find data, if you don't give it enough information to tell it where to look. At least not accurately, which I assume is the most important consideration. The simplified input idea will have to go.' He jerked his head towards Becky-blue-hair and Lucas-citrus-shirt. 'These guys are living in cloud cuckoo land.'

'Now wait a—'

'How dare you—'

'Ryan,' Sam's voice cut through whatever crap they were about to throw at him. 'A word in private. Please.'

She stood up smoothly and walked towards the door, not once looking in his direction. Like a kid being summoned to see the headmaster, he followed her.

Once in her office, she indicated for him to sit down. Then flashed her blue eyes at him. 'We work as a team here. We're polite to each other and treat everyone with respect.'

He shrugged, trying to act indifferent. As if she wasn't making him feel two foot small. 'You're paying me to develop your app. Not make friends.'

'Seems to me you're not prepared to do either.'

Ouch. He was really cocking this up. Then again, that respect thing went both ways. 'Don't think you respected my privacy much when you told Becky about last night.'

Sam froze, a satisfying flush creeping over her cheeks. 'Okay, you're right.' She rubbed at her forehead, as if she had a headache. He guessed gallons of champagne could do that. 'I was so shocked to see you this morning, I just blurted it out. Becky isn't only my marketing director, you see, she's my best friend. We tell each other things.' Her eyes met his and for the first time that day he saw the woman, not the company CEO. 'But I apologise if it's made you feel awkward. If it helps, she'll keep it to herself. And the awkwardness goes both ways.'

He could see she was genuinely sorry. Still, she wasn't the one having the piss taken out of her behind her back. Saying that would be admitting he cared though, and he'd far rather people believed he didn't give a rat's arse what was being said about him. 'Apology accepted. But back to your issue. You don't need a genius app developer. You need someone not afraid to tell you what can and can't be done. Either your Sebastian guy was too terrified of you to say no, or he wanted in your pants.' She blinked, and he wondered if she was just realising something about dear Sebastian. 'Yeah, exactly. As you seem about as scary as a toothless wombat, I'm going with the second idea.'

She blinked several times before leaping to her feet, and this time she didn't seem quite so collected. 'We should rejoin the others to discuss next steps. And what *can* be done.'

'Happy to. Luckily you don't scare me.' He smirked. 'And I've already been in your pants.'

She paused and then surprised him by smiling, even if it did look forced. 'Considering your earlier point about me not respecting your privacy, I'll let that slide, but now we're even.' The smile slipped. 'Take another cheap shot, and you're out.'

With a toss of that glorious red hair, she marched out ahead of him. He almost remembered to keep his eyes on the back of her head. Almost.

Chapter 7

'The guy's a jerk.'

Two weeks into Ryan Black's employment, and he was still creating waves. Unsurprisingly, Lucas was the one moaning about him today. He was also the one who needed to work the closest with Ryan at the moment.

'I know he is.' And boy, did she. Sure, there were moments when those eyes watched her, and Sam felt the rush of arousal. Moments when his dour expression lifted, bringing a small curve to his annoyingly sensuous lips. On those occasions, she felt the powerful attraction that had led her to invite a stranger back to her apartment. Thankfully for her equilibrium, the moments were few and far between.

'This isn't what we've been working towards for all these months.'

Sam sighed as Lucas pouted at her. Yep, the guy could put on one heck of a pout. 'I know. But if Ryan's to be believed, some of what we've been working towards has been the pot of gold at the end of the rainbow. Shiny and gorgeous but totally unattainable.'

'You trust his judgement over Sebastian's?'

Sam felt a ripple of unease as snippets of conversation with Ryan's predecessor wormed their way into her consciousness. The flirting she'd thought was just part of Sebastian's character. The looks she'd chosen to ignore, thinking she'd just been imagining things. Had Ryan been right? Sebastian certainly hadn't been scared of her, so had he tried to do the impossible just to impress her? And if so, how had she not seen that? Was her judgement now totally flawed? 'I know Ryan isn't likeable, but we have it on good authority that he's one of the top developers in his field.' Thankfully not her assessment this time, but that of Becky's brother. 'I can't see why a person like that, who's clearly well aware how good he is, would say streamlining the input to the app can't be done, if it can.'

Lucas let out a dramatic sigh and crossed one pink-chino-clad leg over the other. 'I guess you're right. Cocky sod like him wouldn't like to admit he's beaten.'

'So will you work with him, please?' She gave Lucas her most endearing smile. 'You know how important the next few months are. For better or for worse, we're stuck with relying on Ryan Black to develop Privacy 2. If the company is to succeed, we need him working with us.'

'I'm not the one with the issue, sweet cheeks.' When she narrowed her eyes, he gave her a cheeky grin. 'Okay, okay, I'll go and play nice, though he's the one who keeps telling me to piss off when I try and connect with him.'

Suddenly she became aware of Ryan standing in the doorway. The unfortunately open doorway. 'Having fun talking about me?'

Though his expression was one of careful uninterest, his

eyes flashed with a ... resigned anger, if there was such a thing. It was as if being talked about was nothing new to him. Desperately she thought back to what he might have overheard. *I know Ryan isn't likeable*. He hadn't been there since then, had he? She felt herself starting to blush, which worsened when she saw Lucas give her a speculative look.

Bollocks. She hated being shoved onto the back foot.

Lucas, thank God, spoke into the awkward silence. 'I'm having more fun talking about you than I've had talking to you, sweetie.' He swung round in his chair to face Ryan. 'Not that I don't think we could have fun together,' he added. 'But every time I try and speak to you, you cut me dead.'

Ryan let out a frustrated exhale. 'It's called concentrating, mate. You should try it some time.'

'Enough.' Sam threw up her hands. 'Will the pair of you please sort your petty squabbles out privately? I'm rather busy here sorting out a presentation for our next investor meeting.'

Lucas immediately looked contrite. 'You're right. I'm sorry. We'll leave you to your important CEO stuff.' He eased to his feet and headed for the door, flashing Ryan an overly friendly smile. 'I'm sure Mr Black and I can sort out our differences over a cup of mochaccino.'

Ryan didn't follow him out. Just watched cautiously as Lucas walked past him.

Sam's pulse skittered. She'd carefully avoided being alone with him since that first day, but now her body seemed very aware that it was just the two of them. 'Was there anything you needed me for?'

Ryan's eyes were still on Lucas. 'Anyone tell him he looks like a frigging watermelon?'

The comment was so unexpected, Sam wondered if she'd heard correctly. Then she clocked the departing view of Lucas' pink trousers and green shirt and had to stifle a giggle. 'I'm not sure telling him that will help your working relationship.'

'Maybe not, but I can tell you what will.' He turned back to her. 'Find me an office, with a door I can lock.'

Sam sighed. Considering his closed personality, she could understand why he wanted it, but it went against what she was trying to achieve. How could they be a team if they worked behind closed doors? 'We work in open plan here. I'm the only one with an office, and even then I only use it for meetings or when I'm working on something sensitive. Like now,' she added pointedly.

He scowled. 'I can't work with fruit-features breathing down my neck every ten minutes.'

Anger zipped through her, and she jumped to her feet. 'Take that back this instant. I won't tolerate name calling—'

'Relax.' He cut her off, raising his eyes to the ceiling. 'Words aren't my strong suit. Neither are jokes, from the sound of things. I only meant fruit as in watermelon. Not, you know.' Sighing deeply, he ran a hand down his face. 'Look, I get it, you're all used to working as a big, happy, smiley team, but it doesn't work for me. I need quiet and space to think.' He shoved a hand into the pocket of his habitual jeans. 'I'm guessing you do want me to think?'

The anger drained from her and Sam slowly sank back into her chair. Homophobia was a big red flag for her, but a cussed nature she could handle. 'Of course I want you to think. I also want you working as part of the team. It's no good you building something that doesn't fit into Lucas's design.'

'I can work with someone and not sit on his lap.'

So, he was cussed *and* stubborn. It was hardly a surprise. But as it was her job to keep him sweet, at least until they'd worked out if he was as good as was claimed, she plastered a smile on her face. 'I can't give you an office, but you can move your computer to a meeting room temporarily if you need to.'

'Thanks.'

It wasn't just the word that took her surprise, it was the relief on his face. Not *I've won*, but *thank God*. His request hadn't been about one-upmanship, or arrogance, but about genuine need.

The tiny breakthrough gave her the motivation to stop him as he turned to leave. 'About what you might have overheard.'

Ryan froze. In his experience, most people weren't like him. They preferred to shove things they were embarrassed about under the carpet, not put them out there.

'Yeah?'

'I apologise. Lucas came here to vent and I was trying to support him, but in doing so I said things that were unprofessional.'

'Was that the bit about me not being likeable, or you being stuck with me?'

Her eyes held his and she smiled. Actually frigging *smiled*. 'Both?'

It was her sunshine smile, too. The one that lit up her face, shimmered through her eyes and was alarmingly infectious. Determined to remain unaffected by it, he lifted his shoulders in a casual shrug. 'Forget it. It's nothing I've not heard before.' He'd cut off his right arm before admitting how much the first comment had stung. He thought he'd got over being hurt by what people said behind his back, but maybe that was just people he hadn't slept with.

'Well, you shouldn't have heard it from me.'

As he continued to hold her gaze, his control wavered. Whether it was the candour in those blue orbs or the tilt of her lips he didn't know, but the need to kiss the woman who'd only moments ago said he wasn't likeable became almost overwhelming. Shaking off his confused emotions, he walked towards the door. 'Guess I'd better go and find Lucas. What the hell is a mochaccino anyway?'

'A latte with added chocolate.'

He screwed his face up. 'Not happening.'

He stepped out to the sound of her soft laughter. And the realisation that he was smiling.

The smile broadened when he caught sight of Lucas at the coffee machine. Christ. He was all for bucking convention but pink trousers and a green shirt? 'I didn't realise it was dress-as-a-fruit day today.' Lucas's eyebrows shot into his hair-line and as he glared back at him, Ryan belatedly realised he'd used that word. Again. 'What is it with you guys? Don't you eat apples, oranges?' He deliberately ran his eyes over Lucas's attire. 'Watermelons?'

Lucas frowned and looked down at what he was wearing, clearly unable to remember what he'd thrown on this morning. 'The fruit dressed as a fruit?'

Ryan heaved out a sigh. This was why he avoided people. Why he needed to work alone. His social skills sucked. 'Look, mate, I promise I was only thinking watermelon.'

For a few disconcerting moments, Lucas's gaze seared through him. 'You're sure about that?'

'You seriously think I give a flying fig who you sleep with?'

Finally, Lucas dropped his ready-to-strangle-him look. 'Okay, darling, I believe you.' He then proceeded to flash a smile that, if it had come from a woman, Ryan would have called downright flirtatious. 'Do you like watermelons?'

Shit, where was he going with this now? 'Sure. In a fruit salad.'

'Umm, so you are partial to a bit of fruit then?'

As Lucas continued to smile at him, Ryan felt a blush creep up his neck. 'Please tell me you're not hitting on me.'

Lucas batted his eyelashes. *Batted* his damn eyelashes. 'Do you want me to?'

'Christ, no.'

While Ryan went all sorts of hot and cold, Lucas tipped his head back and roared with laughter. 'I'm messing with you, Black.' A sly smile flitted across his face. 'I do have standards, you know.'

Relief made Ryan almost lightheaded. 'Thank fuck for that.'

Once he'd stopped laughing, Lucas turned his attention back to the drinks machine and pressed a few buttons. Ryan watched with horror as an obscene amount of white frothy liquid spouted into a mug. 'On the subject of standards, I never drink anything I can't spell. I'll stick to black coffee, thanks.'

Lucas pursed his lips. 'Here was me thinking we were going to be friends.'

Ryan couldn't see that happening if they were the only two left on the planet, but as he and Lucas seemed to have arrived at some sort of truce, he kept quiet.

Lucas carried both drinks into the nearby meeting room and placed them on the table before sitting down with a theatrical flurry. 'So, it seems we've been naughty schoolboys.'

Ryan carefully sat on the chair furthest away. 'At least I didn't go crying to the teacher.'

'Touché.' Lucas took a sip of his mocha crap. 'I wouldn't have needed to if you'd bothered to talk to me on just one of the six occasions I came to run something by you.'

'That's what meetings are for.'

Lucas stared back at him, jaw opening and closing like a goldfish. 'I have to schedule in time to talk to you, do I?' He rolled his eyes. 'And people call me the Queen.'

'I only called you a watermelon.' Ryan huffed out a breath, wondering what the hell he was doing sitting here discussing queens and fruits with a man drinking a mochaccino. 'Look, when I'm working, I need quiet. It's nothing personal.'

Lucas frowned. 'Then how about this for a wacky idea? Tell me that. Don't just growl at me.'

'Fine.' He looked Lucas in the eye. 'When you can see my head's down, please don't disturb me. It really ticks me off.'

'Noted.' Lucas flicked something off his trousers. Probably a confused insect looking for pollen. 'There are still things we need to discuss though, and don't tell me I have to schedule an audience with you.'

'Wouldn't dream of it,' he muttered, taking a swig of his coffee.

'How about we set aside half an hour every morning and every afternoon to ... hook up.' Lucas waggled his eyebrows suggestively.

Ryan decided to play him at his own game. 'You sure half an hour is enough?'

'I'm easily satisfied.'

Lucas's face kept impressively deadpan – for about two seconds. Then his lips twitched and Ryan couldn't help himself. He started to laugh. 'Half an hour it is then.' He drank the last of his coffee and jumped to his feet. Time to make a run for it while they were still on reasonable terms. But as he reached the door, Lucas's question stopped him in his tracks.

'What do you think of our Sam, then?'

Was it a fishing expedition? Or did the guy know something? Ryan couldn't tell from Lucas's impressively blank expression. 'Too early to tell.'

Lucas's expression sharpened as he stood and walked towards him. 'Have you two met before?'

Ryan willed himself not to flinch, not to blink. He rated honesty above all other traits, mainly because he'd been lied to for much of his childhood, but this was a question he wasn't prepared to answer. Even if, by not answering, he raised suspicion. 'Why?'

Sure enough, Lucas's eyebrows rose another inch. 'Just idle speculation. There seems to be an undercurrent between you. I can't work it out.'

Ryan snorted. 'Yeah. She doesn't like me. You were there when she told you.' Before the man could ask anything else, Ryan shot off back to his desk.

Undercurrent? Was that code for sex? And why the bloody hell couldn't he stop thinking about that night? It had been two weeks, for pity's sake.

Maybe his obsession had nothing to do with Sam Huxton, he thought as he logged back onto his computer. Maybe he just needed to get laid again. Then again, considering how much trouble the last hook-up had landed him, maybe celibacy was the way forward.

In fact, considering his to-do list, celibacy was the only viable option.

Chapter 8

'I'm going to throttle Hank. How could he recommend that guy to us?'

It was now four weeks into Ryan's employment with them, and things hadn't got any easier. This time it was Becky chewing Sam's ear off as they walked together to the weekly management meeting. A quick glance along the corridor and it was clear Ryan was already in the meeting room, as was becoming the norm. Obsessive punctuality seemed to be as much his thing as obsessive quietness when he was working.

As if he could sense her, he glanced up and immediately her pulse shot up a gear. Sam groaned inwardly. Here went another hour spent pretending he was just another employee.

Pretending she didn't still find the man impossibly attractive.

'Sam?'

She shook away her errant thoughts. 'Sorry. Miles away.'

Becky gave her a sidelong look. 'Oh boy, please don't tell me you actually still like the guy?'

'What guy?' Becky huffed and Sam immediately caved. 'If you're talking about Ryan, I never said I liked him.'

'But you can't take your eyes off him, either.'

Sam lurched to a stop. 'I can. See, my eyes are on you now.' She gave Becky her best wholesome smile. 'So, what's our newest employee done now?'

Becky sighed. 'He's not easy to work with, you know? Locks himself away in the meeting room all day. It's so frustrating when I have things I need to run by him. He's been here a month now and it's vital we start communicating more.'

'Maybe you should gatecrash Lucas's time slots.' Aware that Ryan was still watching her, Sam started walking again. He probably thought they were gossiping about him. But when did being a responsible manager and listening to her staff's gripes become gossip?

'I said the same to Lucas. He told me he didn't want to share him.' Becky started to giggle. 'I seriously think he's got the hots for Ryan and he's hoping to turn him.'

A memory of Ryan's dark, hooded eyes flashed through her mind. The way they'd burned into hers as he'd moved over her. Then slipped inside her. 'I doubt the man's for turning,' she murmured, feeling heat pool between her legs. Would there ever be a time when she didn't remember every blasted moment of that night?

Thankfully Lucas arrived at the meeting room just behind them, allowing her to keep her interaction with Ryan to a brief, impersonal smile.

'The elusive Mr Black.' Lucas strode into the room and glided elegantly into the seat next to Ryan. Sam stifled a smile as she saw Ryan's forehead crinkle in a frown. 'What's wrong? Don't you want me to sit next to you?' Lucas pouted.

'Sure I do.' He glanced at Lucas's bold pink and white striped shirt, which he'd teamed today with rather conservative beige trousers. 'As long as your wardrobe choice isn't catching.'

Lucas burst out laughing and Sam immediately glanced at Becky, who looked as shocked as she was. Were those two actually starting to get on?

The meeting began with department updates. 'Are we still on schedule to have Privacy 2 finalised in two months?' Sam's stomach knotted, as it always did, when she thought of the rapidly approaching deadline.

It was Lucas who replied. 'Boy wonder here is working his fine butt off.' Ryan briefly closed his eyes, but Sam thought she saw his lips twitch. 'We've managed to streamline the input side of things by providing a consent button to access third party data, like Facebook and Instagram. We've also got the app to monitor the user's junk email, which we didn't have before. If we carry on at the same rate of progress then yes, we should be done in time.'

Ryan raised his hand. 'What Lucas meant to say was, if we don't come across any hitches, if we can persuade you and Becky to be happy with the compromises we've had to make, and if we can agree on the next steps, then maybe there's a chance it will be done in two months.'

Automatically Sam's hands reached into her trouser pocket for the antacids. The thought of not having it ready before Damien's launch ... No, she wasn't thinking like that. They were going to do this. Taking a breath, she pushed a smile onto her face. 'Sounds good.'

Next to be discussed was the upcoming investor meeting. They held one monthly to keep those who'd ploughed a considerable amount of money into the company abreast with how things were going.

'Will your parents be attending?' Becky asked after she'd given them all a brief update on what she was planning to say.

Ryan's head snapped up and Sam was aware of his eyes watching her intently as she replied. 'I don't think so. They said they didn't want to interfere. Just to help.' Why did she suddenly feel as if Ryan was weighing her up, and finding her wanting? Worse, why did she care if he was?

'Mummy and Daddy funding your pet project, are they?'

At the derision in his eyes, she felt her blood boil. 'This isn't a project,' she told him tightly. 'It's my life. My parents didn't give me a penny until ...' She slammed her mouth shut, aware she'd nearly given him further ammunition to laugh at her. 'It's none of your business.' Words she should have stuck to in the first place.

'You're right. Sorry.' Ryan gave her an awkward-looking smile. 'Sometimes crap comes out of my mouth before my brain has a chance to filter it.'

Mollified – and more than a touch surprised – by his unexpected apology, Sam moved quickly on. 'The next agenda item is employee of the month. Does anyone have a recommendation?'

'What?'

The look on Ryan's face was almost comical. 'We have an employee recognition scheme,' she explained patiently, well aware he'd feel as much affinity towards that as he did to open-plan working. 'Anyone can nominate someone for it. They just need to give a reason. We discuss the recommendation in this meeting. The nominated employee gets to keep the plaque on their desk for a month.'

'Whoopee.' Though his tone was sarcastic, his eyes were amused.

'They also earn a fifty-pound voucher of their choosing.'

Ryan's lips curved in that funny smirk. 'Can I nominate myself?'

Becky leant unsubtly towards her. 'Self-nomination is the only way he'll get one,' she whispered, though whispered wasn't quite the right word as Ryan's eyes flashed in their direction.

'Not very teamy of you, Becky.' He gave a slow shake of his head. 'At least direct your sarky comments to my face.'

'Not very teamy of you to shut yourself in a meeting room all day.'

He raised his eyes to the ceiling. 'I don't sit at my desk dreaming up cute ad slogans. I write complex code. It requires thought.'

'Seb wrote code,' Becky retorted, never one to step down from a challenge. 'He also sat in the open plan area and was happy to be interrupted when I needed to ask him something.'

'Is this the same guy who told you he could do the impossible?' Before Becky could reply, and from the way she was practically vibrating, Sam knew her friend was itching to deliver a snappy put-down, Ryan spoke again. 'Look, I'm sorry

I need quiet to work. If you need to talk to me, why not use the same slots as Mochaccino Man.' He pointed at Lucas.

Becky stiffened. 'That's rude.'

Lucas, though, looked far from unhappy, his blue eyes shining with amusement. 'That's nothing. He called me a fruit the other day.'

As Becky gasped, Ryan cut in. 'It's not as bad as it sounds. He's winding you up. And at least I don't talk about people behind their backs. I say it to their faces.'

Sam felt a dart of guilt as she recalled Ryan overhearing her and Lucas talking about him. But God, had he seriously told Lucas he'd looked like a fruit? And was Lucas really as okay with it as he seemed to be?

Time to move the meeting into safer, more professional territory. Sam cleared her throat. 'Okay, enough. While Ryan's working in the meeting room, Becky will use the same time slots as Lucas if she needs to talk to him.' Not that she was going to let Ryan work in isolation for much longer. She fully believed employees who chatted together and socialised together worked better together. *One team, one mission, one heart* wasn't just the company motto. It was a fundamental part of their success. 'Now can we get back to employee of the month?'

'I'd like to nominate Alice.' Becky gave Ryan a pointed look. 'She's been terrific, helping me as much as she can when Ryan's been ... unavailable.'

Ryan's face twisted. 'There's something going on with her.'

Not the response Sam had been expecting. 'What do you mean?'

'Nobody can be that happy all the time. It's not real.'

'Especially not working with you.' Becky uttered the words loud enough for Ryan to hear this time.

He let out a low laugh. 'Good one.'

Sam accepted Alice's nomination and moved hastily to the next item on her list. The conference. 'We've agreed to have a stand at the mobile app conference next month. Becky, I know you and the sales team will be attending on both days. Do you need support from anyone else?'

'In the past we've had one of the development team come, in case we get asked anything technical.' She smiled sweetly over at Ryan. 'Alice did a great job last time.'

He smirked. 'What, you don't want me?'

'If your face can do anything other than glower, then yes. Otherwise, we'd rather have Alice.'

Sam sighed. Here they went again. She was going to throttle her friend. Sure Ryan was a pain in the arse, but Becky knew that. She'd flipping interviewed him. Needling him was only going to make him worse.

'You think this face can't smile if it needs to?' Ryan countered. 'At least I don't have bright blue hair.' As Becky bristled, he held up his hand. 'Hey, don't get me wrong, it's kind of cool, but who's to say it won't put more people off than my sour face?'

Ignoring him, Sam turned to Becky, trying to gauge her thoughts. Did she want Ryan at the conference, or not?

Her friend clearly read her unasked question. 'If he puts on a suit and plays nice, I'm happy for him to come.' She paused a moment. 'Will you be coming?'

'Yes, for a bit.'

'Then it probably makes sense for Alice to come on the first day and for you and Ryan to come for the second day. We can hold an informal Q&A at the stand.' A slow smile crept over Becky's face. 'And I think you and Ryan live near each other, so this way you only need to bring one car.'

Sam's jaw dropped open. What on earth was she cooking up? But Becky just continued to smile.

'Ryan?' With great trepidation, she looked over at him, but he wasn't listening. He was staring down at his phone, a tight expression on his face.

'Sorry, got to get this.'

Without another word, he shot to his feet and marched out of the room.

'Well.' Lucas leant back on his chair and started to laugh. 'I'll say one thing for Black. He certainly livens up a management meeting. Is there anything else we need to discuss?'

'We're done, but before you go, one question.' Sam knew Lucas put on a good game face, but behind it, he was far more sensitive than he let on. 'Are you really okay with Ryan taking the mick like that?'

'Darling, he can call me whatever he likes.' When she continued to look at him, his face sobered. 'If you want the truth, there's something refreshing about a man who's prepared to stare me straight in the eye and say I look like a watermelon. Most of the time that sort of stuff is whispered behind my back. With Ryan I know where I stand. There's no side to him. He's not saying it to be mean, or to goad me. He just says what he thinks.' As he stood up, he added with a wink.

'Don't go telling him I said this, but I'm actually starting to like the man.'

Feeling equal parts surprise and relief, Sam watched him leave before turning to her so-called friend. 'What the hell, Becks?'

Becky had the grace to look shamefaced. 'Sorry about setting you up to travel with him like that, though I'm not sure he heard any of it. He was so focused on whoever was calling him.'

'But why would you? Especially after you'd just spent the whole meeting winding him up, which wasn't cool, by the way. I'm trying to develop a culture of team working. Of being one happy family.'

Becky grinned. 'You have brothers, right? Don't tell me you never wound them up on purpose, just to see how they'd react.'

'Is that what you were doing? Because it seemed to me it was more than that.'

'Hey, he started it. *Not very teamy of you, Becky*,' she drawled in a terrible imitation of Ryan's deep yet oddly soft voice.

'When I said I wanted this to be a family, I didn't mean I wanted squabbling siblings. And I certainly don't want to be Mum.'

Becky snorted. 'No, it's quite clear what you want. He's six-three with big shoulders, dark eyes and an annoying attitude.'

Sam lurched back, aghast. 'I do not.'

Becky gave her arm a light touch, her expression turning from highly amused to concerned. 'Are you sure about that?

Because the way you looked at him before we went into the room sure didn't say *not bothered.*'

Groaning, Sam covered her face with her hands. 'Please tell me I didn't look like that in the actual meeting.'

'You didn't, though I suspect that's just because you barely glanced at him.' Becky sighed, giving Sam's shoulders a sympathetic rub. 'Hey, come on. You like him, he likes you.'

'He doesn't.'

'Of course he does. You think he'd say sorry to any of us like he just did to you?' Her eyes brimmed with understanding. 'I know it's not ideal because of the office connection again, but it's only really a problem if you make it into one. I thought if you travelled to the conference together it might give you a chance to talk things out.'

'Oh no, no, no.' Sam heaved in a breath and sat up. 'No, no, no. There's nothing I have to say to Ryan outside work. What we did was a mistake. I can't see someone from work again. Have you forgotten how badly that went for me last time? And God, Ryan *works* for me, sleeping with him is all sorts of wrong.' A bubble of brittle laughter escaped her. 'Except I did, didn't I, and now I can't stop thinking about it.' Emotions all over the place, she looked glumly over at her friend. 'I don't even know if I like him, Becks, but my eyes can't stop tracking him. My body can't stop remembering what it felt like to be touched my him. What the blazes am I supposed to do?'

Becky took hold of her hands and clasped them in hers. 'Number one, stop worrying. Just because Damien ended in disaster doesn't mean every office-based relationship is doomed.'

'Did I mention the part about me being Ryan's *boss*?'

'You're not the first boss to sleep with an employee.'

'Yeah, but the boss is usually male. I hold myself to a higher standard than that.'

Becky started to snigger. 'If it's like I've read in books, the boss isn't just usually male, he's also usually a billionaire who likes to tie his employee up in all sorts of—'

'Thanks, I get the picture.'

Becky gave her a cheeky grin and started to fan herself. 'Oh my, so do I. You standing by the four-poster in sexy heels. Ryan sprawled out on the bed, arms and legs cuffed to the posts.'

'What's point number two?' Sam interrupted, feeling heat pulse through her body. 'Because number one isn't exactly helping here, you know.'

Becky sobered. 'Number two is spend more time with him. Go to the conference together. You might find you don't like him, and then this crazy attraction will disappear.'

'And if the opposite happens?'

'Ah.' She slid Sam a look. 'You think you could actually like a guy whose default mode seems to be rude and the only smile he knows is a smirk?'

'No.' Yet the man she'd slept with, who'd nearly walked away from a certain one-night stand because he'd been worried she was drunk, and who'd been kind enough to pretend to listen when she'd poured out her grief about her grandad, had been more than that. 'At least I don't think so.'

PART THREE

A Matter of Trust

Chapter 9

Ryan cursed under his breath as he kicked the tyre of his car. Bloody thing was letting him down more and more these days. With a huff of resignation, he threw his jacket on the passenger seat, yanked off his stupid tie, rolled back the sleeves of the one collared shirt he owned, and opened the bonnet.

Twenty minutes later he had the engine of the forty-year-old Triumph Spitfire running again. But now he was late.

Why had he nodded dumbly last week when Sam had asked if he wouldn't mind driving because her car was having its airbags replaced, thanks to a customer recall? Why hadn't he laughed and said airbags, what the hell are they? His car was lucky to have seat belts.

But no, with his brain in a fog of worry because of the phone call he'd just taken, and his mind hung up on the image of them travelling together, just the two of them, he'd meekly agreed to pick her up.

Quickly slipping the tie back on, he jammed himself behind the wheel and set off towards her place. Of course he hadn't needed the address, because he'd been there before, two months ago.

The memory caused heat to prick at the back of his neck and he pulled the tie further down. No point strangling himself all the way to the meeting venue.

She was waiting outside when he arrived, and his heart skipped a beat as his eyes drank her in. Looking wow in a curve-hugging purple trouser suit, her hair neatly coiled into a bun, she dripped sophistication and poise. And he was about to cram her into his battered old car.

Fuck, he was stupid.

Keeping the engine running – he wasn't going to take a chance on it not starting again – he jumped out. 'Sorry I'm late.'

She gave him a polite smile. 'No problem. London traffic is never predictable.'

Averting his eyes, he pulled open the passenger door for her. Was it lying if he didn't correct her? Sod it, for once he was keeping quiet. She slipped inside and he banged the door closed. His mum would be proud of his chivalry, but he knew he'd had no choice. Ruddy door only shut if you banged it from the outside.

'Do you need me to map read?' she asked as he pulled off, waving her hand at the pathetically barren dashboard. 'No GPS, I take it.'

He leant towards her and pulled open the glove compartment, feeling a jolt as he inhaled her familiar scent. Immediately images from that night flooded through him and he reared back. 'GPS is in there somewhere.'

His voice was suspiciously hoarse, something she must have clocked because he saw her swallow before she spoke. 'There had better not be anything in here that might bite.'

As she angled her body to dig around in the compartment, Ryan felt himself starting to smile. 'Nah. It's just where I keep my spare boxers.'

She stilled, but her eyes were alive with humour. 'Dirty or clean?'

'Clean.' He gave her a mock disgusted look. 'I'm not a total slob.'

'Thank heavens for small mercies.'

She smiled and he felt a rush of air leave his lungs. As he reached to take the gadget from her, their fingers touched and he felt another jolt. This was going to be impossible. The car was too small. She was too gorgeous. And he was far, far too aware of everything about her. 'This was a bad idea.'

Those huge blue eyes swivelled towards him. 'Sorry?'

Was she really that clueless? Or was it only him feeling as if he'd been tied into a hundred knots? 'Do I need to spell it out?'

He watched the heat touch her cheeks. 'No.' She swallowed again. 'Maybe it would be better if I got a cab.'

He laughed humourlessly. 'What, you go by cab, I drive, and when we meet up at the conference, I suddenly don't want to have sex with you any more?'

Her breath hitched. 'Please don't say things like that.'

Feeling a mix of annoyed, turned on and helpless, he exhaled roughly. 'Sorry.' After a few humming moments of silence, during which he plugged in the sat nav and stuck it to the dashboard, he handed her a crumpled Post-it. 'It's the postcode for the hotel where the conference is. Can you enter it while I turn the car round?'

She took it from him, carefully avoiding touching his fingers, and within a few seconds the woman on the sat nav was telling him the way to go. He wished she could also tell him how to erase the simmering tension he'd just created.

As he set off down the road an awful thought struck him. Was it sexual harassment if you told your female boss you wanted to sleep with her? Bile flew up his throat as his stomach churned painfully.

'Perhaps we should use the journey to get to know each other.'

He swallowed down the nausea and took a breath. And then another. 'Yeah?'

Out of the corner of his eye he saw her gaze fly to his face. 'Professionally.' A little laugh bubbled out of her. 'Oh God, how ridiculous. We're two grown adults. We can manage an hour in a car together without weirding ourselves out.'

Was she weirded out because she felt the same blinding sexual attraction he felt? Or was hers down to the acute embarrassment of knowing she'd slept with one of her underlings? And yeah, he didn't really need to wonder, did he? He was the only one tied up in knots here.

He had to get over himself. Determinedly he searched for a safe topic. 'So, word on the street is you started Privacy Solutions straight from university. Is that true?'

Her shoulders relaxed a little. A clear signal she was relieved to be talking work. 'Sounds precocious, I know, but yes. Me and ... another student planned it while we were studying. When we graduated, we'd already put a business plan together and had a few interested parties keen to invest.'

'Impressive. This other student was Damien Lynch? The guy who left to set up the rival company you're wetting yourselves over?'

Her stance stiffened again. Clearly she was happy to talk work, but not happy to talk about her ex-partner. 'Yes, though I'd use the term "concerned" rather than "wetting ourselves".'

'Guess that's CEO-speak compared to employee-speak.' Or posh end of town compared to poor end. Either way, he was at the wrong end of the spectrum. 'What did you have a bust-up over?'

Her posture wasn't just stiff now, it was rigid. 'We had a difference of opinion on the way forward.'

'That's the line trotted out to the media. I was looking for the real reason.'

Once again tension hung in the air, but this time it wasn't sexual, thank God. He was a million times more comfortable handling an annoyed boss than an attractive one.

'You don't need to know what we disagreed about. It's irrelevant to the work we're doing.'

'Irrelevant maybe.' He flicked her a look. 'Uninteresting, I doubt it.'

Their eyes caught briefly and he saw a glint of humour before he had to look back at the road. 'I'm not here to entertain you.'

'Shame.' And just like that, the sexual tension was back

again. 'Sorry.' Feeling the stiffness invading him now, he rolled his shoulders. 'I'd offer to put the radio on, but it's broken.'

'Maybe I should ask the questions.' He was aware of her gaze falling on him. 'Why were you fired from your last job?'

He snorted. 'You already know the answer to that.'

'I know that Becky's brother said you refused to work on the next app they assigned you. What I don't know is why.'

Ryan's hands tightened on the steering wheel. Why hadn't he had the radio fixed? 'I don't like gambling apps.'

Sam watched Ryan's hands clench the wheel and realised she'd touched a nerve, just as he'd touched hers when he'd asked about Damien. Was it a misuse of her power to prod at it, when she'd deliberately cut his questioning of her dead? But if they weren't arguing, they seemed to fall into conversations laden with sexual innuendo, and that was even more dangerous. Besides, she was interested in what made Ryan Black tick, what made him so anti-social. Why a man who earnt a pretty good salary was driving a forty-year-old rust heap.

Though it was painful to admit, Becky was right. She was interested in Ryan Black, full stop.

A gentle prod it was, then. 'You've never had a flutter on the horses?'

'I didn't say I disagreed with gambling. I disagree with making it too easy.'

'So much so that you gave up a well-paid job, with nothing in the pipeline?'

He indicated to switch lanes and it was a few seconds before he replied. 'Yes.'

There was history there, but if she probed, it would move their conversation into the personal, and she'd promised professional. 'Why didn't you just ask to work on another project?'

'Simple as that, huh?'

'I can't see why not. I know the company. There must have been other apps you could have been moved to.'

When he didn't immediately reply she turned to study his face. At times, like now, she'd put him down as a thinker. Slow and careful about what he said. It went with his need to work in isolation. He liked to detach himself from others, and from the problem, so he could look at it painstakingly. Logically. It was in direct contrast to her, who liked to talk out a problem, and then go with her gut instinct. At other times though, he seemed quick to blurt the first thing that came into his head. That, she guessed, was when his emotions were involved.

'I probably could have moved apps.' He shrugged his wide shoulders, drawing her attention to the way his muscles shifted beneath the white shirt.

Eyes forward, Huxton. 'I suspect you screwed up any chance of being moved to another project by going, and I quote from Becky's brother, "apeshit".'

Humour danced around his mouth, drawing her eyes again. She really should have gone by cab. It was far too easy to stare at him, knowing he couldn't stare back. 'Why ask the question, when you knew the answer?'

'I only know you lost your temper,' she corrected. 'I don't know why.' Because she wanted it to at least *appear* she was asking the question for professional reasons, she added, 'I don't want the same to happen when you're working for me.'

His jaw tightened, and she suspected he hated her reminding him of their unequal status. 'Are you planning on developing an app that has the potential to feed an addiction?'

'No. The company is all about protecting our customers' privacy.'

His eyes briefly held hers. 'Then I won't be going apeshit on you.' He smiled darkly. 'At least not in work time.'

What did he mean by that? Sam pulled her gaze away, aware yet again of the sexual undercurrent that was never far from the surface. Her slow-burning affair with Damien hadn't prepared her for this raw attraction and she didn't know how to handle it. Add in the fact that Ryan was an employee, and it felt like she'd been tossed into a stormy sea without a life jacket. 'Please stop the innuendos.'

'It wasn't.'

Oh boy. Her heart let out a loud thump. 'There can't be any non-work time for you and me. It would be too awkward.'

'You think I don't know that?' She heard him exhale slowly. 'Doesn't stop me wondering about it.'

Me too, she thought despairingly. She risked another glance at his strong profile, and her stomach flip-flopped. Would it really be so bad to continue their affair, if both parties were up for it?

Continue their affair? Dear God, she was going crazy. They'd had a one-night stand. At the time she'd been so determined they were totally wrong for each other, she'd not even wanted to know his name. To consider falling into that trap again was total madness.

To her relief he turned onto the slip road. 'Not long now.' He flicked a look at the sat nav.

He'd given her an out so she could ignore his previous sentence, but that would be cowardly. She had a grudging admiration for his willingness to face difficult situations head on. 'I wonder about it too,' she admitted quietly. 'But you and me, we'd burn bright and then fizzle out. If you think now is awkward, imagine if we couldn't stand the sight of each other.'

Pulling up at a red light, he gave her a small smile. 'Does that mean you quite like me at the moment?'

'Don't push your luck.' The amused look he gave her caused her stomach to execute a neat somersault. Quickly she dropped her gaze to her hands. 'I can't afford to lose another software developer,' she said finally.

He obviously understood her meaning, because he sighed. 'I read you.'

They were silent as he navigated the final few miles to the hotel. It was only when he'd parked that he turned to face her, and her heart fluttered as those dark eyes sought hers, his body looking huge in the small interior. 'This ex-partner of yours. Will he be here, too?'

Way to kill off the sexual tension. 'I don't know.' But she'd woken in a cold sweat thinking about it. They'd bumped into each other a couple of times in the early days and each time she'd told herself the next time would be easier. Apparently she'd been lying.

Ryan nodded and opened his door. 'Well, you need me to beat anyone up, just let me know.'

The thought was so delicious, Sam started to laugh. 'How do you know he isn't taller and stronger than you?' Damien was about an inch or two shorter, and on the lean end of the body scale.

Ryan shrugged those huge shoulders. 'Doesn't matter if he is.'

She raised a brow. 'Cocky, much?'

He shook his head. 'Not cocky. Just know how to handle myself.' Before she could wonder at the meaning behind his statement, he was walking round the bonnet and pulling her door open. 'Out you get, boss.'

Grateful for her trouser suit as she climbed out of the cramped sports car, she waited while he bent to retrieve his jacket from the back seat. That's when she noticed the side of his shirt. 'Looks like you've got some oil on your shirt.'

He stilled, looking down at the large black smear, then swore under his breath. 'Guess I'll be wearing a jacket all day.'

Carefully he eased into it and jerked up his tie. The transformation was quite something. A brooding hunk in jeans and a T-shirt, in a suit he was … handsome wasn't right. He was more than an attractive face. He was mesmerising.

Willing the butterflies in her stomach to settle, she focused not on the powerful body shape silhouetted by the suit, but on the oil. 'It wasn't traffic that made you late, was it?'

He flushed, avoiding her eye as he did up the button on his jacket. 'No.'

'Hey, I didn't mean to embarrass you. I just wondered why you didn't tell me.'

'Tell you what?' Defensiveness ran through his voice and every inch of his body. 'Sorry I'm late but the forty-year-old rust heap I drive is always breaking down? Think you'd have still come with me?'

Her breath hitched as those eyes burned into hers. *He'd wanted to take her*. Before she could start to think about that too much, she nodded towards the hotel entrance. 'Better get in before Becky sends out a search party.'

The loaded look he gave her told her exactly what he thought about her avoiding his question, but thankfully he didn't call her on it.

Chapter 10

Ryan felt like he was in a straitjacket, with a noose tied around his neck. He might be a geek, but he knew enough about the world outside his computer to understand there were times a suit and tie were needed. Didn't mean he enjoyed wearing them, and knowing he was sporting engine oil down the side of his shirt didn't help.

Nor did standing in three square metres of vivid blue exhibition booth. He felt like he was an exhibit. The sales guy had popped off for a break, and Becky – one glance at her hair, and it wasn't hard to see who'd dreamt up the colour for the Privacy Solutions branding – had somehow managed to rope Ryan in to help her for twenty minutes. So far he'd done four.

'Stop fidgeting.' Becky, looking almost normal in her black trousers and white shirt, with the exception of her Privacy-blue hair, gave him her death stare.

'Who made you my mum?'

She sniggered. 'If I'd given birth to you, I'd have shoved you right back.'

'If you'd been my mum, I'd have crawled back in willingly.'

For a second she looked daggers at him. Then she burst out laughing. 'Like newborn babies can do that.'

'I was very advanced.'

'God, Black, you're such an arse.' She looked him up and down. 'But you scrub up okay.'

He fidgeted again with his collar. 'Careful with the compliments. You don't want me getting big-headed.'

'Too late for that,' she muttered, then straightened up as she saw two men in dark suits walk towards them. 'Hello. Welcome to Privacy Solutions. Can I help?'

Ryan stepped niftily away. He was happy to answer technical questions, but that's where his participation started and ended. Spying Sam on the other side of the stand, he walked over, frowning as he neared her. She looked as if she'd seen a ghost. 'Everything okay?'

She shook herself, causing a tendril of red hair to escape from her neat bun. 'It's fine.' But then she swore, and as Ryan tracked her gaze, he saw a slim, dark-haired man walking towards them, about his age.

Sam continued to stare at the guy, as if she couldn't drag her eyes away, and Ryan felt the penny drop. 'Damien Lynch, I presume.'

'Yes.' The sound came out scratchy, and she coughed. 'What the hell does he want?'

'I'm guessing you're about to find out.' Should he stay, or did she want privacy? From the way his usually calm, collected boss was suddenly looking like a startled rabbit, he'd put money on the relationship between her and Damien being more than just business partners.

Feeling an unexpected surge of protectiveness, and an unwanted bite of jealousy, Ryan squared his shoulders. He was staying put.

'Damien.' Sam had schooled her face into the same polite mask she'd worn when she'd walked up to him in the Privacy Solutions foyer, the morning after *that* night.

Ryan studied Damien Lynch as the guy gave Sam what looked to be a well-practised smile. Grey eyes, about as warm as the North Sea. Wavy dark hair, neatly combed. Unbroken nose – yeah, okay, it was a good, straight nose. Lean body clothed in a charcoal suit that made Ryan's look cheap and ill-fitting. Slim wristwatch that said *I'm discreet and expensive*.

'Good to see you, Sam.' Damien bent and kissed her cheek, and Ryan felt that blasted jealously bare its teeth again. 'How's business?'

'Fine, thank you.'

Her voice was a whisper, her face a slab of marble. Where had his ballsy, animated boss gone? The woman looking back at Damien was like a hollowed-out statue of her, movements wooden, her fire extinguished. Whatever this prick had done to Sam, it had hurt. Ryan took a step forward and shoved out his hand. 'Ryan Black. And you are?'

Damien narrowed his eyes, no doubt wondering at the abrupt tone, but he clasped Ryan's outstretched hand. The handshake was firm, though the hands were soft. 'Damien Lynch. I used to be Sam's ... business partner.'

Ryan nodded, as if he didn't already know. 'What do you do now?' And yes, he wanted to make the guy uncomfortable.

Damien gave him a tight smile. 'I set up my own company.'

'Same field?'

'Yes.' The man had the gall to reach into his inside pocket and draw out a business card.

Ryan read the name out loud. 'Privacy Protect, huh?' He glanced across at Sam, who was giving him a *what the hell are you doing?* look. 'You left Privacy Solutions and set up a rival company called Privacy ... Protect?' He emphasised the word 'privacy' and added what he hoped was a sufficient note of staggered disbelief to his voice.

Damien's smile vanished. 'And what do you do, Ryan Black?'

I'm the guy who's going to develop an app that will bust your shitty venture wide open. Ryan swallowed down the words. Where had all this angst come from? It didn't matter to him what Damien Lynch had done. Hell, if Sam decided to throw him out before his probation period was up, he might end up going to Lynch on bended knee and begging for a job. 'I'm a software developer.'

Interest sparked in Damien's eyes. 'You must be working on the Privacy app update, then.'

Before Ryan could say a word, Sam was elbowing him in the side. As he let out an *umph* sound, she swivelled to face her ex-partner. 'Thank you for your interest in my company, Damien. And good luck with yours.' All attitude and poise again, she smiled sweetly at him. 'Now if you don't mind, we have customers to talk to.'

Her look, her voice, the turn of her shoulders, all effectively dismissed Damien, who was left glaring at the back of her head, before walking away.

'Neat.' Ryan rubbed at his side. 'Could have done without the bruised ribs, mind.'

'I didn't want to risk you blurting anything out.'

Ryan stilled. 'Don't you trust me?'

'Trust is earned.' Her eyes strayed towards Damien's retreating figure. 'I trusted him once.'

'Right. All men are bastards.' It shouldn't bother him. But it did.

'No.' She exhaled softly. 'Maybe.' Those big eyes found his and her expression softened slightly. 'I appreciated you needling him. It was good to see him squirm for a second.'

Still smarting from her lack of trust, Ryan nodded sharply. 'Pleasure.' Then he shoved his hands in his pockets and strode away.

When he felt there was enough distance between them, he let out the breath he'd been holding and glanced back at the stand. Becky and Sam were now deep in conversation, looking occasionally over in his direction.

The feeling of being slapped returned in force. Angry with himself, he spun back round. He was the outsider. He'd always be the outsider. Let them have their fun at his expense, it didn't matter. He'd keep his head down, do his job. Pick up his pay slip. The rest of it, including any half-baked ideas he might have harboured about seeing Sam outside the office, could go to hell.

'He looks angry.'

Sam saw what Becky saw; the scowl on Ryan's face, the hands rammed into his pockets. Yep, even from twenty yards away Ryan could show his displeasure. 'He's just cross because I sort of said I didn't trust him.'

'Ouch.'

'No, it wasn't as bad as that.' Yet the pain she'd seen flash across his face niggled at her. Her barb had been intended for Damien, not Ryan. 'Damien came over.'

Becky's eyes widened. 'Bugger, I'd forgotten he might be here. He was at the sister conference six months ago. I remember him having the balls to come onto the stand and talk to Alice until I sent him packing. What did the weasel want?'

Sam might have felt the force of his betrayal most, but Becky and Lucas had both been hurt when Damien had set up a rival company. It was hard to conceive that the same man they'd built the company with, who'd been there through numerous all-nighters, who'd eaten pizza and kipped on the office floor with them, got stupidly drunk on launch day with them and ended up dancing in Trafalgar Square fountain, had gone on to coldly abandon them. Then set up a rival company. 'I don't really know what he wanted. Probably just to get under my skin.' For a few sickening moments, she'd let him, too. It had taken Ryan stepping in to help her recover her balance.

Becky touched her arm. 'He's not worth it, Sam.'

'I know.' And she did. Damien's betrayal had successfully extinguished any romantic feelings she'd had towards him. Sadly, it had also left her feeling less: less of a businesswoman, less of a *woman.* Eighteen months on and she was still recovering from it. Of all the things he'd done, that was what she hated him most for.

'How'd he look?'

Unconsciously Sam's mouth curved into a smile. 'A bit thin, to be honest. And his hair was too long.'

Becky sniggered. 'You do realise why you're saying that, don't you?'

'Because I've just seen him?'

'Because you're comparing him to Ryan.'

Sam let out a noise that she hoped conveyed her disgust. 'You marketing types have a vivid imagination.'

'And *you* business types often can't see what's in front of you.' She nudged Sam's arm. 'How was the journey here? Decided you don't like him yet?'

'Stop it, Becks. I'm confused enough without you stirring the pot.'

'Umm.' Her friend glanced at her, a smile hovering on her lips.

Sam resigned herself to more mickey taking. 'Come on, out with it.'

'Just wondering what there is to be confused about. Unless you really are starting to like him, as well as fancy him.'

'I wouldn't go that far.' She inhaled a deep breath, but her mind wouldn't settle. 'He offered to beat Damien up.'

Becky's eyes flew open. 'You told him about what happened?'

'No, of course not.'

'I'd pay good money to see that fight.' Becky's lips twitched. 'From the look of Ryan, he'd pulverise the twerp.'

Sam had a sudden image of Ryan standing over a prostrate Damien, tie askew, shirt sleeves rolled up over bulging biceps, broad chest heaving, sweat dripping from his brow and down his crooked nose. She caught Becky's eye, and started to laugh.

It was late afternoon and they'd all had enough. Sam's face felt like it had gained a hundred wrinkles from all the smiling she'd done. Becky and the sales team looked like she felt. Knackered.

Ryan simply … looked. His eyes sought her out whenever he wasn't with a customer. A dark, brooding gaze, simmering with an edge of resentment, it sent goosebumps racing across her skin. It was a gaze that was hard to ignore. Harder still to feel indifferent towards.

And she still had the journey home.

As she gathered up the feedback forms, Sam watched as a tall, good-looking man marched towards the stand. Early forties, she hazarded, and a face she was certain she'd seen before. His eyes flicked past her before zeroing in on Ryan.

'I'm looking for Sam Huxton. The man in charge of this company. Is that you?'

Ryan shifted on his feet. 'Who am I talking to?'

Fizzing with frustration, Sam dropped the forms back on the table. '*I'm* Sam Huxton. This is Ryan Black. One of my software developers.' She enjoyed seeing the surprise register. That's until she glanced at Ryan's flushed face, and realised how her words had come across. Like she owned him.

Regret washed through her but she had no time to dwell

on it because now a pair of interested blue eyes were raking over her as if she was wearing a tasselled bra and a G-string. 'Well, well. Jeremy Whittaker, at your service.'

Now she remembered who he was. A tech journalist. The woman in her wanted to give him the same once-over, see how he liked it when her eyes lingered on his crotch. The businesswoman knew he could be useful, so she pasted a cool smile on her face.

Ryan pushed his way in front of her. 'Show some respect or make yourself scarce.'

Jeremy bristled, though not half as much as Sam. First Damien, now the journalist. When had Ryan assigned himself as her protector?

Summoning her calm, she smiled again at Jeremy. 'Excuse us a moment, please.'

Catching Ryan's eye, she nodded sharply over to the other side of the stand.

'What?' All swagger and attitude, Ryan followed her over.

'Don't ever do that again,' she hissed.

'My mistake.' Temper shot through his eyes. 'Didn't realise you liked being objectified.'

'If you think I can't handle a chauvinistic prick like him, that I need a man to protect me from him, then you're just as bad as he is.'

His jaw tightened. 'I think you shouldn't have to.'

'Yeah? And I think he's a journalist who could, if I smile sweetly at him, write a cracking article on our new app. So that's what I'm going to do. If you haven't entirely pissed him off.'

Anger flashed across his face, but she didn't have time to mollify him. She had a business that needed all the good publicity it could get.

An hour later, Sam left the cafeteria feeling drained but happy with the way things had gone. Once they'd got down to business, Jeremy had proved to be entirely professional, though there had been an awkward moment at the end when she'd had to dodge his invitation to take her for a drink. Then again, maybe a drink with the flirtatious journalist would have been better than a ride home with an angry employee who made her hormones dance.

When she arrived back at the stand, Becky was supervising its dismantling. 'Ah, our CEO and founder returns. Is Whittaker going to write an article telling the world how great we are?'

Sam rolled her eyes. 'Time will tell.' She glanced around the hive of activity. 'Have you seen my lift home?' Becky bit into her lip, then slowly pointed to the other side of the conference room. Sam followed her eyes and froze. 'How long have they been talking?'

Becky lifted her shoulders. 'I don't know. I only spotted them a moment ago.'

It was nothing to worry about. Even if Damien was pumping Ryan for information, Ryan wouldn't tell him anything, surely.

Yet the man was clearly angry with her. And Damien would no doubt provide a ready and willing ear to any disgruntled employee.

'You can always come back with me.' Becky watched her carefully. 'I'll be done in another hour.'

It sounded appealing, but it was also a copout. Between Ryan's talk with Damien, his earlier attitude to the journalist and his clear anger at her, there was a lot of unfinished business that needed tidying up. 'Thanks, but I'll risk another dose of Mr Black.'

Chapter 11

The tension between them was so heavy, it set Ryan's teeth on edge. An elephant in the room he'd heard of, but an elephant in the car was something else. And right now, there was a herd of the ruddy things stampeding through. But manoeuvring through rush-hour traffic to get onto the motorway wasn't the time to mention them.

'What were you talking to Damien about?'

Ryan exhaled a deep breath. Okay, looks like Sam was going for it. 'Any chance I could get onto the motorway before we start this conversation? Might help us make it home in one piece.'

She snorted. 'You need that long to work out an answer to my question?'

The anger that had been simmering since she'd said she didn't trust him and had ramped up when she'd belittled him in front of the journo threatened to boil over. 'I need that long to calm the fuck down.'

She flinched but kept quiet for the next ten minutes until he was on the motorway – hugging the slow lane, as that's all the Triumph could cope with. When he felt her stare on him, he turned to catch her eyes. 'You really think I was telling Damien about the updates I'm working on?'

He heard her take several deep breaths. Yet her answer, when it finally came, was so quiet he almost missed it above the noise of the forty-year-old engine. 'No.'

The tension in his shoulders relaxed a fraction. 'He asked me if I was happy working for you.'

'Good God, he was trying to *poach* you?'

Her clear disbelief pricked at his ego. 'Thanks.'

She started to laugh, then clearly realised it wasn't appropriate so tried to stop herself, which just made it worse. 'Sorry.' Another round of laughter, softer this time. 'I'm not laughing at you. Just ... the situation. The arrogance of the man who thinks he can just do whatever the hell he likes.'

'He must have been okay once. You set up in business with him.' And yes, he was trying to wangle some gossip out of her. Frustratingly she didn't take the bait.

'Dare I ask what your reply was?'

'I told him you were a kick-ass boss.'

Out of the corner of his eye he saw her head snap round to look at him. 'Wow, how did you work that out? I mean it's a great compliment, so thank you, but you hate my style. You don't agree with open-plan working, you laugh at employee awards. You think the previous software developer managed to successfully lie to me about what he could achieve with the app update only so he could ... how did you phrase it? ... "get into my pants". Need I go on?'

He felt a stab of discomfort. Had he really been that much of a shit to her? 'Aside from all that, you kick ass.'

She let out a bark of laughter. 'I do, huh? Then you must be the master at kissing ass.'

He glanced quickly at her. She had one brow raised in a *got you there* kind of look. 'I'm very particular about whose ass I kiss.'

The reminder of their night together, when he'd kissed every part of her body, including her very fine backside, was all it took for the amusement in her eyes to die. The brief camaraderie now over, he figured he might as well raise the next elephant. 'How did the meeting with the journo go?'

'Good.'

'You know he was a lech, right?'

'He was also a journalist with a strong reputation in the technology field. And I'm not wet behind the ears.'

So she was still pissed at him. Well, that went both ways. 'Point taken. I know you can handle yourself. I just didn't like seeing him look at you like that.'

Resolutely he kept his eyes on the motorway, but he felt her gaze on his face. 'You can't be the jealous boyfriend, Ryan. You're my employee.'

'A fact you've made crystal clear.'

She let out a sharp exhale. 'I know you didn't like the way I introduced you to Whittaker.'

'One of your software developers.' Grimly he repeated what she'd said. Not *a* software developer, or *our* software developer. Not even hers, but *one of* hers. And yeah, he knew he wasn't being rational. If it had been any other boss who'd referred to him like that, he wouldn't have batted an eyelid. But he hadn't slept with other bosses.

'I didn't mean it to sound so arrogant. I was cross that Whittaker had assumed you were the one in charge. I wanted to put him in his place.'

'You succeeded. With both of us.'

'I'm sorry.'

Though she said the words quietly, he didn't doubt their sincerity. Fact was though, he *was* in that place. The one where she held all the cards. And every time he spoke out of turn, he was at risk of losing his job. For a man who only knew how to speak his mind, that was one hell of an edge to be walking along. Especially when every time he looked at her, he wanted her.

The sound of his mobile ringtone cut through the silence. Damn, he meant to turn the thing off. His car didn't have any fancy hands-free system.

Sam angled her head to look at where the sound was coming from. 'It's in my jacket pocket.' Which he'd dumped into the small gap behind them.

'Do you want me to answer it?'

'It can wait.' The sound faded, but then started up again. By the third time of ringing, worry pricked. There weren't many people who had his mobile number. The bank, his landlord. His mum. He felt his stomach start to knot. 'Can you check who it is?'

She reached behind and tugged out the phone. 'It's your mum.'

For her to ring at all meant something was wrong. Not that she'd ever admit it directly. When he'd run out of the meeting last week to take her call, she'd insisted everything was fine, she just wanted to chat. This from a woman who hated talking on the phone. It was only when he'd pressed that she'd admitted she wasn't feeling well. *A bit of indigestion, nothing to worry about*. He'd urged her to go to the doctors. To his shame, he'd not called to check on her, his mind too full of himself: work, making the crappy flat he was renting at least habitable. Obsessing about a woman who was totally out of bounds.

'Can you answer it. Please.' Fear made his voice tight, and his hands grip at the steering wheel.

Sam saw the fear spread across Ryan's face, and her heart bounced. For a private, solitary man like him to ask her to do something so intimate as to answer his phone – and to his mum – spoke volumes about how worried he was.

'Hello, this is Sam Huxton. I'm answering for Ryan because he's driving at the moment. Can I help?'

There was a pause, during which Sam wondered if his mum was still there. Then a young voice came on the line with a faint Midlands accent. 'Tell him it's Erin.'

Sam frowned and turned to Ryan. 'It's not your mum, it's Erin.'

If anything, Ryan's expression became even tighter. 'Put her on loudspeaker.' Sam did as he asked and held the phone up to him. 'What are you doing on Mum's phone?'

His voice, usually smooth, sometimes edging towards a drawl, was so abrupt Sam winced. Whoever Erin was, they weren't friends.

'I'm doing what you should be doing.' Erin's accusing words echoed round the car. 'Looking after her.'

Sam watched as Ryan's face paled, and his knuckles turned white. 'What's wrong?'

'She had a turn; dizziness, out of breath. Pains in her chest.' Erin's tone retained its edge. 'The doc says it was a bout of angina.'

Ryan cursed under his breath. 'Put her on.'

'Bossy, much? I'll do it, but only 'cos *she* wants to talk to you.'

There was a moment of silence. All Sam could hear was the rumble of the car engine, and Ryan's uneven breaths. Then a hesitant older voice came over the speaker.

'I told your sister not to worry you.'

Because she was watching Ryan's face, Sam saw every bit of the emotion he obviously felt at hearing his mum's voice. The pain, the worry, the guilt. And in the tender way he spoke the next words, she heard the love. 'How are you doing?'

'I'm grand, love. It was just a funny turn. The doctor's given me some spray to use if it happens again.'

He breathed slowly, clearly clinging to his control. 'I'm in the car now, Mum. I'll give you a call when I get home. You take care of yourself.'

'Don't you go mithering, now. I'm fit as a fiddle.' There was a pause, and Sam could hear her take a rasping breath. 'Erin tells me a woman answered your phone. Who is she? Anything you're not telling me?'

Pulling up at a red light, Ryan sighed and rolled his eyes upwards. 'She's my boss, Mum. I'm giving her a lift home.' He glanced sideways at Sam, a small smile hovering on his lips. 'And you should know you're on speaker. She can hear every word you're saying.'

'Oh my.' His mum laughed, which turned into a cough. 'Hello, love, nice to meet you. I hope he's behaving himself.'

As Ryan shook his head, Sam started to giggle. 'I think you know your son better than that.'

More breathy laughs echoed down the phone. 'Aye, you're right there. Well, if he gives you any trouble, tell me. I'll give him a good lampin'.'

Sam raised a brow at Ryan and he shook his head again, but the half-smile was still on his face. '"Lampin'" is Midlands-speak for beating,' he clarified. 'Apparently my five-foot-nothing mum still thinks she can tan my backside.'

It was the affection in his voice, the warmth, that Sam found hard to equate with the man she knew. 'Well, thank you for the offer, Mrs Black. I'll let you know if I need your help bringing him in line.'

'It's Maggie, and be sure to do that. I'll be on my way now. Ta-ra.'

The call ended and Sam tucked the phone back in his jacket, her mind a jumble of thoughts. In barely five minutes she'd found out so much more about him. He had a sister he didn't get on with; okay, hardly a shock. Yet other parts of the conversation had definitely taken her by surprise. 'You have a mum.'

His lips twitched. 'Most people do.'

It was hard to imagine the blunt, very male guy sitting next to her as anyone's son, and yet he was clearly a devoted one. A tough outer shell, definitely, but maybe not as hard on the inside as she'd imagined. 'Sorry. I just can't see you as a boy, somehow.'

'Good.' He paused, giving her a quick sidelong glance. 'I'd rather you saw me as a man.'

The words, the way his voice had lowered, combined to cause a slow sizzle in the pit of her stomach. Swallowing hard, she grasped for something to say that would take them out of dangerous territory. 'Are you worried about her health?'

His hands tightened imperceptibly on the wheel, but the look he shot her was one of wry amusement. 'Nice deflect.'

'I thought so.' She smiled back, the sizzle now more of a flutter, and just as hard to ignore. 'The question is a genuine one, though.'

'The short answer is yes.'

'Can I have the long answer, please? We've got plenty of time to kill.' And she really needed him to fill it with conversation that wasn't going to leave her yearning for what she mustn't have.

'That a request or an order?'

'You're off the clock. It's a polite request.'

He heaved a sigh. 'She's got a weak heart so yes – I worry about her.'

'I'm sorry to hear that. Sounds like you have a good relationship.'

'We do.'

Suddenly the car seemed to go quiet. A quick look at Ryan confirmed her fears.

'Damn it, I've lost power.' He angled the steering wheel and they glided onto the hard shoulder, coming to a rather serene stop. His shoulders lifted as he let out a long, deep breath. 'How good are you under a bonnet?'

'About as good as I am at coding an app?'

He huffed softly as he reached for the door handle. 'Wish I could say the same.' A few seconds later he was opening her door. 'I think you need to get out, too. Safer sitting behind the barrier.'

'Sure.' As she stepped over the safety barrier and settled on the grass verge behind it, she was grateful for the warm June evening. And the fact it was still light.

Jacket off, tie off, sleeves rolled up, she allowed herself to watch as Ryan did ... whatever it was people did ... under the bonnet.

A few minutes later, though, he was striding towards her, jacket slung over his shoulder, shaking his head. 'Bloody alternator belt's gone.'

'But you have a spare, right?'

'A spare? What sort of planet ...' He tailed off when he saw her smiling. 'Funny.' Sighing, he dragged his phone out of his pocket and threw his jacket on the ground. 'There, sit on that.'

She eyed the jacket, and then his face. 'Is that a request or an order?' she asked, mimicking his retort from earlier.

He gave her a faintly exasperated smile. 'Please, boss lady, do me the honour of planting your fine arse on my jacket while I call the rescue service.' He grimaced then, staring down at his phone. 'We might be here some time, and I'd hate your bum to get cold.'

Smiling to herself, she shifted onto the jacket. It seemed that somewhere inside the grumpy man, lurking very deep, was a reluctant gentleman. Who'd have thought it?

Chapter 12

Ryan ended the call to the rescue service and hunkered down next to Sam.

'They say within the hour.' It was the stock reply. He should know, he'd called them often enough. So often their number was now in his contact list.

'That's not too bad. At least it isn't raining.'

Typical Sunshine Sam remark. 'That's really what you're thinking? Not angry that you're forced to sit by the side of a motorway for an hour. Just grateful you're not getting wet?'

'Why would I be angry?' She glanced sideways at him. 'You didn't deliberately sabotage the car, did you?'

'Give me some credit.' He grinned. 'If I was going to manufacture some lone time with you, it wouldn't feature a prickly verge and a busy motorway.'

Her big eyes rolled back at him. 'So, where were we? Talking about your mum, I think?'

He winced. 'You're really going to use this time to' – he mimed quotation marks – '*find out more about each other*?'

'Yes.' She shifted, pulling her legs up so she could rest her hands on her knees, her expression quietly determined. 'You have a mum and a sister.'

'Half-sister,' he corrected.

'What about your father?'

He slid her a look. 'You really want to know all this crap?'

Her response was a big, sunny smile. 'Are you kidding? I love finding out about people. The more I know, the more it helps me understand them.'

He wasn't so sure he wanted that. The more she knew, the more she'd find not to like. 'Dad buggered off when I was eight and I haven't seen him since. Can't say I missed him.'

Her eyes watched him carefully and he had the sense she wanted to know more, but his deliberately closed-off expression was stopping her. 'And Erin's father?' she asked finally. 'Was he your stepdad?'

He laughed at the notion. 'Hardly. Never met the guy, neither has Erin. I'm not sure Mum ever told him he was a father.' And because he didn't want her to delve any deeper into his dysfunctional family, he added, 'I reckon it's my turn now. What really happened between you and Lynch?'

He heard her sudden intake of breath. Felt the tension run through her as her back stiffened, and hands that had been clasped loosely round her legs suddenly clutched at them as if they were the only thing holding her upright. 'It's not a secret, though there are plenty of times I wish it was,' she answered finally. 'Damien wasn't just my business partner. He was my partner in every sense. We weren't married, but we were living together. I thought we were happy.' Slowly her eyes lifted to his. 'Then I found out he'd been having an affair with our office manager.'

'Ouch.' Though he'd suspected her fall-out with Damien was more personal than business, it irked him to hear her say it. He wanted to believe his anger was for her, but had an awful feeling it had more to do with jealousy.

'Yeah. Big ouch, considering how I found out about the pair of them.'

It didn't take a genius to guess. 'You caught them at it?'

'I'd been out all day, meeting with one of our investors. I knew he had to work late so instead of heading straight home I decided to go and see him. I found him bending our office manager over his desk.'

He cursed. 'Christ. Guess it explains your vendetta against offices.'

She huffed. 'It's part of the reason, maybe, but I still believe open plan—'

'Makes us all one big happy family,' he cut in. 'Yeah, I heard you the last time.'

Her eyes caught his and when she gave him a small smile, he felt something flutter in his chest. Shit, what was she doing to him? 'Was today the first time you'd seen him since then?'

'Pretty much, yes. We bumped into each other a few times after it happened as he cleared his stuff out of the office and I cleared my stuff out of the place we shared. After that, everything was done through lawyers.' She paused and he thought that was it, but then she seemed to come to a decision and carried on. 'I made him sell his share of the company, but of course I couldn't afford it, so I went back to the investors. It soon became clear they saw Damien as the major brain behind the operation. He was a man, after all,' she added in a rare display of bitterness. 'It looked like I was going to lose the business, but then my parents stepped in to rescue me.' Her gaze met his. 'That's why Becky asked if they were coming to the investor meeting.'

Shame rolled through him. 'Yeah, the bitchy remark about Mummy and Daddy funding your pet project. Not one of my finer moments.' He nudged her, giving her what he hoped she could see was a genuinely apologetic smile. 'Sorry.'

She smiled back. 'As you've got a cute smile, when you bother to use it, you're forgiven.'

Cute? He laughed quietly to himself. He'd take it.

Silence descended, except for the hum of the traffic as it sped by. He felt her shiver and shifted closer to her so she could share his body heat. 'Lynch is clearly not very bright,' he said after a while.

She blinked up at him. 'Why do you say that?'

'Come on, he has you to go home to every night and he starts looking somewhere else?'

Her breath hitched and he wondered if he was going to get a bollocking for veering from the professional into personal. Instead a small frown settled across her face. 'I didn't think you thought of me like that.'

He gave her his best *you've got to be kidding* look. 'Thought I'd made it pretty obvious.'

God, those eyes of hers. They were luminous against the descending darkness. 'No.' She shook her head. 'You were just talking sex.'

Had he been? Sure, he wanted to tumble into bed with her again. And again. But his reaction to Lynch earlier, and then to that sleaze of a journo? The pricks of jealousy, the sudden urge to protect her even though he knew very well she didn't need protecting? They weren't feelings associated with just sex. 'I guess there's only way to know if it could be more.'

Once again he felt her stiffen. But when she looked at him, he didn't see anger, or annoyance. He saw distress. 'I can't have another office-based affair. The last one nearly ruined me.'

He lurched backwards, stung. 'You think I'd cheat on you?'

'No, no. That's not what I meant.' She grabbed his arm and drew him back to her side. He wished he knew whether it was for warmth or the connection. 'I can't bear to have another relationship acted out in the office goldfish bowl. The way the last one ended ... it was ... God, it was humiliating. Excruciating. Bad enough to suffer the pain of a betrayal, but to know everyone knew what had happened. To have to go in each day pretending everything was okay when really I wanted to curl up in a ball and hibernate for the next two years.' Another shudder ran through her. 'Work should be a safe haven. A place where you can distract yourself from any pain that might be taking place in your life. I lost that haven. Everywhere reminded me of him. It's why I agreed to let him keep the apartment. I desperately needed a place to go that held no memories.'

The anguish in her voice almost did him in. Aching for her, he wrapped an arm around her. When he couldn't think of anything he could say that would help, he settled for planting a kiss on the top of her head. Soppy, hell, yes. But this woman made him want to be that man. The one who got to share more than a bed with her. The one who got to comfort her.

Ironic, as she'd just told him he had no chance of doing either.

As Sam felt his lips press against the top of her head, a surge of warmth, of longing, of *hope* ran through her. The warmth could be mistaken for the fact his body felt like a furnace but she thought it was tied into pleasure and an unlikely, yet growing, affection. Longing was surely the desire to feel a connection to someone again; for what she'd had with Damien before he'd cruelly trampled all over it. But hope?

Was she seriously beginning to think she and Ryan could be more than a night of hot sex?

People don't need to know.

The thought bounced wildly through her head. Thrilling, exciting. Scary. Could they have a secret liaison?

It was something to think about.

Before she could mull it over any further, a truck with orange flashing lights pulled up next to the Triumph.

'Looks like help's arrived.' Ryan stood and glanced down at her. 'You wait here until we're ready to go.' His lips curved in the half-smile she was starting to really enjoy. 'That's a polite request, for your own safety.'

'And as it's polite, I'll do as you suggest.'

He raised his eyes heavenwards but as he headed down the slope towards the car, she heard the low rumble of his laughter.

Twenty minutes later the alternator belt had been replaced and they were on their way again. The noise of the engine made continuing any conversation, never mind one with a subject matter as delicate as the one they'd been discussing, too difficult. It did, however, give her time to think. To wonder about possibilities. If she was to – what had Ryan said? – *find out more* about him ... well, if she was to do that, it wasn't a decision to be made lightly. Once bitten, twice very flipping wary about starting anything again.

Except that each time she turned to look at him, she felt a squirmy sensation in her belly. Her mind might be wary, but it seemed her body was willing her to take another chance.

Finally, he turned the car into her road.

'About your mum,' she ventured as he pulled up outside her building. 'If you need some time off to go and see her, take it.'

'That would screw with your deadline, but thanks.' He cut the engine and immediately the car fell quiet, except for the ever-present sexual tension that hummed between them.

'Well, thank you for the lift.'

He turned to look at her, his eyes searching her face. 'That stuff you said about not wanting an office-based affair.'

Oh boy, where was this heading? 'Yes.' Her gaze clashed with his, and her pulse scrambled.

'You agree we're not in the office right now?'

She swallowed. 'I guess so.'

'Good.' With that his mouth swooped down on hers and he kissed her. He *kissed* her. Full of heat, of longing, his hands reached to clasp her face as he deepened the kiss and it was all she could do to simply hold on while he swept her away on a tide of sensual desire. Her mind stopped thinking; her body was on fire.

Slowly he drew back, dropping his hands from her face and giving her a wry smile. 'I just wanted to see if it was as good as I remembered.'

Sam struggled to get her breathing under control. 'And was it?' No, she shouldn't have asked. She should have ignored him and got out of the car.

He let out a long, ragged breath. 'No. It was better.'

Pleasure mixed with arousal, mixed with fear. Where was all this taking them? 'I don't know what to say,' she whispered, afraid to encourage, yet also burning with a need to agree with him. To say to hell with being sensible and invite him up to her place to finish what he'd started.

'If I'd known it would shut you up, I'd have done it earlier.' Abruptly he pushed open his door and hauled his big body out of the cramped interior. Within seconds he was opening her door and reaching to help her out.

As she clasped his hand, she felt the zing from his touch all the way through her already fevered body. Torn between the desire to pull him towards her and slide her hand under his white shirt, and the desire to flee to the safety of her apartment where she could think, she glanced up at him.

Immediately she saw his eyes darken, and her breath hitched. 'Ryan ...'

He exhaled sharply, dragging a hand through his hair. 'It was just a kiss, Sam. No need to get your knickers in a twist. I'll go back to pissing you off again tomorrow.'

His words put a pin in the tension, effectively bursting it, and a bubble of laughter caught in her throat. 'That isn't compulsory, you know.' He gave her one of his precious smiles and she felt another unwanted tug on her heart. Shaking it off, she took a step back. 'I meant what I said about your mum. If you want to see her—'

'You want this app launched in four weeks. I've got a shed-load to do. I'll visit her at the weekend.' He jammed his hands in his pockets, his expression warning her off discussing it any more.

'Right.' Yet still she hesitated.

'Sam.' His voice carried a warning. 'Unless you want to get kissed again, you need to go.'

She gulped, her heart in danger of bursting through her chest. 'Okay.' On instinct, she stepped forward and kissed his cheek, inhaling a lungful of pure male smell: a dash of pine, a hint of engine oil, a huge dollop of Ryan.

Surprise shot across his face before his eyes smouldered down at her. 'Go.'

The rough command sent need pulsing through her. Hastily, her legs trembling, she dashed up the steps to the front door.

Chapter 13

Saturday morning and Ryan climbed gingerly out of the Triumph and slowly straightened his back. He really needed to invest in a decent car. One that didn't break down, forcing his classy boss to spend an hour sitting on a motorway verge. Though that had provided some unexpected benefits, he thought with a smile, as he remembered their closeness while they'd waited for the breakdown truck. And the following kiss.

A glance up at the rotting window frames of the semi-detached house he'd parked up outside and he sighed. The car was about seventy-second on the list of things he needed to spend money on. Hauling his bag from the boot he walked up to the front door. After ringing the bell, he cast a cursory eye over the neat front garden, noting with relief the flower-pots bursting with colour and the freshly mown grass. His mum was clearly going through a good patch.

The door swung open and he stooped down to hug the short, slightly overweight lady with the pretty, lined face who stood in the doorway.

'Ryan.' His mum's arms briefly tightened around him before

she stepped back and gave him a wobbly smile. 'I'd almost forgotten what you look like.'

'It's been nine weeks. I've not changed.'

Her eyes swept over him. 'You've lost weight.'

Smiling, he wrapped an arm around her shoulders. 'That's because it's been nine weeks since I've had one of your gut-buster puddings.'

Her elbow connected with his ribs. 'Less of the cheek. Now come on in and sit down. You're making the place look untidy.'

As they walked towards the living room a tall, slim figure jumped up from the sofa. 'I was just leaving.'

Ryan sighed. 'Hello, Erin.'

His half-sister said nothing, just looked at him with a bucketload of seventeen-year-old attitude.

'Stay and have a cup of tea with us. Please?' His mum, ever the peacekeeper, gave her daughter a pleading look. 'It's been a while since you've seen each other.'

'Not long enough.' Erin glared at him from hazel eyes that were warm and pretty, when she was looking at anyone else but him. Then she bent to give her mum a kiss. 'I'm off to Hayley's. Dunno when I'll be back.'

'Text me.'

'Yeah, yeah, I know the drill.' With a flick of her long dark hair, she sauntered out of the room. A second later, the house shook as the front door slammed shut.

His mum glanced sadly at him. 'When are you two going to sort this out?'

'It's not me who has the issue.'

'I know, but maybe if you make the effort to talk to her,

she'll listen.' His mum's eyes, hazel like her daughter's, glistened as she took his hand and led him over to the sofa. 'You used to get on so well as kids. When she was a baby you'd fuss over her something rotten.'

'I was ten. She was something different to look at.'

His mum let out a hiss of frustration. 'Hogwash. You doted on her. And she on you. The moment she learnt to walk she'd follow you everywhere.'

That, Ryan thought wretchedly, had been a big part of the problem. Erin hadn't been able to follow him when he'd left home at eighteen to work in Manchester. And she'd never forgiven him for it. 'Well, now she can't tolerate being in the same room as me.' It hurt to say it. Had hurt even more to watch her walk out the moment he'd walked in. 'If she stays around long enough for me to catch her, I'll have a word.' It was a fob-off. He knew very well there was no real hope of it happening.

'Good.'

She smiled up at him and he studied her carefully. Still attractive, but the eyes weren't as clear as they should be. The face too hollowed, the skin on her cheeks riddled with small blood vessels, giving her a flushed appearance.

'How are you, Mum?'

Her eyes darted briefly away from his. As always, she found it hard to look him in the eye when it came to her health. 'I feel good.'

'Aside from the dizzy spells.'

'Just a bit of angina. Doctor said it's not unusual.'

'In alcoholics.'

His voice was clearly harsher than he'd intended because she flinched. 'I know I am one, Ryan. I'll always be one. You don't have to rub it in.'

Anger burned, at both her and himself. 'How many times have we been through this? You choose to be one. If you wanted to, you could stop. There are groups that can help you. I can help you. I *want* to help you.'

'You're acting like I haven't tried.' She became agitated then, shifting around on the sofa and wringing her hands.

Ryan sucked in a deep breath, trying to calm himself. Getting her worked up never achieved anything. 'I know you have.' *But just because it didn't work, doesn't mean you should bloody give up*, he wanted to yell. Had yelled, far too often.

All it had resulted in was her throwing him out, or retreating into herself, depending on the mood she was in. It had taken a shameful number of years for him to realise he couldn't bully her into it.

Seemingly mollified, she finally looked at him again. 'Enough talk about me. What about this new job?' A sly smile came over her face. 'And your new boss.'

He'd expected the change of topic, just as he'd expected the inquisition. It had been three years since he'd introduced a woman to his mum. Fiona hadn't turned his life into one giant fluffy marshmallow, or whatever love was supposed to do, but he'd thought they had something. Clearly she hadn't, because she'd dumped him three months later. Women like to talk, and to share, she'd told him. Seems he was pretty crap at both. 'Sam's just that. My boss.' Maybe if he said it often enough, he'd convince himself.

'She sounded like a real bobby dazzler.'

He snorted. 'You can't tell what a woman looks like from her voice.'

'Maybe not, but what *you* think she looks like is written all over your face.' She squeezed his arm. 'You've got a soft spot for her.'

Ryan leapt to his feet. 'As a boss, I like her just fine. Now where's this brew you promised me this morning when I told you I was coming up? You said it would be waiting as soon as I stepped inside.' His mum wasn't the only one who knew how to deflect a conversation.

She rose slowly to her feet, and Ryan tried not to notice the effort it took her. 'I'll sort you out a cuppa. But don't think I haven't twigged there's something between you and this Sam lady you're not telling me about.'

We had sex before I knew she was going to be my boss. Now all I can think about is having sex with her again. And again. Yeah, he didn't think his mum was ready for that. 'There's nothing going on.' It was pretty much the truth. Except that he'd kissed her after giving her a lift home, and she'd seemed as into it as he'd been. But also as conflicted, he reminded himself as he recalled the way she'd hesitated outside her place, her eyes swirling with fear, with desire, and a tonne of other emotions he couldn't begin to guess at because, unlike him, Sam hadn't just shared a bed with her ex. They'd shared a life.

Sam spent the weekend entertaining her parents. Entertaining was probably too strong, but as they'd made the effort to drive all the way from Cornwall to see their daughter, she thought it only fair she gave them her undivided attention. Which meant for once, she put her laptop away.

Saturday had been spent doing a little shopping down the Fulham Road (to please her mum) and the Science Museum (to please her dad). Sunday they'd spent walking round the Serpentine. Now they were back at hers, pleasantly tired and more than a little hungry.

'What would you like me to make you for dinner?'

'Oh.' Her dad coughed and stared at her mum. 'We don't want you to go to any trouble, do we, Helen. Why don't we eat out?'

'Yes, good idea.' Her mum gave her a too-wide smile. 'Let us treat you.'

Sam eyed them both suspiciously. 'You don't want me to cook for you again, do you?'

'Nonsense.' Her mum's reply was too fast to be believable. 'The lasagne you made last night was very nice. Just a tad on the runny side.'

Her dad spluttered out a laugh. 'It was soup. Our girl's an amazing businesswoman but she can't cook for toffee.'

'Thanks.' It was hard to act hurt when she knew she totally sucked in the kitchen. 'I'll focus on the amazing bit and suggest we leave cooking dinner to the pub across the road.' It would be the first time she'd gone back there since the night she'd met Ryan.

A night that stuck stubbornly, and vividly, to her mind, refusing to fade no matter how hard she tried to shake it off.

The pub was busy when they arrived. As Sam sat with her

parents in a booth at the back, she couldn't help glancing at the bar. She told herself it was to make sure to avoid Ryan if he came in. Introducing her parents to her one-night stand, the same man she was pinning all her business hopes on, and the one she was considering having a hot secret affair with, wasn't something she was ready for.

She froze as a broad-shouldered male wearing a white T-shirt and black jeans strode through the door. A pair of dark eyes flicked round the room before landing on hers. He gave her a small crooked smile before heading towards the bar.

'Shit.'

Her mum reached across the table and touched her hand. 'What's wrong?'

Sam struggled to hear her above the wild beating of her heart. 'Nothing.' Because that was clearly untrue, she shook her head. 'What I meant is nothing important. I've just seen our new software developer walk in. It's always a bit embarrassing seeing people outside work.'

'Nonsense. You go out with Becky and Lucas all the time.'

'Sure, Mum, because we're *friends*.' Sam didn't know what she and Ryan were, but it wasn't friends.

'Which one is he?' Her mum was angling her head, totally uncaring how obvious she was. 'The one with the dark hair, white T-shirt and big muscles?' Her eyes dropped down. 'Ooh, and rather delightful bum.'

'Mum!' Mortified, Sam put her head in her hands. 'How would you feel if Dad objectified one of my female employees like that?'

Her dad cleared his throat. 'Well said. For the record, I only have eyes for your mother.'

Her mum burst out laughing. 'Okay, okay. I was just admiring from afar, that's all. I may be old, but I'm not blind.'

Just then Ryan glanced in their direction. To Sam's utter embarrassment, her mother waved. And then signalled him to come over.

'Oh my God, Mum.'

'What's wrong? We've met your other employees.'

It was true. Last time her parents had come to visit they'd popped into the office to say hello. But still.

'Besides.' Her mum bent towards her. 'I want to meet the man whose presence has brought a blush to my daughter's cheeks.'

Sam swallowed, feeling those same cheeks now burning. There were times she hated being a redhead.

'Sam.' Ryan nodded towards her, amusement dancing in the dark depths of his eyes. He knew very well she was hating every minute of this.

'Ryan.' She smiled tightly. 'Meet my parents, Robert and Helen. They're visiting from Cornwall. Mum, Dad, this is Ryan. Our new software developer.'

Ryan stuck out his hand to shake first her dad's hand and then her mum's.

'So Ryan, what's it like working for our daughter?'

While Sam cringed at her mum's question, Ryan smirked, his eyes drifting over her face, then deliberately down to her lips. 'It has its moments.' His eyes snared hers and she felt the connection pulse through her. A beat of uncomfortable silence followed before Ryan turned back to her parents. 'Good to meet you. I'll leave you to your meal.' He'd started to leave when her mum's voice halted him in his tracks. And made Sam's heart leap into her throat.

'Have you eaten?'

Oh no, she couldn't be about to suggest ...

'If not, why don't you join us?'

Sam groaned, only just managing to stop from banging her head against the table. As she watched the surprise settle across Ryan's rugged face, she thanked God the guy was about as social as a grizzly bear.

But then his eyes met hers, and the devilish gleam she saw made her heart pound.

'Actually, that would be great. Thanks.'

She was left to watch in horror as he slid into the place next to her.

'Are you a regular here, Ryan?'

Sam swallowed her gasp and sank a little lower on the bench. Her mum was really coming out with the questions today.

'It's not my local but I come here now and again.' He glanced sideways at Sam. 'It's always worth the trek out.'

Heat crept across her face, something she knew her mum hadn't missed. Why was he, the anti-social one, looking so in control and she was the one left squirming around like a worm on a hook?

For the next few minutes they studied the menu and made their order, Ryan surprising her by going for the fish pie.

'Don't tell me,' he said when he caught her expression. 'You expected me to order steak and chips?' He shook his head, tutting. 'Just when you thought you'd got me sussed, eh?'

She was a long way from sussing him, she realised, but did she want to inch closer? Did she want to invest the time and energy, even though it might explode in her face again?

She was horribly afraid she did.

After their orders had been taken, Ryan surprised her again by turning to her parents. 'So, you live in Cornwall?'

'We do.' Her mum smiled at Ryan. 'Have you been?'

'No. Maybe one day.'

'Oh, yes, you must. It's stunning. Get Sam to bring you.'

Sam stared wide-eyed at her mum, who simply smiled serenely back.

Ryan, the bastard, started to chuckle. 'I might just do that.'

'Do you sail? Or surf? Sam's a good surfer, she could teach you.' God, she loved her mother, but right now she wanted to bop her one. Anything to shut her up. 'Cornwall's got some excellent surfing beaches.'

'Afraid I don't do either, but I'm up for learning.' Ryan glanced at Sam and gave her his trademark little smirk. 'With the right teacher.'

She tried not to blush again. Flipping heck, this was unbelievable. Her mum and Ryan were actually having a conversation. She caught her dad's eye and he gave her a curious look. One she read as *do I have to grill this man? Is there something going on between you?*

Sam raised her eyes to the ceiling and gave him a small shake of her head. No.

Not quite the truth, but clearly there was no need for him

to grill Ryan because her mum was doing a fine job all by herself.

'Do you play any other sports?' Her mum continued the interrogation, after the briefest of pauses to sip at her wine.

Ryan shook his head. 'I'm a geek, remember.'

'Poppycock.' Heaven help her, was her mum now *fluttering her eyes*? 'You look like a man who keeps fit.'

Ryan laughed softly. 'Well, I go to the gym, and I run and swim. Just no good at anything that requires skill.'

Her mother smiled. 'From what I hear, you save your skill for the computer keyboard.' She leant forward and tapped his hand lightly. 'And I hope you're going to use it to help my daughter defeat the man who's trying his best to destroy her company.'

Ryan's face sobered and he looked her mother straight in the eye. 'You can count on it.'

There was a beat of silence, during which Sam scrambled her brain for something to say but found she couldn't get past the determination in Ryan's face. The sincerity of his words.

In the end it was her dad who spoke first. 'Lynch is a temporary blip. We're incredibly proud of what Sam's achieved at Privacy Solutions.'

Proud? Sam felt the emotion catch at her throat. It was hard for her to see what her dad could be so proud of, considering the way she'd misjudged Damien so badly. And then dropped the ball for eighteen months.

Ryan's voice broke the silence. 'From what I've seen, you're right to be proud of her.' He leant across the table and added in an exaggerated whisper, 'But don't tell her I said that.'

As the laughter died down and the conversation moved on, Sam was forced to wonder who, exactly, was Ryan Black? The curt loner who'd so annoyed them all when he'd first started at Privacy Solutions, or the man who'd sweetly laid his jacket out for her when his car had broken down. And who was right now, against all the odds, charming the socks off her parents. Well, her mum, anyway. Her dad was quietly listening and assessing. Because she knew how angry he'd been at Damien's treatment of her, and how badly he'd blamed himself for misjudging the man he'd welcomed into their family, she couldn't blame him.

'It was lovely to meet you,' her mum said to Ryan after the bill had been taken care of, Ryan insisting on paying his share.

'And you.' He shook her dad's hand and then reached out to shake her mum's. When she ignored it and reached up to kiss him on the cheek, a faint blush crept up his neck.

'You go on ahead,' Sam told her parents, still trying to make sense of the evening. 'I'll catch you up. I just want a quick word with Ryan.'

When they were out of earshot, she faced him head on. 'What was all that?'

'All what?' he countered, his expression all innocence.

'You being all smiley and *nice*?'

He looked put out. 'I am nice.'

'When it suits you.'

'Hey, your parents are fun. Well your mum is, anyway. Your dad looked like he wanted to have a poke around inside my head. See what made me tick.'

'He'd have to be either very brave or very stupid,' she muttered.

'True.' He paused, his eyes searching hers, a small smile on his face. 'Well then. Guess I'll see you tomorrow.'

'I guess so.' She hesitated. 'Why did you agree to join us?'

He shrugged. 'I was hungry.'

'It wasn't because you wanted to wind me up?'

Amusement flickered in the depths of his eyes. 'I was hungry, Sam.' He started to walk back to the bar before halting and looking back at her, that half-smile curling his mouth. 'And I thought it would wind you up.'

Chapter 14

Ryan scowled as Alice knocked on the door to the meeting room he'd claimed as his office. He hated interruptions. His brain was wired in a way that meant he needed space and quiet so he could analyse a problem rationally and logically before determining the solution. He didn't want to talk to people about it; he did his thinking in private. One mumbo jumbo course he'd been on told him he was an introverted thinker. Whatever. All he knew was that the woman now entering his 'space' was about to put him further behind schedule.

'What?'

He must have snapped because she flinched. 'I just wanted your help on the coding you asked me to do.'

'Does it have to be now?'

She bit into her bottom lip. 'Well, I can't progress unless you help me. I'm stuck.'

'I thought people with degrees were meant to be smart?' When she flinched again, Ryan cursed inwardly. He was being a git. It wasn't her fault he had a chip on his shoulder about not going to university. Nor was it her fault he wasn't going to finish this flaming app within the ridiculous deadline he'd been given. Heaving out a sigh, he climbed to his feet. 'Fine. Show me the issue.'

They walked back to her workstation in an uncomfortable silence. 'Look, sorry I barked at you.'

'It's okay.'

She stared straight ahead and Ryan knew it definitely wasn't okay. Distractedly, he shoved his hands in his pockets. He was tetchy – okay, even more tetchy than usual. He should have worked over the weekend. He'd known he was behind, yet going to see his mum had scuppered any chance of catching up. It had also reminded him she was a hell of a lot sicker than she was letting on. And that Erin was never going to forgive him for what he'd done. The only high spot of the weekend had been bumping into Sam in the pub on Sunday evening, and seeing her all twitchy because he'd accepted the offer to eat with her parents.

Even now it brought a smile to his face. Worth every penny of the astronomical sixteen pounds fifty for a bit of fish pie he could have bought from the supermarket for a few quid.

'If you look here, maybe you can see where I've gone wrong …'

Ryan snapped his attention back to Alice.

Ten minutes later, he'd fixed the issue.

'Thank you.'

She kept her eyes on the screen. When he'd first met her, she'd smiled at him so much it had made him antsy. Now she couldn't look at him. It was one thing not being a team player.

Another being a total arse. He hesitated, then forced the next words out. 'If you need my help again, just knock on the door.' Her eyes flicked over to him and he gave her what had to be the most awkward smile in the history of man. 'I'll try not to bite your head off next time.'

'Okay.'

Her answering smile was about as hesitant as his. The uncomfortable moment was broken by the appearance of a tall, lean figure walking past Alice's desk, and heading towards Sam's office.

'Who's that?'

Ryan frowned as he stared at the guy's back. 'The bloke Sam started the company with.'

Alice hissed in a breath. '*That's* Damien Lynch?'

'Yeah,' he answered distractedly. 'Haven't you seen him before?'

'Once,' she answered quietly. 'At a conference. I didn't realise who he was.'

Ryan was only listening with half an ear. His main focus was on Lynch as he knocked on Sam's door. What did the man want with Sam? Unconsciously, Ryan straightened. He'd taken two steps towards her office when he remembered how she'd reacted to his last attempt to protect her, that time from the journo at the conference ... *if you think I can't handle a prick like him ...*

Frustrated with himself, he turned away. Why did he feel this burning need to muscle in on any other guy he felt was getting too close? She was a one-night stand who, in her own words, would never be anything more. Oh, and a boss who, for all he knew, was planning to ditch him at the end of this week when his probation period was up.

Still, his hands twitched with the desire to storm into her office, grab Lynch by the scruff of the neck and haul him out.

Carefully he forced himself to relax.

'I'm going to ... umm, get myself a drink. Do you want one?'

Alice's voice drifted over to him and he forced his attention back to her. 'I'm good, thanks.' He watched as she jumped quickly to her feet. 'Thirsty?'

Clearly still wary of him, she gave him a strained smile. 'Sorry?'

'You seem to be in a hurry for that drink.'

'Oh, right, yes.' Another forced smile and she scampered off.

Great. Now he could add pissing off Alice to the long list of reasons Sam could use to release him from his contract. That's if being behind target with the modifications that weren't even those they'd originally asked for wasn't reason enough.

'Upsetting the staff again?'

Lucas grinned as he walked towards him. 'No more than usual.' Ryan eyed the guy's outfit of pink trousers, topped with a shirt covered in black-and-white swirls. 'I want to make a comment about liquorice allsorts.'

Lucas rocked back with laughter. 'Keep them coming, geek boy.' Ryan worked hard to keep his expression neutral, but he must have done a crap job because Lucas immediately sobered. 'Seemed like that touched a nerve.'

'No more of a nerve than my fruit comment to you.'

Lucas eyed him speculatively. 'True, but I'm a sensitive soul. I didn't think you would be.'

'I'm not.' God knows, he'd learnt not to be. Learnt to ignore the regular barrage of insults thrown at him as a kid. He even used geek to describe himself, before others did. But it seems he wasn't quite as indifferent to the term as he wanted to be.

'Sure.' Lucas started to smile. 'I'm beginning to realise you and I aren't as different as I first thought.'

Ryan deliberately ran his eyes up and down Lucas's colourful ensemble, and then down his own plain black T-shirt and grey jeans. 'You think?'

Lucas patted him on the back. 'I'm talking about what goes on *inside*, you hunk of beefcake.'

Ryan was almost afraid to ask. 'Go on, I'll bite. What do we have in common?'

Lucas gave him a look that seemed to see right through to Ryan's soul. 'I think we've both been treated as outcasts for being different.'

It touched too close to home for comfort, so Ryan forced a laugh. 'Right, sure. Whatever you say.'

Lucas just smiled. 'Deny it all you want, but I've sussed you, Ryan Black. You're not half as much of a grouchy loner as you claim to be.'

Sam swallowed hard as Damien carefully closed the door behind him. Whatever he'd come here to say, it didn't matter. This man had lost the ability to hurt her any more.

'Kerry said you wanted to see me?'

He smiled, and she noticed how practised it looked. 'She seemed very nice.'

'She is. She's also smart and loyal. Unlike our previous office manager.'

The barb found its mark, though only someone who knew him as well as she did would have noticed the flash of annoyance on his otherwise smooth features. 'No need to be a bitch.'

'Better than being a cheating bastard.'

His stance stiffened, a sure sign that annoyance was turning to anger. Good. She'd spent too long wallowing in her own anger, in her hurt and betrayal. It was about time she came out fighting.

'I came here in the spirit of friendship,' he said tightly. 'Not to rake over old coals.'

She rose to her feet – she'd had enough of him looking down on her – and smiled sweetly. 'You've decided not to launch an app you know very well is a poor imitation of the Privacy app?'

His eyes narrowed. 'I can assure you we won't be launching a poor imitation. I came here out of courtesy to let you know that tomorrow we launch the Privacy Protect app. You'll find it does everything the Privacy app does. And more.' He withdrew a sheet of paper from his pocket. 'Here's the advance press release. I wouldn't normally share this with a rival company, but I'm doing so now out of my regard for you, and what we built together.'

Sam froze, her mind having trouble grasping what he was saying. *Launch tomorrow* were the only two words that stuck, and they were enough to send a wave of nausea rolling through her. 'Get out.' Her words sounded feeble. She swallowed down the nausea and tried again. 'Get out.' Better, but not as strong as she'd like. She sounded like a woman who'd taken an emotional hit. Not a woman unconcerned by his petty attempt to derail everything she'd worked so hard for.

He nodded. 'I'm sorry it had to come to this, Sam.'

Sorry? He'd broken her heart, now he was breaking her company. He didn't look sorry at all. He looked ... superior. Arrogant. Keeping her eyes down, she sat back down on her chair and turned her attention to her computer. He wasn't going to get the satisfaction of seeing her cry. Of seeing her beaten and bowed.

Her hand trembled as she reached for the mouse, but she kept clicking. Kept pretending an interest in what was on the screen even after she'd heard him leave. Maybe if she stared at it long enough, she could pretend the last five minutes hadn't happened.

'What did he want?'

She jerked her head up to see Ryan's big bulk framing the doorway, Lucas behind him.

'He came to tell me I'm screwed.'

'What?' Lucas muscled his way in, pushing past Ryan.

'Oh, he said it politely, because apparently he really respects me, which is funny considering how he keeps shafting me at every turn, but anyway, that's besides the point. The key message is I'm screwed.' She looked at them both through a blur of tears. 'We're all screwed.'

Just then Becky appeared, too, her face worried. 'I've just seen Damien. What's he doing here?'

'Telling us we're all screwed, apparently.' Ryan frowned over at Sam. 'Is that all we're getting, or are you going to elaborate?'

'Oh, I'll happily elaborate. That app you've been working on, the one that was due to be finished at the end of this week but isn't going to be?'

Ryan's jaw clenched. 'Yeah?'

'Well, we might as well not have bothered.' All the anguish, the anger, the gut-wrenching despair she was feeling poured out of her. 'Damien came to tell me that Privacy Protect will be launching their app tomorrow.' She waved the press release in the air. 'And guess what? It looks remarkably similar to the one we've spent the last year and half working on. It's almost as if they knew exactly which updates we were incorporating.'

She didn't mean to, she really didn't, but her eyes focused straight on Ryan. She saw the exact moment the implication of what she was saying hit home. 'You think someone told him what we were doing?' His dark eyes flashed with anger. 'You think *I* told him?'

'Did you?'

She heard Lucas inhale sharply. 'Now, now. Let's not start throwing around accusations. Not while emotions are running so high.'

Sam cringed inwardly. What was she doing? This wild woman wasn't her. She was calm, considered. She *trusted* people.

'It's okay, Lucas.' Ryan's voice was so cold she could almost see the shards of ice forming around it. 'Obviously I'm number one suspect. I'm the newcomer.' His eyes, when they met hers, caused her to gasp inwardly. Oh God, he wasn't just angry.

He was hurting. 'I've been here three months.' A bitter smile touched his lips. 'Just under. During that time I've met Mr Lynch only once, a month ago, at the conference. I've already told you what we spoke about.'

Sam felt the shock start to drain out of her, and along with it a lot of the anger. 'You did. I'm sorry—'

'You must really rate his abilities,' he cut in, 'if you think he's been able to achieve in one month what I've not been able to achieve in three.' She wanted to dive in, to stop him and apologise, but for once the uncommunicative Ryan Black wouldn't stop talking. 'Or perhaps that's not it. Perhaps you think I've been deliberately slow, giving him time to launch his app with all the updates I told him about in the three-minute conversation we had?' His eyes hardened. 'Or maybe it's not that either. Maybe you think this whole thing is a set-up. That we planned that I'd get fired from my last job so I could sneak my way in here.' His hurt and anger were now boiling over into his voice. 'Hell, maybe you think I'm just as much of a traitorous bastard as the guy you used to shack up with? The one who literally screwed you over.'

'Enough,' Lucas snapped, his gaze going from her to Ryan, as if trying to work something out. Beside him Becky winced, her expression one of complete and utter sympathy. And behind Becky, oh God, there was Alice, who just stared and stared, her face as white as a sheet. This was going from bad to worse to totally destructive.

Ryan heaved in a deep, shuddering breath, his gaze darting from the ceiling, to the floor before finally landing back on her. 'No need to fire me. I quit.'

Before Sam could say anything, he'd turned and walked out.

There was a moment of stunned silence during which Sam tried to unscramble her brain. She didn't know what she wanted to do first. Punch a hole in the wall, scream at the top of her voice. Or bury her head in her hands and weep. Before she could do any of it though, Alice stepped forward. 'You have to call him back.' Her voice trembled as she avoided Sam's eyes. 'It wasn't Ryan who talked to Damien. I have a terrible feeling it was me.'

Chapter 15

Ryan was seething as he marched back to his temporary office. Both at Sam and at himself. Her for kicking him exactly where it hurt, and him for letting it hurt so much. So what if she didn't trust him? If he wasn't part of her hallowed inner circle? It was a job, that's all.

And now, because of his hot-headedness, he didn't even have that. But how could he stay, after what he'd said? It didn't matter how belittled he'd felt, how angry and upset, he had no right to throw her previous relationship in her face. No right to embarrass her like that in front of the others.

Cursing, he yanked open the door to the meeting room. Grab his jacket, his stuff – flask to keep his coffee hot, his wireless mouse, the Tupperware box he put his sarnie in – and get out of here, pronto.

Then spend the rest of the day finding another job. And avoiding all bars, because no way in hell was he going to risk shagging his next boss.

He was in the process of jamming his mouse into the Tupperware box, when Lucas burst in.

'Stop right there.'

Ryan glanced up. 'I'm not pinching anything. The mouse is mine. The company ones are crap.'

Lucas lifted his eyes to the ceiling. 'Take that chip off your shoulder for a moment. It's weighing you down.'

'Fuck off.'

Lucas sighed. 'Wow, you really are turning on the charm today, aren't you?'

'Being told you're a backstabbing traitor does that to a man.'

'Umm. Was it the accusation that has you riled though, or the person who delivered it?'

Ryan snatched at the flask and shoved it into his jacket pocket. 'Did you come here for something specific, or just to piss me off?'

Silently Lucas turned and shut the door. Then he pulled out one of the chairs from under the table and plonked himself on it. 'I came to stop you from leaving.'

'Why? Going to miss me too much?'

'Actually, I would, yes.'

His admission pulled Ryan up short. He studied the man's face, looking for signs of irony, but couldn't see any. Letting out a deep sigh, he slumped onto the nearest chair and faced Lucas. 'I appreciate that. More than you can know, if I'm being honest, though don't go getting any ideas.'

Lucas waggled his eyebrows suggestively. 'Too late.'

Ryan shook his head, but he couldn't stop a smile from forming. 'Whatever gets you through the day. But I'm done here, mate.'

'Alice has just admitted it was her who gave Damien the

information on the updates. Apparently she talked to him at a conference she went to last year, two weeks after joining the company. Not knowing who he was, when he expressed an interest in what she was working on, she told him she was trying to get the app to show the user not just who held personal information on them, but what that information was. She didn't think any more of it, until now.'

Ryan thought back to Alice's reaction when she'd asked who Damien was a few minutes ago. 'Figures.'

'We're good then? You can plug that special mouse of yours back in?'

'That wasn't the reason I'm leaving.'

Lucas's forehead wrinkled. 'Then enlighten me.'

'*Enlighten* you? Who the heck uses that word any more?'

'Non philistines.' Lucas narrowed his blue eyes. 'If you prefer it in simpler terms, spill.'

Ryan shifted on his chair, uncomfortable with the conversation. 'That's my business.'

Lucas's expression sharpened. 'Does it have anything to do with your rather stunning over-reaction to Sam's question? Or maybe it has more to do with your unsubtle reminder to everyone of what Lynch did to her?'

Ryan felt the heat of embarrassment creep up his neck. 'Thanks. You've helped a lot.'

Lucas sighed, threading a hand through his wavy blond locks, which fell back into exactly the same place. 'Sam asked me to stop you from leaving.' His eyes tracked Ryan's. 'So whatever is between you two, and however annoyed she is, she doesn't want you to go.'

'Yeah.' Ryan wasn't convinced. He'd seen the horror in those vast eyes of hers when he'd thrown her history with Lynch at her. She probably didn't want him to go *just yet*. Not until she'd pinned him into signing a statement to the effect that he was forbidden to work for Lynch. Ever.

'If you're wondering why she hasn't come to find you herself, it's because she's trying to console Alice.'

Ryan winced. Poor kid. First she'd had him barking at her, then she'd found out she'd unwittingly put the company in jeopardy. And he thought he was having a bad day. 'How is she?'

'Sam or Alice?'

He'd meant Sam, but because he didn't want to admit that to a guy he could sense was bursting with curiosity, he lied. 'Alice.'

Lucas gave him a knowing look. 'Alice is, as I believe I've already hinted, understandably upset. She thinks she's ruined everything. Sam's trying to convince her she hasn't, even though Sam secretly believes it is all over.'

'Bollocks she does. She's got more fight in her than that.'

Lucas smiled and rose slowly to his feet. 'Maybe you should go and tell her that. I'm sure she needs to hear it.' His smile dimmed and he fixed Ryan with a steely blue glare. 'If you are going to waltz off like a prima donna and leave us high and dry, at least have the decency to stay until she can find someone to replace you. She deserves that, at least.'

'Ouch,' Ryan muttered, feeling every sharp, serrated edge.

Lucas turned his smile back on, before turning and walking out.

Sam gave up passing tissues to Alice and handed her the box.

'Please, you have to stop blaming yourself. You weren't to know who he was. If anyone is to blame here, it's me. I should have briefed you before you went to the conference.' And she would have done, if she'd believed for one minute that Damien would stoop that low. Chalk up yet another flawed judgement on her part.

'You're being very kind.' Alice wiped her eyes, then blew into the tissue. 'Is all the work we've put into Privacy 2 really for nothing?'

'Of course not,' Sam lied. 'I just said it in the heat of the moment. I didn't realise you were listening.' She'd thought she'd been talking to friends. Oh, and to Ryan, who might or might not be a friend, but whom she knew she'd hurt. It was hard to blame him for lashing out at her. Even though it had felt like a public slap round the face.

'So we'll still launch our app?'

'We certainly will.' But the initiative had now been yanked from under them.

'Right then.' Alice lurched to her feet. 'I'm going back to work. The quicker we finalise it, the better, yes?'

'Yes.' Or to put it another way, the longer it took them to launch, the more customers they would lose, and the quicker they would go under.

The moment Alice stepped outside the office, thankfully

closing the door behind her, Sam put her head in her hands. What a bloody mess. She didn't want to feel this down, this beaten, and maybe tomorrow she wouldn't. Maybe tomorrow she'd square her shoulders, take a deep breath and come out fighting, but right now?

Tears welled and Sam's face crumpled. Bugger it, right now she needed to wallow. To hang her head and let all the anger, frustration, the crushing disappointment, drain out of her.

But first, she had to check on Ryan. Wiping furiously at her eyes, she was about to stand when Lucas popped his head round the door.

'How is he?' she blurted, any cool she had now long gone.

Lucas stepped further in. 'Funny, he asked the same of you. Though being a devious devil, he pretended he was asking about Alice, but I know he actually wanted to know about you.'

'Or he could *actually* have wanted to know about Alice.'

Lucas smirked. 'Do you want to hear how our chat went, or not?'

Sam groaned and sagged back against the chair. 'I really don't know. I think I'd prefer to sit here in blissful ignorance than learn that the guy we need to finish Privacy 2, which apparently is no better than the rival app launching tomorrow, has just walked out of the door.'

'He hasn't. I told him the least he can do is stay until you'd found someone to replace him.'

Sam gaped at Lucas. 'You seriously had the nerve to say that? I've basically told Ryan he's a lying toerag who betrayed this company. I believe the least he can do is sue me for slander.'

'What can I say, I'm very persuasive.' He flashed her a cocky grin before perching on the chair opposite and giving her a long, quiet look. 'He's not considering leaving because of what you said.'

'He's not?'

'Nope. It's because of what he said. He thinks he's embarrassed you so much he can't stay. At least that's what I think he thinks, reading between the lines.'

Sam started to laugh. 'Flipping heck, Lucas. You're basically making up a story to fit your own agenda. You have no idea what he's thinking.'

'I know more than you think, sweet cheeks,' he countered. 'There's something going on between the pair of you, isn't there?'

'No,' she mumbled, not wanting to go there. She was still reeling from Damien's bombshell. She didn't need to pick over her disaster of a one-night stand. What she needed was to get her head straight so she could find her way through the mess she was in right now.

Once again she felt the prick of unshed tears.

Okay, while she was on this roll, maybe it wasn't typical CEO behaviour, but what she also needed was a bloody good cry.

First though, she had to put herself and Ryan back on the right footing. Sighing, she rose to her feet. 'Look, you're right, there is an attraction, but the last thing I need right now is another office relationship. I've got enough on my plate dealing with the fallout from the previous one.' Angrily she swiped away a stray tear. 'Do you think Ryan will still be in that stupid meeting room he's locked himself in?'

Lucas stared at her in horror. 'Please tell me you're not going to see him now?'

'Why not?'

He waved his hand in the direction of her face. 'Darling, your eyes are all watery, your face is like a heavy grey cloud on a wet weekend in November. You look like all you want to do is hide in a dark corner and burst into tears.'

She sniffed. 'That's probably because I do.'

'Then Ryan can wait. You don't want him to see you looking like a misery bucket, do you?'

More tears leaked. 'God, Lucas, whatever you're thinking, stop. I told you, there's nothing going on between us.'

'No?' He eyed her speculatively. 'Regardless, you're a woman, and you're the boss. You don't want him to see you cry. So do what you have to do in here, put your game face on and then go and see him.' Clasping her shoulders, he gave her a quick kiss on the cheek. 'And after that, sweet cheeks, you need to get back to your day job. You still have a company to run.'

But for how long?

She gave him a watery smile and watched as he carefully shut the door behind him. Then she slumped back in her chair and allowed the misery to take over.

Chapter 16

Ryan told himself he was just taking the scenic route back from the gents. He didn't have to stop by Sam's office. Didn't have to take a peek inside and see if she was in there. He could just walk on by, back to his desk ... well, to his table, since he hadn't had the balls to move his desk into the meeting room.

And anyway, why should he make the first move? He was the employee she'd publicly accused of being a traitor. He deserved the apology.

Puffed up with righteous indignation, he stalked past her office. And careered to a halt.

Crap.

Was that really Sunshine Sam sitting at her table with her head in her hands? Crying?

Pretend you haven't seen her. It wasn't even cowardice, as there was no way his boss would want him to see her like that.

But though his mind told him to walk by, his feet wouldn't budge.

Double crap.

What was this weird pull he felt towards her? Somehow this woman had got under his skin. Straightening his shoulders, ignoring the race of his pulse, he knocked on the door. Then walked in before she had a chance to reply.

She looked up with a start, her cheeks wet, those beautiful eyes swimming with tears. And snapping with annoyance. 'What the hell, Ryan? It's bloody rude to walk into someone's office when their door is shut.'

He shrugged. 'I never pretended to be a gentleman.'

Clearly embarrassed at being caught crying, she snatched at the tissue box sitting in front of her on the table. Then dumped it back in disgust. 'Flipping Alice used up all the tissues.'

Ryan indicated at his T-shirt. 'You can use this.'

She rolled her teary eyes. 'Oh yes, sure I'm going to use my employee's shirt to blow my nose on.'

He didn't want it to sting, but it did. 'I'm not here as your damn employee.'

She blinked. 'No?'

Exhaling in frustration, he sat on the chair next to her. 'No.' And now she was flustered, but it sure as hell beat crying or annoyed. 'I didn't expect to find you blubbering. Expected to find you sticking pins in a doll.'

She let out a strangled-sounding laugh. 'That would have been less embarrassing.' Her gaze shifted to his face. 'Who did you think the doll would look like?'

'Me.'

'Usually you'd be right.' The flicker of humour left her eyes as fast as it had entered them. 'But not this time. Ryan, I need to apologise for—'

'It's fine,' he cut in, embarrassed. 'I get it. I'm the outsider. Figures you were going to think of me first.'

'No.' Her voice was firm, but the breath she inhaled was shaky. 'That wasn't it. I don't think of you as an outsider.'

'Right,' he answered tightly. 'You just think of me as a snake in the grass.'

'For pity's sake Ryan, no!' Frustration etched across her face. 'There's a lot about you I don't understand, but I know this. You're brutally, usually painfully, honest.'

'So, if I'm not an outsider, and I'm *painfully* honest' – he emphasised the word, not knowing whether it was meant as a compliment or an insult – 'why accuse me?'

She slumped back on her chair, her eyes downcast as her fingers drummed on the table. 'I was intimate with Damien,' she said finally, 'and he betrayed me in the cruellest way.'

'And you've been intimate with me.'

She met his gaze head on. 'Yes. I was in full *every man I've slept with is a betraying bastard* mode.' Her face froze for a fraction of a second and then she groaned and put her head in her hands. 'And now you're wondering if that makes you only the second guy I've ever slept with.'

'I'd say I wasn't, but you've just called me honest.'

Slowly she raised her head. 'I believe I said painfully honest. Quite apt, it turns out.'

'I can be the third, fourth and fifth guy too, if it would help.' He gave her a wry grin, even though inside he was feeling all sorts of strange, mushy feelings at knowing he'd had the honour of being only the second man she'd invited to her bed. 'I'm all for helping my boss.'

'Now you want to help, huh?' For a split second a smile played across her lips and he felt the warmth of it curl around him. He wanted to lean forward and kiss the tears from her cheeks. Then move to her sexy wide mouth and kiss her, again and again, until she didn't give a stuff about Damien Lynch or what he'd done to her.

As if she sensed his desire, her lids slammed down and her face lost its humour. 'Was there a reason you came to see me?'

Frustrated with her, he cursed and rose to his feet. 'We're back to that again, are we?'

'What do you mean?'

'Back to the professional bullshit, when you know there's something more between us.'

He expected a fiery response, but instead she gave a slow shake of her head. 'Cut it out, Ryan. Please.' The defeated look in her eyes cut him to the quick. 'I can't handle anything else today.'

'Fine.' He shoved his hands in his pockets, battling to get his unruly emotions under control. 'I dropped by to apologise for blurting out that stuff about you and Lynch. It was out of order.' He gave her an ironic smile. 'Guess you could say it was unprofessional.'

'It was, but Becky and Lucas already know what went down with me and Damien, and I suspect Alice does too, considering how office gossip spreads, so no harm done. At least no more than was already done by Damien himself.' Her eyes bounced from the ceiling to the floor as she inhaled a shuddering breath. 'He's beaten me, Ryan. I can't see how we recover from this. It'll be weeks until we're ready to launch.' Snatching up the empty tissue box, she threw it at the wall and let rip a choice swear word. 'Lying, cheating, spawn of the devil, man-whore bastard.'

Ryan felt his lips twitch. God, she was beautiful when she was angry. Especially when, for once, the outpouring wasn't directed at him.

Sam watched Ryan as he struggled not to smile. Typical. The one time she wanted him to glower, to empathise with her shitty mood. 'Stop it.'

'What?'

The look he gave her was all innocence. 'You know what. This isn't funny.'

'No.' But his dark eyes glittered and his mouth curved upwards.

She shot to her feet. 'If all you're going to do is laugh at me, Black, you can piss off back to your hovel. I'm not in the mood.' She needed to stay angry, because angry felt strong.

'I'm not laughing at you,' he said quietly.

She was only a few feet away from him. Close enough to see the sincerity in his eyes, and the sympathy. 'Damn you,' she hissed, shoving at his brick wall of a chest. 'I prefer you laughing at me than pitying me.'

He swore, stumbling back a step. 'Stop telling me what I can do. How I can feel.'

The anger, the hurt, the embarrassment at what Damien had done to her reared again and she started to pummel Ryan's chest with her fists. In the back of her mind she knew it was unfair, that she was taking it out on the wrong man, but she couldn't stop. Tears streamed down her face as she shoved at Ryan, the emotions pouring out of her.

Dimly she became aware of his arms wrapping round her, holding her so close that he trapped her hands between them. She fought against his hold, trying to break free, but he was far too strong.

Slowly the fight drained from her.

Instead of feeling suffocated, now she felt secure in his arms. Safe. As she dragged air into her lungs, the fresh outdoor smell of his aftershave filled her nostrils and calmed her further. Gradually her body relaxed into his hold, and she sighed.

'You done hitting me now?'

His dryly amused voice entered her consciousness and she tried to wriggle out of his hold, but he held her firm. 'Let me go.'

She felt the rush of air against her hair as he exhaled before dropping his arms to his sides.

Hugely embarrassed, she stepped around him. His eyes watched her and when she went to stand behind her desk, he smirked. 'Is the desk for your safety, or mine?'

She couldn't be cross with a man who'd let her use him as an emotional and physical punchbag. Especially one who looked as sexy as Ryan did right now, with his amused dark eyes and crooked smile. But she could, and should, be cautious, hence her need to distance herself. 'I'm sorry. I don't know where all that came from.'

'Feel any better for it?'

She sighed, slipping onto the chair. 'I don't feel like crying any more, which is good. But it hasn't changed the facts. The company is still screwed.' Sadness rolled through her. 'All that effort wasted. Snatched away by a man who hasn't even had the decency to come up with his own ideas. He's just copied ours.'

'You're assuming his app will be a success.' Ryan frowned, his dark features taking on their more usual brooding look. 'What if your customers are more loyal than you think? What if their app isn't as simple to use as ours? What if there's a bug?'

Sam snorted. 'He's a software genius. There won't be any tech issues.'

'You seem to have an awful lot of faith in a man you claim to hate.'

Ryan's sour tone made her look up. He clearly wasn't happy with her view of Damien's ability. In fact, she'd almost say he sounded jealous. 'As a person, he's a lying, cowardly, cheating bastard.'

'You forgot man-whore and spawn of the devil.'

'How remiss of me. Okay then, as a person, he's a lying, cowardly, cheating, spawn of the devil, man-whore bastard.' She smiled grimly. 'Sadly, as a software developer, he's still a genius.'

Ryan seemed to fill her office as he straightened his shoulders and jutted out his chin. 'No more of a genius than I am.' He caught her eye, almost as if he was daring her to disagree. 'You reckon his new app is a copy of the original Privacy app, together with the updates we've been working on?'

'Aside from simplifying the user input, which you say nobody could do—'

'They can't.'

'I believe you, so yes, his press release states they're going to launch with an app that can tell the user what information is being kept on them, and by which companies. Exactly what Privacy 2 will do.'

'Then don't launch with Privacy 2 as it stands. Go one better.'

'One better?' As his words percolated through her brain, Sam began to feel a small kernel of hope. A teeny, weeny, buzz of excitement. 'Hold off the launch until we have an app that outdoes his,' she murmured.

'Exactly.'

'We'll lose our customers as they switch over.' Even as she said it though, her mind was racing. What if they could stem off some of that loss by sending out a press release of their own tomorrow, talking of their plans for the updated Privacy app? An app that would do everything Damien's app claimed to do, and more? They didn't need to say what the *more* was, at this stage. Just have the confidence that they would be able to find it, then develop it. In a ridiculously short space of time. Yet there was no reason why they couldn't. She trusted her team. Trusted in the company she'd helped to build.

Reaching for a pen, she started to scribble some notes, her mind racing as the excitement began to build; no longer a buzz now, more a zing. They could do this. It would be bloody hard work. Time wasn't on their side as their current users wouldn't wait for long, but Ryan was right. Who wanted to keep swapping apps? It was a hassle, and it was costly.

She scrawled another note. *Offer a discounted rate for those who stayed with them.*

Her head in a spin, she glanced up to thank Ryan, but he'd already gone. All that remained was the lingering pine of his aftershave, and the impression he'd made.

In her hour of need, he'd been there for her, a shoulder to cry against, a solid wall of muscle to thump out her anger on. But he'd also given her something even more precious.

He'd given her hope.

wouldn't wait for long, but Ryan was right. Who wanted to keep swapping apps? It was a hassle and it was costly.

She scrawled another note: *Offer a discounted rate for those who stayed with them.*

Her head in a spin, she glanced up to thank Ryan, but he'd already gone. All that remained was the lingering pine of his aftershave and the impression he'd made.

In her hour of need, he'd been there for her, a shoulder to cry against, a solid wall of muscle to thump out her anger on, but he'd also given her something far more precious.

He'd given her hope.

PART FOUR

The Idea

Chapter 17

Ryan stared out of the minibus window, watching the scenery change from motorway to countryside. To sea. He was in frigging Cornwall.

Lucas, whom he'd had the dubious pleasure of sitting next to during the four-plus hours of tedious travel, elbowed him in the ribs. 'I hope you've brought your trunks.'

There was a gleam in the man's eye. Two months ago, it would have freaked Ryan out. Now he rolled with it. 'You want to ogle me, you'll have to get up early. I plan to swim before breakfast.'

Lucas gave him a wicked grin. 'I'm sure the view will be worth it.'

Ryan shook his head, but laughter bubbled in his chest. Lucas was unbelievable. One minute he could deliver an eye-wateringly flirtatious comment, the next a blisteringly astute, professional summary. The second Ryan respected, the first kept him in stitches.

'Hey, Sunshine Sam,' Lucas shouted from the back of the minibus to the front. 'Are we nearly there yet?' Ryan shot him an *I'm going to kill you for that* look, and Lucas feigned innocence, whispering. 'She doesn't know it's your nickname for her.'

'*Sunshine* Sam?' Sam popped her head round.

Lucas gave Ryan a sly look before replying to Sam. 'Of course. You bring sunshine into all our days, boss.'

Beside him, Ryan slunk further into his seat. It served him right for letting the nickname slip. Lucas knew very well it had nothing to do with bringing sunshine into their lives, and everything to do with Sam's wide, beautiful, blinding smile.

Sam's laughter bounced round the minibus. 'I hope you'll still be saying that after the next few days. And yes, we're nearly there. About another fifteen minutes.'

Lucas smirked at Ryan before settling back against the seat. 'See, she likes the name. You'd earn brownie points if you used it.'

'I don't need any blasted brownie points.'

'No?'

'I'm still here, aren't I? Officially two days past my probation period.'

Lucas sighed, his expression pained. 'You don't need the points to keep your job, you muppet. You need them if you're ever going to persuade her to go out with you.'

Ryan swore under his breath, rubbing a hand over his hair and down his face. 'For Christ's sake, keep your voice down.' Why the hell had he ever thought telling Lucas he fancied Sam was a good idea?

He'd been drunk, that's why. Not blinding drunk, more loose-tongued drunk. It had been the day that Lynch had come over and made Sam cry. Having been hit, then cried on, Ryan had left her office relieved to see her back to her old self, yet oddly put out that she'd snapped back so effectively, clearly not needing him. Of course he'd also been quietly seething about her faith in Lynch's technical ability. Genius? He'd show her who the blasted genius was.

That was when he'd bumped into Lucas, who'd suggested a drink. That had turned into two, then three. Before he knew it, under Lucas's subtle-as-a-brick probing, Ryan had admitted he liked Sam. A fact Lucas had, predictably, found hilarious.

'Nobody can hear me.' Lucas pouted. 'And stop being such a grump bucket. I'm trying to help.'

Ryan snorted. 'You seriously think I need your help to get laid?'

Lucas was unfazed. 'To get laid, no. To get any further with Sam?' He gave him a smug look. 'You've not exactly made a great deal of headway in that direction.'

'Thanks.' Thank God he hadn't been so drunk that he'd told Lucas that he had, in fact, already made quite a lot of headway in that direction. Before she knew who he was, admittedly.

Lucas smiled serenely. 'Don't you worry, big boy. I'm all over this. I happen to think a hot affair might be just what our Sam needs.'

A hot affair? Was that all Lucas thought he was capable of? Or all he thought Sam would ever want from him?

Not that it mattered, because Sam wasn't prepared to give them a try. Still, it wouldn't harm his cause to have Lucas in his camp, so he clamped his mouth shut.

'Hot damn, look at that.'

At Lucas's irreverent words, Ryan looked out of the minibus window. They'd left the road and were heading up a winding driveway towards a big sprawling farmhouse nestled on a small hill, overlooking a beautiful bay. 'You reckon that's it?'

'Not bad, huh?'

Ryan felt a burst of unease. He'd been on team-building events before, and that's what Sunshine Sam had decided they needed, apparently. Even though what they actually needed was to get a new version of their app out yesterday. What he hadn't done was have a team-building do at the house of his boss's parents. Nor had he ever wanted to date the boss he'd gone on the team building with.

Briefly he had an image of his mum's house. The semi with the broken roof tiles and peeling paintwork. Even the idea of a hot affair between the pair of them was totally frigging ridiculous.

Maybe that's why Sam had been so adamant she didn't want it. Not because she didn't want another work-based relationship, but because she didn't want one with him.

An hour later they'd stowed their stuff in their rooms – most of them were in the converted barn, Sam and Becky in the main house – and were sitting out on the huge patio. Lucas was next to him.

'We're almost an item,' he remarked as he took a pair of designer shades out of their case and settled them on his face. 'Sitting together on the minibus—'

'You sat next to me,' Ryan cut in.

Lucas ignored him. 'Sharing a room.'

'You shoved your case in the room I'd chosen.'

'Details,' Lucas scoffed. Then he peeked at him over his shades. 'Admit it, big man. You've got a soft spot for me.'

'It's soft all right,' Ryan muttered, causing Lucas to burst into laughter.

'Touché.' Lucas eyed Sam pointedly as she walked through the French doors from the farmhouse to join them. 'For how long, though, I wonder.'

Ryan glared back, not interested in discussing the finer parts of his anatomy. Still, as he watched Sam throw back her head with laughter, red hair glinting in the sunlight, sexy curves outlined by her T-shirt and cropped trousers, he crossed his legs. Just in case.

Sam scanned the group walking along the cliff path ahead of her. They must think she was bonkers. And yes, she didn't need to look at Ryan to know he thought that, too. In fact, *not looking* at him was a good idea. Currently striding ahead with his new pal, Lucas, and wasn't that a surprise combination, Ryan was wearing a white T-shirt that showed off his dark looks, and a pair of cargo shorts that drew the eye to his muscular legs. Her stomach dipped and she had to remind herself not to stare.

Since her meltdown in front of Ryan last week, she'd managed to avoid him. Partly because she'd been arranging these days away. And because she was embarrassed to face him.

Mostly because the sight of him made her wish for stupid, foolish things, like his arms around her again. One of his rare smiles, directly into her eyes. Those tantalising lips brushing across her skin.

'Sam?'

At the sound of Becky's voice, Sam shook her thoughts away. These next few days would make or break the company. That was what she needed to be concentrating on.

'Sorry, miles away.'

Her friend snorted and stared pointedly at Ryan. 'Hardly. You're about fifty yards away.' Before Sam had a chance to say anything, Becky was yelling at the men ahead of them. 'Hey, wait for us.'

They turned, Lucas looking like an Abercrombie model in his board shorts and sunglasses. Ryan looking ... like a man who sent goosebumps flying across her skin each time she glanced his way. Big, muscular, rugged, his dark eyes seeing more than she liked.

'This walk is supposed to be part of the team building,' Becky protested when they caught them up.

Ryan angled his head to the group walking ahead. 'Tell that to them.'

'Calm down, Becks,' Sam soothed. 'The team building will come later. This is a walk to stretch our legs, take in the scenery and just' – she shrugged – 'breathe?'

They set off again, and Sam shook her head as she noticed Becky thread her arm through Lucas's and ease away from them. Traitor.

'Is this where you grew up?' Ryan asked after a few minutes.

'Cornwall? No, though we had a lot of family holidays here when I was a child.' She paused and decided, considering what she knew about his mum, it was only fair. 'Dad had a heart attack a few years ago. Overworked, overweight, over-stressed. They decided to sell their business and move down here.'

His gaze drifted over to her. 'I can see the attraction.'

As his eyes held hers, dark and full of double meaning, she felt an awkward blush sting her cheeks. She was used to men; flirty, chauvinistic, arrogant, she'd faced them all. How could this one unsettle her so easily?

They walked on in silence for a while, navigating a stile and disturbing a field of sheep. Above them the sun shone in a cloudless blue sky. Below them the sea frothed against the cliffs. All around them was quiet, calm. Tranquility.

It would be so easy to simply walk and enjoy, to steer clear of anything heavy, but Sam knew there was something she needed to say to Ryan. 'I didn't get around to thanking you properly.'

He quirked a dark brow. 'For?'

'Allowing me to use you as a punch bag.'

He laughed. She didn't know whether it was the sun, the setting, or just being out of the office but he seemed lighter today. 'You can use my body any time.' His smile turned sensual, his gaze hotter. 'In any way.'

Though her heart began to pound, Sam tried to keep the conversation casual. 'I do believe we've been here before. And decided it wasn't a good idea.'

'You decided.' He tapped his chin with his finger in an

exaggerated thought pose. 'What was it again? Oh yes, you can't have another office-based affair because we're going to crash and burn and then it'll be awkward.' His dark eyes snared hers. 'How about this. If it comes to that, I promise to quit.'

Thump, thump, thump went her heart. 'I can't have you quitting.'

'You value my tech prowess more than my sexual prowess?' His expression turned to one of mild disgust. 'I'm not sure how insulted to be.'

'Don't be.' Because she needed to make the connection, to show him the attraction was still there for her, too, she squeezed his arm. 'I value both, Ryan. I just need the first more than the second right now.'

He glanced down at her hand on his arm, then over at her, his chest lifting and falling as a rush of air left his lungs. 'Okay.'

This time the silence didn't feel quite so peaceful. He was tense beside her, the light-heartedness of a moment ago now gone. She racked her brains for a way to bring it back.

'You think this is a bad idea, don't you?'

They'd reached a stile and he climbed over first, his movements agile and economical. 'Walking with you in the sun, across the cliffs?' He held out his hand to help her down.

'Not exactly.' She felt the zing from his brief touch hum all through her body. 'More taking the company out of the office for three days.'

'Ah.' He rubbed at the back of his neck as they set off

again, and her eyes were drawn to the flex of his bicep. God, she was turning into a Ryan Black groupie. 'We need to have a new app out yesterday, and we're swanning about in Cornwall. Guess you could say I'm confused, but what do I know?'

'You know more than you think. In fact, broadly speaking, this was your idea.'

'Whoa, hold on.' He held up his hand. 'Where did you get that from?'

'You told me we needed to go one better, and you were right. Tomorrow's brainstorming session is going to give us that.' It had to. She was betting everything she had on it.

'A bunch of hungover people with sunburn are going to come up with the next big idea for your app?'

'I can't be responsible for whether you've all put sunscreen on today, but I can restrict the alcohol tonight.' She grinned over at him. 'Should have kept your big mouth shut, Black.'

He caught her eye and, though he didn't laugh, amusement glinted in those dark pools, and humour relaxed the harshness of his face. Set against the rugged coastline, with the sun bringing out his tan, he was gorgeous enough to make her breath catch.

It was with a mixture of relief and disappointment that she saw they were catching up with the group ahead of them.

'Did you ever consider only bringing a few of us here?' he asked.

'Which few? How can we know where the next idea will come from? Besides, how motivated would you feel if half of the company were, what did you call it, swanning off in Cornwall, and you were left behind?' She hated the thought of anyone believing there was a them and us.

'As long as you kept paying me, I'd keep working.'

'That's what Damien used to say. You tech guys must have no heart.'

She felt him stiffen. 'Lump me in the same category as your lying, cheating ex. Nice.'

'I didn't mean it like that.'

'Sure.' He gave her a sidelong look. 'Have you heard from him since last week?'

She hesitated. 'No.' When he carried on staring at her, she huffed. 'Okay, he did send me a bunch of apology roses.'

'And they're different from *I want to get back in your pants again* roses?'

'Of course. Apology roses have a card with them saying sorry.' A single word followed by his name. Since she didn't much like flowers – something Damien would have known, if he'd ever listened to her – Sam had given them to Kerry to take to her mum, who was recovering from a knee operation.

Ryan shook his head. 'Roses are roses. They always say I want to get into your pants.'

'Send a lot of them, do you?'

He smirked. 'I prefer the direct approach.'

In a flash she was back in that bar, being propositioned by a dark, sexy stranger. *All I care about is whether your bedroom is less of a shithole than mine.*

Ryan Black hadn't needed roses to seduce her. Just a smouldering glance from his magnetic dark eyes. And a terrible chat-up line. She'd been that easy.

Perhaps it wasn't surprising then that she was finding the man she knew now, the one who'd been charming to her parents, who'd held and comforted her even after she'd raged at him, after she'd *thumped* him, increasingly hard to resist.

Chapter 18

Ryan found himself sitting between Becky and Alice at dinner. How he'd managed to cock that up so badly, he didn't know. Of everyone here – and of course Sunshine Sam had invited the whole company, why not? Can't have anyone feeling left out – of everyone here, Becky and Alice would have been bottom of his list of desirable dinner companions.

Becky, because he was pretty certain she didn't like him. The concept wasn't new but being liked by the friend of the woman you had a thing for seemed quite important.

As for Alice, he didn't want to sit next to her because she kept looking at him with wary eyes, as if she was expecting him to tear her off a strip at any moment.

Christ, he needed a drink.

'Is there any beer?' He directed the question at Alice without thinking.

She immediately leapt to her feet, all desperate to please. 'I'll go and find out.'

'No.' Her eyes widened, like a startled deer, and he cursed inwardly before making a determined effort to gentle his voice.

'No need. I'll have some red.' He reached for the wine bottle in front of him and was about to pour himself some when he belatedly remembered his manners. 'Do you want some?'

'Please.' A cautious smile. 'Thank you.'

He tried to smile back, though he probably came off as only marginally less sinister than Hannibal Lecter.

Having poured out their wine he sat back and took in his surroundings. They were sitting on the terrace outside her parents' house. Fairy lights were strung around the nearby trees and solar lights shone from the various flower-pots lining the patio area. The long table was littered with tea lights, bottles of wine, chunks of fresh bread, dishes of olives and plates of various meats. It had a real continental feel, yet here they were, in Cornwall.

Her parents had put in a brief appearance, just long enough to say a general hello – not long enough for either of them to catch his eye – before they drove off in their Range Rover, leaving Sam and the caterers to it.

'Still think coming out here is a bad idea?'

He turned to find Becky giving him a curious look. 'I never said it was.'

'You didn't have to. The expression on your face when Sam announced it said it for you.'

He let out a huff of annoyance. 'Can we cut out the needling for one night, huh? It's tiresome.'

She pursed her lips. 'It wasn't a dig. More an observation. You looked like you were taking everything in. I wondered what you were thinking.'

'I'm thinking her parents have taste. It's a nice place.'

Becky seemed to relax at that. 'Yeah, it is, isn't it? They moved here five years ago, along with Sam's grandparents, who lived in the barn you're staying in. Sadly, they've both passed away.'

'Is that Grumps?'

Surprise flickered crossed her face. 'Yes. Sam's grandma died two years ago. Grumps was never the same after that.' Becky glanced towards the end of the table where Sam was talking animatedly with Kerry. 'It was tough on Sam. She doted on him.'

'Yeah. I know.'

'You do?'

'Why so shocked?'

She gave him a long, cool study. 'Because you're not exactly Mr Conversation.'

'We're talking now, aren't we?'

She looked like she wanted to scowl, but her innate sense of fun won over and she laughed. 'Fair point. So, in the spirit of talking, have you still got the hots for Sam?'

The wine in the glass he was holding sloshed alarmingly up the sides as Ryan lurched back on his seat. 'None of your business.'

'True, but you can't blame a girl for being interested. Especially considering how you two met.'

It was his turn to scowl. 'Keep your voice down. Nobody else knows about that.'

'Sorry.' Becky sighed, playing with the stem of her glass. 'Look, I just wanted to tell you not to mess her about. Damien's betrayal hit her really hard.'

The implied comparison to her ex set his teeth on edge. 'I'm not that kind of guy. Besides, she's my boss. Pissing her off is hardly a smart move.'

There was a beat of silence as Becky's heavily outlined dark eyes flicked over his face. Then she surprised him by smiling. 'It must be really awkward for you, huh? I hadn't really thought about it until now. I'd been more focused on how weird it must be for Sam.'

'Tell me about it,' he returned heavily. Awkward didn't even begin to describe the feeling of being hugely attracted to a woman who not only outclassed him but was the boss of him. Yet when he was with her, like on the walk this afternoon, he forgot all that. She simply became a woman he desperately wanted to get to know more. A woman he wanted to taste again, to touch, to feel beneath him, on top of him. All around him.

Becky turned to answer a question from the guy sitting to her right, and Ryan allowed himself a peek at Sam. She looked especially hot tonight in cropped white trousers and a blue shirt that matched the colour of her incredible eyes. Despite the pressure she was under with the company, tonight she looked ... energised. Buzzing. Totally in her element as she bestowed a smile here, a funny comment there. She didn't pay lip service to the whole team philosophy, she lived and breathed it.

She chose that moment to glance up and catch his eye. He raised his glass, toasting her, and she smiled before continuing her conversation with the lucky sod she was sitting next to.

His study of her was interrupted as a plate piled high with seafood pasta was placed in front of him. Welcoming the excuse to eat rather than talk, Ryan tucked in.

It was only after he'd finished that he realised he probably should do the conversation thing with Alice, so he turned to her. She was staring down at her phone, tears in her eyes.

Crap. He should leave her to it. Yeah, that was best. He wasn't like Sam. He didn't have a natural warmth, or empathy. Ignoring would be less embarrassing for both of them.

He snuck another look at her, saw a tear roll down her cheek and swore silently. 'Alice?' She jerked her head up and he could see she'd been so engrossed in whatever she'd been reading, she'd forgotten where she was. 'Everything okay?'

Her cheeks flushed and she clattered the phone onto the table. 'Yes, fine.' Her hands trembled as she put them in her lap. 'It's just my boyfriend.'

Upset, he could ignore. Scared, he couldn't. 'Let me reword that. What's wrong?'

She shook her head, rubbing a hand over her wet cheeks. 'Nothing.'

'Well, you're crying for some reason.' He gave her a wry smile. 'I hope it's not that you're stuck with me to talk to.'

'What? Oh, no … I mean sitting next to you is fine.'

He figured 'fine' was about what he deserved. 'What made you cry then?' He made her hold his gaze. 'And don't fob me off. I know a scared look when I see one.' When she still didn't say anything, he inhaled, let the breath out slowly and then admitted something he hadn't told anyone. 'You know how I can spot when a woman's scared? My mum had that look on her face for a lot of my childhood. Until my dad did the decent thing and left.'

Alice jerked her eyes away from his. 'I don't know why you're telling me this. What does it have to do with me?'

He searched her face, wondering how he'd missed it up till now. Her eagerness to please. The way she flinched when he raised his voice. 'He didn't hit my mum, but he liked to bully her. Probably because he was a bad-tempered, small-minded, insecure bastard who bossed her around at home to hide the fact he was a failure outside it.' The memories made his blood boil and he had to take a moment to unclench his fist. Soften his voice. 'What's your boyfriend's excuse?'

She bit into her lip, and her eyes welled again. 'I don't know,' she whispered. 'I don't know why he does it.'

Sam caught herself staring at Ryan. Again. Only this time he wasn't looking at her. Instead he seemed to be in a heavy conversation with Alice. And Alice appeared to be upset.

Excusing herself, Sam slipped off her chair and walked round the table. As she neared Ryan and Alice, she glanced at Becky, who shot her an *I don't know what's going on* look.

'You need to get out.' Ryan's head was angled towards Alice, his expression fierce. She was avoiding his eyes.

Whatever was wrong, Ryan was clearly trying to help, but either he was going about it the wrong way, or Alice wasn't ready to receive it.

'Hey.' They both turned to face her, Alice now looking embarrassed as well as upset. Ryan's expression was more one of relief. 'Is there anything I can help with?'

Ryan looked at Alice, who shook her head before lurching to her feet. 'Excuse me. I need the toilet.'

'Would you like me to show you where they are?' Sam asked softly. Alice was one shaken-up young lady.

'I went earlier. I'm fine. Thank you.'

Sam was filled with concern as she watched her dash off. 'What's wrong?'

Ryan sighed, pulling his chair out so he could rest his elbows on his thighs. 'It's her business.' He glanced up. 'But she could do with talking to someone who's better at this stuff than I am.'

'She looks really upset.'

'She is.' Suddenly Ryan sat bolt upright. 'Hey, wait a minute. You think I upset her?'

'Of course not. At least not deliberately.'

He let out a crack of unamused laughter. 'Thanks for the vote of confidence.'

She slid onto the chair Alice had vacated, anxious to make sure he understood where she was coming from. 'She's young and sensitive, Ryan. Even more so now she believes Privacy Solutions is in trouble because of what she said to Damien. It would be easy for anyone to upset her.'

'Yeah.' His expression sharpened. 'Tell me this. If it had been Lucas or Becky talking to her instead of me, would you have come over?'

He had her there. 'No,' she admitted reluctantly.

'Thought not.' He climbed stiffly to his feet. 'Give Alice my apologies when she comes back. I need to be somewhere that's not here.'

'Now wait a minute.' Sam shot out her arm to hold him back. 'Don't just stalk off like a highly strung teenager. Stay and discuss this like an adult.'

'Discuss what? How you think I'm some sort of bully?' Though his voice was low and controlled enough not to catch the attention of the others round the table, it vibrated with anger.

'No. Of course not.' How had he twisted her meaning so badly?

She opened her mouth to say more, to plead with him to stop being ridiculous, but he was already striding off. Unless she was prepared to embarrass them both by running after him, she had to let him go.

'I think you've poked the bear.' Becky, who'd clearly been listening to everything but pretending she hadn't, shifted to face her.

'Apparently,' Sam said glumly. 'For a big hulking bruiser of a man, he's stupidly easy to hurt.'

'Funny, I thought the same. Maybe the badass attitude he's so keen to show us isn't the real him at all.'

Sam eyed her friend. 'Since when did you become so perceptive?'

Becky grinned. 'I've hung around with you for nearly twenty years. It was probably time something useful rubbed off. Do you want me to go and find Alice? Or Ryan for that matter.'

'No. I think both of them would rather be left alone right now. Hopefully they'll come down to the beach for the rounders game.' Sam rose dejectedly to her feet. Half an hour ago she'd been flying high. Having the team around her, her company, her family, seeing them all round the table, laughing and having fun. It had been invigorating. More than that, for the first time in months she'd had a real feeling of optimism. A belief that they could turn everything round.

Now the doubts were creeping in. Was bringing everyone out here just a vain indulgence on her behalf? A bit of sea air, a game of rounders on the beach ... was Ryan right? Would it really help?

Maybe she should have stuck to doing the thinking in the office, where Alice could have licked her wounds in private. And she and Ryan would have been able to avoid each other.

An hour later, they gathered on the beach in the fading light for the rounders game. Alice had made it and was talking to Kerry. Though her sparkle was missing, Sam was pleased to see her looking more composed.

'I don't have to be Einstein to guess who you're looking for,' Becky remarked dryly.

Embarrassed at being caught out, Sam tore her eyes away from the cliff path. 'He's not going to show.'

'Yes, he is.' Becky nudged her and pointed in the opposite direction to the one she'd been looking. A tall man, athletic build, hands in his pockets, baseball cap on his head, was walking along the beach towards them.

The knot of tension slowly loosened in her stomach.

After asking Becky to sort everyone into two teams, Sam walked slowly over to him. 'It's good to see you.'

Beneath the peak of his black cap, his eyes narrowed. 'Worried I wouldn't show?'

Honesty was what he valued, so honesty is what she gave him. 'Yes.'

He tutted. 'Thought you knew me better than that.'

She didn't, though she was learning, she thought as she watched him jog over to where Lucas was waving. An introverted, blunt-speaking loner at times, but an honest, principled one. And a man more in tune with the feelings of others than he liked to let on.

The rounders game was fun, with everyone in good spirits. Even Ryan, who surprised her by taking it on himself to captain their team. Perhaps his competitive streak was stronger than his desire to remain on the periphery.

'Go on, you big popsicle,' Ryan yelled to Lucas from third base. 'Give it your best shot.'

Lucas, wearing red, blue and green shorts with wide horizontal stripes, topped with a yellow and red striped T-shirt, shot Ryan the middle finger as he stepped up to bat.

One giant swing later and the ball rocketed up into the air. Sam, fielding deep behind Ryan, called for the catch but Ryan darted past her. 'Mine. You'll catch like a girl.'

The ball started to fall from its high trajectory and Ryan splashed through the waves to get beneath it. Seeing her moment, Sam barged into him, sending him crashing into the sea.

As he spluttered and cursed, she promptly took the catch,

then waved the ball under his nose. 'Caught like a girl, I believe.'

Sitting in the sea, elbows on his knees, he smiled blandly up at her. 'Well played.'

'I thought so.' She turned to throw the ball back to the bowler, then yelped as she felt a pair of wet hands slide under her legs and lift her up.

He wouldn't.

His dark eyes danced mischievously, and the bland smile turned into a grin of pure evil as he strode further into the sea. Then dumped her into it.

She screamed, letting out a string of swear words as she staggered to her feet.

'You squeal like a girl, too.' He tossed back his head and laughed – a full-on belly laugh that drew more of a gasp from her than the cold dunk in the sea.

Ryan Black was attractive when he was snapping angrily or brooding silently in his office. With his face lit up with laughter, wet T-shirt clinging to the muscles of his chest, he was far more than attractive.

He was dangerous.

Damien had hurt her, but this man? If she let this man get any closer, she was afraid he could destroy her.

He reached out a hand. 'Come on, boss.' His grin held a touch of wicked. 'Let's get you out of those wet clothes.'

Despite the chill, a warmth settled in her stomach, fanning out to the rest of her body. *If* she let him get closer? Who was she kidding? Right from that very first night, when she'd thrown off her caution and taken him back to her place, the choice hadn't really been hers. There was a saying, something about the heart wanting what the heart wanted.

She had to hope this was only her body doing the wanting. That her heart would, please God, remain safely protected behind the wall of hurt Damien had created.

Chapter 19

Ryan was sitting round a fire pit on the beach with the rest of the team feeling mellow; lapping waves, a gentle breeze, the crack of the fire, a cool beer in his hand. He'd changed into dry clothes after his unplanned dunking, as had Sam, though he hadn't had a chance to speak to her since she'd taken his hand and allowed him to lead her out of the water. Mainly because Becky had rushed over to them and given him the evil eye while she'd flapped all over her friend. Deciding to take the path of least resistance, he'd quietly retreated.

Did he deserve Becky's condemnation? Had he felt guilty seeing Sam wet and shivering? A bit, maybe, but she'd started the whole dunking episode. Maybe a gentleman wouldn't have retaliated, but Ryan reckoned today's world was all about equality. He'd happily take a woman running the country, a woman boss, but he wasn't going to take a woman dumping him in the sea and then getting arsy when he dumped her back.

To be fair, it was Becky who'd got the hump with him. Sam might have shaken her head as he'd tugged her out of the sea, but he'd seen the amusement in her eyes, the flush on her cheeks. She hadn't minded. Just as he hadn't minded her pushing him over.

He figured if she didn't like him, she wouldn't have done it.

Not that he wasn't still cross with her over Alice, he reminded himself as he deliberately kept his eyes on the fire, so they wouldn't stray in her direction.

Slowly people began to leave, pleading tiredness. Soon only he, Sam, Lucas and Kerry remained.

Kerry was clearly drunk on fresh air, exhaustion or alcohol – or maybe all three. Whatever it was, she wouldn't stop talking.

'Best part of the day?' she demanded.

'Easy.' Lucas batted his eyes in Ryan's direction. 'Finding I'm sharing a bed with Ryan.'

'Sharing a room,' Ryan corrected quickly, which set Kerry off on another round of giggling.

'Same question to Ryan,' she announced when she'd stopped long enough to draw breath.

Immediately a show reel of images flashed through his mind. Walking with Sam along the cliffs. Watching her as she'd held court at her end of the table at dinner, all warmth, humour and spellbinding self-assurance. Seeing her rise like a bedraggled mermaid out of the water after he'd dunked her.

Clearing his throat, he glanced back at Lucas. 'Finding the room I'm being forced to share with Lucas has two single beds set at least three metres apart.'

Three months ago, there would have been a strained silence

at his cutting words. Now there was laughter. Was it hopeful thinking, or were these people were finally starting to get him?

'Your go, Sam,' Kerry prompted.

Ryan's gaze shifted over to Sam, and when her eyes met his, she gave him a slow smile. 'Shoving Mr Black into the sea.'

Another round of laughter, louder this time.

'That was my favourite, too,' Kerry said and giggled. 'Not so much the shoving, more the part when he walked out with his wet T-shirt clinging to his chest. I mean, I always thought he looked fit, but wowzer. He'd give Magic Mike a run for his money.'

Ryan shifted awkwardly. 'I am here.' He wasn't averse to being ogled – heck, he was flattered – but this was Kerry. Cheery, sweet. She was going to be mortified tomorrow. And he wasn't going to know what to say to her.

Kerry slapped a hand over her mouth. 'Oops.'

Lucas leapt to his feet. 'I think it's time we headed back. Big brainstorming day tomorrow.' He clasped Kerry's hand and pulled her to her feet. 'Come on, sweetheart. You can make sure I get back safely. We'll leave Ryan and Sam to sort out the fire.' Just as Ryan was about to give Lucas points for tact, the guy glanced over his shoulder at him. And winked.

Quiet descended as they strolled off, the sounds of Kerry's giggles growing fainter and fainter until all Ryan could hear was the roll of the waves and the crackle of the fire.

'That's him being subtle.'

'As a brick.' Ryan's pulse hammered as he looked at Sam,

desire burning through him. Christ, she was sexy, sitting there with her legs crossed, her red hair tumbling around her shoulders. The light from the fire making her eyes appear luminous.

'I guess we should put out the fire.'

The irony of her words wasn't lost on him. The fire in his blood would be a hell of a lot harder to extinguish. If he felt her naked body tremble around him just one more time, could that be enough? 'Why the rush?'

She didn't answer him straightaway. It was almost as if she was having her own internal battle. 'You and me, out here together. People will talk.'

'You really care that much about what they think?'

She looked at him as if he'd just asked her a stupid question. 'You have to ask, given my relationship history? Of course I do. You don't?'

'I used to.' He poked at the fire with a long stick, causing sparks to flurry around them, bright red against the inky night. 'It screwed with me for a while. Now I think, stuff 'em. There are only a couple of people whose opinions I value. My mum.' He raised his head to look at Sam. The woman who only a few hours ago had thought he was being mean to Alice. Yeah, that had really, really stung. 'And you.'

Sam looked taken aback. 'Me?'

'Yes.' He tried to shrug off the crushed feeling in his chest. 'I tried not to care, but it seems I do.'

Shock was the first thing she experienced, quickly followed by something akin to a swarm of butterflies flapping in her stomach. 'I'm not sure what to say.'

He gave her a small, dry smile. 'Doesn't usually hold you back.'

God, he was gorgeous. Arms hugging his muscular legs, swarthy dark looks glowing in the firelight. 'If you value my opinion, you need to know what I thought when I came up to you and Alice earlier.'

His jaw tightened. 'Forget it.'

'No, I won't. I can't.' She was supposed to be good at reading people, at dealing with them, so how did she keep getting it so wrong where Ryan was concerned? 'In a way you were right, I wouldn't have come over had it been Lucas or Becky talking to Alice.' He flinched, and she reached out to touch his arm, her eyes drawn to the scattering of dark hairs that added to his powerfully masculine vibe. 'That doesn't mean I thought you'd upset her.' His expression said *do I look stupid?* and she huffed. 'Okay, you can be blunt, and I know Alice is sensitive, but that's not the reason I intervened. I thought she might find it easier to talk to me.'

He stared at the fire for a few seconds before turning to face her. 'You didn't think I'd be any good handling a crying female?'

'Just because I thought Becky, Lucas or I would have found it easier doesn't mean I thought you couldn't do it.' She smiled. 'After all, you coped with me just fine.'

He caught her eye and laughed softly. 'More by luck than judgement.' He paused, his face growing serious. 'My father was a bully.'

Slowly his words, and their meaning, sank in. 'That's why you were so upset when I came up to you. You believed I thought you were *bullying* Alice?' Emotion caught at her throat and this time when she touched his arm, she clung to it. 'God, Ryan, no. A million times no. You speak your mind and when you work you don't like to be interrupted. You can also be curt, but you're not, I repeat not, a bully.' He looked down at her hand on his arm, pale against his tanned skin, then nodded, once, though his eyes remained on the fire. 'That's why you said you didn't miss him.'

'Yeah.' He reached for a stick and banged the fire back into life.

The ease, the lightness he'd carried with him earlier had vanished and he was back to brooding and quiet. At least now she was starting to understand the reason for that. Growing up with a bully of a father can't have been easy.

'How did your mum feel when he left? Did she love him?'

'She must have done once.' The fire cast shadows across his face, making it seem more angular. 'But by the end she loved the drink more.'

Sam winced. A bully of a father *and* a mother who drank too much. 'Does she still drink?'

His jaw tightened. 'I've tried to get her to quit. She's tried to quit. But she just ...' He shut his eyes, pain etched across his face. 'She keeps going back to it.'

'God, I'm so sorry.' It explained her heart troubles. His worry for her. His reaction to the gambling app, because, like alcohol, it had the potential to be addictive.

Slowly but surely she felt her heart open up to him. There was so much going on beneath his blunt surface. So many layers she was starting to reveal.

And so many reasons why she didn't want to push him away any more.

They fell into a companionable silence, her hand still on his arm. Now they weren't talking, she was fully aware of the strength beneath her fingers. The warmth of his skin. How much she wanted to slide her hand down to clasp his.

He must have read her thoughts because when he turned to look at her, his eyes flared. 'Sam.'

Her name on his lips sounded full of heat, of longing, and her heart began to race. 'The sensible thing to do right now,' she whispered, 'is head back.'

He nodded, but his gaze skimmed her face, searching. 'Fuck sensible.'

His bluntness made her laugh. 'That is one option.' Unconsciously she leant into him, resting her head on his shoulder. 'What about tomorrow morning?'

Finally, a return of his wicked grin. 'I'm game for a repeat if you are.'

Laughing again, she nudged his side. 'You know what I mean.'

'We're on a beach, Sam. Just you and me. No job titles, no office.' He bent his head, his mouth a tantalising few inches from hers. 'It's not as if it's the first time.'

'All true.' Yet nothing about sleeping with him would be simple now.

As she was bombarded with conflicted thoughts his mouth touched hers and a bolt of lust surged through her. Even as she fought to stay in control, to keep it at just a kiss, she found herself lying back on the blanket, his large frame leaning over her, hands caressing, lips nibbling, tongue dancing with hers. She heard a faint moan, her, then a deep, husky groan. Him. The sound sent further heat rushing into her blood.

Chest heaving, he drew back a little, dark eyes smouldering, reflecting the flames from the fire. 'Tell me you want this.'

'I want you.' When she stripped everything else away – the fear of falling for him, the fear of another relationship going up in flames, all under the bright glare of the office – that was the simple truth.

He groaned again, his mouth finding hers with more urgency now, his warm hands unbuttoning her blouse and smoothing over her stomach, then up to her breasts. 'God help me, I can't get enough of you, Sam Huxton.'

She arched her back as his mouth moved to her breasts, sucking them over her bra. 'Are we really going to do this?' she panted. 'In the open. On a sandy beach.' His answer was to slip the blouse from her shoulders, and then undo the clasp of her bra. 'I guess we are.'

He stopped for a second to stare down at her. 'You really think a bit of sand is going to stop me?'

Mesmerised by the hunger in his expression she slowly reached for the button on his shorts. 'I guess we'd better get your clothes off, too.'

'Hallelujah.' With that he lifted his T-shirt over his head, the glow from the fire playing across his rippling muscles. Her breath caught, eyes drinking in his rugged beauty, and his lips twitched. 'Still think I'm nicely packaged?'

She smiled, remembering that first time. Then he'd been an exciting stranger. Now he was a man she'd cried on. A man she'd opened up to. A man she'd hit, managed to upset, yet who somehow still wanted her. Reaching out, she ran her hand across his hard pecs, feeling the rough dusting of dark hair, the smooth heat of his skin. As she lowered her hand to his taut stomach his muscles tensed, and his breath came out in a hiss. 'I think you're the most beautiful man I've ever seen.'

He laughed, low and seductive. 'Thank you, though we've already established I'm only the second man you've slept with. Still, it means I'm better than your git of an ex, so I'll take it.' With that he shrugged off the rest of his clothes, reached into the back pocket of his shorts for his wallet and gave her a dry smile as he pulled out a condom. 'Remembered where I put it this time.'

At the sound of the packet tearing, an unpleasant thought ran through her – unfair, too, because they weren't dating. She hadn't offered anything beyond now. Catching her expression, he reared forward and took her face in his hands, forcing her to look at him. 'You're the last person I slept with, Huxton,' he told her fiercely. 'You're the only woman I think of.'

Delight and smug satisfaction coiled in her belly. 'Good to know.'

In a flash he'd sheathed himself and was lying on the blanket, lifting her up and onto him. 'Don't want sand rubbing against your fine backside.'

She rolled her eyes, gazing down on him. Hair messed by the sea and the wind, lips curved in a crooked smile, dark eyes devouring her. 'I call you beautiful, but my backside only merits a fine?'

He shifted his hips, causing her to gasp. 'Thought you'd be

all over the word "fine". Fine as in the wine. Outstanding quality.'

Clasping his hands around her waist he started to move beneath her. Sam let out a moan of deep, sensual pleasure, losing herself to the moment, to the romance of the setting.

And slowly but almost inexorably, to him.

Chapter 20

Ryan woke gradually, slowly realising where he was. Not in his big bed, in his crummy flat, but crammed in a small single bed, in a freshly painted room. The walls were decorated with paintings of the sea, an artfully distressed set of drawers stood by the window. And a man stared at him from the bed across the room.

'You made it back then.' Blond hair flopping messily over his forehead, Lucas raised himself up on his elbows.

'Obviously.' Memories from last night flooded back to him. The feel of Sam's lithe body. The way she'd moved over him, her hands sliding over his chest. His body twitched and he shifted in the bed, desperately blocking any further images. Bad enough waking up in the same room as a bloke. No way would he add hot and aroused to that scenario.

'Took your time leaving the beach though, you and Sam,' Lucas added pointedly.

Ryan rubbed his eyes, both to wake himself up and to avoid looking at Lucas. 'How do you know Sam didn't come back earlier?'

Lucas laughed. 'Come on. You think I wasn't messaging Becky? She's staying in the room next to Sam.'

Ryan tucked that information away for future reference. If – and he knew it was a big if – he saw Sam tonight, make sure to get the right bedroom.

'So?' Lucas persisted. 'Anything to tell me?'

'Yeah.' He skimmed his eyes deliberately up and down the part of Lucas that was exposed above his duvet. 'Nice pyjamas.'

Lucas frowned down at the blue-and-white striped top he was sporting and then glanced pointedly at Ryan's bare chest. 'Some of us show appropriate decorum when sharing a room.'

Ryan chuckled and eased his long legs out of the cramped bed. 'Chill. I kept my boxers on especially for you.'

'I wouldn't have complained if you'd taken them off for me,' Lucas countered, making Ryan laugh even harder.

'You're all talk, Baker. You wouldn't know how to handle me.'

'If you gave me half a chance, I'd show you,' Lucas muttered, then sighed and sat up. 'All of which conveniently sidetracks me from my original question.' He gave Ryan a hard look. 'What happened with you and Sam?'

Ryan rolled his eyes in an effort to appear casually unfazed by the question. 'She's your friend, ask her.'

'I will.' Lucas's expression turned serious. 'I like you, Black, I really do. And as I said earlier, a hot affair could be just what Sam needs. But know this. If you hurt her, I'll throttle you with my bare hands.'

Ryan flashed him a grin. 'I'll consider myself warned.'

Lucas didn't smile back. In fact, the look he gave Ryan reminded him of a tiger, snarling to warn potential predators away from her cub. 'Don't be fooled by my appearance, or my mild manner. When it comes to protecting those I love, I'm every inch a man.'

Ryan held his gaze. 'You think I see you any other way?'

Lucas's expression lost some of its fierceness. 'Okay then. I just wanted to make sure.'

Feeling unsettled, Ryan rose to his feet and grabbed the towel from the end of the bed. Tension still hung in the air and Ryan knew that however much he and Lucas had bonded, the guy was still very much in Sam's camp. Ryan would always be the one on the outside. 'You assume it's Sam who'll get hurt,' he threw at Lucas as he stood in the doorway. 'Yet she's the one who holds all the power.'

The words stuck with him as he headed down the corridor towards the shower. He suddenly had this vivid picture of him panting after Sam, like a mongrel on heat. Was that how it felt to her? The scruffy mutt, desperately chasing after the glossy red setter?

He shook the image away, pretty certain it wasn't how Sam saw him. Yet equally she didn't think enough of him to want to risk more than a quick, though he had to say bloody incredible, tryst on the beach.

The thought stung, because he wanted more than that.

Yet as he soaped himself down in the shower he acknowledged that such was his fascination with her, if the chance for a repeat presented itself, he'd dive straight in without a second thought.

The meeting that was to decide the future of the company – Sam's words, not his – was to be held in the main house. Ryan walked over with Lucas, and they bumped into her parents in the kitchen.

Lucas, who clearly knew them well, immediately shook Mr Huxton's hand – Bob's hand – and gave Sam's mother a kiss on both cheeks. Ryan wanted to scoff and call him smarmy, but Lucas's style was effortless, much like Sam's. As he stood watching him, Ryan felt rough and unsophisticated.

'Hello, Ryan.' Sam's mum – Helen – caught his eye and smiled over at him.

'Hello.' He cleared his throat. Should he kiss her cheek like Lucas had? Like she had when she'd said goodbye to him after the meal? But knowing him he'd miss and get her ear. Worse, her mouth, and she'd think he was coming on to her.

Moving easily towards him, she took the whole initiative out of his hands by reaching up on her toes and kissing both of his cheeks. 'It's lovely to see you again.'

Christ, he could feel a flush creep up his neck, just as it had the last time she'd done that. He didn't even know why. Embarrassed because he'd not taken the initiative, like Lucas had? Maybe.

Or maybe it felt good to feel accepted by the mum of the woman he was fast becoming obsessed with.

He had no time to freak out about which it was because now Bob was shaking his hand. Not as warm as his wife, his manner more reserved. More cautious. His questions asked more out of politeness than genuine curiosity. Had Ryan had a chance to see much of Cornwall yet – no. Had he swum in the sea yet – yes, last night. *Because I smelt of your daughter, and I didn't want my roommate getting suspicious.* Words he managed to keep to himself.

'Well, we must dash.' Helen went to pick up her handbag from the kitchen worktop. 'We don't want to get in trouble with our daughter. Sam expressly told us she wanted us out of the house by 9.30am.'

Lucas laughed. 'I see you're scared of her, too.'

'Of course.' Bob's gaze drifted over to Ryan. 'She may look soft and easygoing, but she's a demon when crossed.'

Was it his imagination, or had Sam's dad just fired him a warning shot? Lucas waited until they were out of earshot before starting to laugh. 'Well, well, looks like Bob has you on his radar.'

Ryan swallowed his unease. He'd had the same feeling during dinner at the pub. Not dislike, exactly. More a sense the man was watching him carefully. 'Must think I'm some thug out to damage his daughter's company.'

Lucas eyed him speculatively. 'Or maybe he thinks you're some thug out to sleep with his daughter.'

Ryan made himself laugh. 'Good try, but I'm not daft enough to rise to that bait.' He glanced down at his watch, more to avoid Lucas's prying eyes than to see what the time was. 'Better head to the meeting before she turns demon on us both.'

Sam tried to keep her enthusiasm levels high. Tried to keep the smile on her face, and the optimism in her voice.

Inside, her hopes for the day were plummeting fast. They'd

been at this for seven hours, and all they'd come up with was more of the same. Most ideas boiled down to altering the user input into the app. Something Ryan stubbornly, and consistently, told them wasn't the answer.

'I've told you before. The app can't find information if you don't give it a hint where to look.' Hours of building frustration had begun to give his voice a hard edge. 'Do you know how many companies are out there? I can't programme an app to look at every frigging one of them. We've got the input part right, especially now the app can use the email address to search through the user's junk mail. Don't you think Lynch would have simplified the user set-up on his own app, if he could?'

'Fine.' Becky looked as frazzled as Sam felt. 'We hear you. But it would be nice if we also heard some solutions, rather than the same old negative comments.'

'I'm a software developer,' Ryan shot back. 'I write code, programmes, applications. Ideas are your job.'

As Becky squared her shoulders ready to retaliate, Sam held up her hand. 'Enough. We're not going to get anywhere if we snipe at each other.' From her seat on the sofa Becky caught Sam's eye, her expression full of apology. Ryan just clenched his jaw and stared down at his notepad. 'Why don't we take ten minutes to cool down and get some fresh air.'

There was a murmur of approval as everyone stood and stretched their legs, following each other out through the open French doors and onto the patio.

Becky hung back. 'Tough day.' She walked up to Sam and squeezed her hand. 'Not quite going to plan, is it?'

'We'll get there.' Though Sam was starting to fear it was an empty platitude. They had some ideas, sure, but none would fulfill the *it will deliver more* promise she'd made to the market in her press release. At this rate Privacy 2 was going to be nothing more than a dull copy of Damien's app. 'I see you and Ryan are back to being squabbling siblings again.'

Becky snorted. 'I can't help it if the guy winds me up. This is a brainstorm. He's supposed to be adding ideas, not shooting them down.'

'To be fair, his job is to tell us what's possible and what's not,' Sam replied mildly. 'There's no point us getting excited about something if ultimately it can't be done.'

'I know.' Becky grinned wickedly. 'Doesn't mean I can't wind him up now and again. A girl has to get her kicks somewhere.' She gave Sam a sly look. 'And considering how late you finally made it back to your room last night, I can guess where you're getting yours.'

Sam cursed her fair skin as she felt heat sting her cheeks. She might have known Becky would bring up her nocturnal activities at some point, but she couldn't cope with a dissection of them now. Not when she had so much resting on the outcome of today. And not when she was so confused about what she was doing with Ryan.

Automatically her eyes sought him out. There he was, sitting alone on a bench outside, staring out to sea. Was he thinking about last night, too? Thinking about her? Or was he just frustrated with the whole two days away and wishing he was back at his desk, with his codes?

Sam pushed the thoughts away. Ignoring Becky's curious look, she strode over to the flipchart, which looked incongruous alongside the turquoise velvet sofas and tasteful mahogany furniture of her parents' sitting room, and turned to a clean page. Picking up a marker pen, she drew four large boxes. The first she labelled 'user experience', the second 'accuracy', the third 'outputs'. In the fourth, she put a question mark.

As she wrote, she was aware of people making their way back inside. Though her back was to them, she knew immediately who had walked up to her. Who was standing behind her now, his body not quite touching hers, his unique smell sending ripples of awareness down her spine.

'I can see why you didn't go into art.'

Slowly she turned to face Ryan. 'There's beauty in everything, if you know where to look.'

His dark eyes swept over her face. 'Trust me, I know.'

The husk of his voice sent her insides into a fluttering, squirming, chaotic mess. Pressing a hand to her stomach, she cursed her giddy reaction to him. She was more collected, more steady, than this.

Taking a deliberate step away, she poured herself a glass of water from the jug on the coffee table. By the time she looked up again, he was sitting in the seat he'd commandeered – the armchair by the fireplace. It suited him. His own personal space, away from everyone else.

Sam dragged her eyes away. 'Okay, guys, one last push before dinner.' She pointed to the flipchart, and the wonky boxes she'd drawn. 'So far today we've focused very much on the first three boxes, which are all about modifying what the Privacy app already provides. In this session I'd like us to focus on box four. Getting the app to do something entirely different.'

'Like order a pizza?' The joke came from Kerry and everyone laughed.

'Preferably something aligned to our company mission.' Sam smiled at Kerry. 'But I like your thinking. Let's get all those mad ideas out there. You never know, one of them may spark an idea we can build on.'

For the next hour they fired all their wild thoughts at her. By the time the smell of barbecue wafted through the patio doors from where the catering crew had set up, Sam had a full flipchart and an exhausted team.

What she didn't have, she acknowledged with a sinking gut, was anything she could take back to the office to work into a plan.

But that was her worry, not theirs, although if she couldn't come up with something soon, it would be everyone's worry. All their jobs would be on the line. Shaking off the despondency, she plastered on a bright smile and sent them off to wind down before dinner.

As she walked past her, Becky looked pointedly over to where Ryan was still standing at the back of the room, hands in his pockets, and gave Sam a knowing wink.

When the last person had left, Ryan strode over. 'Did you get what you wanted?'

'There are some great off-the-wall ideas.' It wasn't an answer, and they both knew it.

Ryan sighed. 'Crap.'

A ball of emotion lodged in her throat. Whether it was from the crushing disappointment of the day, fear of what it meant, or simply the concern in his eyes, she didn't know. 'Yeah, crap is about right.' She forced a smile. 'But we're in Cornwall, it's a sunny evening and the barbecue smells flipping awesome. I'm off for a shower and then to have a very big drink.'

'You don't have to pretend, Sunshine Sam,' he said quietly, running his index finger gently down her face. 'Not with me.'

The emotion returned, slamming back into her, this time bringing with it the prick of unshed tears. 'Please, don't. I can't take you being kind right now.'

He frowned, studying her for a second, before shaking his head and slipping his hand back into his pocket. 'Well, I don't know about you, but I've had a shit day sitting on my arse and being forced to listen to you lot spout a load of hot air. I'm heading to the sea to swim off my frustration. Catch you later.' He paused just before stepping outside. 'Oh, and you should check on that *awesome* barbecue. Smells like they're cremating everything.'

When he'd gone, Sam slumped down on the sofa, not sure whether to laugh or cry. In the end she managed a bit of both.

Chapter 21

The swim had done its job and Ryan felt a lot better as he strolled back up to the house. Relaxed enough, he figured, to tackle the two women who'd been in his thoughts today, for two very different reasons.

Sam, he'd approach later. He'd seen how on edge she was at the end of the meeting. What she needed right now was someone who'd make her laugh and take her out of her head for a while. Though it gutted him to acknowledge it, that man wasn't him. From the way Lucas was making a beeline for her, Ryan knew he didn't have to worry. The guy, as always, had her back.

It was daft to feel jealous as he watched the easy way Lucas hugged her. Or the way her face lit up a moment later as she gave him a playful shove.

Didn't stop him feeling it.

Spotting Alice standing alone, staring down at her phone again, Ryan strode over to her. Just because he was crap at handling difficult, emotionally charged situations didn't mean he shouldn't try.

'Can I get you a drink?'

Her head shot up. 'Umm, thanks, but I've got one.' She nodded to the untouched glass of wine on the table behind her.

Great. Now what did he say? 'Looking forward to heading back tomorrow?'

A cloud crossed her face and Ryan mentally smacked himself round the head. *She's scared of her boyfriend, dimwit. That's what you've come to talk to her about.*

She avoided his eyes. 'Not especially. I like it here.'

Silence descended.

'Have you been to—'

'Did you have a good—'

Ryan winced, wishing once again that he had Lucas's charm. Sam's easy way with people. 'You first.'

'I just wondered if you enjoyed your swim.' Alice slipped the phone she seemed glued to into her jeans pocket. 'Lucas told us that's where you'd headed.'

'Yeah. Bracing, I think, is the word they use. Frigging freezing, too.'

It squeezed a smile out of her. 'I bet.'

Another round of silence, though this time less tense. Ryan dragged in a lungful of air and decided to go for it. 'Look, about what I said yesterday at dinner.' Ignoring the way she stilled, he pushed on. 'I'm not here to pry. It's your business. But I'd hate you to go through what my mum did.' As her eyes looked everywhere but at him, Ryan's heart sank. Stupid to think he could help, just plain stupid. She was probably as scared of him as she was her boyfriend. 'Just know I'm here if you need me for anything.' When she said nothing, he let out a long, slow breath. 'Okay. I'm going to check out the food.'

He'd taken three steps away when he heard her quiet voice behind him. 'Thank you.'

He turned, nodded and gave her a small smile, which she reciprocated. Holding tight to the small victory, he ambled over to the giant barbecue, his stomach rumbling as he sniffed the smoky, chargrilled aroma.

Becky appeared at his side, smirking up at him. 'That's the most animated I've seen you all day.'

'I'm hungry.'

'So I see.' Her heavily lined eyes appeared to dissect him. 'Sam didn't get what she needed out of today.'

'I know.' The accusation in her stare pierced right through him. 'You're putting the blame for that on me?'

Becky shrugged. 'I don't think you helped.'

Annoyance vied with frustration. 'You think I wasn't trying?'

She didn't back down from his glare. 'Let's just say I'm reserving my judgment.'

Yeah, he could see where this was heading. 'You're not just talking about today.'

She gave him a small smile. 'You're smart. I'll give you that.'

'Smart enough to know when to leave a conversation.' He nodded tightly over to where the caterers were now serving out the food. 'Have a good evening.' He'd only taken two steps when Becky's words brought him to a halt.

'It's not personal, you know.' She gave him a genuine smile.

'I don't think you're half as miserable as you make out. Plus, I have a sneaking admiration for your particular brand of honesty. It's refreshing.' Her smile faded. 'But I told you before, if you hurt Sam, I'll cut off your balls.'

Inside his shorts, he felt them shrivel. 'Only if Lucas hasn't throttled me first.'

Becky put a hand to her mouth and started to laugh. 'Poor you, looks like you've had a two-pronged attack. Better make sure you don't screw up.'

He laughed bitterly to himself as he turned away. Hard to screw up something he wasn't being given the chance to start. And seems both Becky and Lucas thought if he ever did get lucky enough to go out with Sam, he'd be dumb enough, mean enough, *bastard* enough, to hurt her.

Clearly he still had a long way to go to earn their trust.

Of course, though their reactions didn't say much about him, they said volumes about the woman who inspired that sort of fierce loyalty.

After the food had been eaten, the wine drunk and people had started to make their way to bed, Ryan wandered into the kitchen to get himself a glass of water. That was where he finally found Sam, putting containers of leftover salad into the fridge. She looked weary. Not defeated, like the time he'd seen her crying in her office, but down.

'Most people I know go out of their way to avoid salad.'

Her head shot up and she rolled her eyes. 'Let me guess. Real men don't eat salad?' She frowned. 'No, wait, that was quiche, not salad, wasn't it?'

'I'm not a fan of either.'

'No, you wouldn't be. Then again, I had you pegged as a steak and chips man, yet at the pub you ordered fish pie.'

He could hardly tell her it was because he couldn't afford the steak. 'Both beat a custard pie with dodgy savoury filling.'

A smile broke across her face, lifting some of the sadness from eyes he could stare into all day. 'Good description.'

She continued to fuss around in the kitchen, putting leftovers into plastic boxes and shifting things round in the fridge to squeeze them in. Ryan shoved his hands into his pockets, feeling frustrated. He couldn't talk to her here, in her parents' kitchen, and she seemed in no hurry to leave. Finally, he blurted. 'Do you fancy a walk?'

After slotting yet another container into the Tardis-like fridge, she slowly turned to face him. 'A walk?'

'Yeah, you know. One foot in front of the other.'

'Where?'

'The beach. The cliff. Anywhere.' Even round the ruddy garden would be better than standing in the kitchen knowing anyone could walk in. It wasn't just that he wanted her to himself. Not just that he wanted the chance to put into action all the thoughts he'd had every time his eyes had drifted to her sexy, wide mouth. Or her curvy backside.

He actually wanted to talk to her, too. Becky had been right; he'd been shit in the meeting today. Not because he hadn't tried, but because his mind didn't work like that. It was logical, not creative. Still, he thought he might be able to help her, if she'd let him.

* * *

Sam knew she was stalling. Truthfully, she was scared to go walking with Ryan, in the dark. Scared it might lead to a repeat of yesterday. At the memory of what had happened on the beach, a sharp thrill ran through her, perfectly highlighting the problem. His touch was addictive, and addiction was rarely a good thing.

'Just to talk.' His jaw tightened. 'You don't have to worry.'

'I'm not worried about spending time alone with you.'

'No?'

She looked him straight in the eye. 'No.'

He gave her a crooked smile. 'Maybe you should be.'

Her insides flip-flopped, and she could no more refuse him than she could look away. To hell with it. She could do with a tall, dark, devastatingly attractive distraction right now. 'Okay, let's head to the cliffs.'

She received another of those small, resolve-melting smiles. 'As long as you promise not to shove me over.'

Laughter burst out of her. 'Now who's scared?'

'You scare me all right, Sam Huxton.' His dark eyes rested on hers, brimming with emotion she couldn't define, but which caused an answering flutter in her stomach.

They walked to the footpath in an amicable silence, her hyperaware of him: his scent, his long stride, the occasional brush of his arm against hers.

When they were out of sight of the house his hand reached for hers, clasping it in his warm grip. As her fingers settled around it, her heart bounced against her ribs.

Wordlessly he led her to the bench overlooking the beach, and with a light tug he settled her down next to him. The sea looked almost black, the moon glinting off the water like a thousand tea lights. What with that, the warm evening, the quiet, it felt romantic. She wondered if Ryan felt it too. He had a raw, sexual energy, a rugged bluntness that seemed at odds with the idea of romance.

Yet here he was, holding her hand in the moonlight.

Taking a breath, she tried to calm her racing pulse. 'What did you want to talk about?'

A half-smile played on his lips. 'And they call me blunt.'

She laughed quietly, her body acutely aware of him as he rested their clasped hands on his thigh. 'Sorry, I can do small talk if you like. How did you find the barbecue? Cremated enough to your liking?'

His smile broadened. 'Let's stick with blunt. Did you get anything from today you can work with?'

Okay then. She wasn't sure what she'd been expecting, but it hadn't been that. 'Bluntly, no.'

He nodded, glancing down at their hands, his thumb tracing distracting circles across her knuckles. 'Whose idea was the Privacy app in the first place?'

She tried to focus on his question, and not on the gentle caress. 'Does it matter?'

He glanced sharply at her. 'Yes.'

So much for the romantic setting. It looked like she was going to spend this moonlit night talking about painful memories. 'I can't remember exactly what happened. Damien wanted to create an app that would make us millionaires. We bounced lots of ideas around one evening. The drunker we got, the crazier they became.' Her throat tightened as the memories flooded back. It was the night they'd both found out they'd passed their first year at uni. They were young, in love, the world at their feet.

'But who had the idea first?' Ryan insisted.

She wanted him to make her forget everything, not hash it over. She wanted him to *kiss* her. 'What's the point of this?'

'Just answer me.'

She wriggled her hand free. 'Not if you speak to me like that.'

He heaved out a sigh, raking a hand through his hair. 'Please, for the love of God, just tell me who came up with idea of designing an app that could let the user know which websites held personal data on them.'

Not angry, she realised belatedly, but frustrated. 'It was my idea,' she answered quietly. 'Damien thought we should devise an app; I came up with the Privacy app.'

'Exactly.' He straightened, turning to look at her, amusement dancing in his eyes. 'That wasn't hard, was it?'

'It would be easier if you'd tell me what you're trying to achieve.'

'Damien was just like me. A monkey.' His eyes flickered over her face, landing directly on hers. 'You're the organ grinder.'

'Is that supposed to mean something to me?'

He gave his head a light shake. 'Do you really not see where this is leading?'

'If I did, I wouldn't be asking you the flipping question, would I?'

Laughter rolled out of him. 'You're hot when you're riled, you know that?'

'I'm about to get even hotter then, because you're really starting to piss me off.'

'Okay, okay, let me tell you what I thought was plainly obvious.' He waved his hand behind him, indicating her parents' house. 'All this off-site stuff is very nice, but you didn't need it.'

'Now wait a minute—'

'You're so intent on getting the team involved,' he continued, speaking right over her, 'you've forgotten that you're the brains behind this operation.'

His last few words brought her up short. And then his hands cupped her face and the anger drained from her.

'The idea for the next app is in you, Sam,' he said softly, sincerity ringing through his voice. 'You just have to trust yourself enough, believe in yourself enough, to pull it out.'

She couldn't think, couldn't process what he was saying, couldn't even breathe. His eyes were so fierce, yet his expression, his voice, so gentle. As what he was saying began to sink in, her heart lodged in her throat and a muddle of emotions battered her senses. Shock, because she'd assumed he'd wanted to talk about *them*. Not to discuss work. Fear, both that he was right and that he was wrong. Gratitude, great swathes of it, because even if he was wrong, his faith in her was almost overwhelming.

Threading through them all was an emotion that pulled at her heart. He cared, she realised. And that, more than anything else, made the tears start to fall.

'Hey.' He used his thumbs to wipe her wet cheeks. 'Don't frigging cry on me.'

She let out a strangled laugh. 'It's not like I can control it. Would you do me a favour?'

'Anything.' He looked over at the cliff edge. 'As long as it doesn't involve me walking closer to that.'

'Ryan Black is scared of heights?'

'Nah. Scared of falling from a height.' When she started to laugh, he gave her a mock glare. 'There's a difference. What's the favour?'

She shifted, leaning in to him. 'Hold me for a while?'

Within seconds he'd lifted her onto his lap. As his arms wrapped around her shoulders, she rested her head against his chest, listening to the steady beat of his heart.

'That do you?'

She smiled against his T-shirt. 'Perfect.' *And so, quite possibly, are you*, she thought with a start.

Maybe perfect was pushing it, considering his more annoying habits. Yet right now, there was no denying, he was exactly what she needed.

Chapter 22

When he'd dragged Sam away from the house, Ryan hadn't imagined their talk ending with her sitting on his lap. It was clear she needed support right now, not sex, so he willed his crotch not to react to the soft curve of her buttocks by thinking through the coding issues waiting for him when he got back to the office. When that failed, he guessed he could always imagine he was standing on the cliff edge, looking down on the waves as they crashed against the rocks.

'How long is a while?'

She shifted, burrowing further into him. 'What do you mean?'

'You said you wanted holding for a while.'

'Umm.'

She was gazing out to sea, a thoughtful expression on her face. He'd like to bet she was already starting to click through all the possibilities for her app. A good thing, he told himself, as it meant she'd listened to him for a change. Still, it was a dent to his ego to think she was sitting on his lap, in the moonlight, and the only thing on her mind was business.

'Talk to me,' she said after a while.

And now she seemed to have forgotten whose lap she was sitting across. 'Err, hello. It's me, Ryan Black. Talking's not really my thing.'

Her body shook with silent laughter. 'I know, but can you give it a go, just this once?' Those big eyes, almost violet in this light, looked pleadingly up at him. 'It might spark something.'

'What's the subject?'

'Anything you want. But no coding mumbo jumbo.' She wriggled, and he caught a whiff her shampoo. 'How about you describe your typical day to me?'

'You're not looking for excitement then?'

'I don't care what you say. I just want to take myself out of my head for a while.'

'Fine.' He looked down to find her watching him, a small smile on her lips. He had a sudden urge to bend and kiss her, to suck on that sexy bottom lip.

Sod it. Groaning with need, with want, he did just that, driving himself mad for a few crazy seconds before dragging his mouth away.

He took some satisfaction from seeing the dazed expression on her face, though a snatched kiss fell well short of what he really wanted.

'Well.' She coughed to clear the husk from her voice. 'That's another way to take me out of my head.'

'It beats anything I have to say.'

She laughed softly. 'Oh no, you're not weaselling out of this that easily. Come on. Start with breakfast.'

'You don't want me in the shower?'

It was too dark to see if she was blushing, but he liked to think she was. Liked to think she was imagining him naked. 'For the purposes of this exercise, pretend it's a Saturday. You've been through the bathroom and now you're in your kitchen. Fully dressed, before you ask. Now go.'

Feeling daft, he tried to think back to last weekend. 'Okay. I grab myself some cereal.'

'Muesli? No, somehow I can't see you with anything too healthy. Chocolate hoops?'

'Am I telling this, or you?' He shot her a mock glare and she mimed zipping her mouth closed. 'While eating my *cornflakes*, I slap on the TV and search for some sport. Not fussed what. Football, rugby, cricket, snooker.' He paused. 'Is this boring enough for you?'

'Keep going.'

She looked genuinely interested, go figure, so he carried on. 'It usually takes half a bowl before I realise the milk was out of date, so I head to the supermarket. Buy a load of crap that only needs taking out of a packet and nuking in a microwave. Not that I can't cook,' he added, stupidly wanting to impress her. 'But this new boss is a tyrant so I don't have the time.' He grunted as her elbow found his ribs. 'Bags full of milk and ready meals, I head back to the flat.'

'The shithole.'

'Yeah, the shithole.' She meant it as a joke, he knew that, but it was hard to smile when he considered the thought of inviting this woman he fancied, he respected ... damn it, he wanted to date, back to his grotty flat. Not that his salary was anything to be ashamed of – God willing it would continue to rise, and his considerable outgoings continue to fall. Still, the difference between her elegant apartment and his dump of a flat was an uncomfortable reminder of the gulf between them.

'And?'

He shook himself. 'And, guess what? I unpack the crap.' His pause resulted in another prod, gentler this time. 'Then I might grab the computer and check my personal emails. Don't know why I bother as it's usually full of spam.'

'You're the tech wizard, don't you bother to—' Suddenly she lunged to her feet, shrieking into the night. 'Oh my God, that's it.' Face bursting with excitement, she turned to him and gave him a big, loud kiss before doing a jig in front of his eyes. 'You and your boring Saturday have only gone and cracked it,' she said breathlessly, half laughing, half crying.

He didn't have a clue what she was banging on about, but he was happy if she was. 'It has, huh?'

'Yes!' She dragged him to his feet and, keeping hold of his hands, proceeded to dance to a beat that only she could hear. 'This could really be it. I mean it might not be possible, but you keep telling me you're a genius, so if anyone can do it, you can.'

He stilled, fear slithering down his spine. Fuck. He didn't want to be the one responsible for wiping the smile off her face. 'Sam, hold on a minute. You've lost me. What's the big idea?'

She gazed up at him, her face so alive, so beautiful, he felt a punch to his gut. 'What do you do if you get a spam email?'

'Delete it?'

'No. Well, yes, of course you do, but what should you do first, if you don't want another one? What should you look for at the bottom of the email?'

'The unsubscribe link?' He blinked, suddenly getting it. 'You want the app to have an unsubscribe option.'

She beamed. 'Imagine this. You're looking at a list of websites holding personal information on you that you haven't agreed to, or no longer want them to have. How cool would it be to just click on an unsubscribe button? Better still, a delete button? Bam.' She clicked her fingers. 'Just like that, no phoning companies up, no emailing them or spending precious time on their websites trying to find a page that allows it. In one click, it would be done.' Clapping her hands together, she did another twirl. 'Damien flaming Lynch, eat your heart out.'

Though he was thrilled she was excited, thrilled that, in some small way, he'd helped her come to this moment, two threads of dread coiled round his gut.

Did he really have the talent, the skill, to programme the app to do that?

And why the hell was she still thinking of that Damien creep?

Sam felt giddy, like her six-year-old self on Christmas Day when she'd seen all her presents laid out under the tree. This was it. The idea she'd been waiting all day for, and what do you know, Ryan had been the one to inspire it. Ryan, who'd held her when she'd asked him to, who'd talked to her even though she knew he'd been uncomfortable. Ryan, whose surprising faith in her might just have turned out to be justified.

A shadow crossed Ryan's face and she halted her exuberant jigging. 'Hey, are you still with me?'

He glanced down to his feet, then back up at her, his smile just a little too forced. 'Looks like it.'

Nerves jangled in her stomach. 'Please tell me you think you can programme a delete function into the app?'

He rubbed his chin. 'I don't know until we start drilling down into it.' Unconsciously she held her breath, so much resting on his answer. 'Possibly, yes.'

Her breath rushed out and she flung her arms around him. Right now, he was far more than a man she'd slept with a couple of times. More than an employee she'd developed this big, terrifying crush on. He was a friend. One who might, just might, help her save her company. 'Can you change possibly to probably?'

His hands settled on her hips. 'Possibly.'

Every instinct screamed at her to push him on it – she really needed to know whether there was a chance, or not – but she held her tongue. He wasn't that guy, the one with flowery phrases and puffed-up promises. He'd give her his opinion only when he'd had time to consider it properly. Rising onto her tiptoes, she kissed him, very gently, on the mouth.

He gave her a quizzical look. 'Not complaining, but what was that for?'

'Helping me. Believing in me.'

'Hard not to.' His mouth quirked upwards. 'Seems you're freakishly smart.'

Grinning foolishly, she rested her head against his chest. His hands were still holding lightly onto her hips, and what with their gentle pressure, and the solid feel of his chest against her cheek, a familiar sizzle began in her stomach. It was more than a sexual connection. More than gratitude. It was that emotional tug again. Was she at risk of losing part of her heart to him? She had an awful feeling she already had. Yet here, in the moonlight, with the sound of the sea below them, and the excitement pulsing though her, she didn't care. 'At the risk of sounding too forward,' she whispered, 'would you like to come back to my room?'

His answer was a deep, almost guttural groan as his arms tightened on her hips, drawing her core against his hardness.

'Is that a yes?'

His eyes zeroed in on hers, twin lumps of molten lava. 'It's an *I thought you'd never ask*.'

In a flash she was lifted into the air and thrown over his shoulder, just as he had that first night. 'Oh my God, you great hulking Neanderthal. Put me down.'

She felt his laughter rumble through him and it started her giggling. He didn't show enough of this playful side, though maybe that was just was well. She was already alarmingly hooked on the dour Ryan Black.

'How's that fireman fantasy coming along?' he asked.

Placing her hands on his delicious backside, she grinned. 'Can't wait to slide down his pole.'

He stumbled, almost choking with laughter, then slowly

he slid her down his body and onto the ground. 'Christ, if we weren't so close to the house.'

'What?' But she didn't need to ask what. The burning desire in his eyes was her answer.

They walked the rest of the way quickly, sexual tension sparking between them. The house was quiet and when Sam checked her watch she realised why. 'They must have all gone to bed. We've been gone nearly two hours.'

'Lucas will wonder where I am.' He glanced sideways at her. 'Just as he did yesterday.'

Sam knew what he was telling her. 'Does that worry you?'

He let out a huff of laughter. 'Hardly. Though he has promised to throttle me if I hurt you.'

She winced. 'That's Lucas for you. He wears his heart on his sleeve. Since Damien did ... what he did, Lucas has become very protective.' She raised her chin. 'Not that I need anyone going into battle on my behalf.'

He gave her a wry smile. 'So you've made very clear.'

'If you're not worried about Lucas then ...'

'The more important question,' he cut in, 'is are *you* worried?'

Her racing pulse told her she was. Their first time had been out of her control – she hadn't known who he was. Yesterday, on the beach, she could put down to alcohol, to the balmy evening, the intimate setting. If she took him back to her room now, there was no excuse. 'It's like a holiday fling,' she said softly. 'A little daring, a little risky, but we're away from the office. We can let our hair down.'

His dark eyes held hers, magnetic, mesmerising and totally unreadable. 'Okay. Lead the way.'

They walked silently through the house to the stairs. It didn't matter if her parents saw them, she told herself, or if Becky did. She was a mature, professional, single woman. If she wanted to sleep with a man, she could. Even if he was one of her employees.

A shudder ran through her. Was she really going to do this again? Sleep with a man she worked with? And wasn't this worse than with Damien, because she was Ryan's boss. Maybe he felt like he *had* to do this. After all, if she'd been a man, and he a woman, wouldn't this be sexual harassment?

Feeling uneasy, she stepped inside her bedroom. When he closed the door behind them, she turned to him. 'Look, I don't want you believing—'

He silenced her with a deep, drugging kiss. 'Stop over-thinking this,' he said quietly. 'I'm here because I want to be.'

She bit into her lip. 'You promise you're not going to sue me later?'

He laughed softly. 'Jesus, turn your frigging brain off. I'm a man, you're a woman. We want to have hot, frantic sex together. End of.'

The sizzle from earlier started up again in earnest. 'Hot and frantic, huh?'

'For starters, yeah.'

His hands smoothed up and down her arms as his hips pressed sensually against hers, making her suck in a breath. 'What's the main course?'

Another husky chuckle. 'Guess that depends on how filling the starter is.' His mouth trailed down her neck. 'Though where you're concerned, I'll always be hungry.'

As her hormones puddled onto the floor, Sam melted against him.

Chapter 23

Ryan stirred. Forcing his eyes open, he took a moment to appreciate his surroundings – oak drawers, pale-lavender walls, fresh flowers in a simple glass vase. Nice. Turning his gaze to the bed, he took another moment to appreciate the woman he had his arms around. Awesome red hair, wide, usually smiling mouth, a scattering of freckles across her nose, luscious pale breasts spilling into his hand. More than nice. Frigging incredible.

More woman than he'd ever had the pleasure of holding.

More than he deserved, more than he could ever hope to hold again.

Stop with the dubious poetry. Get out, before she wakes.

He forced his body out of the bed and into last night's clothes, knowing if she blinked those incredible eyes open, he'd be lost. He'd want her again. And though he might not care if he was caught sneaking out of her room, he knew she would.

With a final, longing look at her, he eased the door open, crept along the corridor and down the stairs. What would it feel like to be her lover for real? Not just a few furtive couplings, but a relationship where he didn't have to sneak away at dawn.

And that, he thought grimly, was the road to madness. She'd already told him she needed his app development skills more than she needed him. And if that hadn't convinced him he had no chance with her, last night's holiday fling comment was the bucket of cold water on any paltry remaining embers of hope. She wasn't interested in anything beyond a quick distraction.

He had to accept it, deal with it. And try to move on.

With a heavy heart, he headed towards the kitchen, and the side door he knew had been left unlocked.

'Oh my goodness.'

Ryan froze at the startled exclamation. Shit. What on earth was Sam's mum doing up at 5am? 'Sorry. Didn't mean to startle you.'

She held a hand to her chest, the terror slowly receding from her face. 'No, that's fine. We left the door open so you guys could come and go as you wanted. I just wasn't expecting anyone this early.'

And yes, Ryan wasn't so dense he couldn't hear the silent question in her words. 'I ... lost my wallet yesterday. Thought I might have left it in the sitting room.'

'Oh dear. Did you find it?'

'No.' Christ, he hated lying. Disagreed with it, was useless at it, but it wasn't himself he was trying to protect. Sam would not want her mum knowing where he'd spent the night. 'I'll probably find it in my room, lying under a pile of dirty washing.' Great. Not just a shitty lie, but one that made him sound like a slob.

'Well, I hope you do.' She smiled, and by God, she looked just like her daughter. The same warm, embracing, sunshine smile. 'Feel free to use the washing machine in here. I don't want you losing anything else.'

'Right, thanks.' He eyed the door longingly. Would it be rude if he just started to walk towards it?

'Early to be up and about.' Her statement halted his hope of an immediate escape. 'Did Sam not work you hard enough yesterday?'

Telltale heat crept up his neck. Flustered, Ryan jammed a hand through his hair. *She means the brainstorm, you idiot. Not what you were doing to her daughter, in her bedroom.* 'Thought I'd go for a swim,' he managed.

'Oh, I see. A lovely morning for one.'

There was a faint smile on her lips, but it was impossible for him to tell what she was thinking. Was she suspicious? Wondering whose bed he'd just crawled out of, Becky's or her daughter's?

A horrible thought hit him. Did she think he'd come in to snoop? To nick something?

'I hope the water isn't too cold for you.'

'Thanks.' He mustered a smile, hoping like hell it didn't look as guilty as he felt.

Then fled as quickly as he dared.

A bracing forty minutes later, he snuck into the room he shared with Lucas. As he foraged around in the dim light for a towel and fresh clothes – the curtains were still closed – he heard Lucas stir. 'Only me. Just been for a swim and now I'm heading for the shower.'

Silence. Figuring he'd got away with it, Ryan reached to open the door.

'A swim, huh?' Lucas's voice was heavy with scepticism. 'That's what you're calling it?'

Ryan turned, pointing to his wet shorts. 'A swim,' he repeated.

'In the same shorts you wore last night?'

Why couldn't Lucas be a normal bloke? One who didn't notice what frigging clothes a guy wore? 'Saves on the washing.'

'You're not kidding.' Lucas gave him an ominous look. 'Remind me to tell Helen not to bother changing the sheets on your bed. You've hardly slept in it.'

'Funny,' Ryan muttered before stepping out and shutting the door firmly behind him. He'd deal with Lucas later, once he'd got the ocean out of his hair, and the memories of last night out of his mind.

Sam woke feeling happier than she had in months. Twenty-one months, to be precise, as that was how long it had been since Damien had torn her heart with his infidelity, then knocked the stuffing out of her with his betrayal in setting up a rival company.

Now though, life was looking up. She had, fingers crossed, a new direction for the app. And a new man in her bed. At least there had been last night. She hadn't heard Ryan leave, but for most of the night, when she'd stirred, he'd been there, his body tucked firmly behind hers. His right arm around her, hand cupping one of her breasts.

Where you're concerned, I'll always be hungry.

The memories triggered a swarm of butterflies in her

stomach. The last two nights might have felt like a holiday fling, but she'd be naïve to think it was that easy to pigeonhole. After the closeness of the last two days, the way he'd looked out for her, helped her and yes, made love to her, could she really stick to a purely professional relationship back at the office? Did she *want* to?

Now was the time to focus on the business, not on her personal life, but she also needed to be honest with herself. Her feelings for Ryan weren't going away. If anything, the more she saw of him, the more she wanted to spend time with him. In and out of bed.

Did she dare to give it a try? If she was careful with her heart. If they could see each other quietly, so she didn't have to suffer the humiliation of her personal life being scrutinised and picked apart when it all went wrong. If they could remain on good terms afterwards. Oh, and if it wasn't just about sex for him. If he really wanted to give this undeniable *thing* between them a proper try.

Sam groaned, banging her head back on the pillow. That was one heck of a lot of ifs.

Still, as she stepped into the shower, the lightness remained. Following last night's epiphany, she had a fresh purpose. Shedloads of work to do, sure, but that had never troubled her.

It energised her.

So, it was with a bounce in her step that she walked downstairs to grab some breakfast before the morning's final meeting. Humming to herself she stepped into the kitchen, finding her mum and Becky deep in conversation.

'Morning.' She gave them both a bright smile. 'Any coffee going?' The pair of them exchanged a glance that smacked of secrecy and collusion. 'What?'

Becky looked like she was finding it hard not to giggle. Her mum, who was a far better actress, smiled serenely. 'Coffee, you said?'

'Yes, thanks.' Sam sat on a kitchen stool, her eyes swinging back and forth between the pair of them. 'Come on, out with it. You're both too old for sniggering.'

'Sorry, darling.' Her mum set a mug of coffee in front of her, then squeezed her shoulder. 'I was just telling Becky how I found Ryan in the kitchen at five o'clock this morning.'

'Oh?' Sam schooled her expression into one of polite interest.

'He told me he was looking for his wallet.'

Sam took a sip of the coffee, nearly scalding her tongue. 'Did he find it?'

'Sadly not. When I asked him why he was up so early, he said he was going for a swim.' Her mum caught her eye and smiled, mischief in her eyes. 'It struck me as odd that he needed his wallet to swim in the bay.'

I will not blush. I will not flaming well blush. 'You're just trying to create trouble, Mum. He probably threw on his shorts to walk down for a swim, realised his wallet wasn't in them and thought he'd check it wasn't in the house on the way down.'

'That's one explanation.' She kissed the top of Sam's head, whispering in her ear. 'Though I'm rather hoping there's another.'

'Why would you say that?' Sam hoped her game face was firmly in place. That she didn't look as guilty as she felt. 'Ryan and I work together. We all know how well that combination turned out with Damien.'

Her mother simply smiled. 'Your father and I worked together.'

'This is different. I'm his *boss*, Mum.'

'Even better. You make the rules. If you want a hot office affair with your sexy new employee, there's no one to stop you.' Before Sam could recover from that bombshell, her mother deftly changed subjects. 'Right, time for me to disappear before the rest of your crew turn up. Come and say goodbye before you leave.'

As she glided out of the kitchen – yes, her mother definitely glided when she thought she'd won an argument – Becky doubled up with laughter. 'Flipping heck, Sam, your mum is priceless. And as for you, sneaking a boy into your room. You are so busted.'

'Shut it.' When her demand was met with more laughter, Sam couldn't help it, she started to giggle. 'Oh boy, I'd like to have been a fly in the wall when Ryan bumped into Mum.'

That sent Becky off again. 'Can you imagine the look on his face?' Becky was laughing so much, she had tears in her eyes. 'If it had been Lucas, he'd have had no problem explaining it away. Ryan probably looked dead shifty.'

'I'm surprised he didn't just blurt out the truth. You know what he's like.'

'Yeah.' Becky put on a gruff voice. 'Morning, Mrs H. I've

been shagging your daughter all night. Now I'm off for a swim.'

Sam groaned, shoving her head in her hands. 'Please. Enough.'

'Well, was he? Shagging you all night?'

Sam rolled her eyes. 'That's my business.' It hadn't been all night, she thought with a flash of heat, but it had been enough for her to lose count.

'Well, whatever he was doing with you, it seems to have done you good.' Becky's gaze skimmed over Sam's face, no doubt noticing her flushed cheeks. 'You're like the Duracell bunny. You might have been going all night, but you're still very ... perky.'

'Perky? First I'm a bunny, now I'm a pig?' When Becky looked at her quizzically, Sam huffed. 'Come on, you've heard of *Pinky and Perky*?'

'Err, hello, that was from the Fifties.'

'I'm not saying I watched it.' Sam threw her hands up in the air. 'And why am I having a conversation about cartoon pigs when there are far more important things we need to talk about.? She paused. 'Like the app.'

Becky, who'd started buttering herself some toast, stilled and looked up at her. 'Was that a dramatic pause? As in *I've had an idea that's got me so excited I'm almost wetting my pants?*'

Sam chewed on her bottom lip. 'Maybe.'

Becky clattered her knife down. 'It's really that good?' She rushed up to her, gripping her by the shoulders. 'Oh God, just tell me. I'm dying here.'

Sam sucked in a breath. Last night she'd been so sure, but now she worried she'd been caught up in the romance of the setting, the joy of an idea after a day of disappointment.

Ryan.

Becky's views could send her fantasy bubble further into happy space or burst it in her face. Becky, who'd been with her from the start, who knew the customer feedback inside out, who had a sense for these things. 'The user goes into the app, gets given a list of all the websites the app can find that hold personal data on them.'

'That's what it does now.'

Sam smiled at Becky's frustration. '*And* when you tap on one of the websites, you can see the data it has on you.'

Becky hissed. 'That's what we've been working on. That's what Lynch has done with his app.'

'*And,*' Sam interrupted, 'next to that data, you find a delete button.'

That, at last, made Becky pause. 'To remove your information from the website?' she said slowly.

'Exactly.' Sam felt her pulse race as she tried to read Becky's expression. 'What do you think?'

Her friend started to smile. Before long, the smile turned into a full-blown grin. 'That's bloody genius.'

'Isn't it?' And suddenly they were jumping up and down, squealing and hugging each other.

'When did you come up with that?' Becky asked when they'd exhausted themselves.

'Last night.' She lifted her gaze to meet Becky's. 'With Ryan. He was actually really helpful.'

'Uh huh.' Becky's black-rimmed eyes searched hers, and whatever she saw caused her to frown. 'Oh boy. Your expression's gone all dreamy. Please tell me you're not falling for him?'

'What? No, of course not.' She paused, decided it was time to be truthful. 'But I am finding I like him more and more.'

Becky continued to look at her. 'You're serious, aren't you?'

'Don't look so shocked. When you get to know him, he's actually pretty funny. And kind.'

Becky snorted. 'Bloody hell, it's like he's put some spell on you. He must be good in bed.'

The words made Sam pause. Was Ryan another colossal error in judgement? Was this Damien all over again, and she was allowing her hormones to rule her head?

'Hey.' Becky nudged her. 'What's wrong?'

She shook herself. 'Nothing.'

'It's something. You went all pale there for a second.'

Sam sighed. 'What do you think of Ryan, honestly?'

'I told you before, he's like an annoying big brother. Thinks he's always right, refuses to do things any other way than his way. Tells you exactly what he thinks, whether you like it or not.' She patted Sam's hand. 'But if it helps, I think he's the exact opposite of Damien.'

'Oh?'

'No way would Ryan cheat on anyone. No way would he betray anyone. If he wanted out of a relationship, he'd look you in the eye and tell you.' She gave Sam a wry smile. 'He wouldn't do it gently, wouldn't try and safeguard your feelings, but he would do it honestly, because that's the only way he knows how.' She darted a look at the clock and shook her head. 'That's enough boy talk for now. We have a meeting in ten minutes.' She winked at Sam. 'And I have a feeling the boss is going to tell us all about a cracking idea she's had to put this company back on the front foot again.'

'She is.' Sam straightened her shoulders, putting all crazy thoughts of Ryan aside. She'd already allowed one man to unbalance her enough to take her eye off the ball. She couldn't afford to let her attraction to Ryan do the same.

PART FIVE

A Secret Affair

Chapter 24

Ryan stared miserably at his computer. Two days they'd been back at the office, and already Sam was annoyed with him. So much for his hopes of getting back in her bed. He couldn't even get into her good books.

First, there had been the issue with the delete button.

'We can't do a delete button.'

Not the words to say to a woman who was pinning all her hopes on the idea. Especially when he'd been hoping that woman would find him so irresistible, she'd abandon her crappy notion about them only having sex when they were in flaming Cornwall.

As he'd given her the bad news, he thought he'd broken her. For a split second her face had drained of colour, her usually dazzling baby blues had dulled and she'd looked like she was going to howl. But then she'd straightened her shoulders and asked him. 'What *can* you do?'

His version, a *request to delete* button, wasn't as sexy, apparently. 'Wordy' and 'wishy-washy' were the actual adjectives she'd used, said with such clear disappointment he'd felt like a total failure.

Which, in turn, had pissed him the hell off.

'I'm not hacking into any systems, even for you, Sunshine,' he'd countered flippantly.

A response that had, unsurprisingly, got her back up. 'I asked what you can do,' she'd reminded him coolly. 'Not what you won't do.' Oh, and then she'd added scathingly. 'And please stop using Lucas's ridiculous nickname.'

The scathing words had felt like a punch in the gut, though of course they'd been fully deserved. The nickname – *his* nickname for her – had been intended as an affectionate tribute to her glorious smile. The one he was never going to see again at this rate. He should never have used it in such a demeaning way.

After that he'd scurried away to his 'office', a.k.a. the meeting room he'd still not vacated, and spent the rest of the day trying to come up with a way to get around the 'wishy-washy' comment. Best he'd come up with was agreeing to call it a delete button, even though what actually happened was it triggered a request to delete.

Yeah, yeah, turns out he wasn't a genius after all.

After firing her an email confirming his cunning plan, he'd hung around, sad git that he was, hoping to catch a glimpse of her; to apologise, to pick a fight, just to gawp, he couldn't be sure. By nine o'clock, when she still hadn't returned, he'd sloped home, tired, dejected and frustrated, only to find mice droppings all over his kitchen worktop.

Nice. The bastards had clearly been used to having the place to themselves while he'd been having sex on the beach.

And now here he was, the afternoon of day two, and Sam wasn't just annoyed with him. She was seething.

It had started when he'd come back from lunch after a walk around the park to get away from staring at a computer screen and four walls. Deciding he'd play nice and see how Alice was doing with her part of the process, he'd turned the corner to her desk, only to find Damien Lynch strutting past.

Something in him had exploded. How dare the bastard walk in here like he owned the place after what he'd done to Sam? And yes, there had also been a healthy dose of *how dare the bastard think he's got a chance of getting her back?* jealousy, too. So, he'd done what he was famous for and opened his gob without thinking first.

'What the hell are you doing here, Lynch?' he'd demanded which, now he'd reflected on it for a few hours, had been a tad confrontational.

The guy had swivelled on his shiny Italian leather shoes – it was a guess, but wasn't that what all slick bastards wore? – and pinned him with a glare. 'In charge now are we, Black?'

The retort had neatly put Ryan in his place, which had only served to annoy him more. 'Just making sure you don't nick any more ideas.' His eyes had flicked to Alice's computer screen and then back to Lynch. 'You've done enough damage here.'

A gesture not missed by the visitor, who'd narrowed his eyes and replied in a voice dripping with cold fury. 'What, exactly, are you accusing me of?'

To make the moment complete, Sam had popped out of her office, taken one look at them and asked Ryan the killer question. 'What's going on?'

He should have shrugged and said nothing. Or maybe smiled at Damien, said something along the lines of *it's all good, just ribbing him*, and slunk off. But no, gut churning with jealousy and plain old dislike, Ryan had decided it would be a good idea to tell the truth. 'I was wondering what Lynch was doing, walking past Alice's unattended desk.'

In hindsight, he should have left out the unattended part.

Sam's eyes had rounded in horror, but before she'd had a chance to tear him off a strip, Lynch had gone in for the kill. 'You'd better have some evidence to back up that remark, Black, or I'll sue you for slander.'

Ryan had smirked (again, perhaps not a great idea) and replied, 'Your track record of being a douchebag speaks for itself.'

At which point Sam had politely asked Damien to come to her office before turning her cool blue gaze on Ryan. 'I'll talk to you later,' she'd told him in a tone so cutting, it had sliced right through him.

Feeling dismissed, and fizzing with self-righteous anger, he'd decided to find the evidence by accessing the server.

It turned out that nobody had logged onto Alice's computer since she'd logged out for her lunch break.

All that had happened half an hour ago. His humiliation now complete, Ryan was back at his desk, ruing the moment the universe had decided it was a good idea for Sam to come and sit next to him in that bar all those months ago. If she'd not been drowning her sorrows in champagne, her judgement temporarily clouded, he'd not have seen her naked, not had her incredible legs wrapped around his waist. And not have felt like punching Lynch's face when he'd seen him.

Following that logic through, he then wouldn't have felt compelled to confront the guy, and wouldn't now be sitting here feeling like a clumsy oaf who'd just hugely embarrassed himself in front of the girl he desperately wanted to impress.

Staring gloomily out of his office/meeting room, his mood plunged further at the sight of Sam walking Lynch out. How could she be so polite to the git, after what he'd put her through?

Because she still has a thing for him.

Why else had she been so knocked for six when she'd seen him at the conference? Then there were the tears when he'd come to her office. Not forgetting that when she'd had the idea about the app on the cliffs in Cornwall, among the first words out of her mouth had been Lynch's name.

He was so lost in his thoughts he didn't hear Lucas knock on his door. Or maybe he hadn't knocked, Ryan thought testily as the guy waltzed right in. All pink trousers and lime-green shirt.

'You're making my eyes hurt,' he grumbled.

Lucas struck an exaggerated pose. 'Don't be such a whinger. You know it's a good look on me.'

His expression dared Ryan to contradict him, pulling a reluctant laugh from him.

Lucas gleefully clapped his hands. 'God, I'm good. I've only been here a few seconds and already I've turned your glower into a smile.'

Ryan raised his eyes to the ceiling. 'Fine. Good job. Now get lost, I've work to do.'

'We all have work to do. As you'd know if you sat in the open plan area with us, at the desk you were assigned, instead of hiding away in here.'

Ryan drummed his fingers on the table. 'You done with the lecture?'

'I didn't come to lecture. That was a bonus. I came to get rid of the scowl from your face, which I believe I've achieved.' He angled his head, giving Ryan a long scrutiny. 'What caused it?'

Easy would be to say, 'Nothing.' It would also get Lucas out of his hair quicker. But it would also be lying. 'Did you see Lynch and Sam?'

Lucas frowned. 'Yes. She was showing him out. Shame she didn't use the tip of her pointy shoe against his arse, but hey, that's Sam for you.'

'Exactly. Why is she so frigging polite to him?'

'It's her way. She figures cool politeness is more powerful than anger.' Lucas gave him a sharp look. 'Anger shows you care.'

'You're telling me that seeing him strut around here doesn't turn your stomach?' Ryan asked incredulously. 'After what he did to her?'

'I can't stand the man,' Lucas agreed affably, walking towards the door. 'But seeing them together doesn't trouble me.' He gave Ryan another loaded look. 'The question is, why does it trouble you so much?'

Sam fixed an icy smile on her face as she saw her ex out of the building.

'Goodbye, Damien. I appreciate the information, but next time feel free to email me.'

Damien gave her a wounded look. 'Seeing me in person is that bad?'

Once the hurt in his eyes might have softened her. Now it just made her mad. 'Seeing you in person takes up too much time. Time that would be better spent protecting the company you're trying to destroy.'

He let out a huff of bitter laughter. 'What was I supposed to do? You made it quite clear you no longer wanted me at Privacy Solutions. I had no choice but to set up a company in a field I knew. Anything else would have taken too long and required money I didn't have.'

'You had a choice, Damien,' she countered coldly. 'You could have chosen to keep your pants zipped in the first place. You could have chosen to move far away. You could have chosen to work for someone else. But no, you were angry that I found out about your tacky little affair, angry that I didn't forgive you, so you *chose* to try and destroy me.'

His face paled. 'You're right, I was angry you threw me out for one lapse in judgement, after all we'd been through together, but to say I set out to destroy you?' He gave a slow shake of his head. 'Come on, you know me better than that. I still ... care for you.'

She steeled herself against the softness of his voice, the tender expression on his face. To allow him to hurt her once was poor judgement on her part. To allow him to do it again would be total madness.

Silently she turned and walked away, striding purposefully towards the meeting room Ryan was still hiding in. Ryan, who'd embarrassed the heck out of her with his unfounded accusations towards Damien. God, the man could be annoying sometimes. Which was good, actually, because it meant she didn't have to worry about jumping back into bed with him.

Yet as she turned the corner, she caught sight of his insanely sexy face through the glass wall of the meeting room and her traitorous heart skipped a beat.

Annoyed, she reminded herself. She was *annoyed.*

One sharp tug at the door handle and she walked straight in. 'I'm not knocking on a door you shouldn't have.'

His face was carefully blank as he stared back at her. 'Fair enough.'

'Why are you still in here, anyway? I said you could work here temporarily, while you got up to speed. You've been here over three months. Get back out with the others.'

His eyebrows flew upwards. 'Scrapping for a fight, huh?'

'No. Just finding it hard to keep my temper while you're doing your best to annoy me.'

He let out a low, humourless laugh. 'You think that's what I'm doing?'

'I think you can't help yourself.'

'Just one of my superpowers, I guess.' With a grunt of frustration he pushed away from the desk. 'Look, I can't be the guy you want me to be, okay? I can't work out there, with everyone chatting in my ear all day. I can't make your ruddy app do everything you want it to do. I can't ignore how I feel about you. And I can't sit back and let your fucking ex stride back in here like he owns the damn place.' He glared back at her. 'Not after what he did to you.'

Somewhere in her chest, her heart squeezed, but now wasn't the time to dwell on his words. She desperately needed to be his boss. Not the woman afraid she was falling for him. 'Do you have any idea how much your little display in front of Damien embarrassed me? Especially as he'd only come to give me a heads up on rumours he'd heard about a similar app in development.' She glanced away, taking a moment to draw breath. 'What happened with Damien is my business, not yours. I don't need you defending my honour. I don't need you protecting me.' Her eyes sought his again. 'I need you doing your job.' He flinched and instantly regret surged through her. 'Sorry. That came out wrong. I didn't mean to—'

'Put me in my place?' A small, flat smile. 'Sure you did.' He refused to meet her eyes. 'I'll move my stuff before I go home.'

And now the squeeze on her heart was painful. Yet as strong as the desire was to forget the reality of their situation, she knew it was better this way. There was so much work ahead of them. She couldn't afford to let ... whatever it was between them divert her focus. Or his.

'Thank you.' Carefully she closed the door behind her. Being the boss, providing the strategy, the inspiration, cajoling, nurturing, driving the team on to do more, be better than they'd ever believed. All that, she enjoyed.

Hiding her feelings, pretending she didn't care for the man she knew she'd just hurt? That truly sucked.

'Everything okay?' Lucas fell into step alongside her. He took one look at her face and grasped her arm. 'Nope, don't say anything, sweet cheeks. Come with me. I know exactly what you need.'

Ten minutes later she found herself in a small café, complete with plastic red and white check tablecloths and an air of down to earth and ordinary. After taking a sip from her mug of tea, she bit into the toasted bun Lucas had ordered for her, melting butter running over her fingers. 'You figured a teacake was what I needed?'

He grinned as he watched her lick her fingers. 'You're not a flowers and cupcake kind of girl. You like practical. A good, simple but delicious teacake is right up your street.'

He wasn't wrong, she thought as she munched on another mouthful. 'How come you know me so well, yet Damien still thinks I like roses?'

Lucas looked affronted. 'That's obvious. I take notice. Damien was always far more interested in himself.' His expression turned slightly cunning. 'Now Ryan, on the other hand. He takes notice, too.'

Sam wanted to scoff, but instead she found herself asking, 'Why do you say that?'

She didn't miss the glint that appeared in his eyes. 'I hear after the brainstorm he took you for a walk on the cliffs. Told you to start believing in yourself.'

'You and Becky are a right pair of gossips.'

He pouted. 'Only about important stuff.'

'And you think Ryan helping me is important?'

'You tell me.'

Oh no, she wasn't going there. Finishing off the teacake, Sam sat back in her chair. 'What's important is getting Privacy 2 launched.'

'If you say so.' He crossed his legs, flicking at a non-existent crumb. 'Still, there's no reason why you can't work hard and play hard.' He winked. 'At least I hope not.'

Sam's eyes widened. 'Oh my God, Lucas, you've found someone?'

He went all coy on her then, dropping his eyes, his cheeks flushing slightly. 'Maybe.'

Reaching across the table she gripped at his arm. 'Tell me everything.'

'There's nothing to tell.' He smiled across the table at her. 'Yet.'

'Where did you meet him? What's he like?' She gave his arm a playful slap. 'Come on, give me something.'

'We met at the gym. He's fiendishly attractive and nearly as funny as me.' He swigged back the last of his mochaccino and eyed her thoughtfully. 'Tell you what, come out with us tomorrow. You and Ryan. Then you can tell me what you think.'

Sam spluttered. 'Me and Ryan?'

'Don't get all twitchy. He's a friend, you're a friend.' When she still glared at him, he threw his hands up in the air. 'Okay, we'll get some others in the office to come along. Maybe Becky and her drummer guy.'

'I don't know.' It still sounded way too much like a couples thing. Whatever she and Ryan were, they couldn't be that couple that everyone at work gossiped about. She wouldn't go through all that again.

'Come on.' Lucas gave her his pleading look. 'I want you to meet Jasper. Tell me if lust is impairing my judgement.'

She was hardly the one to give him that advice, she thought despairingly. But as she'd never been able to say no to Lucas, she gave him the answer he wanted. 'Fine.'

Chapter 25

Somehow he'd found himself in a swanky club on a Friday night, talking to his gay co-worker about the positive and negative attributes of a bloke called Jasper. From what Ryan had seen so far, Jasper seemed decent – unpretentious (a bit of a surprise, given his name) and affable. He just wasn't the person Ryan wanted to spend his evening thinking about.

Once again, his attention shifted to the woman currently talking to Jasper. The one with red hair, currently tied back in a simple ponytail, huge blue eyes and a smile that made even the glummest man in the room – and yeah, that was probably him – sit up and take notice.

'Don't you agree?'

Shit, that was the third time Lucas had asked him a question. The last two times he'd had to ask him to repeat. Lucas would have a hissy fit if he asked a third time. 'Yeah.'

'Thought you would. Hard not to agree with a great ass, dynamite smile and sexy lips you want to feel all over your body.'

Ryan continued to stare at Sam. 'Definitely.' Belatedly he

realised where Lucas's focus was. 'I mean, if you're into that type of thing.'

Lucas slid him a look. 'If you're into six-foot-two hot men who answer to the name Jasper?'

Ryan took a swallow of his beer. 'Exactly.'

'As opposed to five-foot-ten beautiful redheads?'

Ryan shook his head, laughing under his breath. 'Okay, I'm busted.' He forced his attention back on Jasper. 'Seems like a good guy. Bit earnest, but better than being flip. Weird sense of humour, but same as yours, so I can see the attraction for you.' He shifted his gaze back to Lucas. 'You slept with him yet?'

Lucas rolled his eyes. 'I can always rely on you to voice the question everyone else has been too tactful to ask.' He glanced down at his bottle of beer, then back up to Ryan. 'Would it surprise you if I said no?'

Ryan shrugged. 'What, I'm supposed to think because you're gay you were shagging each other before you'd even swopped names?' His eyes slid unconsciously back to Sam. 'Don't have to be gay to do that. Just dumb.'

Lucas followed the direction of his gaze. 'Why do I get the feeling there's something you're not telling me?'

Ryan blew out a breath. 'All you need to know is she's not interested.'

Lucas sighed, his expression pensive. 'In some ways, I hope that's true. Damien didn't just break her heart. The humiliation of everyone knowing what he'd done almost broke her.'

'I'd never—'

'I know,' Lucas cut in. 'But how much easier for her to date a guy she's met on Tinder. Or at the gym.'

Gutting though it was, Ryan couldn't disagree. Yet as he stared gloomily down at his beer, he couldn't help but think that if she liked him enough, if she felt for him half as much as he felt for her, she wouldn't let stuff like that get in the way. She was his boss, for Christ's sake, but he was prepared to stomach the sniggers, the jibes, for a shot at dating her for real. Then again, he was probably more used to being jeered at behind his back than Sam was.

'You know I didn't just invite you out to meet Jasper tonight.' Lucas eyed him speculatively. 'I thought it would give you and Sam some time together outside the office. Things seem a little ... tense between you since Cornwall.'

'I embarrassed her in front of Lynch.'

The edges of Lucas's mouth turned down in a grimace. 'Yikes. Please don't tell me you went all caveman. She hates that.'

'Yeah, so I've discovered.' He wanted to protect her. Why was that so wrong? It wasn't like he could control how he felt.

'Hey.' Lucas gave him a solid nudge. 'Much as I'm enjoying watching you brood into your beer, it's time I reminded Jasper he came here with me. Why not see if you can clear the air with Sam?'

Ryan wasn't sure there was any air left to clear. She'd made her feelings perfectly plain: she was annoyed with his treatment of her ex, annoyed with his lack of team spirit and probably annoyed she'd ever lowered herself to having sex with him. Still, as the rest of their party – Alice, Becky and Becky's anaemic-looking other half – looked set in their current huddle, it at least gave him an excuse to sit next to her.

It's not like he could make things any worse.

The moment Lucas dragged Jasper onto the tiny dance floor, Ryan eased onto the stool he'd vacated, next to Sam. 'If you move away now, it'll be obvious you want to avoid me.'

She blinked, slowly lowering her wine glass. 'Why would I want to avoid you?'

'Beats me.'

Her breath escaped in a sort of ladylike snort. 'Anyone ever tell you how annoying you can be?'

'Yes, you. Frequently.'

Another noise, this one like someone was strangling her. 'Was there a purpose to you coming over to talk to me, or is it just wind-up-the-boss time?'

His frustration bubbled over. 'And there it is.'

'What is?'

He laughed, heavy with sarcasm. 'The not so subtle reminder of our respective positions.'

She didn't reply immediately, forcing him to actually look at her. Something he found hard to do, without wanting to kiss her. And now she was biting into her lip, which sent a pulse of lust straight to his groin.

'I'm sorry.' She was so close, he was sure he could feel her sigh against his skin. 'I'm not finding this easy. Cornwall felt like another world. Now it's back to reality. I don't think we can carry on where we left off. Not without getting into a tangled mess.'

'A hot, tangled mess.' He caught her eye and smiled. 'Sounds epic.'

She started to laugh. 'It does, doesn't it?' Then her face became serious again. 'But would it be wise?'

He wanted to tell her to stuff wise. If being wise meant he was left feeling like he did now, with an ache in his groin, and what seemed like a hole in the middle of his chest, it bloody sucked. But before he could say it – well, words along those lines – they were interrupted by Becky. 'Is this a private talk, or can we butt in?'

'Private.'

'Of course you can join us.'

Typically, Becky ignored him and within seconds his private chat with Sam had become a group chat. Strike that, it was a girl chat, because Becky's man seemed about as keen to join in the conversation as Ryan was. With a resigned sigh, he signalled to the bartender. Then realised he could hardly get himself a drink without asking the others.

A round of drinks later, he reluctantly handed over the equivalent of his grocery bill for the week. Looked like he was heading for a diet of jacket potato and baked beans.

It was after eleven when Lucas finally said he was heading home. Or, more precisely, that he and Jasper were heading off. Sam would have to quiz him tomorrow about where they ended up. How much easier to talk about someone else's sex life than her own. Not that she had one now, because she and Ryan had agreed that was off the table.

Or had they? The words 'hot, tangled mess', said in a low, husky tone, kept running through her head. Easy to talk about doing the sensible thing. A heck of a lot more difficult to stick to it.

Especially when the man she imagined being in a hot, tangled mess with kept looking at her like he was now. All simmering sexual intensity from across the cab they were sharing with Alice. And as Alice was the first stop, it meant she and Ryan would be alone when they arrived at her place – or his, because she still didn't know exactly where he lived. Not that it mattered, both had a bed.

Her belly fluttered.

Wise. She needed to be wise.

'This is me.' At Alice's instruction, the cab came to a stop and Ryan stepped out, holding the door for her. But as Alice bent to climb out, she froze, her eyes fixed on a man sitting on the top step to the entrance of a modern block of flats.

'Who is it?' Ryan, too, had spotted the figure.

'Shaun. My ex,' she whispered, her hand trembling as she reached for the door to steady herself.

'The one we talked about in Cornwall?' Ryan asked.

'Yes.'

'And you finished with him?' Ryan's tone was matter of fact, but Sam could tell from his expression that he wasn't happy.

'Yes, I realised you were right.' Alice kept darting looks over at the dark figure. 'He was a bully. I told him I didn't want to see him again.'

'Looks like he didn't hear.' Ryan ducked his head into the cab and spoke to Sam. 'You go home. I'll deal with this.'

Sam ignored him and climbed out, asking the cabbie to wait for them.

Ryan stared back at her, his expression tight. 'Don't trust me?'

'Don't be stupid.' She put an arm around Alice's rigid shoulders. 'I want to make sure Alice is okay.'

She could tell he was put out, but she didn't care. There wasn't a chance in hell she leaving Alice on her own if Ryan started anything with Shaun. Judging from the tension emanating from him as he strode on ahead of them, Ryan was more than ready to lock horns.

'Shaun?'

The guy on the steps jumped to his feet as Ryan reached him. Shorter than Ryan, but bulkier, stockier. Sam would have said Shaun wasn't bad looking, if she wasn't aware of the tremors running through Alice.

'Who are you?' Shaun shoved his hands onto his hips, his eyes flickering between Alice and Ryan.

'Irrelevant,' Ryan shot back. 'What are you doing here?'

'None of your business.'

From her position at the bottom of the steps, Sam saw Ryan smile. Not an amused curve of the lips, but a cold twist of them. 'I've just made it my business.'

'I'm here to see Alice.' Shaun stood his ground.

Ryan turned to Alice, his expression taut, like an over-coiled spring. 'Do you want to see this guy?'

Alice shook her head. 'No.' Her voice sounded scratchy and

Sam gave her hand an encouraging squeeze. 'No,' she said more firmly. 'I told you, Shaun. It's over. I don't want to see you again.'

'Come on, honey.' Shaun started to take a step towards her. 'You don't mean—'

In a flash, Ryan had Shaun with his arm pinned behind his back. 'I just heard Alice say she didn't want to see you.' His voice was so harsh it sent a shiver down Sam's spine. 'Did you hear that, too?'

Shaun struggled against the hold. 'Let go of me, man.'

'I'll let go,' Ryan bit out, 'when you reassure Alice that you won't be troubling her again.'

Sam's heart was going at a gallop. She'd seen Ryan angry, amused, gentle, sarcastic. She'd never seen him like this.

Shaun grunted and swung his body round, fists flying as he tried to punch Ryan, though his action was hampered by the hold Ryan had on his arm. But then Shaun got dirty, moving out of Ryan's grasp enough to lift his knee to slam it into Ryan's groin. Ryan swore and let go, leaving Shaun free to aim another punch. Ryan swerved, then grabbed at Shaun's arm again, this time turning so Shaun was in front of him. His groin out of harm's way.

'Go near Alice again,' Ryan told him in a cold, flat tone, tightening his pressure on Shaun's arm, 'and you'll have me to answer to. Understood?'

Shaun nodded, once, and Ryan dropped his hold.

For several taut moments Shaun glared back at Ryan before swearing under his breath and walking away.

When he was out of sight, Ryan bent over, hands on his knees.

'Are you okay?' Sam asked him, shaken from what she'd seen. Call her life charmed, but she'd never seen two men fight before. It was brutal.

'Yeah.' Slowly he straightened, wincing. 'My nuts are somewhere in my throat, but yeah.'

'That was ... that was horrible.' The tremor in Alice's voice wasn't hard to miss. Nor was the way she remained several feet away. As if she was scared to come closer.

Ryan glanced from Alice, to Sam and back to Alice. Whatever he saw on their faces caused him to duck his head and thrust his hands in his pockets. 'I'll leave you two to it.'

'Wait.' Sam touched his arm. 'Aren't we sharing the cab?'

He wouldn't look her in the eye. 'You take it. I need to clear my head.'

'But Ryan—'

'Leave it.'

She watched as he marched off down the road, a big, hulking, possibly upset, definitely stubborn male.

Next to her, Alice started to cry. 'He's annoyed with me, isn't he? I shouldn't have said it was horrible. It's like I was telling him what he did was wrong.' She heaved in shuddering a breath. 'It was Shaun who tried to punch Ryan. I know that, just as I know Ryan was trying to help. It's just, it was frightening to watch.'

'You were right to say it. Violence is horrible.' Sam gathered Alice to her, draping an arm around her shoulders. 'I suspect, going out with Shaun, you may have seen it before.'

Alice twisted her hands. 'He didn't hit me. But ... he made me think he might, and that scared me.'

'Well, horrid as it was to watch, I don't think Shaun will be troubling you again. Funny thing about bullies, they don't like it when somebody turns the tables on them.'

A short while later, having reassured herself Alice was okay, Sam got back into the miraculously still waiting cab. As it set off towards her place, she slipped out her phone and texted Ryan.

Just checking up on you. Sam

A moment later, she received a text back.

Worried about me or my balls?

She let out a short laugh.

Both.

When his reply finally came, not until she was letting herself in to her flat, she frowned down at it.

Both are fine.

Funny how she could sense his mood from only three typed words. He was clearly still upset with how she and Alice had reacted. A second later he sent her another text.

Are you back at yours?

Immediately her heart jumped into her throat. Was he checking so he could come over? Oh God, she wanted that, so much she almost couldn't breathe. She wanted to reassure herself he was okay, that he wasn't hurt. To hold him, too. To just be with him.

With shaking hands, she typed,

Yes

Quick as a flash, he replied.

Good. See you on Monday.

The rush of disappointment she felt confirmed what she

already knew. She was kidding herself if she thought she could keep Ryan in a neat, tidy box marked 'Employee only. Do not touch.' She was in too deep.

Taking a breath, she pressed call. He answered on the first ring.

'Sunshine?'

He'd used the name earlier in the week and she'd hated it, feeling like he was talking down to her. Now he said it softly, the word coming across as a caress, a term of affection. And it caused a band to tighten across her chest. 'I was wondering ...' Oh God, this was much harder to do than she'd thought. What if he said no? What if he'd decided she wasn't worth the angst?

'You were wondering if my balls really were okay?' he supplied for her. 'Because I've got to tell you, there's really only one way to find out.'

'Then would you get in a cab and come here, so we can do just that?'

Silence. Well, except for the muffled sound of him breathing. Sam's skin started to prick with embarrassment. Oh God, she'd totally misjudged this. He didn't want—

'You're seriously inviting me over, after ... after what just happened?'

What was he saying? Did he really think this was all about sex? That she was worried whether he could perform or not? 'Yes, I'd like you to come over. If that's what you want, too.'

The sound of his laughter echoed down the phone. 'Try and stop me. I'll be there in ten. If I can't find a cab, I'll run. Don't, for God's sake, fall asleep on me.'

Chapter 26

Ryan blinked his eyes open. Not his own shabby bedroom, but one he remembered. An elegant room, dominated by a striking bay window with elegant wooden shutters.

As his gaze drifted down, he saw a cascade of red silk hair across a pristine white pillow. Pale cream skin. The curve of a shoulder. The smooth warmth of one of her breasts, cupped in his left hand.

His heart jumped, then settled in his chest. Why had Sam invited him over last night? Because she wanted company, because she wanted sex. Because she wanted him?

It hadn't mattered. When the offer had come, he hadn't needed to think twice. He'd walked away from her and Alice feeling like a thug. Worse, like his *dad*. But then Sam had phoned. And though they hadn't done any talking, the way she'd kissed him, the way she'd touched him, let him touch her, suggested maybe his thuggery had been forgiven.

He leant across and kissed her shoulder. When she murmured sleepily back at him, he kissed her again. This time on the back of her neck.

She turned and smiled up at him. And his heart went into freefall. 'Hey.'

'Hey yourself.'

He drank her in. The huge blue eyes, wide, sexy mouth. He was falling for her, fast and hard, and there was nothing he could do about it but cling on for as long as he could.

A frown appeared between her eyes and she reached to trace her fingers across his face, along his jaw. 'Is everything okay?'

'I'm in your bed. Everything is about as good as it can get.' He swallowed, then said what was on his mind. 'I didn't think I would be again. Especially after last night.'

'What do you mean, especially after last night?' Her eyes roved over his face and he found he couldn't hold her gaze. 'God, Ryan, what's going on in that head of yours?' When he didn't reply, she let out a strangled groan. 'I was right. You thought I just wanted you for sex.'

What? 'No. I mean I hoped, yes, but that's not what I'm talking about.' Had he got this wrong? Was she really not upset by what she'd seen?

He watched as understanding bloomed in her eyes. 'We're back to me thinking you're a bully, aren't we? That I'm horrified at the way you manhandled Alice's ex?' Once again he found he couldn't meet her eyes. Instead he lowered them to her mouth, holding his breath as she planted a soft kiss on his lips. 'I don't and I'm not, okay? I'd never seen two men fight close up and I didn't like it.' When he flinched, she added quietly. 'But you weren't the aggressor, he was. And I wasn't frightened of you. I was frightened *for* you. At times it looked like you were a different person. That your head was somewhere else.'

His stomach clenched. Stupid to think she hadn't noticed. 'I guess that's fair.'

'Where were you?' she asked softly.

He glanced away again. 'It's what I always wanted to do to my dad. If I'd been big enough.'

He heard her sharp intake of breath. 'You said once that he was a bully. Did he hurt you? Hurt your mum?'

'Me, no. Mum ... you don't have to hit someone to hurt them.' His eyes snared hers, brimming with clearly still painful memories. 'There's a reason she turned to drink.'

Compassion was etched on her face. 'I'm sorry.'

'What are you sorry for, Sunshine Sam? You aren't responsible for him being a git.'

'And you're nothing like him,' she shot back. 'You looked out for Alice, both in Cornwall and last night.' Her eyes turned soft as her hands captured his face. 'Not bad for a guy who claims he's not good with people.'

'I'm not.' He caught her hand and laid it on his chest, over his heart. 'You're making me better at it.'

Her eyes glistened and she shook her head. 'Don't say things like that to me.'

'Why not? It's the truth.'

Her gaze searched his. 'Who are you, Ryan Black?'

'What do you mean?'

'Are you the grouchy guy who just wants to be left alone,

or the sweet guy who looks after people like you did with me in Cornwall, and Alice last night? The guy who melted my heart just now with that comment?'

He shrugged awkwardly. Truth was, he didn't know. He wanted to be the latter, but for too many years he'd been the former. 'I'm not known for melting hearts. As for being *sweet*? Christ.' He shook his head. 'Not even my mum would call me that.'

'And yet I suspect you're very sweet to her.'

He thought of the rows they'd had over the years, the way he'd shouted at her about the drinking. 'Don't go imagining I'm something I'm not,' he replied roughly. 'I've done plenty I'm not proud of.'

She didn't reply straightaway. Instead she plumped up the pillows behind her and settled back against them. 'Tell me about thirteen-year-old Ryan Black. What was he like?'

He had a feeling his eyes were bugging out of his head. 'Do we have to do this?'

She sighed gently, a resigned sort of sound, as if she'd been expecting his response. Then suddenly she jumped out of bed, giving him a quick yet incredible view of her naked body as she raced to snatch a framed photo from the large oak chest of drawers before diving back under the duvet. 'Here.' She pushed the photo into his hands, pointing to the girl in the middle. 'This is twelve-year-old me.'

Gazing down at the photo he saw a grinning girl with red hair in pigtails, braces on her teeth, surrounded by what he guessed were her parents and her siblings.

'I looked pretty gross, right? I hated those braces.'

'Yet you've still got that killer smile going on.'

She shrugged. 'I learnt to pretend they weren't there. I wasn't going to let them stop me enjoying myself.'

What an attitude. And it worked. He could see the happiness on her face. The love that shone from her face and her parents' as they stood with their arms around their children.

His attitude had been totally opposite, he realised grimly. He'd given in, let others stop him from enjoying life.

Sam gave him a nudge. 'Come on. What were you like? You told my parents you were a geek, yet I have this image of teenage Ryan strutting around town in a gang, attracting all the girls with his brooding looks.' She tilted her head, studying him. 'Which were you?'

Ryan tried to keep the smile on his face. Tried not to let his mind wander too much into the past. 'Both.' He let out a long, slow breath, knowing that if he was going to convince Sam he had more to offer than sex, he had to open up to her. 'Mum being an alcoholic' – he sucked in a breath, then decided to get the words out there quickly, before he lost his nerve – 'it made going out hard. I'd plan to meet up with my mates, and yeah, sometimes with girls, then go home and ...' find his mum drunk and incapable of looking after Erin. He rubbed a hand down his face. 'Find I couldn't go out, after all. After a while I let people down so much they stopped asking.'

Sam's heart went into freefall. She'd posed the question for a bit of fun, to lighten the mood after the heavy conversation about last night's altercation with Shaun. Stupidly she'd not thought it through. Not taken the information he'd given earlier, about his mum drinking, and made the connection to how tough that had to be on her teenage son. It was no wonder he'd turned into a bit of a loner.

Her heart hurting for him, Sam shifted to kiss him. And kiss him again. 'You don't want to talk about this, do you?'

His laugh had a desperate edge to it. 'Not if I don't have to, no.'

'Then how about we go out somewhere for breakfast? Take a walk around a park, or along the Thames?'

The eyes that met hers were dark and intense. 'What are we doing, Sam? You told me a relationship with you wasn't on the table, yet now you're talking about spending the day together?' His mouth curved slightly. 'Don't get me wrong, I'm all for it. I just want to know where I stand. Am I an occasional sex buddy when you're in the mood? Or are we something more?'

She swallowed the lump in her throat. 'What do you want us to be?'

He placed a hand on her chin, smoothing his thumb gently across her lips. 'I want as much of you as I can get.'

Her heart shifted, wanting that too. As much of him as he was willing to give. But she couldn't give him all of her – the thought of losing herself all over again, like she had with Damien, was too terrifying. So she couldn't expect all of him back.

Would that be enough, for either of them?

'I want to try,' she whispered. 'But I'm scared to make another mistake. Can we go slowly? Keep it to ourselves?'

His eyes flicked away from hers. 'You want me to be your dirty little secret?'

Ouch. He made it sound so sordid, when she was thinking of sexy looks at the coffee machine when nobody was watching. Of whispered words, and the thrill of knowing no matter how serious the work got, she had him, had them, to look forward to when she climbed the stairs to her apartment. 'That's not fair.' She grabbed his shoulders, forcing him to look at her. 'You know how much Damien hurt me, and not just my heart. My pride and my confidence both took a battering. For a long while I didn't even want to date again, never mind date someone I worked with.' Feeling horribly unbalanced, she sucked in a ragged breath, not above pleading with him. 'Please understand where I'm coming from. I like you, Ryan. Really, really like you. I've tried to ignore what's happening between us and look where it's got me. Naked and in bed with you.' She tried to smile, but her mouth wasn't working properly. It was too bogged down with emotion, like the rest of her.

'You don't see me complaining.'

'No, but I do see you hurt because right now I can't give you more.'

His expression was too guarded for her to read. 'If I've got this right, you just offered me more. As long as we keep it quiet.'

'Yes. If you're willing.' Her heart seemed to falter as she waited for him to reply.

His eyes drifted over her face before settling on hers. 'It's not what I want. No point pretending otherwise. And I'm not a fan of lying.'

Of course he wasn't. How could she have been so stupid? She'd just asked Mr Painfully Honest to lie for her. Any second now he was going to shoot her down, and then what was going to do? Could she really give him up? Then again, could she survive another traumatic public break up?

'But I told you earlier' – his gruff voice cut through her panicked thoughts – 'I'd take as much as I can get.' Her heart began to pick up pace, understanding what he meant before her brain could work it out. And then all she could feel was the press of his mouth on hers. The strength of his arm as it slid around her shoulders, pulling her against him. 'Yes, Sunshine Sam,' he whispered in between kisses. 'I'll be your dirty little secret.'

'It's not like that—'

He cut off her protest with another searing kiss.

In the end, she dragged him off to Kew. Dragged wasn't the right word, because he went willingly enough, though he made it clear it wasn't his first choice of venue.

'You're taking me to a glorified garden centre?' he complained as they walked up to the entrance. 'What happened to the walk in the park?' Then he spotted the price. 'Bloody hell. What are these plants? Rare species from Mars? Diamond-encrusted?'

She reached for his hand, loving the way his fingers immediately curled around hers. Warm, intimate. 'Come on, my treat.'

He stopped abruptly, his face back to the stubborn lines she was so familiar with. 'That's not how this works.'

Instead of locking horns, she decided to go for the subtler approach. Reaching up on her toes, she kissed him on the mouth. 'This' – she waved her hand between them – 'works how *we* agree it does. My choice, I pay. Your choice, you pay.'

He seemed to consider it for few moments before giving her a slow smile. 'And if my choice is we always stay in bed all day?'

She laughed, pushing him towards the ticket booth. 'If I'm enjoying it, you won't get an argument out of me.'

'That'll be the first time,' he muttered under his breath, but when she turned to him and asked him to repeat what he'd said, he gave her a dazzling smile. 'Hurry up, Sunshine. Those plants aren't going to wait all day.'

He had a playful side, she found out, as he yelped in mock pain after putting his finger inside the Venus Fly Trap, making the little girl who'd been watching him giggle.

And a tender side as he held her hand as they walked along the treetop walkway.

Yet still there were times, when he thought she wasn't watching, that she caught a pensive look on his face. Brooding, almost sad. It was those times she realised that while she felt closer to him than she ever had, she was a long way from knowing what he was really thinking.

But then he'd surprise her by kissing the top of head or squeezing her hand, and she reassured herself whatever it was on his mind, he was happy to be with her.

For now, at least.

Chapter 27

Working in open plan was Crap. And yeah, that was with a capital C. It was two weeks since he'd shifted his stuff back to his originally assigned desk, and Ryan still hadn't come to terms with it.

It wasn't the only thing he was struggling with. And compared to the thing that niggled at him day and night, like a toothache that wouldn't stop throbbing, putting up with the sound of ringing phones, laughter and chatter from outside his booth was a doddle.

Was she ashamed of him?

It was the question that wouldn't go away. Oh sure, he understood why Sam thought she needed to keep their affair secret. Knowing Damien's betrayal had been front-page gossip for the whole company must have been brutal for her at a time when she already felt kicked in the teeth.

But was that the real reason she wanted to keep their liaison quiet? Or was she actually, deep down, ashamed of dating a guy who worked for her? Ashamed of dating a guy who wasn't exactly the life and soul of the place?

Ashamed of dating *him*?

And considering he knew he'd done things he was ashamed of. Things she didn't even know about yet.

Yeah, it wasn't surprising the thought continued to nag at him. Not enough to stop seeing her. No bloody way. The chance to be with a woman as incredible as Sam wasn't going to come again, that's for certain. And when they were together? When he turned his brain off and just lived in the moment? Suffice it to say, he'd take what she was offering, for as long as she was offering it.

'How are you enjoying life out here in the real world?' Lucas popped his head over the paltry divide. 'Made any friends yet?'

'Too busy.' He gave Lucas a pointed look, but the guy just laughed.

'How about *special* friends?' Lucas bent towards him and whispered. 'You know, like a certain redhead you've got the hots for?'

Ryan froze, guilt making his reply too snappy. 'I told you before. She's not interested.'

Lucas frowned. 'No need to get your boxers in a twist. I'm only being neighbourly.'

'Sorry. I'm just frustrated with the beta.' Christ, this sucked. It had been a long time since he'd had a friend he could confide in, and in Lucas he hoped he'd found one. Yet he wasn't allowed to talk to him about the one thing he desperately wanted advice on.

Worse, he had to lie to the guy. Something that didn't just make him feel horribly uncomfortable, but he was totally crap at.

The sound of his phone vibrating on the desk cut into the moment and Ryan reached for it gratefully, giving Lucas an apologetic smile. When he glanced at the screen to see who was calling him, though, his heart sank. Erin. Rising to his feet – he wasn't taking this call where others could overhear him – he waited until he'd walked past the reception desk, on his way out, before pressing answer.

'What took you so long?'

'Hi to you, too.'

Erin made an agitated noise. 'Fine, hello. I'm worried about Mum. She's been complaining of indigestion on and off all day, and she doesn't look good.'

Ryan pushed his way out of the heavy door and into the August heat. 'What do you mean, not good? Does she have a temperature? Is she flushed, pale?'

'Pale.' Ryan heard the muffled sound of his mum's voice in the background. 'I've just felt her forehead and it doesn't feel hot, but it's a bit sweaty.'

Shit. Ryan kicked at the wall. 'You're right to be worried, I think. Put her on.'

'Is that please put her on?'

Ryan gritted his teeth. 'Yes. Erin, please put Mum on the phone.'

A few jarring seconds later, his mum's voice sounded in his ear, her upbeat tone managing to allay some of his nerves. 'I told your sister not to call you. I've got a bit of heartburn, that's all. Probably the sausage sandwich I had for lunch from that mobile greasy spoon on the market. Haute cuisine it isn't. More like haute coli.'

It was relief, more than the joke, that made Ryan laugh out loud. 'What the hell were you doing eating from there?'

'It's cheap.'

Ryan leant back against the wall of the office block and drew a hand down his face. 'Shit, Mum, if you need more money—'

'We don't,' she interrupted firmly. 'I should have eaten before I went out, but time ran away from me. I won't make the same mistake again. Now, aren't you supposed to be busy?'

'I am.' Since Cornwall it had been early starts and late nights for all of them. He knew, they all knew, that time was crucial. While the Privacy 2 app wasn't out there, customers were leaving to the rival app, Privacy Protect – Lynch's frigging app. Plus those rumours of yet another similar app in development continued to circulate. Ryan could put his hand up to feeling frazzled. Strung out on caffeine and lack of sleep, his mind was a jangle of codes and algorithms. And Sam, because between their snatched moments in bed, and the secret smile she'd give him in those rare moments she was in the office when nobody else was around, he couldn't stop thinking about her.

'Then stop mithering me and get back to work.' His mum's voice pulled him back to the present.

'It was Erin who phoned me, because she was concerned about you.' Once again the worry niggled, because Erin, who hated his guts, wouldn't have phoned him just for the crack. 'This indigestion. Is it like the last time, when it turned out to be angina?'

'You think I don't know heartburn when I feel it?'

He thought she was good at trying not to worry him. 'Did you take anything for it?'

'Of course.'

'And it's still there?'

'It comes and goes. Stubborn bugger.'

'Okay, let Erin know if it gets any worse. And let me talk to her again.'

'Fine. But don't you go hatching any plans to have me airlifted to hospital. I'm telling you now, I'm right as rain.'

'I promise no helicopters will be involved. Now put Erin on.'

There was another pause, before the sweet sound of his loving sister's voice. 'What?'

Ryan forced in a breath. Clung to his control. 'Are you planning on sticking around tonight?'

'I'm always around. I live here, remember.'

'Damn it, Erin.' He looked skywards, slamming his mouth shut until he was sure the words that came out would be civil. 'You know what I'm asking. I'm worried about her. It could be indigestion, could be something else. I'd feel happier if I knew you were around to keep an eye on her.'

'Of course I'm staying in. Unlike you, I won't abandon my family.'

The barb wedged deep and he clenched his jaw. 'Let me know if she gets worse. Or if she doesn't get better.' He inhaled a ragged breath. 'Just phone me and let me know how she's doing. Please.'

He was left listening to the disconnect sound.

Frustration bubbled and he kicked the wall again, though

this time more with defeat than with anger. Then he walked back inside.

The morning had been hell. Sam could totally understand why the investors were getting antsy. They had her sympathy, they really did. Just as she was seeing her sales line falling, they were seeing their investments taking a dip, too. But for heaven's sake, how many times did she have to tell them she had it in hand? Apparently it wasn't enough that she'd held monthly meetings with them for the last six months, nor that she'd phoned each of them in turn every week with an update. Now she had to go and see them in person. It was exhausting.

It was times like this, she thought as she eased off her shoes – the kitten heels might look cute, but they didn't half pinch her toes – that she wondered why on earth she'd ever thought running her own company would be fun.

Spending all day soothing the ruffled feathers of stupidly rich men was not her idea of fun.

'You got a minute?'

Sam's eyes flew over to the doorway with a start. Ryan. Her heart gave the usual bump at the sight of his tall frame. His dark, magnetic eyes. 'Sure. Come on in.'

By the time he sat down opposite, her office felt half as big and her senses were on full alert. Why did this man have the ability to send goosebumps racing over her skin just by looking at her?

Leaning forward, he rested his forearms on his thighs. 'How serious are you about this no fraternising at work rule?'

Where was he going with this? 'Very. Why?'

'Because I really want to kiss you right now.'

She felt a flush of heat, along with the goosebumps. 'That's ...' She had to clear her throat and start again. 'That's good to know.'

His gaze left hers briefly to flick over to the glass wall, with the frosted bottom portion. 'You could always drop your pencil on the floor. I could help you find it.'

She laughed softly. 'Tempting, but a little too risky.' He shot her a look and though his lips were smiling, his eyes weren't. They were hot, intense and a little bit pissed off. They hadn't discussed her need to keep their relationship quiet since that morning two weeks ago when he'd agreed to be her, in his words, dirty little secret. She knew he wasn't happy about lying, especially to Lucas, but so far he'd not complained. At least not verbally. It's just that every now and again, like now, his brown eyes were like those of a puppy shoved out in the cold. 'Please, don't look at me like that. You know why we can't.'

'Yeah.' He glanced down at his clasped hands. 'One public betrayal is humiliating enough.' Again those puppy eyes caught hers, filled with hurt and reproach. 'Kind of assumes I'm going to betray you, doesn't it?'

Emotion balled in her throat. 'It's not that. I don't want everyone knowing my business. Not again. I feel too vulnerable, too raw.' At the prickle of tears, she bit into her bottom lip. 'I explained all of this and you agreed. If you want to change your mind—'

'About seeing you?' He gave a sharp shake of his head. 'Not a cat in hell's chance.'

Slowly she felt her muscles unclench. 'Okay then.' She looked straight into those dark eyes and decided it was time he knew how much he was starting to mean to her. 'You have no idea how happy that makes me.'

This time his smile reached right into his eyes. 'Maybe you can show me tonight.'

Her belly fluttered. 'Maybe I will.'

'Deal.' He shifted to sit back in the chair, his eyes falling to the floor before coming back to meet hers. 'Need a foot massage?'

'What?' Suddenly she realised he'd seen she'd taken her shoes off. 'You weren't meant to notice my feet.'

He started to laugh. 'Relax. I've seen plenty more of you naked.' He nodded to the frosted glass. 'And it's something I can do without anyone knowing.'

At the thought of having his big warm hands touching them, her feet tingled. Did she dare?

As if he could read her thoughts, he bent suddenly and tugged both of them onto his lap. 'So, these meetings that keep taking you away from the office.' He spoke as if his strong fingers weren't massaging her soles, sending waves of bliss rolling through her. 'Am I allowed to ask what they're about?'

'Umm.' She wanted to close her eyes and give in to the pleasure.

'Boss?' His eyes were alive with mischief.

'Yes, sorry.' She shifted, trying to focus on his question. 'The investors are getting twitchy. I've being doing the rounds, trying to allay their fears, which is hard when I'm feeling twitchy myself.' Some of the pleasure vanished as she recalled the conversation from this morning. 'Please tell me the beta version will be ready soon. I desperately need something to show them before they start turning words into actions.'

His busy hands stilled. 'They're threatening to pull out?'

'It's been mentioned by one of them. Maybe just a bluff. Maybe not. I can't tell.' She used to be able to read people at will, she thought crossly. Now she doubted her judgement too much to make the call.

Something flickered across his face. Worry? Resignation? 'It's not quite there but it can be, if I work on it tonight.'

'Would you?' It was hard to keep the hope out of her voice. 'I know it's a lot to ask—'

'Sure.' He eased her feet back onto the floor. 'I'd better get back to it.'

'Wait.' There was something off with him. He wasn't Mr Chatty, but this was crazy. 'You haven't even told me what you came to see me about.'

He shook his head, eyes not looking at her. 'Doesn't matter.'

'Ryan.' Her voice pleaded with him. 'Come on, what is it? Talk to me.'

He smirked then. 'What do you think I've been doing?'

She rolled her eyes. 'God, you exasperate me sometimes.'

'Only sometimes? I really must be growing on you.' As he rose to his feet, his face straightened. 'The reason I came to see you is no longer important. You need the beta version finishing. I'll sort it.'

As *exceedingly stubborn* was one of his more annoying

traits, she decided not to push it. 'Thank you. And for the foot massage, too.'

Those dark eyes held hers. 'Next time maybe you'll consider dropping the pencil, after all.'

Though he smiled, his statement held enough of that stubbornness to warn her he hadn't accepted her argument about keeping their relationship quiet. He was going to keep pushing. Well, she could be stubborn, too, when it was important enough. And right now, with everything going on with the business, protecting herself came under that category. 'Will I see you later?'

He shook his head, hands slipping into his pockets. 'It's going to be a late one. I don't want to disturb you.'

He wouldn't if you gave him a key. It stunned her that she was even contemplating it, considering they'd only been officially, albeit secretly, dating for two weeks.

While she was inwardly debating with herself, he quietly let himself out.

PART SIX

The Unscheduled Visit

Chapter 28

Ryan glanced at the clock on his screen; 8pm. Five hours since Erin had phoned, worried about their mum. Five hours since he'd told her to let him know how she was doing. And still no phone call.

Probably he was fretting about nothing. Probably her indigestion *was* just a frigging stomach ache and not the huge heart attack he'd been having nightmares about ever since Erin had called. Sadly his plan to zoom up the motorway to check on his mum for himself tonight had been aborted the moment Sam had told him about the investor meetings, and the need to have the beta version ready ASAP.

Hard to refuse the boss when you were more than halfway in love with her.

So now he was stuck with useless worrying. He bloody hated that. With a grunt of frustration, he focused back on the programme.

'Hey.'

He jerked his head up to find Sam standing behind him. 'Checking up on me?'

Her eyes flashed back at him. 'Wondering if you wanted a coffee. I'll take that as a no.'

Yep, he deserved that. 'Crap, sorry. You caught me at a bad moment.' He wanted to take her hand. Hell, just to touch her, and it frustrated him hugely that he couldn't. That out here he had to pretend nothing had changed between them, when actually *everything* had. He was falling so fast he was spinning out of control.

'Anything I can do to help?'

Stop standing where I can smell your perfume. Stop making me hide my feelings. 'I'm good.'

He heard her gentle exhalation. 'You're not.'

'Fine. I'm not.' Frustrated with her, with himself, with Erin's lack of communication, he pushed his chair away from the desk. 'The beta's still a mess. At the moment, it's more likely to convince people to disinvest than keep the faith.' He sighed, hanging his head. 'Sorry, but I can't fix it tonight. I'm going to need a few more days.'

'Then we'll have to live with that.' Her head tilted as she studied him. 'There's something else. The reason you came to see me, which got sidetracked by the investor meetings.' She lowered her voice. 'And the very welcome foot massage.'

He found he couldn't make a flirty comment back. His worry was too acute. 'Erin phoned earlier. Said Mum's had indigestion on and off all day.'

'Has she taken any antacids? I get it from time to time ...' She trailed off, a frown creasing her forehead. 'You think it's something more?'

'Probably nothing.' But he knew it could also be something, especially considering the angina.

Sam's expression looked troubled. 'It's enough to have you sitting here fretting, though?'

'Maybe.'

She screwed her face in disbelief. 'What happened to the famous Black honesty?'

'Look, I'd thought of shooting off early to go up and see her. You need this done urgently, so I knocked the idea on the head. I'll go up at the weekend, when this is finished.' God, those bloody eyes of hers were almost drowning him in sympathy.

'Your mum is more important.'

'Well, yeah, but she's only got indigestion.' Keep telling himself that and he might believe it. Suddenly Sam jumped off the desk and turned off his monitor. 'What the hell?'

'Go and see your mum. If you're satisfied she's okay, you can come back to this tomorrow.'

Just as he was deciding whether to be outraged by her bossy manner or pathetically grateful for it, his phone rang. Erin.

Heart racing like a pack of wild horses, he pressed answer. 'Hey.'

'Mum's in hospital. She's had a heart attack.'

There was both panic and accusation in his sister's voice. As the blood drained from his face, Ryan felt the cold hand of terror press against his chest. 'Is she ...' Christ, he couldn't say the words. As he sat, frozen to his chair, immobilised by fear, Sam calmly slid the phone from his hands. Vaguely he heard Sam talk to Erin, but his mind was on overload and he couldn't take anything else in.

'Ryan.' Those incredible eyes shone through the fog in his brain. 'Your mum's having tests but her condition is stable.' He felt the comfort of Sam's hand as it pressed against his face. 'Come on, I'll drive you up there.'

Heart attack. He seemed stuck on the words, unable to speak, to move.

Then Sam's hands were on his face, cupping it in their soft, warm hold. 'Ryan, look at me.' Once again he felt the power of her gaze. 'She's going to be okay. Now move your arse so you can go and see her.'

The cloak of fear lifted a little, at least enough that he felt he could breathe. 'Right, yes, sorry. I need to go.' Numbly he stood, automatically reaching for the wallet and car keys he always left on the desk. 'Which hospital is she in?' He rubbed at his face, trying to get his brain working again. 'Shit, you said she was stable, yes?'

'That's right.' Once again she clasped his face. 'You're not driving, I am.'

'What?'

Ignoring his confused question, she took hold of his hand and started to propel him out of the office. Woodenly he followed, still not sure what was going on but relieved someone was taking charge because he sure as hell couldn't.

It was only when they were on the motorway, him sitting in the comfy leather passenger seat of a snazzy Mercedes coupé, that he fully realised what was happening. 'Shit.' He leant back against the headrest, feeling the weight of the last hour dragging down on him.

'Are you okay?' She winced. 'I mean, apart from the fact that you're stressing out about your mum.'

'You forgot the bit about me making you drive two hours up the motorway at nine o'clock at night.' He looked over at her, but her eyes were fixed on the road.

'Nobody made me.'

'True, but did anyone see you? Or is this the type of service you'd provide for all your employees, whether you're sleeping with them or not?' And why the hell was he trying to pick a fight with her over this now?

Because you need to take your mind off what you'll find when you get to the hospital.

'I'm not going to argue with you. Not now.' She gave him a fleeting sidelong glance and gentled her voice. 'I'm driving you to the hospital because the alternative, staying at home and wondering how you are, how your mum is, was unthinkable.'

Emotion flooded through him and he shut his eyes, turning his face away from her so she wouldn't see how close he was to totally losing his shit and bawling like a baby. 'How long till we're there?'

'The sat nav says another hour.'

'Right, thanks.' He focused on breathing for a few seconds until he felt, not steadier exactly, but less likely to break down on her. 'I'll phone Erin and get an update.'

* * *

Sam tried not to listen to the tense conversation between Ryan and his sister, but it was hard not to when he was sitting right next to her.

And when she felt every ounce of his pain, his frustration, each time he spoke.

'I'm sorry you had to cope alone.' He hung his head, squeezing his eyes with his thumb and forefinger. 'I should have been there.'

And wow, now the guilt he was so clearly feeling wound its way through Sam, too. Why hadn't he told her he wanted to leave when he'd first come into her office?

Because you pressured him into staying. How could he say no to you when you're not just dating him, you're also his boss?

Oh God, what a mess.

'Can we not have this argument now?' His voice sounded heavy, dragged down by worry, sorrow and whatever it was Erin was beating him up about. 'We'll be there in an hour.'

His sigh, when he ended the call, seemed to come deep from his soul.

'How's your mum doing?'

'They've taken her into surgery.'

His whole body shuddered and Sam desperately wanted to wrap her arms around him. It was so hard, watching him hurt like this and unable to help. 'What's the story between you and Erin?' She blurted after a few minutes tense, silence. 'Before you tell me you don't want to talk about it, remember we've still got sixty minutes to kill and you could do with a distraction.'

'I can think of better distractions.' Instead of his usual

smirk, he sighed heavily and leant his head against the headrest. 'Erin thinks I abandoned her.'

When no other words were forthcoming, Sam prodded. 'Why?'

'Because I did.'

She swallowed her frustration – he was going through a tough time. 'That's not an answer. Come on, talk to me.'

'I wasn't being difficult. I did abandon her.' From the corner of her eye she saw him turn his head away to stare out of the side window. 'She was eight when I left home.' The words were spoken slowly, reluctantly. 'Sounds simple enough, but it wasn't. Mum was ... hell, she was a mess. The drinking led to her being fired, so then she had nothing to do all day but drink and wallow.' He gave a bark of humourless laughter. 'Buying booze when you've got no income isn't recommended.'

It wasn't hard to fill in the parts he hadn't said. 'You left home to work?'

'Yeah. Not many places are prepared to pay an eighteen-year-old kid a decent whack, but I'd been doing some stuff from home now and again for this tech company up in Manchester and they offered me a good job. Just basic programming, but it was a lot more than I'd been able to earn up to then.' His head turned again, this time to stare down at his hands. 'I told myself I was doing it for the family. You know, earning money to send back to Mum so she and Erin would be okay.'

'You were doing that.'

He shook his head, letting out another sharp laugh. 'I was escaping. Fact. I was done with babysitting them both. I wanted to get on with my life, so I buggered off to Manchester and left the pair of them to it.' His head dipped again, and he rubbed at the back of his neck. 'Six months later social services got involved and Erin was taken into foster care.'

Sam could feel his remorse, his guilt. It was a living, breathing thing that went beyond the droop of his shoulders and the hanging of his head. 'That's not on you,' she told him softly.

'Yeah? That's what I kept telling myself, too, but you know what? It's a load of bollocks. They both needed me at home more than they needed the money I sent them.'

His guilt was buried deep, she realised. It would take time to get him to see he was being too hard on his younger self. 'How long was Erin with foster parents for?'

'A few months. Just long enough for Mum to sort herself out.' He paused and she heard him inhale several deep breaths. 'Mum knew she needed help, it was done voluntarily, but if I'd been at home, it wouldn't have happened.'

'If you'd been at home your mum would have had no reason to sort herself out, either.'

He laughed, quiet and humourless. 'Or maybe I could have helped her give up the booze for good, instead of just ... managing.'

'Only she can do that, Ryan.' She cast a quick glance his way and saw that his head was tipped back, his eyes shut. 'Did you and Erin get on before you left?'

'She's my baby sister. Of course we got on.'

His face looked so strained, her heart ached for him. 'I'm guessing you went from hero to zero in her eyes.'

'Something like that.' Suddenly he shifted, sitting bolt upright. 'What junction are we up to?'

'Is that your subtle way of saying you've had enough of the conversation?'

He exhaled heavily. 'I just want to see her.'

And there went another sharp tug on her heart. 'I know you do.' She reached across and squeezed his hand, the contact as much for herself as for him. 'She'll be okay. Erin said your mum's in surgery so she's probably having an angioplasty. Maybe a stent inserted. That's what happened to my dad after his heart attack. And you saw him in Cornwall. I'd say he's back to his old self yet better, because he's fitter.'

Ryan didn't say anything, just nodded, but his hand continued to hold hers, his thumb rubbing gently over her knuckles.

Chapter 29

Ryan fought to control his emotions as he walked into the small side room his mum had been put in. There she was, looking horribly fragile as she lay in a bed surrounded by monitors and intravenous drips. The back of his eyes stung as he bent to kiss her.

Her eyes fluttered open, and he felt a vice-like grip on his chest. 'You gave us a scare.'

She smiled, face as pale as the pillow she lay on. 'The things I have to do to get my son to come and see me.' Guilt washed through him and she immediately snatched at his hand. 'You visit me plenty. That was me making a joke.' She glanced around. 'Where's your sister?'

'She went to take a piss.' He took comfort from her frown. Maybe his mum was still his mum, despite the fright. 'Fine, she went to powder her nose, or whatever other crap you women use. She's been here with you the whole time.' Unlike your son, who only arrived when the drama was over, he thought heavily.

Her hand, bonier than the hand he'd held on the journey up here, the skin not as soft as Sam's, but the grip still strong, tightened round his. 'I know what you're thinking, and you need to stop. You're twenty-eight, you daft sod. I'm thankful you live only a couple of hours away. Grateful you could drop everything to come and check on me, even though you didn't need to.'

'Shit, Mum, you had a heart attack.' A shudder ripped through him and as his legs started to tremble, he grabbed at the chair and shoved himself into it. 'Of course I needed to be here.'

'You're busy at work, you told me that. I don't want you getting in trouble with that boss of yours.'

He began to laugh then, hysteria, relief and amusement all rolled into one. 'She's the one who drove me up here.'

'She's here?' In an instinctive gesture that would have had him laughing again, if her face hadn't contorted in pain the moment she tried to sit up, she patted at her hair. 'Where is she?'

'Where's who?'

Erin walked back into the room. When she'd first seen him walk onto the ward, she'd given Ryan such a heart-wrenching hug he'd begun to hope they could find a way back to each other. But since then her answers had been monosyllabic and the accusing stare she'd cast his way every now and then had seen his hope turn to dust.

'Ryan's boss, Sam, drove him to the hospital.' Either his mum was oblivious to the undercurrent between him and Erin, or she was determined to ignore it. 'It's late. You two need to get some sleep. The staff here will keep an eye on me.'

'I don't want to leave you.' Erin's voice caught as she strode up to the bed and bent to give her mum a hug. 'You scared the crap out of me, Mum.'

'I'm sorry, darling.' She kissed Erin's head. 'But I'm a tough old bird. I'll be fine now.'

Erin refused to budge, just lay across the bed, holding on tightly to her mum, and Ryan's heart went out to her. He'd been a mess when he'd got the call. If it hadn't been for Sam insisting on driving him here, he'd probably be in a mangled heap at the side of the motorway by now. How much harder had it been for Erin though, watching their mum suffer the heart attack, calling for the ambulance? Waiting alone in the hospital while the staff operated, not knowing if she was going to be okay?

And while he was on this monstrous guilt trip, there was also Sam herself, whom he'd left sitting in the stark hospital waiting room. He'd told her to go home hours ago but she'd refused to budge, insisting the hard plastic chairs were actually quite comfortable.

A nurse came in to check the monitors, reassuring them everything was fine. Soon Erin's hands relaxed and her breathing became more even.

'She needs to sleep at home,' his mum whispered to him a few minutes later.

'I'll take her.'

'Will you stay with her?'

'You're certain you'll be okay here?'

She smiled tiredly. 'I've got all these monitors checking me, nurses checking me. I don't need you, too. But your sister does.'

'Fine. I'll kip at home and come back to see you in the morning.'

Relief washed over her face. 'Good. Thank you.'

Ryan leant forward, holding onto one of her hands. 'Since when do you thank me for looking after my sister?'

'Since things have been strained between you.' Before he could say anything, she added. 'Erin's wrong to blame you for leaving when you did, but she was only a child. Still is, in many ways. She needs her big brother more than she'll ever let on.'

He didn't doubt that, but needing and wanting were two different things. She might need him, but she didn't want to need him. Didn't want him in her life at all. It was a hard thing to move past.

Reluctantly he stood, easing Erin off the bed. As soon as she realised who was touching her, she bristled and squirmed away from his touch. Sighing heavily, he dropped his hands. 'Time to go home. Mum needs her rest, and so do you.'

She put up a bit of a fight but was clearly knackered because it wasn't long before she was following him out of the ward, her steps sluggish. He wanted to put his arm around her because she clearly needed someone to lean on, but he didn't want to risk another argument so he kept his hands in his pockets.

As soon as they entered the deserted waiting room, Sam looked up. Her eyes skimmed over Erin before falling on him. 'Is your mum okay?'

As Ryan nodded, Erin halted, staring at Sam. 'Are you the boss?'

Sam looked uncomfortable. 'I'm Sam.'

'You're the one I spoke to. The one who drove him up here?'

'I am, yes.' She glanced back up at Ryan, her eyes soft with compassion. 'Do you want taking home?'

And shit, he didn't want to use her as chauffer service, but what was the alternative? Send her off into the night while he and Erin waited for a cab? 'Thanks, yes.' So much more he needed to say; thank her for driving him here, for waiting. Tell her how frigging amazing she was, but Erin was watching them closely, so he settled for giving her a small smile. One he hoped conveyed at least some of his gratitude.

The journey to the house was quiet; the only words spoken were directions from Ryan, delivered in a flat voice that seemed designed to put off any further conversation. Not that Sam knew what to say, what with Erin sitting in the back seat, staring out of the window, her face looking horribly harsh for someone so young. The tension pinging between Ryan and his sister – half-sister, if she recalled correctly – was so taut Sam was sure she could hear the air cracking.

It was with a great deal of relief she pulled up outside a redbrick semi.

'This is us.' Ryan unclipped his seat belt, his actions slow, as if he didn't want to get out of the car.

'Is she coming with us?'

Erin's sharp question hung in the air. Sam glanced at Ryan who shook his head, and for a moment Sam thought it was in reply to Erin, but then he turned round and glared at his sister. 'Yes, Sam, who's spent all night either driving or sitting in a shitty hospital waiting room just so she can take you home, is coming in with us.'

Erin didn't reply, just flung the car door open and leapt out, slamming it behind her.

Ryan heaved out a breath. 'Fuck, sorry.'

'Don't be. She's upset about her mum.'

'Yeah, but she's acting like a right cow. I deserve it. You don't.'

Before she could tell him he didn't either, he'd climbed out of the car. Sam took her time grabbing her handbag and locking the door, giving the siblings a few moments to themselves before she followed them up the path.

'Where's she going to sleep?' she heard Erin ask as she stepped into the house.

'In my room,' was Ryan's terse reply from the sitting room.

'You're sleeping with your boss? Classy, bro, real classy.'

Standing in the doorway between the hall and sitting room, Sam cleared her throat. Erin looked over and stared coolly back at her, all attitude and simmering hostility.

Ryan dragged a hand over his face, seeming to be at the end of his tether. 'Not that it's any of your business but I'll be kipping on the couch. Now go to bed, Erin. I'll see you in the morning.'

'You don't get to tell me what to do in my house.'

Tell her it's your house too, Sam willed him. Tell her you're paying for it, because she was pretty certain that's where most of his wages ended up. It explained why he lived in a shithole of a flat, as he'd memorably called it that first night they'd met. She knew what she was paying him, and it was enough for a decent flat, and a new car.

Yet Ryan didn't say anything. He was like a boxer who'd taken one hit too many and was now clinging to the ropes, no fight left in him.

Thankfully Erin seemed to have had enough, too, because she turned away and trudged up the stairs, heavy footsteps making clear her anger, or perhaps her fatigue.

Ryan sagged against the wall. 'Do you want a drink of anything? Tea, coffee?' His mouth settled in a grim line. 'Something stronger? There's bound to be some.'

She walked over to him and laid a hand on his arm. 'I'm good,' she told him softly.

'Good doesn't begin to describe you.' He wrapped his arms around her, drawing her tight against him, and her heart melted. She was falling for him, and there was nothing she could do to stop it. 'I'm sorry, but I think you're stuck here for the night. Too late to drive home and it's a fair drive to the nearest decent hotel.'

'I'm not stuck here. I want to be here.'

He groaned. 'You must be bloody bonkers, but I'm so flaming grateful you're here.' His arms tightened and she felt his need. It wasn't sexual, not this time. It was a need for comfort, for connection. The same things she'd needed from him that night on the cliffs in Cornwall.

After a while she felt the press of his lips against the top of her head. The gentle gesture, coming from this hulking, taciturn male, touched places deep inside her. 'You need to get to bed.' He eased her away. 'I'll show you.'

'Aren't you coming too? I know you said you'd take the couch, but—'

'That was mainly to keep Erin quiet.'

'Mainly?'

His eyes darted away from hers. 'You've seen the way Erin is with me. You've heard why she hates me. I figured you might not be up for sharing my bed.'

'Because you left home at eighteen to work so you could send money home?' She wound her arms back around his waist. 'If anything, I like you more now.'

'Yeah?' He shook his head. 'You're kind of crazy, you know that?' He tugged at her ponytail, drawing her mouth towards his for a brief kiss. 'But it seems I'm a fan of crazy.'

Taking her hand he led her upstairs. His room was small, the bed taking up nearly all the room. 'I bought a double for it a few years ago. Got fed up with wedging myself into a single every time I came to stay. Didn't think I'd get a hot woman sleeping in it with me.' Bending, he touched his lips against hers again, the kiss deeper this time. 'Strip.' Her expression must have betrayed her surprise because he laughed. 'Yes, I want you naked. I also want to shove our clothes in the wash so we have something to wear tomorrow.'

And God help her, she felt her heart open up for him that little bit more. A practical man, who could make her laugh, and make her knees tremble. How was she supposed to resist?

When he finally eased into the small double bed beside her, all naked hot skin and hard muscles, resisting was the last thing on her mind.

Chapter 30

Ryan woke early, his mind immediately back at the hospital. There'd been no phone call, which had to be a good sign. Still, he felt anxious to go back and see for himself. His gaze fell on the woman curled up next to him in the bed. The woman who'd given him more support, more comfort in the last twelve hours than he'd ever had. He loved his mum, but thanks to the booze she'd never really been there for him when he'd needed her. It had always been him, worried about her.

For the first time in his life, last night, someone had taken care of him.

Emotion welled, churning around in his chest, tightening his throat. Sam was the gutsiest, kindest, sexiest woman he'd ever met, no doubt would ever meet. He was one lucky sod to be going out with her.

Even if it was on the quiet.

Even if it meant lying to people at work. To Lucas. To Erin.

Shaking off the unwanted thoughts he pushed himself out of bed and took a quick shower in the tiny cubicle – a far cry from Sam's swanky walk-in version with the multiple jets.

Wrapping the towel around his waist, he went to wake her. 'Hey, Sunshine. Time to get moving.' She grunted in an unladylike fashion, turning away from him. 'Whoa, no, you don't. Not if want to have a shower before Erin wakes up.'

Sam blinked open her eyes. 'What time is it?'

He looked down at his watch. 'Six thirty.'

She groaned. 'Four hours isn't enough sleep.'

'Not all of that was my fault,' he reminded her smugly.

Her cheeks turned pink, which made him feel even smugger. 'Fine. I'll get up.' She pulled back the duvet, and his body reacted instantly to the sight of her naked one. This time it was her turn to smile and she did, flashing him a provocative look over her left shoulder as she walked out of the room.

Shaking his head, he sat on the bed and dialled the ward. Hearing his mum was stable and still asleep sent a wave of relief through him. Another good sign, surely.

After dragging the clothes out of the tumble dryer, he shrugged his on and dumped hers on the bed. Then thought twice and made a reasonable attempt at folding them, his fingers lingering on the lacey underwear longer than was strictly necessary. It was only when he thought of Erin barging in and finding him perving over his boss's knickers that he dropped them onto the pile and headed downstairs to find something for breakfast.

'I see she's in the shower. She'd better not nick all the hot water.'

Erin stood in the doorway, wrapped in an oversized dressing gown, the scowl she reserved just for him already on her face.

Ignoring her comment, he filled the kettle. 'I've rung the hospital. Mum's still asleep.'

'That's a good thing, right?'

There it was, he thought, the vulnerability beneath the bluster. It was signs like that, and the way she'd clung to their mum yesterday, that hinted at the sister he knew was still in there. 'It's a good thing,' he reassured. 'Fingers crossed she'll be allowed home soon.' But what was he supposed to do about Erin in the meantime? She'd be okay by herself – she was seventeen, after all – but he didn't want to think of her stewing at home, worrying. 'Have you got any friends who can come and stay until Mum gets back?'

She quirked a brow. 'Worried about me?'

'Of course I am.'

'Not enough to stay around though, eh?'

He sighed, leaning against the counter. 'I work, Erin. You know that.'

'What, you can't wangle a few days off, even though you're clearly shagging your boss?' She let out a sharp crack of laughter. 'A fact you haven't even got the guts to admit to me?'

'Cut it out,' he answered tersely.

'Hit a sore spot, did I? Must be really weird, having sex with someone who's the boss of you. Still, I guess that's the only way you can get on in the company, with you having no qualifications or anything. Can't see what's in it for her, mind. You'd have to be one hell of a lay.'

'I said cut it out.' Ryan felt the anger burn through him, tinged with a hint of shame, because some of what she was saying was true. He didn't have any qualifications. And he was terrified that part of the reason behind Sam's desire to keep their relationship secret was that sex *was* all she wanted from him. 'What happened to you?' he asked Erin sadly. 'When did you become so hard?'

'Maybe when I was forced to live with a foster family for a while 'cos my brother upped and left me with an alcoholic mother? Or maybe during the last nine years of living with Mum, seeing her struggle with the booze and depression. Wondering every time I woke up if this was going to be the day she'd have another major meltdown and I'd have to go back into care.'

Tears filled her eyes and Ryan felt his heart break for her. Shit, he hadn't realised. How easy it had been for him, just checking in on them every few weeks. Blissfully ignorant of how hard they were both finding day to day life. 'I'm sorry,' he croaked, swamped with guilt.

'Yeah, sure you are.'

At the sound of a creak they both looked up to find Sam had entered the kitchen. Ryan swore under his breath, humiliation rolling through him. How long had she been listening?

Sam stood awkwardly in the doorway, wishing for all their sakes that she could unhear the last few minutes. And unsee the tortured expression on Ryan's face as he'd issued his choked apology to Erin. For a man who already wore his guilt like a heavy chain around his neck, his sister's words must have really sliced through him.

'The bathroom's free.' She glanced over at Erin, saw her

stony expression and clamped down on the other things she'd planned on saying. Like *your brother is far more than just a good lay.*

As Erin flounced up the stairs, Ryan turned, leaving her staring at his rigid back, his hands clenched so tightly to the worktop she half expected to hear it snap.

Must be really weird, having sex with someone who's the boss of you. Erin's words seemed to echo around the room, leaving an awkward silence in their wake. The feelings she had for him, woman to man, were hard enough to cope with, without the added complication of their work situation.

'What happened with Erin isn't your fault.' Though she ached to put her arms around him, she held back, unsure if he'd accept that from her now Erin had shoved their boss–employee status down his throat. 'I feel for your sister, I really do, but you have to stop blaming yourself. If you need to throw the blame at someone, hurl it at your dad.'

'Sam.' She heard the breath rush into his lungs, saw the rise of his shoulders and then the fall. 'Leave it. Please.'

She wanted to push. To shake his stubborn body and yell at him for being so accepting, so meek when it came to defending himself against Erin's barbs. But he didn't need any more angst right now. 'I'll leave it, when I've said this. You are one hell of a lay. But you're also far, far more than that.'

Slowly he turned to face her, his smile going a long way towards dissolving the awkwardness Erin had put between them. 'Come here.'

Three steps and she was sliding into his open arms. As

she wrapped hers around his waist she felt the tension leave his body. Guessing he needed the contact more than words, she kept quiet, just holding on to him as he held on to her.

Finally he eased away, but not before he'd planted a soft kiss on her lips. 'You want some breakfast?'

'I'll take a coffee, if you're offering.'

'Cereal? Eggs? Toast?'

He was so subdued still. Upset about his mum, Erin? Or smarting from Erin's implication he was sleeping his way to the top? 'Whatever you're best at.' Nope, still nothing, just a nod of his head. 'Shall I ask Erin what she wants?'

Gratitude shot across his face. 'Thanks.'

Warily Sam climbed the stairs. She could do this. If she could face down angry investors, she could tackle a stroppy teenager. Finding the bathroom door still open, she walked to the room Ryan had pointed out to her last night – the one at the end of the small landing. Squaring her shoulders, Sam knocked on the door. 'Erin. Ryan wants to know what you'd like for breakfast?'

A second later the door swung open. 'I don't want his shitty breakfast.'

Sam took one look at Erin's wet cheeks, her red-rimmed eyes, and held back the sarcastic retort she wanted to deliver. Still, the thought of Ryan downstairs, weighed down by misery, was too painful for her to leave this alone. 'Why are you so mean to him?'

Erin shrugged, the casual gesture not fooling Sam. 'Don't act like you didn't hear what I said downstairs.'

'I heard what a tough time you've had, yes, and I'm sorry.' She paused. 'Have you ever considered how it was for Ryan, when he was your age?'

'What do you mean?'

'I mean it's tough, living with an alcoholic parent, I can see that. But he had to go through it too. The difference is, I suspect there were many times he had to take care of you, as well.' She made sure to catch Erin's eye. 'That's a lot to put on a teenage kid.'

Erin moved to shut the door on her. 'I don't need to listen to this.'

Sam put her foot in the way, stopping her. 'I think you do. I think you need to ask yourself why Ryan has no qualifications. Why he left you when he was eighteen, because it sure wasn't to do what most smart guys his age would do and go to university.'

'Just goes to show what you know. He didn't like school or studying. Didn't even go out with his mates. He preferred sitting in his room, playing on his computer.'

'Maybe he didn't prefer that,' she countered quietly. 'Maybe he felt he had no choice.'

Erin blinked, then turned away sharply. 'Go away.'

Sam sighed. What had she expected? That Erin would magically start to soften a stance built from nine years of resentment? 'Okay, I'll leave you to get ready.'

She was halfway down the stairs when she heard Erin shout through the closed door. 'Tell Ryan I want a cup of tea and eggy bread.'

Feeling the pleasant hum of a small victory she went to

rejoin Ryan, who was stirring a pan on the small hob. 'Erin says she'd like tea and eggy bread.'

His head snapped round, his expression a curious mixture of shock, puzzlement and tentative hope. 'She did?'

'Yep. Why the surprise?'

'Eggy bread.' A small smile curved his lips. 'It's what I used to make her years ago.'

'When you still lived at home?'

'Yeah.'

'When you used to get on?' she added softly.

He nodded. 'She was easy to please in those days. She'd have had eggy bread for breakfast, lunch and dinner if she could.' His face twisted. 'Sometimes she did.'

'But look at her now,' Sam said firmly, desperate for him to stop beating himself up. 'At the young lady you helped to nurture. How strong and capable she is. How beautiful.'

'How stubborn. How mouthy.'

Better. Sam smiled. 'She's not afraid to stand up for herself. It's a good thing. Not unlike her brother.'

He laughed then, a sound that warmed her inside. 'Careful, Sunshine. You're close to admitting you like me being a stubborn git.'

'No, I'm not.' Shaking her head, she pressed a gentle kiss on his lips. 'I'm saying I like you. All of you. Very much. Even the parts that make me want to scream.'

The sexy smirk was back. 'I like making you scream.' But then his face turned serious, his eyes more intense. 'You know I like all of you, too, don't you?' He trailed his thumb across her lips, his eyes darkening. 'More than like, in fact.'

Her heart jumped, but before she could reply, before she could tell him it was more than like for her, too, they were interrupted by the smell of burning.

'Bugger, bollocks.' He lunged at the pan of charred scrambled eggs, lifting it off the hob. 'Shit.'

She couldn't help it. She started to laugh. 'I think I'll take the eggy bread instead.'

'You seriously think that'll go any better?' He proceeded to scrape the eggs out of the pan and onto the waiting toast. 'Serves you right for distracting me.'

He shoved the plate at her and she bit into her lip, desperate not to giggle because he looked so frustrated. 'Thanks,' she managed. 'I love burnt scrambled eggs.'

'Piss off and eat it.' The warmth in his eyes, the affection in his tone, drowned out the sting of his words.

'Are you allowed to tell your boss to piss off?' Erin appeared in the doorway, dressed in skinny jeans and a T-shirt, her dark hair still wet, her face looking finely beautiful without makeup.

Sam gave her a level gaze. 'I'm not his boss here.'

Ryan clattered the egg pan into the sink. 'Sam tells me you want eggy bread?'

Erin raised her chin as she answered, as if daring him to comment. 'Yes.'

He ignored the bait. 'Coming right up.'

Half an hour later they were back at the hospital. While Erin rushed ahead, Ryan held onto Sam's arm. 'You should head back. I've taken you away from the office for long enough as it is.' He jammed a restless hand through his hair. 'I'll catch the train when I know Mum's okay and Erin isn't on her own. Then I'll work through the night to get the beta version finished.'

'I'm not going back until you come and tell me how your mum is. Take as long as you need.'

She sensed his hesitation. 'If you don't go back soon, everyone in the office will know where you spent the night.'

Anxiety knotted her insides, but it wasn't enough to change her mind. She didn't just want to stay until she knew everything was okay, she *needed* to. 'We'll worry about that later. Go and say hello to your mum. I'll be in the waiting room when you're ready.'

Still he didn't move. Instead his eyes travelled over her face, before staring into hers. 'I don't know if I said it enough, but thank you.'

'You've said it plenty. Go.'

Still he hesitated, his gaze drifting to her mouth, as if deciding whether to kiss her or not. Just as she started to anticipate the feel of his lips, he turned and strode off. Leaving her feeling acutely disappointed.

Chapter 31

He'd wanted to kiss her. It was only the realisation that kissing her in public was a no-no for her that had held him back. Even as Ryan raced through the doors of the hospital entrance though, desperate to see his mum, part of him was back with Sam.

I like you very much.

It wasn't the first time she'd told him that, and like was good, right? Especially considering it was only a few months ago he'd overheard her saying to Lucas, '*I know Ryan isn't likeable.*'

But. But.

His feelings had moved on from like. In fact, he was pretty certain he'd tumbled head-first into love. Considering Sam was only just coming out of a traumatic breakup, that she was so hesitant about their relationship she wanted to keep it quiet, oh, and that she was most definitely way out of his league, falling in love with her was neither clever nor sensible.

Yet from the day he'd realised he was working for the woman he'd had an unforgettable one-night stand with, falling for her had been utterly unavoidable.

And now he was left with his mind a mass of jumbled emotions, and his heart so full it hurt.

He shoved aside the messy thoughts as he approached his mum's bed, relieved to see her sitting up and chatting to Erin.

'You look a lot better.'

She glanced up and smiled. 'I feel a lot better.'

'Good.' He bent to kiss her cheek.

Immediately she touched his face, her familiar brown eyes searching his. 'Thank you for coming back to see me. For taking care of your sister.'

He sighed, placing his hands over hers. 'I told you before. Don't thank me for being a son, or a brother.' When she nodded, he stepped back and went to sit on the opposite side of the bed to Erin.

'I've talked to Erin and we agree you need to get back to work.' He opened his mouth to protest but his mum held up her hand. 'Erin's friend Hayley is coming round to stay with her tonight and the doctor said I can go home tomorrow.'

'She did? That's great.'

'Apparently I'm a model patient.' A cloud passed over his mum's face. 'Shame I'm not a model mother.'

'Hey.' Ryan clutched her hand. 'Don't ever think that. You went through a crap time. It would have broken most people but you pulled through.'

'Booze pulled me through.'

The heavy pressure on his chest was a familiar sensation. It was how he always felt when he thought of her drinking. 'You don't need it now. Maybe the heart attack is the shove you need to make you realise that.'

'Maybe you're right.' She looked him straight in the eye. 'I'm going to try.'

He'd heard it before, but Ryan gave her an encouraging smile. One day, he kept telling himself. One day, she'd mean it. 'I can't ask for more than that. I love you.' He glanced over at his sister, who for once wasn't looking at him as if she couldn't stand the sight of him. 'Erin loves you. We both want you around for a long time to come.'

His mum sniffed, eyes welling. 'Since when did you turn so mushy?'

'Since he's met Sam.' Ryan snapped his gaze to Erin, who shrugged. 'Come on, I'm not stupid. She's more than your boss.'

He could feel his mum watching him. His sister watching him. Crap. What was he supposed to do now? Look them in the eye and lie to them both? 'She's a friend.'

Erin rolled her eyes. 'A friend you want to sleep with. If you're not doing it already.'

Rubbing at his forehead, he wondered how the hell to get out of this conversational minefield. He almost wanted Erin to go back to not talking to him. Almost. 'Look, it's true I fancy Sam. She's strong, ballsy, funny and incredibly attractive. She's also smart enough not to get involved with the likes of me.' It wasn't far from the truth. She certainly didn't want to get involved with him publicly.

'Yet she took time away from running her company to drive you here last night.' His mum frowned. 'Hang on, where is she now?'

Ah. Uncomfortable with the question, Ryan shifted on the

bed. 'She's in the waiting room. She wants to hear how you are before she leaves.'

A look he couldn't quite decipher came and went in his mum's eyes. 'Would she mind ... I mean, do you think I could ...' She trailed off, shaking her head, eyes avoiding his.

'Do you want to meet her?'

Her eyes darted back up to his. 'Only if you wouldn't be embarrassed.'

'*Embarrassed*? Because you're in a hospital bed?' When she shook her head, he leant forward, choosing his next words carefully. 'Don't start making stuff up in your head that isn't real. If you want to meet my boss' – he emphasised the word – 'I'm sure she'd love to drop by.' Because he now guessed what was worrying her, he added. 'And I'd be happy for her to meet you.'

Pleasure trickled into her eyes and she smiled. 'Right then, you go and fetch her. Erin, love, be a sweetheart and bring me a mirror. And a hairbrush. Oh, and have you any blusher in that handbag of yours? Maybe some lipstick?'

Chuckling to himself, Ryan went to hunt Sam down.

Sam made two calls while waiting for Ryan to come back. The first to Becky, letting her know where she was, and why.

'Is this a new service you're providing to all of us, or is it reserved for special employees?'

'Very funny. He wasn't in a fit state to drive and even if he was, his car is a heap of junk. It would have been lucky to make it.'

'Think he managed the drive a few weekends ago.'

Sam huffed. 'Okay, okay. I ... he ... look, I was there when he got the call. I wanted to help.' If there was one thing worse than lying to a friend, it was knowing the need to lie was entirely self-induced.

As if she knew she wasn't getting the full story, Becky let out a soft sigh. 'Tell him I'm glad his mum is okay.'

The next call she made was to the investor who'd threatened to pull out yesterday – was it really less than twenty-four hours ago? 'We're working on a beta version which we'll have with you shortly.'

'You know I only deal with hard facts. When, Sam, when?'

She winced, unwilling to lay more pressure on Ryan's shoulders. 'By the end of the week.' It gave them two working days, and potentially the weekend because she could always argue she'd not specified the end of the working week.

'Fine. I look forward to finally seeing this updated app I have so much money invested in.'

Feeling horribly conflicted, she ended the call and sat back against the seat. She loved her company, but right now she resented it for making her hassle a man who was trying to take care of his family.

'Hey.' At the sound of Ryan's voice, she lurched back upright. 'What's wrong?'

'Nothing.' She pasted on a bright smile. 'How's your mum?'

'Good, thanks. In fact ...' He glanced down at his feet, rubbing the back of his neck with his hand. Then laughed softly. 'Shit, this is probably going to freak you out, but she wants to see you.'

'She does?' Surprise mixed with pleasure, alongside a hefty dollop of *oh my God*. This was Ryan's *mum*.

'You don't have to.' He'd obviously taken her muted response as a lack of enthusiasm. 'I can see it's weirded you out.'

'Don't be daft.' She gave herself a mental shake. 'I'd love to meet your mum. I mean, you've met mine.'

He smiled, but it didn't reach his eyes. 'True. Look, I've not told Mum you're ... we're ...' He sighed, shifting on his feet. 'She knows I fancy you. That's it.'

Guilt pricked at her. 'I'm sorry. I know you hate lying. It's okay if you want to tell her.'

'Tell her what, exactly? We're having an affair but actually it's all a big secret so I can't say anything?' He huffed, glancing away. 'It's easier this way.'

And there it was again, she thought as he led her back towards the ward. The unease she knew he felt at being asked to keep their relationship quiet. She hated that she was the one making him do that. Making him go against his moral code.

But people were human. They talked. Secrets accidentally slipped out and before long everyone knew your business. People who were supposed to respect you, people you worked with, who worked for you, suddenly knew you'd been cheated on, maybe even before you did. They knew when you'd been humiliatingly betrayed. And slowly the respect turned to pity.

Her stomach churned and she placed a hand on it, trying to quell the rising nausea.

'Are you okay?'

She gave the past a determined shove. 'I'm good.'

His eyes narrowed. 'Something's up, but I'll have to let it pass. Mum's just round the corner.'

What did it mean that he knew her so well he could tell she was lying? She couldn't remember Damien ever reading her like that.

He pushed open the door to a small room, just inside the ward.

'Mum, this is Sam Huxton, my boss—'

'Hi, Maggie, I'm Ryan's friend,' Sam cut in, hating the boss reminder, even though he was only using it to protect her desire for secrecy. 'We spoke on the phone once but it's lovely to meet you in person. How are you doing?'

Maggie shook her hand and gave her a warm smile. 'Grand, thank you, lass.' She glanced at Erin, then at Ryan. 'Why don't you two go and get yourselves a drink? Leave me and Sam to have a chat.'

Sam bit down on a smile as she saw Ryan's expression turn wary. 'Now wait a minute.'

Maggie waved her hand at him. 'Shoo. Sam and I are going to talk in private.'

He wasn't happy, that much was obvious, but he dutifully walked out, Erin trailing behind him. Sam gave a low whistle. 'That's impressive. He never does what I ask him to do.'

Maggie smiled gently. 'Oh, I doubt that very much. From what I can see, he's got a real soft spot for you.' Before Sam could panic about how to reply, Maggie was talking again. 'I know I must seem daft, wanting to meet my son's boss when I'm laid up here in a hospital bed.'

There was something about Maggie's searching look that drew the next words from Sam. 'I'm more than his boss.'

Maggie gave her hand a quick squeeze. 'I know, dear. Not that he's said anything, mind, but why else would you bring him here last night?' She watched Sam carefully. 'I think you have a soft spot for him, too.'

It wasn't hard to admit. Not when her actions had made it so obvious. 'I do.'

Maggie's smile was one of quiet satisfaction. 'Then I hope you won't mind me telling you a bit about what he had to put up with when he was a kid. He'd hate me for saying it, but you're the first woman I've seen him show a real interest in and I don't want him to scare you off. Not before you've had a chance to see the real him.'

Sam started to laugh. 'Oh, he's shown me plenty of his scary side, trust me.' She gazed at Maggie steadily. 'And I'm still here.'

Maggie grinned broadly. 'I knew, even from that short chat we had in the car, that I'd like you. You have backbone. Just like he does.' She sighed, sinking into her pillow. 'Now then, what has he told you already? That I'm an alcoholic? That he had to leave home to work because I'd lost my job and the bank was threatening to kick us out of the house?'

'I know you've had a tough time,' Sam replied quietly. 'And that he loves you.'

Tears welled in Maggie's eyes and she wiped at them, shaking her head. 'He's a daft sod.'

'Actually, he's incredibly bright,' Sam cut in and Maggie laughed.

'Aye, you're right.' Her face sobered. 'But that's not thanks to me. He thinks I don't know he was bullied at school because he couldn't go out with the other lads. Not while he was taking care of me and Erin. And of course the things they'd say about me, calling me names. It can't have been easy for him to hear all that. It's no wonder he ended up in so many fights. No wonder he used to bunk off school and shut himself in his room, just him and his computer.'

The image of teenage Ryan, isolated from friends, brought an ache to her heart. No wonder he'd kicked up such a fuss about working on his own. It was what he was used to. 'Thank you for telling me. It explains a few things.'

'I hoped it would. Has he ever spoken about his dad?'

Sam shook her head. 'Only to say he was a git.'

Maggie rolled her eyes. 'Guess that's no worse than my name for him – lying, cheating scumbag. I won't bore you with details, but he wasn't a nice man, not to me or to Ryan.'

'I suspect that's where Ryan's blunt honesty comes from,' Sam mused. 'He's determined not to become his father.'

Maggie caught her eye and held it for a few moments before speaking. 'He's nothing like his father. Never will be. Beneath the tough shell Ryan has a heart of gold. I wanted you to know that.'

Sam reached for Maggie's hand this time, giving it a gentle press. 'I already know. I've seen that side of him.' She thought of how he'd been there for her when she'd had her melt down. Of what he'd done for Alice. 'You raised a good man, Maggie. Be proud of that.'

This time the tears didn't just well, they crept down Maggie's cheeks. 'Bless you, love, but he raised himself. I'm the one who's proud.' She wiped her face, then patted Sam's hand. 'Now, enough of the past. Why don't you tell me about this company of yours? I can't believe a young thing like you owns her own company. You must be so smart.'

Smart to set up a company, perhaps. Not so smart in her choice of partner. 'I just got lucky. The company is called Privacy Solutions ...'

Chapter 32

Ryan fretted as he sat down opposite Erin in the hospital café, placing one hot chocolate and one dubious-looking coffee in front of them. God knows what his mum was saying to Sam. He tried to tell himself she knew the worst of it. Knew about his dad, about his mum and the booze. Still, there was stuff no man would want a woman he was trying to impress to know.

'Chill.' Erin rolled her eyes at him. 'Mum's not going to say any stuff that'll put her off you. She's trying to matchmake.'

'That's what I'm afraid of.' He took a sip of the coffee and winced. How the hell could they make it taste that bad?

'I thought you fancied the pants off your boss?'

'Fine. I do.' He rubbed a hand down his face. 'Can we drop the subject now?' He'd had enough of people dissecting his love life.

'She likes you.' Erin paused. 'I mean, like, really likes you.'

'That's a lot of likes.' Her foot kicked him under the table. 'Ouch.'

'I'm trying to tell you Sam has a thing for you.'

'Sure she does. What can I say? I'm a good-looking guy.'

Erin groaned. 'I'm serious. I think you could have a shot with her, if you want.'

Hope trickled through him as he realised he and Erin were actually talking. 'And you know this how?'

'Because she chewed me out this morning while you were making breakfast.'

He jerked upright. 'She *what*?'

'You heard. She asked why I was being so mean to you.'

He swallowed down his emotion. Keep it light. Keep her talking. 'What did you say?'

'I told her she already knew, because she'd overheard what I'd said to you. How I resented you buggering off and leaving me to take care of Mum.' Erin sighed, pushing away her drink. 'Then she pointed out you'd had to take care of Mum *and* me. She said I should ask myself why you left to get a job. Why you didn't go to uni.' Her hazel eyes sought out his, and this time they weren't snapping at him in anger or freezing him out. They were troubled but warm. 'It wasn't a choice, was it?'

He didn't want to get into this. Not to the extent that she'd level her blame at their mum instead. 'Sure it was a choice. I could probably have found a job locally.'

She huffed. 'Yeah, eventually, by which time we'd have been kicked out of the house.' When he stared at her, she shrugged. 'I'm not completely stupid. I knew we had no money. I was just so upset at you leaving me.' She blinked then, looking away from him. 'Crap. Now you've bloody made me cry.'

She looked so indignant, glaring at him in between wiping her eyes, that Ryan couldn't help himself. He started to laugh. 'I didn't make you, shortarse. You did that by yourself.'

She reached for a napkin, scrunched it up and threw it at him. 'Piss off.'

'I don't think so. I'm having way too much fun watching you.' Sobering, he grabbed her hand across the table. 'I'm sorry me leaving meant you had to go in temporary care. Really bloody sorry.'

She sighed, her hand gripping his. 'And I'm sorry for being a bitch all these years and blaming you for it.' She gave him a small smile. 'I needed to be angry at someone, and you were the one who left.'

'Fair enough.'

'No. It wasn't fair. I've said some really shitty things to you.' She groaned, tugging her hand away. 'Like yesterday. All that stuff about you having no qualifications and having to sleep with Sam 'cos there was no other way you'd get on.' She covered her face with her hands.

'Forget it. We're looking forward, not back.' Please God, this was the start not just of him and Erin talking, but of his mum sorting herself out. Of them being a family again. Draining the last of his awful coffee, he focused back on Erin. 'Right, shortarse, let's get back to Mum.'

'I'm not short any more.'

'You are compared to me.'

She huffed as she stood up. 'So I'm always gonna have that dumb nickname?'

'Yep.'

Falling in step beside him, she sighed dramatically. 'Suppose I can put up with it.'

He saw the smile she couldn't hide and it sent joy barrelling through him. He was going to get his sister back. Thanks to Sam.

That tight feeling returned to his chest. She'd not just been there for him last night and today, she'd gone beyond. Even risking gossip at work. Was Erin right? Did he really have a chance with Sam? Something beyond this secret affair she'd convinced herself was a good idea.

Only time would tell. One thing for certain though, if there was a snowball's chance in hell for them, he was going to give her that time.

Sam walked out to the car park with a reluctant Ryan.

'Stop dragging your feet.'

'I'm not.' He turned back, eyes scanning up the hospital building to the floor his mum's ward was on.

'She'll be fine.' Sam touched his arm, bringing him back to face her. 'You know I'm happy for you to stay here, right? It's your mum who's kicked you out.'

He scratched at the dark one-day-old stubble on his chin. God, this guy was sexy. Really, stop and stare, made your heart pound, sexy. 'It doesn't feel right, leaving her in there.'

'I know.' She took his hand. 'But she's not on her own. Your sister is with her. And the doctor said she'll be good to go home tomorrow.' He nodded and carried on walking with her towards the car, but Sam knew he felt bad, which was enough to trigger her own guilt. 'Look, maybe you should stay. I mean, what can she do? Make you sit on the naughty step?'

Finally, he cracked a smile. 'Been there a time or two.' He glanced her way, his expression conflicted. 'If I stay, your beta version gets put back another day.'

'I can live with that.' Whether her investor could, was another matter, but she could hardly dump that on him.

'You shouldn't have to.' He straightened his shoulders, picked up the pace. 'I'm not going to be responsible for you losing your company. Mum's good.' He gave her a searing look. 'Erin's finally talking to me again, too, so I can trust her to let me know if they need me.'

Sam felt a ripple of relief roll through her. 'That's great.'

'It is.' His eyes remained on hers, dark, compelling. 'Erin told me what you said to her. Thank you.'

Once again she felt the pull of him. More than an attraction, more than heat, she felt it where it mattered, in her heart. 'I only pointed out things that deep down she already knew.'

He nodded. 'And Mum? What's she been saying?'

Oh boy. He definitely wouldn't be happy about her knowing some of that. 'Just that your dad was, in her words, a lying, cheating scumbag.'

They reached the car and Ryan paused. 'Can't argue with that. I was only a kid, but some of the stuff he said to her.' He placed his hands on the car roof, leaning against it, his movements taut and restless. 'I knew it wasn't right, the lies he told. The way he got into her head.' He looked bleakly at her. 'I hate that I have his DNA.'

'You share his hair colour, his eyes. Probably his build, looking at your mum.' Her eyes pressed his, willing him to believe her. 'Your heart, your strength, your decency. It all comes from your mum.'

'Yeah, right.' His tone told her he wasn't convinced. 'What else did she say?'

'She asked about the company, about how I founded it—'

'About me, Sam,' he cut in roughly. 'What did she tell you?'

He hated lies more than anything, and now she could understand why. So she looked him in the eye and told him the truth, even though she knew it would mean a tense car journey. 'She said you were bullied at school, because you had to look after her.' His eyes remained fixed on hers, demanding she told him everything. 'She figured that's why you spent most of your time in your room, on your computer.'

'Goddamn it.' He pushed away from the car, stalking a few paces before turning abruptly. 'She shouldn't have said anything. I didn't want you to know this stuff.'

'Why not?'

'You know why.' His nostrils flared and he looked away. 'This will affect how you see me.'

Confused she touched his arm. 'What do you mean?'

The muscle in his jaw clenched. 'You'll see me as weak.'

She wanted to laugh at how preposterous the notion was. As if anyone could see this big, tough guy as weak. But having had her own self-confidence battered by Damien, she knew all too well that the face you showed the world wasn't always what you saw when you looked in the mirror. So she took his hands and stared him straight in the eyes. 'I could never see a boy who took care of his family, and a man who left home to work at eighteen to continue to do that, as anything other than what they are. Steady and strong,' she told him quietly.

His shoulders rose and fell as he sighed, leaning forward to rest his forehead against hers in a connection she felt pulse all the way to her heart. Then he finally looked up, eyes tracking the keys in her hand. 'Do you trust me with your fancy car?'

Taken by surprise at the change in conversation, Sam replied without thinking. 'Of course.'

He prised the keys out of her hand and walked round to the driver's side, grinning over to her. 'How's that trust level now?'

Before she could say anything, he'd opened the door and slipped into the driver's seat. She had no option but to climb in beside him. 'This feels like kidnapping.'

He laughed, which was a million times better than the tight expression he'd worn a few moments ago. 'Or it's me driving you back so you can kip in the car.'

It was typical of the man that he hid his kindness in a defiant gesture. 'I like that version better.' She waved at the dashboard. 'Are you sure you can cope with all this modern technology?'

'I spend my days working with technology. I think I can cope.' As he started the engine, his gaze rested on her. 'Thank you, for, you know.' He let out a frustrated huff. 'For the kind words.'

'True words.' The look he gave her was so full of emotion, as if he couldn't believe what he was hearing, she had to avert her gaze before she blurted out words like *it's why I'm falling in love with you*. Easing the seat back, she shut her eyes. 'Wake me up when we get there.'

'Yes, boss.'

She opened an eye at that and found him giving her an amused smile. One that settled over her like a caress. Her heart feeling full, she nodded off to sleep.

Sam spent the rest of the day on the phone, in meetings, or on her computer. In between fending off Becky and Lucas. At first, they'd pounced on her individually:

Becky: *I can't believe you drove him there. That is not the action of a woman who only likes him.*

Lucas: *Darling, Becky told me what happened. Are you now moonlighting as a chauffeur service?*

Many hours later, they both pushed their way into her office to tell her to go home. And proceeded to prise more information out of her.

'You met his mum?' Becky looked startled. 'Was she as scary as I imagine? Did she have fangs?'

Sam burst out laughing. 'She was lovely, actually. Warm, funny. I liked her.'

'Aren't you doing this backwards?' Lucas drawled. 'Shouldn't you meet the mother *after* you start dating him?'

Her heart thumped. She knew how Ryan felt. Lying, especially to people who were close to you, really sucked. She wasn't sure how long she could carry this on. 'Very funny. I was just glad I was around to help. Now get out of here.'

'What about you? Are you heading home now?' Becky smirked. 'Or are you going to check on Ryan first?'

Her friends weren't stupid. They knew something was going on. But Sam felt too vulnerable to open up to them just yet. Her feelings for Ryan too new. There was still the chance it could explode in her face, and she wasn't emotionally ready to cope with the fallout. But she would be, she promised herself. Perhaps once the app was launched she'd feel more like the confident woman she'd once been. More ready to take another risk.

Ignoring Becky's question, she waved to the door. 'Out.'

After giving it another half an hour, Sam checked her reflection, tucked a few wayward strands of hair back into place and walked towards Ryan's workstation. There he was, eyes fixed on the screen, shoulders hunched forward. 'Occupational health would go nuts to see you working like that.'

His eyes remained on the screen. 'Maybe, if you employed an occupational health team.'

'I'm responsible for your health and safety.'

He glanced up at that, a small smile hovering on his lips. 'You're offering to give me a back rub?'

Instantly her hands itched to touch those big, muscled shoulders. 'Maybe.'

The smile grew wider. 'I've got to finish this first, or the boss will never forgive me.'

She wriggled her fingers. 'When you do, I think you'll find

the boss in a very grateful mood.' Pleasure gave his dark eyes a warm glow. Bending closer to him, she whispered. 'Come over as soon as you're done.'

Then she walked back towards her desk. Making sure to wriggle her hips.

PART SEVEN

The Conclusion

Chapter 33

Ryan closed the door gently behind him. It was the fifth night in a row he'd snuck out of Sam's apartment at dawn.

Which meant it was also the fifth night in a row he'd followed her home after work.

They were practically living together.

Of course there was little of the stuff that proper couples living together encountered. They were both working so hard they barely had time to grab a takeaway before falling into bed. Weekends didn't exist.

Work, sleep, work, pretty much summed it up. It might not sound like much of a life, yet he was the happiest he'd ever been. His mum was out of hospital, off the booze for now, and doing well. His sister was talking to him again, *and* he got to spend every night in the arms of the most frigging amazing woman he'd ever met.

If only the actual work wasn't proving to be a monumental pain in the butt.

He worked steadily at his desk all morning, poring through the endless lines of code. The beta version was finished, but bugs remained that needed to be sorted out. Bugs that were making his brain spin.

He jumped when he felt a tap on the shoulder and turned to find Sam smiling down at him. 'Have you forgotten the team meeting?'

He glanced at the time on his screen. Three hours he'd been going at this, and no further forward. 'Course not.' With a sigh he leant back and stretched out his back.

'You need to stop hunching over.'

'So you said.' His eyes lingered on hers, and he felt the kick of his heart. 'Sleep well?'

She scanned around before leaning toward him, her breasts pressing into his back. 'You know I did.' All too soon she'd stepped back. 'Now shift your arse into the meeting room. We're all waiting for you.'

She strode on ahead of him, those hips swaying in a way that was both sassy and classy. He groaned inwardly. Sassy and classy? What was he, a frigging poet now?

They all stared at him when he walked into the meeting room. 'What?'

Lucas smirked. 'Don't get your panties in a twist. We're just gratified the great Ryan Black finally decided to turn up.'

'Now wait a—'

'Enough.' Sam's quietly controlled voice cut him off mid-bluster. 'The next few weeks are crunch time. We're all going to be stretched beyond what's comfortable, so we all need to look out for each other.' Her gaze bounced from Lucas to him. 'Which means playing nice.'

'I'm always nice.' Lucas sat back in his chair, running a

hand through his blond locks, looking like a poster boy for Ralph Lauren.

Before Ryan could respond to that, Sam was talking again. 'You all know the beta version is out for user testing. Within the next two weeks we need to have the results back, make the modifications and finalise the app so it's ready for the quality check.' As a wave of *you've got to be bloody kidding* raced around the room, Sam put up her hand. 'I know it's not fair of me to ask, I know it's too little time, but my analysis shows if we leave it any later, there's a good chance we'll lose so much market share we won't be viable any more.'

Ryan instantly felt the change of atmosphere in the room. The collective shift from *bloody hell*, to *no problem, boss, we've got this*. Such was Sam's authority, her magnetic pull. 'I can get the results from the public beta testing back by tomorrow.' Becky started the ball rolling. Soon everyone was pitching in, committing themselves to absurdly tight deadlines.

'Ryan?'

Sam's eyes swung to him. Clear, huge. The colour of the ocean he saw in all those travel adverts. Eyes it was impossible to say no to. He knew there was a major bug he still couldn't solve, knew he was already so strung out from sixteen-hour working days that the likelihood of solving it was shrinking rather than improving. 'Sure.'

She smiled, warm, trusting, and his heart swelled. 'Great, thank you, everyone. Your commitment to this project, to the company, is humbling.' She cleared her throat, and Ryan could see the emotion on her face. 'Before we go, one final item. Employee of the month.' As her hand grasped the plaque, her gaze sought out Alice. 'I'm delighted to announce that this month, our award goes to' – her eyes swung in his direction – 'Ryan.'

He sat bolt upright. 'Pardon?'

Sam's mouth twitched as she glanced down at the sheet of paper in front of her. 'Ryan was nominated for this award for his support of a colleague that went beyond what was reasonably expected. In fact, what the colleague actually said was "Ryan really looked out for me. He saw things even my friends had missed."'

As Sam stood and placed the plaque in front him, his eyes strayed unconsciously to Alice. She stared back, her expression full of such gratitude, he felt a boulder-sized lump jump into his throat. 'I ...' He had to work hard to squeeze even that word out. 'Thanks.' It was all he could manage, but Alice's shy smile told him it was enough.

The meeting came to a close and everyone gathered their things and started to walk out. Becky paused as she walked by him. 'Seems I was wrong.'

'Not like you. Are you sure?'

She shoved at him. 'I'm trying to be serious here. A few months back I remember saying self-nomination was the only way you'd get the award.'

He was still too embarrassingly overcome by it all. The last thing he needed was Becky being kind to him. 'Maybe you weren't wrong. Maybe I'm more cunning than you think.'

She laughed, giving him another hefty push. 'You're not

cunning, Black.' She paused, her expression sobering. 'But you are sort of, kind of, surprisingly, nice.' Just as he feared his emotions would overwhelm him, she ruined the moment, thank God, by winking and adding, 'Sometimes.'

Sam frowned as she listened to what Kerry was saying over the phone. 'Right, thanks.' Remembering what happened at the last visit, how Ryan had accused him of spying, Sam added. 'Would you do me a favour and escort Damien to my office?'

She sighed as she put down the phone. What the flipping heck was her ex doing, darkening her door yet again?

Hastily she cleared her desk and made sure there was nothing of interest on her computer screen.

A few moments later, Kerry tapped on her door. 'Are you ready for him?'

'As I'll ever be.'

The Damien who walked into her office was different to the one she was used to. This Damien stepped inside hesitantly, his manner no longer that of the ex-owner but of an uninvited visitor. 'Is now a good time?'

She laughed incredulously. 'You're seriously going to ask me that, when you know very well you're stealing market share from me left, right and centre?'

He stilled, his expression pained. 'I'm not, actually.'

'That's not what my sales information tells me.'

'May I?' He nodded towards the spare chair.

She wanted to make him stand. To make him feel uncomfortable. To pay him back for the way he'd treated her in whatever nasty, small-minded, vindictive way she could. But he'd already damaged her confidence. He wasn't going to damage her decency, too. 'Of course.'

He crossed one elegantly tailored leg over the other. 'I wanted to tell you in person, before you heard it elsewhere. I sold my share of Privacy Protect.'

Sam gaped. 'Why?'

Damien glanced away, the muscle in his jaw working overtime. When he turned back, all trace of arrogance, of aloofness, had gone from his face. He looked like the boy she'd fallen for that first year at university. 'I couldn't bear the thought of being in competition with you any longer.' He leant forward, clasping his hands together, his face earnest. 'We were meant to work together, you and I. It's what we do. You're the brains, I'm the tech brawn. We inspire each other, motivate, encourage.' He shook his head. 'Without you, it doesn't work.'

'You seem to be doing just fine.'

'Sure, we're taking market share away from you, but it left a bad taste in my mouth. The app was your idea, I just copied it. The modifications were your idea, too. I got lucky, getting your new-join to blab about what you were doing.'

Sam had stored up so much anger against him, it was hard to see through it. 'You're telling me that was *luck*?'

He had the grace to look embarrassed. 'Okay, not entirely luck, but I didn't browbeat her, if that's what you mean. I just asked the right questions.'

Was he tricking her, like he'd tricked Alice? 'This is quite a turnaround.' She didn't try to hide her scepticism. 'A few months ago, you waltzed in here gloating about what you were about to do to me.'

Shame filled his eyes and he hung his head. 'I know. I wouldn't trust me, either. I was such a bastard to you. But' – he jerked his gaze up again – 'and it's not an excuse, just an explanation. You don't know how difficult it was, living and working with someone smarter than I was.' He swore, climbing to his feet and starting to pace. 'Sorry, that sounds like a real pity party. I was the luckiest bastard that ever lived, being able to go home with you every night. I know that now, but for an awful few weeks, when you were basically running the show and I felt more like the forgotten underling than the partner, I lost sight of it.' He let out a short, bitter laugh. 'My ego was snared by a woman who treated me like I was a god.'

Sam's mind was reeling. There was so much she hadn't realised, yet did it justify his affair? Or his treatment of her afterwards? And what did it say about her chances of anything more serious with Ryan, who would surely at some point feel exactly as Damien had?

'I know I hurt you by having the affair, and that I compounded that hurt by setting up a rival company.' Damien's words continued to wash over her as she fought to focus on what he was saying and not on the dread now churning her stomach. 'I felt bitter that you wouldn't give me another chance. We'd been together for eight years and it was one lapse in judgement. At least that's how I saw it. So I harnessed the anger – it was better than feeling like the bastard who'd cheated on the woman he loved – and fought back. I wanted to prove I could do it without you.' His eyes filled with remorse. 'But now the anger has faded, and I realise all I'm doing is continuing to hurt the woman I still love.'

He *still* loved? Shocked to her core, Sam played for time, taking a sip from her now cold coffee. Finally she glanced up at him. 'I don't know what you expect me to say.'

He gave her a faint smile. 'It's a lot to take in, I know. I just wanted to tell you I'm not your rival any more. I'm your ... friend. If you need any help, anything at all, then shout.' Leaning over the desk, he kissed her cheek. 'I want the business we started together to succeed. I want *you* to succeed.'

Her brain too muddled to come up with a reply, she simply nodded, her gaze wandering over his shoulder.

When she caught sight of who was staring at them through the glass door, her heart plummeted.

Damien stood and followed her gaze, nodding stiffly at Ryan as he opened the door to let him in. Sam held her breath, waiting for Ryan to make some sarky remark about following Damien out to ensure he didn't pinch anything, but he remained tightlipped and stony-faced.

It was only when they'd watched Damien walk round the corner, that Ryan spoke. 'I'd ask if he was bothering you, but you didn't look bothered.'

'I wasn't.'

He inclined his head in one tight, sharp movement, then turned and began to walk out.

'Hey, wait.' He stopped but didn't turn around. 'What did you come to my office for?'

'Nothing important.'

When he took another step forward, she hissed in frustration. 'Stop acting like a jerk.' She rose to her feet, causing him to finally turn and face her. 'Damien came to let me know he's pulled out of Privacy Protect.'

Surprise shot across Ryan's stubborn features, quickly followed by understanding. 'Don't tell me, he's sorry he cheated on you, sorry he set up a rival company to ruin you. He realises what a dumb shit he's been and now he wants you back.'

It was so accurate, Sam could only nod.

Ryan cursed crudely.

'It doesn't mean I believe him.'

'Of course. What sane woman would?'

'And I'm not just sane, I'm smart, remember?' *Except where you're concerned.* His expression eased slightly, and she squeezed his arm. 'Come on, Ryan, forget him. Tell me what you came to say.'

He sighed heavily, shoving his hands into his jeans pockets. 'I still haven't fixed the screen freezes. It happens too randomly; I can't find the cause.'

If you want any help ... Damien's words bounced back at her. It would be like pouring petrol on a slow-burning fire, but time was running out. 'Damien offered to help, if we needed it.'

Ryan reared backwards, as if she'd smacked him hard around the face. 'Tell him he can piss off. I don't need his blasted help.'

With that he stalked away, all burning anger and bruised male pride.

Nobody was more surprised than her when Ryan appeared at her apartment later that evening.

'I wasn't expecting you,' she told him as she opened the door.

He huffed, eyes darting away from hers. 'You can tell me to go.'

How little he knew the hold he had over her. She opened the door wider and he took one step inside, then stopped. 'I don't want to talk about it, okay?' She must have looked confused because he added. 'You and Damien. Whatever's going on. I don't want to know.'

Did it mean he didn't care? Or that he cared too much? Taking a chance that it was the latter, she reached up to kiss him. 'Fine,' she whispered against his lips. 'We won't talk about the fact that nothing is going on between me and Damien.'

He groaned, his whole body shuddering as he wrapped his arms around her. 'I'm knackered.'

She smiled against his chest. 'Me too.'

'Wanna go straight to bed?'

Laughing, she peered up at him. 'I bet you say that to all the girls.'

He smiled, but there was a weariness to it, a sadness that tugged at her. 'There's no other girls, Sunshine Sam. Only you.'

Chapter 34

Sam shifted to snuggle into Ryan's chest, limbs heavy in the way that only a blissful orgasm can achieve. They'd been doing this for ten days now. Working late, coming back to hers. Usually he stayed at the office an hour or two later than she did, leaving her to rattle around in her flat, feeling restless, guilty and frustrated with him. He was battling to make sure all the changes from the user testing were implemented, sure, but that wasn't what was forcing him to work later and later, arriving on her doorstep increasingly more shattered.

The bug was still in the programme, and he was too stubborn, and too proud, to ask for help.

'Ryan?'

'Yeah?' He sounded half asleep, the soothing strokes of his hand up and down her back becoming slower and slower.

'Have you made any more progress on the random screen freezes?'

The hand stilled, and his body tensed. 'No. But I will.'

'I know.' She inched up so she could look at him. 'But will you find it in time?'

When he turned his gaze away from her, eyes staring at the ceiling, her heart sank. If even he wasn't convinced he'd do it, there really was only one solution. 'You know we have to get this sorted, don't you?'

'I know,' he replied heavily.

'Should I ask Damien if he can come over tomorrow?' Ryan sat up abruptly, almost pushing her off him in his haste to get out of the bed. With quick, jerky movements he dragged on his jeans. 'Where are you going?'

'Just ... out.' His abs rippled as he reached up to tug on his T-shirt on. Finally he looked at her, face haggard, dark eyes glittering. 'I need some air.'

As he strode out of the bedroom, Sam flopped back on the bed, annoyed, yet at the same time hurting for him. His ego was bruised, she could see that, but what was she supposed to do? Let the company fail because he was too proud to admit he needed help?

It was half an hour later when he buzzed on the doorbell. Slipping on a robe, she went to answer it. 'Feel any better?'

He sighed, resting his arm against the door frame. 'No?'

She pulled him inside, leading him back to the bedroom. There she pushed him onto the bed and leant over him. 'Now listen to me. Asking Damien to help us doesn't mean you've failed. This version of the app is light years better than the original. Thanks to you.'

'The changes were your idea.'

Sam held his face, making him look into her eyes. 'You made them a reality.'

He hesitated, his dark eyes holding a hint of worry now,

along with the frustration. 'Are you sure you can trust him? He's betrayed you before.'

'I know.' Damien had lied to her face, gone behind her back to cheat on her both professionally, via Alice, and personally. 'Honestly, I can't say for certain. My judgement isn't what it was. All I know is he has sold his shares; I saw the press clippings. And you'll be watching him every step of the way.'

Ryan closed his eyes, his chest rising and falling as he heaved out a sigh. 'I frigging hate feeling like this.'

'Like what?'

Slowly he opened his eyes again. 'Like I failed you.'

Oh, man. Her heart crumpled painfully in her chest. 'God, Ryan, you haven't failed me. You haven't *failed* at all. If we had longer, you'd fix it, but we don't, so we need a fresh pair of eyes on the job. That's all.'

He nodded, but she sensed it was just to shut her up.

'Are you staying the night?'

'Are you chucking me out?'

'You know I'm not.' Shifting off him, she climbed into bed and pulled back the duvet. 'Now get in here and go to sleep. You're shattered, and tomorrow is another long day.'

She watched as he pulled off his jeans and T-shirt, his movements weary. He felt like this because of her, because he wanted to help. Once he'd climbed in beside her, she reached for him, kissing him softly. 'One more thing.' He eyed her warily and she smiled. 'Why don't you bring a change of clothes with you tomorrow so we can have breakfast and get ready together in the morning, like a normal couple.'

'Normal couple,' he repeated. 'Is that what we are?'

She couldn't read his expression. Was he questioning it because they were dating in secret? Or because as well as dating her, he worked for her? And why did either of those things matter, if what they felt for each other was real? 'I'd like to think we are, yes.'

Though she didn't expect a reply, it still hurt when he didn't say anything. Yet when he curled his big body around her, hugging her as if he never wanted to let her go, she wondered if maybe he had replied, in his own way.

Ryan knew he had to put up with Damien sitting at his desk, rifling through his code, but he was damned if he was going to let the bastard poke his nose around all the workings of the new app. So he spent the first hour before Damien's arrival making sure the guy only had access to snapshots of Privacy 2.

The realisation caused Damien's first frown of the morning. In reply, Ryan raised an eyebrow – his version of an *up yours, dickhead*.

Their working relationship didn't get any better, though Ryan had to concede, most of the angst was on his side. It wasn't just that he felt a failure, the pretender to the crown, left to watch uselessly as the real genius sorted out his mess. No, sitting next to Damien caused every one of his insecurities to rear up and laugh sarcastically down at him. This guy was better looking – if you liked smooth, with an unbroken nose. Better dressed – although, come on, what muppet wears a tailored suit to sort out a programming error? Better qualified – that cut deep. Not as deep as the knowledge that the man was far more Sam's type than he'd ever be.

Yet he'd cheated on her, something Ryan knew he'd never do. Not in a million years.

'You want a drink?'

Damien looked startled by the admittedly abrupt question. 'Thanks. I'll take a white coffee. Number three on the machine, if I remember correctly.'

Yeah, Ryan knew exactly what that little remark was all about. Damien's snide reminder this had once been his stomping ground.

Ryan muttered to himself as he shoved the cup under the machine and jammed his finger on the buttons.

'Ouch.' Lucas appeared at his side. 'What has that poor machine done to upset you?'

'Nothing. Yet.' Ryan slid the cup out and put the next one in more carefully, making a conscious effort to unclench his muscles.

'Then it must be our visitor that has you all tense and quivery.'

'*Quivery*?'

'Sure.' Lucas was totally unfazed by the glare Ryan was giving him. 'You're trembling like a newborn lamb.'

'For Christ's sake. Do not compare me to a frigging lamb.' He yanked the other cup out, slopping half the contents in the drip tray. 'Sod it.' Lucas tutted and slowly removed the cup from his fingers before dumping the contents into the nearby sink. 'Hey, that's my drink.'

'Watch the master.' Lucas proceeded to gently press the

button, then carefully remove the full mug, placing it next to the other one on the worktop. 'Now, tell Lucas why you're letting Douchebag Damien get you all riled up.'

'Douchebag Damien, huh?' Ryan allowed himself a small smile. 'I've been using Dickhead Damien, but I can work with Douchebag.'

'It's what Sam and Becky called him. I just jumped on the bandwagon.' Lucas peered over at him. 'Now answer the question.'

'How would you feel if Sam got another designer in to do your job because you couldn't.'

'You're angry at *her*?'

'No. Of course not. It has to be fixed, and I ...' Shit, it rankled to say this. 'I was getting nowhere.'

Luke studied him, and Ryan knew he was seeing far more than he should. 'This is more than you being pissed you've had to get help. You're jealous. You think Sam still likes him.'

'I think you can butt out and go psychoanalyse someone your own size.'

'I think you're falling in love with her.'

Ryan lurched back, stumbling as he tried to steady himself. Seems he wasn't just crap at keeping secrets. He was crap at keeping his feelings to himself. Avoiding Lucas's eyes, he stepped towards the cups. 'I'm not that dumb.'

'Why would it be dumb? She's immensely loveable.'

'Yeah, she is.' The best way to lie, so they said, was to stick to the truth as much as possible. 'She doesn't see me like that though.' Sure, Sam liked him enough to let him almost move in with her. But not enough to let anyone know about it. Not enough to date in public like a real couple. And yes, like a *normal* couple, because no matter how she tried to convince herself last night, she had to know they weren't that. Not while she was too wary, too untrusting, too unsure and, hell, probably too ashamed to tell her friends about him.

Before Lucas could fire any further incendiary statements at him, Ryan snatched at the cups and hotfooted it back to his desk

Rounding the corner towards his workstation, he halted when he saw Damien wasn't alone.

Sam was leaning over him, eyes on the screen, her breasts way too close to Damien's back. Douchebag's back, he reminded himself.

But did Sam still think of him as that? The guy had sold his share in the rival company, no doubt also told her he loved her and wanted her back. Had definitely come running as soon as she'd asked him to. Was he more Dynamic Damien now? Delicious Damien. Maybe even Damn-he's-wonderful Damien.

Ryan's stomach knotted and he had to force himself to keep walking. Keep breathing.

He clattered the mug on the desk, making them both jump. 'Find anything yet?'

And yes, it wasn't lost on him that while he'd been demoted to drink bearer, Damien was sitting in his chair, at his desk, saving the day.

'Not so far.' Damien turned to smile at Sam. 'But I'll get there, don't worry. Never come across a bug I couldn't shake out.'

Ryan opened his mouth – phrases like *fuck you, you arrogant prick* bouncing around his head. But then he caught Sam looking at him, those big blue eyes pleading with him not to say anything, and he clamped it shut again.

It was going to be one hell of a long day.

Five hours later, Damien clenched his fist and jumped up from the chair. 'Found it.'

'Yeah?' Ryan tried to act cool. As if this man hadn't just achieved in a day what he'd spent a month trying, and failing, to do.

Ryan shifted into the vacated chair – his blasted chair – and restarted the app. He wasn't going to believe the bastard until he saw it with his own eyes.

'You check everything's working to your satisfaction.' Damien's smile could only be called smug. 'I'll go and tell Sam the good news.'

And joy of joys, the moment Ryan discovered the random screen freezing really had gone was also the moment he chose to look across into Sam's office.

His heart shrivelled as he watched her face light up, and her arms wind themselves around Damien's neck.

It was nine o'clock, and Sam had been home for over an hour. When she'd left the office, Ryan had still been at his desk. He'd looked so absorbed in what he was doing she'd decided not to disturb him, figuring he was giving the app the final go-through before they sent it to be checked by the QA vendor. He couldn't still be there, could he? Not being the type to sit around and wait for things to happen, she picked up her phone and dialled his number.

He answered on the second ring. 'Hi, Sunshine.'

Automatically her mouth curved upwards at the nickname. 'Hi yourself. Are you still at the office?'

He hesitated before replying. 'No.'

'On your way here?'

Another hesitation, longer this time. 'Not exactly. I'm at my place.'

'Oh.' Hurt and disappointment crashed through her in equal measures. 'I thought you were coming over. And bringing some clothes with you?'

She heard him let out a sharp breath. Imagined him rubbing at the back of his neck. 'I wasn't sure it was a good idea tonight.'

'Again, why?'

'You know why.'

'You're going to have to spell it out.'

More breathing, heavier this time. When his words finally came, it was as if they'd been wrenched from him. 'Look, I wasn't sure if he'd be there, okay?'

'Who'd be here?' As if she didn't know. 'Lucas? My dad?'

'Damien,' he hissed.

And now she was starting to get angry. 'You think I'm the type of woman to sleep with more than one guy at a time?'

'No, of course not, but ...' He swore under his breath. 'Look, you think we're a normal couple, but normal couples don't skulk around in secret. I come to yours every night and you don't kick me out, so I guess you don't mind, but ... I didn't want to assume.' He paused and all she could hear was the sound of his agitated breathing. 'I wasn't sure you'd want me there after today.'

The vulnerability in his voice slayed her. He was so confident when it came to sex, yet so unsure when it came to his value beyond that.

And her insistence on keeping their relationship quiet wasn't helping him understand it.

She opened her mouth to tell him of course she wanted to see him, but before the words were out her door buzzer sounded.

Something he clearly noticed. 'You've got a visitor, so I'll hang up and see you tomorrow. Sweet dreams, Sunshine Sam.'

Frustrated, she went to answer the buzzer.

'Sam, it's me, Damien. Can I come up?' When she hesitated, he added. 'I'll be quick.'

Typical. Ryan hadn't come over because he'd feared Damien would be here. Damien had turned up, blithely assuming she was alone.

She used the few moments it took Damien to climb the three flights of stairs to collect herself. She might be annoyed he'd turned up at her home, but today he'd gone out of his way to help her. 'Come in.'

She led him through to the sitting room and indicated for him to sit down. 'Before you start, there's something I need to get straight. Today, in my office, when I hugged you—'

'It was a thank-you hug,' Damien gave her a sad smile. 'I know that.'

'Good. I was relieved, and grateful. I still am. But it doesn't wipe out what went before. The betrayal I felt.'

He winced, leaning back against the sofa. 'I realise that, though if I'm honest, I still have hope that one day you'll forgive me.' He held up his hand. 'Please, you don't have to say anything. In fact, I'd rather you didn't, because then I can live in blissful ignorance.'

Time to move the conversation on. 'What did you want to see me about?'

He shifted, looking awkward, which was rare for him. 'I know you don't trust me yet, but working with you today, you have no idea what that meant to me. How much I enjoyed it.' His eyes zeroed in on hers. 'I want to work with you again.' Once again, he put up his hand. 'I know it can't be like before, and I accept that. I ruined what we had and that's a shame I'll always have to live with. Just do me a favour and don't immediately dismiss the idea. I'd happily work for you, rather than with you.' Her face must have betrayed her shock, because he smiled. 'I know, the idea came as a surprise to me, too. But my time with Privacy Protect has shown me I'm not a businessman. You were the business brains. I was only the tech guy. But I was one hell of a tech guy. It's not too late for us to give it another shot, professionally. Just think what we could achieve together.'

While she was reeling from his words, he rose to his feet. 'I've taken up enough of your evening. Please think on what I've said. I don't need a quick decision.' He gave her a wry smile. 'After the success of today I thought I'd try my hand at consulting for a while.'

When he'd left, Sam closed the door behind him and leant against it, her mind spinning. How had they gone from bitter rivals to him offering to work for her, in the space of a few months?

Then again, they'd gone from lovers to enemies in a day, so perhaps this was normal for a couple who shared as much history as they did. It was certainly better having him on her side than against her, but it didn't mean she was interested in resurrecting the past.

It hadn't been Damien she'd wanted to see tonight.

And it wasn't Damien she thought of as she climbed into bed.

Chapter 35

The following evening, Ryan scanned his eyes across the dimly lit bar, the place packed with hippy young Londoners out for a good time.

He felt old, and it wasn't just the crippling exhaustion from the last few weeks. He'd never been these people. His idea of a good time in his early twenties had been a quiet drink in the local pub.

It still was.

The thought of paying a small mortgage for the privilege of drinking a daft-coloured drink while wedged in a loud crowd didn't sit well with him.

'Hey, Black, drink up.' Lucas had to shout to be heard over the music. 'You're letting the side down. Bad enough you're on lager. Don't embarrass us further by sipping it like a grandma.'

Figuring it was easier to do as he was told than argue above the din, Ryan sighed, grabbed the half-filled glass and drank it down.

'About flaming time.' Lucas put his hands on Ryan's shoulders and turned him towards the exit. 'Right, team, off to the next bar.'

'Thank God.'

Lucas raised an eyebrow. 'This one not to your liking?'

'Can the next place be less ...' He fished around for the right term.

'Trendy?' Lucas supplied. 'Cool? Wicked?'

'Loud? Expensive? Crowded?'

Lucas sighed dramatically. 'How old are you? Fifty?' He flung his arm around Ryan's shoulders and herded him out of the bar. 'Come on, grouch, tonight we're letting our hair down. The app passed its quality checks and is ready to go live on Monday, the launch plans are in place. For once we have a Friday night, followed by a weekend, a whole two days, when we don't have to be in the office.'

It was something to celebrate, all right. If only it hadn't needed *Damien's* help to get to this stage. Automatically his eyes fell on Sam, who was in the group ahead of him, her arms linked with Becky on one side and Kerry on the other. Alice was next to Kerry.

'How come I get to walk with you?' he muttered, causing Lucas to double up with laughter. Clearly the guy was well on his way to being buzzed.

'Poor Ryan. You'd rather be linking arms with the girls, huh?' Lucas waggled his eyebrows. 'Or was it one girl in particular you had your eye on?'

'Leave it.' Ryan knew his reply had been too curt when Lucas frowned and dropped his arm from Ryan's shoulders. He had a right to feel sorry for himself for a bit though, didn't he? He'd gone and fallen in love with a woman who was still, even though she'd never admit it, at least part way in love with her ex. Why else would she be so quick to forgive him? To hug the bastard who'd so cruelly cheated on her?

Maybe it also explained her continued obsession with secrecy. She didn't want their relationship to get back to Damien, because some part of her wanted him back.

Or maybe it was just that she didn't want people knowing she'd lowered her standards from dating the joint owner to dating *him*.

'Are you all right?'

Lucas's voice shook him out of his shitty introspection. 'Yeah, sorry about snapping. I'm just ... beat.'

Lucas eyed him carefully for a moment before calling to the group ahead of them. 'Hey, ladies. How about we have a change of pace and find a pub?'

Following a chorus of agreement, they headed down the next side road and into the Fox and Hounds. Ryan put one foot inside the quiet, slightly scruffy interior, and immediately felt his muscles start to relax, his mind to quieten. Lucas nudged him. 'Better?'

'God help me, I could kiss you right now.'

Lucas grinned. 'If I wasn't looking forward to seeing Jasper later, I'd hold you to that.'

The evening got even better a short while later when Ryan found himself at the end of the table, wedged next to the wall and Sam. 'Bet you're almost gagging to kiss me now, huh?' Lucas whispered in his ear as he placed a long, cool pint in front of him.

It was a measure of his relief, his joy and his general state of punch-drunkness that Ryan briefly considered it.

'So.' Sam looked over at him, and Ryan's eyes immediately focused on her lips. Yeah, that was the mouth he really wanted to kiss. She cleared her throat, and guiltily he forced his eyes up to hers. 'How are you feeling?'

Sick. Terrified. Feelings he couldn't admit to, because then she'd want to know why, and he'd have to tell her he was in love with her. Then she'd have to stop herself from laughing … No, this was Sam, she'd stare at him with compassion, those gorgeous eyes full of pity. And shit, that was worse, way worse. He'd take the laughter any day.

'Ryan?'

He gave himself a mental shake. What the blazes was he doing? If he carried on like this, she'd be dumping his arse sooner rather than later. No way was he going to give her up without a fight. No frigging way. 'Sorry, I'm kind of feeling spaced out. Like I could sleep for days.'

'Me too.' She checked nobody was listening before leaning towards him. 'I missed you last night.'

His heart jumped. 'Missed you, too.' The need to kiss her, to feel those soft lips against his, to stake his claim in front of everyone, was almost overwhelming. Reaching for his glass, he tried to drown the urge in a mouthful of beer before finding out the answer to the question that had haunted him all night. 'Who was the visitor?'

She wouldn't look at him. 'Nobody important.'

'It was him, wasn't it? Dickhead Damien.'

'Douchebag Damien.' She smiled. 'But yours works, too.'

'Does it? Still?' God, he sounded needy.

'Yes.' Her gaze locked onto his. 'How many times do I have to say it? I'm not interested in Damien.'

On one level he thought that was true. It was what she believed. It was just he could see things she couldn't. Still, he forced a smile. 'A dozen more times won't hurt.'

'You said yesterday you weren't sure if I'd wanted to see you last night. Just to be clear, I did. And I want to see you tonight.' Her eyes flickered away for a moment before resting back on his. 'If that's okay with you.'

Ryan gave a low laugh. 'You have to ask?'

'Assumptions work both ways. I can't assume you want what I want, either.'

He didn't, he wanted more, much, much more. Yet if this was all he was going to get, he'd grasp it with both hands and cling on with everything he had. 'If me turning up on your doorstep every night wasn't a big enough hint, let me spell it out. I want you, Sunshine Sam. For as long as I can have you.'

Her answering smile did full justice to her nickname. 'I'm glad we cleared that up.' She nodded to his almost full glass. 'Now drink, before Lucas has another go at you.'

What with the exhaustion and the alcohol he'd already consumed, he was feeling light-headed enough as it was. Still, now he had something to celebrate. So he lifted the glass and sank the pint.

She'd drunk too much, but what the hell. After all the trauma of the last few months – no, wait, the last eighteen-plus months

– she deserved a bit of crazy. Of course, the last time she'd felt this tipsy was the day after Grumps's funeral, when she'd ended up taking a stranger back to her place and having wild, fabulous sex.

She eyed the man standing up at the bar talking to Alice. Hand in his pocket, plain black T-shirt topping a pair of snug-fitting black jeans. Battered brown leather jacket slung over the back of a nearby chair. The same sexy stranger she'd met all those months ago, though now she knew him. Blunt, taciturn, stubborn, solitary. Yet also kind, honest, decent through to his core, and with a wit drier than the desert. A man who loved his mum and his sister – who'd given up his childhood for them. Was still giving up things for them.

A man it had been scarily easy to fall in love with. Whether he was ready to hear that yet, or she to say it, she couldn't be certain.

I want you for as long as I can have you. Her heart gave another little jig as she recalled his words from a few hours ago. Maybe admitting her feelings out loud to him wasn't such a big step, after all. Yet what he felt now and what he might feel further down the road were two different things. Damien had wanted her once. Until he'd become – what had he said? – *a forgotten underling*? Would Ryan feel that way too, once the excitement had worn off?

The sound of giggles brought her out of her trance and she turned to find her supposed friends, Becky and Lucas, laughing at her.

'If you carry on looking at him like that' – Becky followed

the direction of her gaze, eyes landing on Ryan – 'everyone is going to think you two are shagging.'

Lucas shuddered. 'Please, less of the vulgarity. I have sensitive ears.'

'Aw, I'm sorry.' Becky placed her hands over his ears before looking back at her. 'You are shagging, aren't you?'

Sam dropped her gaze. 'Maybe.'

Becky clapped her hands. 'I bloody knew it. Why the big secret?'

'You know why.' Sam took in a deep, shaky breath. 'I didn't want a repeat of Damien. Everyone being privy to my humiliation.' She still didn't, still felt too raw, but she also felt ashamed. Ryan deserved a lot more from her than a clandestine affair.

Becky's gaze softened. 'I guess I can understand.' She reached for Sam's hands, clasping them gently. 'Is it serious?'

'It is on my side.'

Lucas let out a soft exhale. 'Not only on your side.'

Sam flashed him a look. 'He told you about us?'

'No, of course not. But I have eyes.' Lucas took a swig of his rainbow-coloured cocktail. 'You want to know how a man feels, don't listen to what he says. Watch what he does. Ryan was seriously cut up when Damien came in. And it wasn't just his ego that was hurting.'

Sam mulled over Lucas's words. If she went by actions, Ryan had demonstrated how he felt, many times over. The way he'd tried to protect her, the fits of jealousy, the support he'd given when she'd needed it. The faith he'd shown in her.

Yet what had her actions shown him? She'd been there for

him when his mum was taken to hospital, true, but what about her insistence on keeping their relationship secret? What impression had that given?

'I once told him not to hurt you,' Lucas continued. 'I said if he did, I'll throttle him with my bare hands.' At her gentle tutting, Lucas gave her a sheepish smile. 'I can be macho when I want to be. The thing is though' – he paused, clearly considering his words – 'I think the power base has shifted. You have the ability to hurt him.'

'I have no intention of hurting him. I—' She clamped her mouth shut, but it was too late.

'You love him.' Becky finished for her. 'It's not a shock to hear you say that. Damien left you so bruised it had to take something special for you to risk dating again.' She winked. 'Even if it was in secret.'

Sam groaned. 'I feel terrible about that now. Not just for lying to you guys but for treating Ryan like he was something I was ashamed of. I was trying to protect myself.'

Becky nudged her gently in the ribs. 'We know. And I'm sure Ryan does, too.'

In the beginning, she'd thought he understood. But now she wondered if her selfish need for privacy had damaged the chance of anything more serious between them. He wanted her, he'd said, but that wasn't the same as loving her, was it?

She squeezed her eyes shut and took a deep breath before looking at her friends. 'Please, I don't want to talk about this any more. How about we talk about Damien' – she paused, enjoying the look of anticipation on their faces – 'and what he said to me last night?'

Becky's eyes were like saucers. 'Oh my God, he came round?'

Sam smirked. 'Not only that, he offered to work for me.'

Two hours later, she found herself in the back of a cab with Ryan. A rather drunk Ryan.

'I can make my own way back,' he slurred, his head rolling from side to side as the cab weaved its way through the backstreets. 'I'm not totally rat-arsed.' He hiccupped. 'That's the right term for pissed, yeah? 'Cos it's not clear where the rat's arse comes into it.'

God, why did her heart turn to mush when she looked at him? Drunk men were usually loud, boorish and annoying, yet it seemed Ryan turned into a pussycat. A cute, sexy, pussycat.

'I know you can manage, but we're sharing a cab. What's your address?' She asked again.

'Shithole.' He started to laugh. 'I told you, Champagne Lady. I live in a shithole.'

Hearing him call her that brought back a raft of delicious memories. 'What's the address of this shithole?' She pressed. 'The cab driver needs to know.'

Sam relayed Ryan's answer to the cabbie. If it wasn't right, they could always go back to hers. Yet she was curious to see where Ryan lived, and yes, she was taking advantage of his drunk state, knowing full well if he was sober, he'd never agree to it.

The cabbie pulled up outside what looked to be a second-hand electrical shop, though God knows why anyone would want to buy anything from the place. Rundown was putting it politely. She nudged Ryan, who had his eyes closed. 'Is this where you live?'

Ryan peered out of the window. 'Ah, home sweet home.'

After hauling him out of the cab, she put an arm around his waist and helped him round the corner to the side entrance. He fumbled about with the key, sniggering when he failed to get it into the lock. 'I'm usually good at, you know, sliding things into holes.' He leant against the wall, chest heaving as he laughed at his own joke.

'I know you are, Casanova.' Taking the key off him, she opened the door and carefully helped him up the stairs.

'Honey, I'm home.' Ryan sniggered again. 'I say that to the rats. Makes them scarper.'

As Sam walked warily into the small living area, taking in the stained carpet, the unshaded light bulbs, the chipped formica of the small kitchenette, she couldn't be certain he was joking about the rats.

It was tidy though. A throw spread over the sofa, a stack of magazines neatly piled on the coffee table. This morning's washing-up drying by the sink.

'Bedroom?'

He gave her a sloppy smile. 'Thought you'd never ask.' Lurching upright, he started to walk towards the door to the left of the kitchen. Then he swayed, gripping the beige formica worktop. 'Bloody floor. It's moving.'

Wrenching the door open, he staggered into the bedroom and face-planted onto the bed.

Smiling to herself, Sam followed him in. Carefully she

tugged off his shoes, peeled off his jacket. Removed his belt.

He stirred then, giving her a drunken smile. 'I may have lied about the not being totally rat-arsed bit.'

'You think?'

He frowned. 'Hey, don't you worry. It won't affect my perf … perfo …' He trailed off and she thought that was it, he'd gone to sleep. But then he blinked open an eye. 'I can still get it up.'

Laughter shot out of her and she bent to kiss the frown from his face. 'I'm sure you can.'

After a quick trip to the bathroom to wash off her makeup, she stripped to her underwear, yanked at the duvet and slid into bed next to him. He shifted, pulling her back against his chest, sliding his hand over her stomach and under her bra until he found her breast. 'Hmm, you feel good.'

Seconds later, all she heard was the faint sound of his snoring.

Chapter 36

His head was pounding, a thousand jackhammers going off inside. Oh, and did he mention his mouth was as dry as the flaming Sahara?

Blearily Ryan struggled to sit up. Then froze when he realised he wasn't alone. Not that he was ever going to complain about finding Sunshine Sam in bed with him, but not *this* bed. Soft pale skin, silky red hair, she was made for expensive bed linen, for bright modern furnishings, elegant surroundings. No way on God's earth should she be in his grotty flat, in this crappy bed.

His stomach heaved and he lurched to his feet, staggering to the bathroom. After splashing cold water on his face, he gripped the sink, squeezing his eyes shut so he wouldn't have to see the mould on the tiles, the tatty plastic shower curtain.

When he thought his stomach had settled, he fumbled in the medicine cabinet for a couple of painkillers and washed them down with a handful of water. Then he stood under the dribble that was his shower, and prayed he'd feel better afterwards.

He didn't.

He walked slowly back to the bedroom, towel wrapped around his waist, and stood in the doorway, staring down at the woman in his bed and feeling unbalanced. Between Erin's sharp tongue and his mum's blabbering mouth, Sam had seen sides of him he'd rather have kept hidden. His flat was another of those sides. Knowing he lived in a shithole and actually seeing him in it felt different. Just like he hadn't wanted her to picture him as a weak kid being bullied, he hadn't wanted her to picture him living here.

Maybe his ego was more fragile than he thought.

'Ryan?' Sam propped herself up against the hardwood headboard. 'How are you feeling?'

He exhaled roughly, leaning back against the doorframe. 'Crap.'

She smiled. 'I have to say, you look like crap, too.' She waved her hand in his direction. 'All those sexy muscles aside.'

'Thanks.' His gaze skimmed over her messy hair, her makeup-free face. 'You look beautiful.'

Her big eyes widened further and a slight flush stained her cheeks. 'Hangover must be affecting your eyesight. I look like a woman who drank too much last night.' She gave him a sly smile. 'Though I think you beat me on that one.'

He stepped inside and sat on the end of the bed, every part of him, his mind, his heart, aching. 'What are you doing here, Sam?'

She frowned, shifting higher. 'What do you mean? I came back with you last night.' Her eyes clouded and she wrapped her arms around her knees in a gesture that looked horribly defensive. 'Do you want me to go?'

'No, God, no. That's not what I meant at all.' His alcohol-addled brain tried to pick through his messy thoughts. 'Why did you follow me in? Why not just dump my drunken ass on the doorstep like most intelligent women would do?' He glanced round the drab bedroom with its white MDF drawers and peeling floral wallpaper. 'Why stay *here*?'

Her posture relaxed, her face softening. 'Because you're here. And because you promised me drunken sex. I think your exact words, before you passed out, were that you could still get it up.'

He winced. 'Looks like I'm a smooth talker drunk and sober.' He started to shake his head, then hissed as his brain collided with his skull. 'What on earth do you see in me?' And damn, he hadn't meant that to slip out. Clearly having a hangover loosened his tongue.

Her gaze skimmed over his face, seeming to caress wherever it fell. 'It turns out I have a real soft spot for blunt men with magnetic dark eyes who take care of their family and love their mum.'

He wanted to accept the compliment, the reasoning, but it wasn't the whole picture. 'The unsocial git who started to work with you four and a bit months ago. The one you said was unlikeable, who everyone found difficult to work with because he said what he thought even when it upset people. It's still me.'

'I know. Just as I know it's not all you.' Her eyes sought

his, a frown appearing between them. 'What's brought this on?'

I can't work out why a gorgeous, smart, bubbly woman like you is with an antisocial git like me. Words he couldn't say, because they made him sound like an insecure prick and he didn't want to be that man. He wasn't so old-fashioned, or so unsure of himself, that he couldn't handle being with a woman smarter and richer than he was. Yet Sam wasn't really with him, was she? Not while they were still tiptoeing around in secret. 'Forget it. Just the alcohol withdrawal making me melancholic.'

She leant forward, resting her hand against his cheek, and everything inside his chest tightened. 'Have you ever been in a relationship before?'

He swallowed. 'I dated a woman a few years ago.'

'How long for?'

He looked past her, eyes zeroing in on the patch of damp on the wall behind her. 'A few months.'

'Define a few.'

'Three,' he muttered, leaping to his feet, feeling both embarrassed and ... inept, inadequate. Hell, while he was on a roll with words beginning with in-, add inferior, too. 'I guess I'm not what you'd call relationship material.'

'Is that because you don't want one?'

'I didn't say that.'

'What then? Talk to me, Ryan. Please.'

Fool that he was, he glanced over at her, and his heart crumpled at the hurt expression on her face. He was ballsing this conversation up big time, but what did she expect from an emotionally retarded guy with a hangover? Sighing, he moved up the bed to sit next to her. 'Look, I don't have your way with people. I've spent too much of my life being on my own.' And now he was terrified he didn't have what it took to gain the respect, the love, of a woman like her. Groaning, he flopped backwards on the bed with a thud. 'I'm too hungover for all this crap.'

A heartbeat later her smell – some sort of flower – drifted up his nose and her warm body snuggled up against his. 'Don't let whatever happened to you as a kid define how you see yourself now,' she whispered.

He stiffened, hating the reminder of that part of his life. Worse, the reminder that she knew about it.

But then her arms wrapped around him and she pressed a kiss against his neck, sending a giant boulder flying into the back of his throat. And that was before he heard her softly spoken words. 'You're not that boy, Ryan, the weird one nobody likes. You're the guy who does everything he can to protect those he loves. Even if it means staying in, losing his mates. Missing out on university.' She kissed him again. 'Getting his nose broken in a fight.'

'You said it was a good nose,' he rasped through a throat that felt too tight. If he didn't dial down the emotion, he was going to make a total arse of himself.

'It is a good nose.' Her lips feathered it with kisses. 'And you, Ryan Black, are a good man. Don't you dare think differently.'

He let her words settle, swallowing again to loosen his throat. Good was ... hell, it was good. And right now, it was enough. 'I'll tell you something I am good at,' he murmured a moment later, twisting so he could face her.

She gave him that wide, beaming smile. The one that sunbeams shot out from. 'Programming?'

'It does involve pushing the right buttons.'

He captured her laughter in a kiss.

Sam sank back against the lumpy pillow. Ryan certainly did know the right buttons to press. And how to tug on the heartstrings. If she wasn't already in love with him, she'd surely have fallen after his heart-breaking question, *What do you see in me*? He really didn't know how special he was.

Shifting onto her side she turned to face him, only to find him watching her. 'What are you thinking?'

His face split into a grin. 'Mainly X-rated thoughts.'

She rolled her eyes. 'You weren't thinking about making me breakfast?'

His grin faded a little. 'I can do coffee. Cereal, as long as you like cornflakes.'

'And if I don't?'

'Coffee.'

She swung her legs out of the bed. 'Coffee and cornflakes sounds perfect. Do you mind if I grab a shower while you make it?'

His eyes darted away from her. 'Any chance I can persuade you not to?'

'Why would you do that?' And then it dawned on her. 'For God's sake, Ryan. Does the shower work?'

'Yes.'

'Then why wouldn't I use it? I'm not a spoilt princess. A few years ago I was a student, sharing a shower cubicle with five others. Your shower will do me just fine.'

He climbed out of bed, his powerful frame distracting her for a moment as he slipped into snug-fitting boxer briefs.

'You don't belong here,' he muttered as he tugged on a pair of well-worn jeans.

'What do you mean?' She didn't belong with him?

'Look at this place. I'm embarrassed to bring anyone here, but *you*?' He exhaled sharply, chest muscles rippling as he pulled a T-shirt over his head. 'I didn't want you to see it.'

'You think I don't know you live like this because you send most of your salary home? I know what I pay you, Ryan.'

He gave her a wry smile. 'Yeah, I guess you do.'

Frustrated with him, Sam leapt to her feet, wrapping the duvet around her. 'I didn't mean it to sound like that.'

'What, that you pay my salary?'

A rush of hot tears stung her eyes and Sam whirled away from him. Why was he doing this? It was like he was trying to put a wedge between them. Trying to show her how ridiculous she was for thinking they could possibly work as a couple. 'You know what, don't worry about the cornflakes, or the shower. I'll get out of your hair.'

She ignored the loud smack behind her, presumably Ryan slapping his hand against the wall, and bent to put on her clothes. She was fiddling with the clasp on her bra when she felt the heat from his body behind her, a beat before his hands rested on hers. 'Leave it.' Slowly he peeled it back off her and turned her so she was facing him. 'Sorry, I'm being a dick.'

After taking in a deep breath he rested his forehead against hers. 'Stay. Have a shower in the minging bathroom. Eat my soggy cornflakes. Please.'

Swallowing her angst, she nodded. Relationships weren't easy, and the fact she was his boss just added another layer of complexity to theirs. It was something they both had to work through, if it was ever going to lead somewhere.

'Do you fancy doing something this weekend?' she asked ten minutes later as they stood in his kitchen, sipping coffee.

He gave her another wry smile, but this time his dark eyes held a glint of amusement. 'I can't remember the last time I had a weekend off. The boss is a real ball-breaker.'

'Funny.' Yet also scarily true. Since Kew, the demands of the app update had meant they hadn't had a real weekend.

'What did you have in mind?'

Was it normal to feel nervous asking the man she was supposed to be dating out on a date? 'How about a trip to Camden Market? We could have lunch by the lock, wander by the canal. Browse the stalls. Maybe hang on and find a club playing live music.' Heart in her mouth, she searched his face. 'What do you think?'

'I think it sounds like something couples would do.'

There was that word again. She was the one who'd put the rules around their relationship, so it was up to her to make it clear where he stood. 'Isn't that what we are? A couple?'

'I hope so. I want to be.' He heaved out a breath, tugging a hand through his hair. 'But last night, in the pub, I couldn't hold your hand. I couldn't kiss you, like I wanted to.'

Emotion hit the back of her throat and she reached up to trace her fingers across his face, smoothing out the frown lines. 'I'm sorry. If it helps, Lucas and Becky know now.'

His eyes remained level on hers, dark and enigmatic. 'Did you tell them, or did they guess?'

Suddenly her gesture sounded trite. 'A bit of both.' It was time to be brave. Time to forget her need to protect herself and prove how much he meant to her. 'Next time you want to hold my hand, or to kiss me, don't hold back.'

Surprise shot across his face. 'No matter who's around?'

'No matter who's around,' she repeated.

A deep smile curved his mouth, pleasure adding a warmth to his eyes. 'Does that mean I can snog you in the office?'

Oh God. 'Well, it's not strictly professional, but—'

He laughed, capturing her face in his hands. 'Relax. I'll keep the kissing to outside work.' His mouth drifted down to hers, and he nibbled gently at her lips. 'Though I may spend an inappropriate amount of time inside work fantasising about it.' With a deep, happy-sounding sigh, he drew back. 'And the answer to your question is yes. Camden Market, the lock, the wandering, the club.' He flashed a quick grin. 'The browsing we can ditch.'

The day was sunny and warm, perfect for a visit to Camden's canal-side market. Despite his protest about browsing, he seemed to enjoy wandering through the maze of stalls, allowing the hustle and bustle of the place to wash over them. Sam was content to let him set the pace and the destination, happy simply to be with him, his hand holding hers.

They stopped for lunch by the waterside, watching the narrowboats glide serenely by as they ate paninis and sipped at cold lager. With his attention on the canal, she took the opportunity to study his face. Now the tension had gone, so too had the harshness. No longer broodingly attractive, today he was blindingly handsome. A fact the women around them had definitely clocked.

He glanced up and caught her looking at him. 'What?'

'Just enjoying the sight of Ryan Black without a scowl on his face.'

'Ouch.' He stared down at his drink, then sighed. 'Have I been that bad?'

'As you value honesty, I'll have to say yes.'

'Maybe your -smile is catching.'

She rolled her eyes. 'I believe Lucas called me Sunshine Sam because I brought sunshine into your lives.'

His eyes darted away and he shifted on his chair. 'I was the one who nicknamed you Sunshine Sam, not Lucas,' he admitted after a pause. 'Because of your smile.'

Delighted, she leant forward, forcing him to look at her. 'You thought I had a nice smile, even before Cornwall?'

A flush tinged his cheeks. 'I thought you had a smile that lit up your face and touched everyone around you.' He took a long swallow of his drink before putting it down and staring back at her. 'I still do.' While she flapped around for something to say, knowing even if her besotted brain could think of the words, her emotion clogged throat would be unable to voice them, he rose to his feet. 'I'm going to settle the bill before I give away any more embarrassing secrets.'

After Camden Lock they strolled to Buck Street Market, where the stalls were less arts, craft and food, and more your typical market clothes and mass-produced goods. He drew to a stop at a stall selling toys. Puzzled by his interest she left him to it, going to look at the scarves on the neighbouring stall.

'There you are.' He joined her a few moments later, clutching a brown paper bag. 'Thought you'd done a runner.'

'Hardly.' She glanced at the bag. 'What did you get?'

He grinned, a touch bashful, which was a rare, but incredibly appealing, look on him. 'Bought you a present.' He handed the bag over to her. 'This reminded me of you. Of what we were talking about earlier.' Intrigued, she glanced inside. And burst out laughing when she drew out a dancing sunflower. 'It doesn't need watering, or even batteries. It's powered by the sun.' His eyes met hers. 'Just like your smile.'

Her heart feeling full to bursting, she clutched the precious gift to her chest and kissed him. 'Thank you. It's the most perfect flower I've ever received.'

Later, as the light faded and the clubs came to life, they found a jazz bar and listened for a while until she pulled him onto the dance floor.

'I'm a watcher, not a dancer,' he grumbled.

But he went with her anyway, and when his arms slid around her, settling on her lower back, she breathed him in and felt her whole body settle. As if this was where she was meant to be.

Later, back in her apartment, after they'd made love, he kissed her gently, gazed at her with those mesmerising dark eyes and whispered. 'Bloody amazing day, Sunshine Sam. Thank you.'

And she fell even further in love.

Chapter 37

Monday morning came around all too quickly. Ryan felt restless, his nerves pulled so tight he half expected to hear a twang and see them catapult across the office. Eighteen weeks of work all boiled down to this moment. Would the media, the investors, the critics, the public, love the new app? Or hate it?

Sam had decided to use the Privacy Solutions office as the venue for the launch of Privacy 2, arguing they couldn't have investors thinking the company was pissing money away –frittering, she'd actually said – on a fancy hotel.

Nervously he fiddled with his collar. God, he'd be glad when this shindig was over.

As he paced the room, he noted Becky bustling about making sure everything was as it should be. Podium in place, check, big screen behind, check. Vases filled with flowers in shades of Privacy blue, check. Sound man hauled over the coals because the speakers at the back weren't working properly, check, and fixed. Rows of chairs, covered in white and bearing big blue bows at the back, check.

'When's the bride due?' he asked her as she tugged at a drooping bow.

She gave him a sort of exasperated glare, if such a thing existed. 'It's tasteful. We're aiming for the sophistication of a smart venue, in the professional setting of an office.'

He had no clue what she was talking about, but he could see her nerves were as shredded as his, so he nodded. 'I see that.'

She narrowed her eyes, her mouth twitching. 'I'd call bullshit on that, but I desperately need the reassurance, so thanks. Have you seen Lucas yet?'

'Seen, no, not technically. I spoke to him through the door of the cubicle in the gents.'

'Oh God, he always hides in the loos when he's nervous.'

'Said he'd be out when his stomach stopped cramping.' Actually, he'd said more, but Ryan had scarpered the moment the word 'shits' had been mentioned.

'Okay, I'm leaving you in charge of hauling him out when the VIPs start to arrive.'

'No problem.' Greeting the great and good, or camping out in the loos? Easy decision. Aware she was still looking at him, a secretive smile on her face, he frowned back at her. 'What?'

'If you're looking for Sam' – another smile, this time more a knowing smirk – 'she's at the reception desk, trying to rearrange an already perfect flower arrangement.'

'Right.'

Becky started to laugh. 'Oh boy, Ryan Black is now officially blushing.'

He gave her a very unprofessional middle finger. And

headed straight over to the reception desk. He'd missed her last night. After the magic of the weekend, of Camden on Saturday and most of Sunday in her bed, his own company had been a major letdown. She'd needed some space to get her head in the right place for today, though. And while he hadn't needed space from her, he had needed space to come to terms with his growing need to spend every minute of every day with her.

Especially now he was officially allowed to call himself her ... yeah, boyfriend sounded a bit soppy, but he was so proud to call himself that, he'd put the word on his name badge if he could.

As he neared her, she looked up and gave him the full sunshine smile. The only hint that this was one humdinger of a big day for her was the way her hands continued to fiddle with the flowers.

'Are you sure you're qualified to do that?'

Immediately she halted, pushing the arrangement away. 'You're right. The florist did a great job and I'm butchering it.'

'The way I figure it, they're already dead.'

She let out a half-laugh, half-groan. 'You're such a romantic.'

'Just speaking the truth.'

Her eyes swept over him, gently assessing. 'You don't believe in giving flowers?'

'Ah.' He rubbed at his neck, uncomfortably aware he'd never bought anyone fresh flowers, not even his mum. But she liked chocolates, so he'd given her them. And he'd bought pots to put flowers in, hadn't he? 'Always seemed stupid to me, giving dead plants to someone.' His mind flashed to Cornwall, and her admitting Douchebag Damien had sent her roses. Had she *liked* them? Of course she had. Women went for that stuff.

While he was fretting, she was laughing. 'Stop panicking, I agree with you. The nicest flower I've ever been given is a cute plastic sunflower that dances.' Her eyes met his, drowning him in warmth before skimming back over the arrangement in front of her. 'But for today, I think they do just the job.'

She stepped back, nibbling at her bottom lip, hand moving to tuck a stray strand of hair behind her ears.

Out of habit, he scanned around him, checking nobody was looking, before reaching for her hands. 'How are you holding up. Nervous?'

She huffed, her hands closing over his. 'I want to say no. That I'm so confident in the work we've done, in the app itself, that I haven't got room for nerves.' She laughed softly. 'Truthfully though, I'm bricking it.' Her eyes flicked towards the entrance. 'Oh God, they're starting to arrive.'

Reluctantly he let go of her hands. 'This is what you were born to do,' he told her quietly. 'Give 'em hell, Sunshine Sam.'

She gave him a smile so full of gratitude and, yes, of affection, it wrapped right around his heart. 'I plan to.'

Then she lightly touched his cheek before walking away, her bearing full of confidence, her hips swaying just enough to bring a grin to his face.

After watching Sam go, Ryan headed back to the gents where he found Lucas standing by the sink, looking washed-out.

'Good job you wore a green shirt today,' he remarked going to stand next to him.

Lucas made a huffing noise. 'Okay, I'll bite. Why?'

'Matches your face.'

'Sod off, Black. I'm feeling too fragile for your shit today.'

Ryan smirked. 'Had enough of your own to deal with?'

Lucas shuddered. 'You have no idea.' He ducked, splashed his face with cold water, then straightened and put his shoulders back. 'Okay. I'm good. Let's go and wow those punters.'

It was Ryan's turn to shudder, but hell, if Lucas could face them with a dodgy stomach and a green face, he had no excuse not to get out there.

They were walking towards the assembled group when Ryan careered to a halt. 'What's *he* doing here?'

Lucas followed his gaze, looking confused. Then he sighed. 'Ah, Douchebag Damien.'

'Yeah. The guy seems to think he belongs here.'

'Well, from what Sam told us the other night, he is looking for a job.'

Ryan felt the blood drain from his face. The bottom fall from his stomach. 'What?'

He must have looked like he was about to pass out, because Lucas gave him a thump on the back. 'Hey, you pillock, just because he wants one, doesn't mean Sam's going to give him one. She's not a soft touch.'

The words flowed over him. All he could think was she'd loved Damien once. Enough to build a company with him. They had years of history together. Even if she really had fallen out of love with him, even if she hadn't forgiven him yet for what he'd done, she'd do what was best for the company she loved.

'I know she's not soft, she's smart.' And a smart businesswoman would employ the man with the proven track record, even if he was her ex. The man whose genius at finding the bug was the reason she had an app to launch today.

His stomach started to knot, and then the knots formed knots, making him feel sick. Shit, he couldn't think about this. Couldn't think how his dreams of a relationship with Sam, of working and playing with her, felt like they were crumbling to dust. How long would Damien need to work here again, before Sam started to question what she was doing with Ryan? Why employ him, when she had Damien? And why date him, when she had Damien smarming up to her again, flashing his smooth smile, buying her fucking flowers.

She hates flowers. She hates Damien.

Yeah, he just had to keep telling himself that. Shove all these blasted insecurities back in their box.

His poker face was clearly non-existent, because Lucas sighed heavily, shaking his head. 'Whatever crazy stuff is going on in your head, forget it. I'm telling you; Sam isn't going to do anything stupid.'

'I know.' Because stupid would be turning down Damien's offer and sticking with the unqualified software developer. Stupid was thinking a woman like her would ever consider more than a fling with a guy like him.

'Ryan?' Lucas's face was etched with concern.

'Sorry, mate, I'm just going to get some air. Won't be long.'

He knew he was acting weird, knew Lucas wasn't the only

one staring at him as he dashed through the office in the opposite direction to everyone else, but his heart was too heavy, stomach too queasy, emotions too raw. He needed air and space to get his game face on.

Sam's face was aching, she'd smiled so much. And people were still coming in. Her nerves jangled, but alongside that the ever-present buzz of adrenalin kept her moving forward, holding out her hand, greeting the guests.

'What a turnout,' Becky whispered to her as she went past. 'All these people just to see our little app.'

'Our groundbreaking app,' Sam countered, satisfaction bumping against the nerves and excitement. They were giving Privacy 2 the best possible chance to succeed. The interest was here. Now they had to hope the app delivered on everyone's expectations.

A man jostled past her, clearly in a tearing hurry. Sam turned in time to see the back of his broad back and frowned. 'Hey, Becky,' she whispered, at the same time smiling over at Jeremy Whittaker, the sleazy journalist she'd met at the conference. The one Ryan had nearly thumped in his desire to protect her. 'Any idea why Ryan's practically running out of here?'

'What?' Becky followed her gaze, just in time to see Ryan racing down the stairs. 'I saw him a few minutes ago and he was fine. Well, you know, as fine as he can manage.'

'He didn't say anything to you?'

'Asked me when the bride was due, cheeky sod, but other than that, no. I left him in charge of Lucas. He might know.'

She could see Lucas's blond head over the sea of guests, but there wasn't time to quiz him because Kerry was coming towards her, reminding her it was nearly eleven o'clock. Time to get everyone seated. Time to deliver the biggest presentation of her life.

Her heart began to beat erratically, and nerves threatened to take over. She wasn't ready for this.

'Darling, we just came to wish you good luck.'

The sight of her mum and dad nearly had her bursting into tears. 'Oh my God, you're here. Thank you so much for coming.'

'Sam, darling.' Her mother patted her cheeks. 'This isn't you. What's wrong?'

'Nothing. I just wish I'd gone through this a few more times.' Guilt trickled through her. 'I should have spent the weekend rehearsing.'

Her mother smiled. 'What did you do instead?'

'I went to Camden with Ryan. We ate, we drank, we danced.' She couldn't stop a wistful smile creeping over her face. 'It was amazing.'

Her parents both laughed. 'Then you chose the right option.' Her dad put his hands on her shoulders, turning her to face him. 'My darling daughter, there's more to life than work, and the sooner you learn that, the better. You don't want to end up like your old dad, frazzled and heading for a heart attack.'

'Oh, Dad.' She swallowed the lump in her throat. 'I hear you.'

'Speaking of hearing, we want to hear about this new

development with Ryan.' Her mother squeezed her hand. 'But first I think you have a presentation to give. And knowing my daughter, it won't matter whether she's gone through it one or seventy-one times because most of it will come from her heart.'

With those words running through her, Sam walked towards the front, unable to resist a smile as she glanced at the rows of people. Ryan was right, it did look like a flipping wedding. But boy, she loved it; the elegance, the simplicity.

As if just thinking of him, conjured him up, she spotted his tall figure at the back, leaning against the wall, hands in the pockets of his suit trousers.

Her heart bounced, relieved to see him, but try as she might, she couldn't catch his eye. Then the moment was lost, because Kerry was signalling at her. It was time.

'Honoured guests,' she began. 'Privacy Solutions is delighted to welcome you into its home to see a demonstration of our latest innovation.'

Twenty minutes later, Sam was drinking in the applause along with the rest of the team. She'd invited them all up to the front not because she felt she should, but because she knew none of this would have been possible without them.

'Well, boss, I think they like it,' Lucas murmured. 'Then again, what's not to like. It's a cracking design. Oh wait, I designed it.'

'Old Jeremy was bowled over by it. Getting him to be a guinea pig for the demonstration was a genius idea,' Becky cut in. 'Oh, wait, it was my idea.'

They all looked at Ryan, who just shrugged. 'It worked, didn't it?'

While the others laughed, now used to his sense of humour, Sam felt a prick of worry. There was something off with him. Since he'd come back from his dash outside, he'd avoided her eyes and his body language seemed to be saying *get me out of here*.

'Are you okay?' she whispered as they drifted off, ready to mix with the guests.

His eyes finally met hers, bottomless dark eyes that tugged and tugged until she was drowning in their depths. 'Don't you worry about me, Sunshine Sam.' He gave her the smallest of smiles, his eyes skimming her face, as if trying to imprint it to his memory. Then he nodded over to the crowd in front of them, clearly waiting to talk to her. 'You were incredible up there. You should hear what they're saying about the app. About you. This is your moment. Enjoy. You deserve every frigging plaudit.'

As she accepted congratulations after congratulations though, the worry niggled. As glass after glass of champagne was thrust into her hand, it still niggled.

Then she spotted Damien walking towards her, smiling at those who greeted him with the proprietary air of someone who thought he still belonged. Maybe now she knew what was getting to Ryan.

'Damien.' He leant towards her, as if to kiss her, and she deliberately stepped back, stretching out her hand instead. 'Thank you for coming.'

Irritation flashed across his face before he smothered it

with a smile and shook her hand. 'Thank you for the invitation. It's quite some app you've got there, better than the one I launched. Congratulations.'

'Thank you. I wanted to acknowledge the part you played in the development.'

'No problem.' He gave her a smooth smile. 'Fixing the screen freeze was my pleasure.'

She bet it was. Getting one over the guy who'd replaced him – he'd probably dined off the story ever since. 'Actually, I meant the work you put into the mark 1 app. But I also wanted to discuss how I see things moving forward.'

Chapter 38

The party had moved to a swanky hotel. Sam might have scrimped on the launch for the VIPs, but when it came to the employee celebration, she'd pulled out all the stops. As Ryan gazed round the room she'd hired, complete with a private bar and enough balloons to sail an airship, he saw not just his colleagues knocking back the fizz, but their partners, too. *They've given just as much to this company*, Sam had argued when she'd mentioned the idea at the last team meeting. *They're the ones who were keeping the home together while we were working late. They should be part of the celebrations.*

That was Sunshine Sam for you. Always going the extra mile for those she cared for. He glanced around the room again, at the happy faces, and his respect for her, his awe at what she'd achieved, grew. This party wasn't just proof of her vision, her commitment to the company. It was proof of her humanity.

'What if the launch is a flop?' he remembered saying to her. 'Your party will be more like a wake.'

She'd shaken her head, those eyes dancing with amusement as she'd asked. 'Where's your optimism, Black?'

Now, leaning against the bar, surrounded by joy, by laughter, he wished he could find a sliver of that optimism. Instead he felt so paralysed by fear, all he wanted to do was slink away and lick his wounds.

Angry with himself, he swigged back the rest of his pint. If he couldn't shrug this defeatist attitude off, he might as well throw in the towel right now. And no way was he giving in that easily. Sam was worth every drop of fight he had left in him.

First, he needed to clear his head. Pushing away from the bar, he made towards the exit.

Once outside he bent over, hands on his knees, heaving in a breath. Second time he'd done this today. He was turning into a basket case.

'There you are.'

He jolted upright at the sound of Sam's voice. 'Hi,' he managed weakly.

'Hi?' She stepped towards him, pushing into his personal space. 'You run out before our launch party has even properly started, and that's all you can say?'

Christ, *our* launch party. She was priceless. 'Your launch party. Your company, your success, your party.' Wait, that wasn't how he meant it to sound. Frustrated with himself he added. 'I'm not having a dig. I mean it. The presentation you gave today. The way you cajoled, directed, steered the company to this point. You're frigging awesome. You've earnt this.'

'We've earnt this.' Her expression softened as she touched a hand to his face. 'It wouldn't have happened without you.'

He so desperately needed to believe it, but honesty was his thing, and honestly? It was bullshit. 'Any software developer could have done what I did.' Maybe not in the same timeframe, he'd give himself a point for that.

'I wasn't talking about the development side of things.'

'No.' He scratched at his head. 'Well, I didn't do anything else. Unless you count sleeping with the boss.' And yeah, if she thought having a healthy sex life had helped her launch the app, he'd take it.

She growled. Actually growled at him. 'Will you stop calling me your boss? It's not how I see you, and it's not how I want you to see me.' Abruptly she stepped away from him, then whirled round to face him. 'The whole idea for the app updates came from that night in Cornwall, remember?' He did, vividly, but before he could say so she was talking again. 'You dragged me up to the cliffs.'

'Led, not dragged,' he pointed out for the sake of accuracy.

'Fine. You led me to the cliffs, held me, talked to me.' Her voice softened. 'You told me—'

'About my boring Saturday, I know. I mentioned the spam emails.'

Her hands grabbed his. 'That was when the idea formed. I don't think you have any clue how much that moment meant to me personally. Not to the company, but me. How much it lifted my confidence. Two days of brainstorming brought nothing, yet you taking the time to talk to me, to listen to me, and bam. We had it.' He opened his mouth to speak, but she pressed her finger against it. 'We had it, Ryan. Not me. Us.'

Us. The word bounced through his brain, and the crushing feeling returned to his chest.

Wide blue eyes searched his, clearly waiting for him to say something. When he didn't, she sighed and stepped back. 'Are you going to tell me why you're out here? And if it has anything to do with Damien I'm going to box your ears, because you know he means nothing to me.'

'Not now, maybe.' Looks like he'd found his voice. 'But in a year, two years, when you've worked together like you did before?' The crushing pain was back again. He almost couldn't breathe, never mind talk.

'Why would we be working together?' Slowly her frown lifted, the confusion clearing from her eyes. 'Oh my God, Lucas told you about Damien wanting to work for me, didn't he? That's why you've been acting all weird.'

'Sure, he told me.'

'You think I'm going to *hire* Damien?' She raised her eyes skywards. 'Oh, man, it's worse than that, isn't it? You think I'm going to hire him and, what, ask you to go? Then jump back into bed with him?'

He forced himself to shrug. 'Why wouldn't you?'

'*Why wouldn't I*? Of all the stupid, ridiculous statements.' She gave him a shove. 'I told him no, Ryan. I told him I only worked with people I trusted. And as for why—' With a huff of exasperation, she grabbed at the collar of his jacket. 'Because you're better than him. More decent, more honourable. Because your blunt honesty keeps things real. Because, despite all your gruff, you look out for people.' She stared him straight in the eye. 'Because I've fallen in love with you.'

He staggered back, banging his head against the wall, his heart clamouring in his chest. 'You what?'

'You heard me.'

He was going to have a heart attack. Right before he blacked out. *She loved him*? Had he heard her right, or was this just some dumb dream, and any minute now he was going to wake up in his crappy bed? Yet when he opened his eyes, she was there, right in front of him, her soft curves pressing against him, her sweet fragrance drifting up his nostrils. Her beautiful face staring at him with such open love, he had to press a hand to his chest to ease the ache. 'I'm not good with people, I told you,' he muttered. 'I'll drive you crazy.'

'You already do. Yet here I am.'

'Yes.' Slowly the ache disappeared, flooded by warmth, by joy. 'Here you are.'

Sam watched as a sense of wonder settled over Ryan's features. She hadn't planned on blurting out her feelings like that, but she'd been so angry with him for thinking she was stupid enough to hire a guy who hadn't thought twice about betraying her.

Yet now she'd told him she loved him, removed her heart from safety and handed it to him, open and vulnerable, she was terrified. Was he ready to take it from her? Did he *want* to take it? Or would she find him carefully, embarrassedly, giving it her back?

'Christ, Sam.' She froze as he shook his head, her heart plummeting. 'I don't know what the hell I'm doing here.'

She tried to laugh, but it sounded brittle even to her own

ears. 'You think I do? My track record in relationships is hardly stellar, either. One previous guy, who was so into me he went and shagged someone else.'

'Don't.' His hand cupped her cheek, his thumb stroking gently across it, his dark eyes intent on hers. 'Don't let what that git did make you feel less about yourself. You're incredible. He forgot that for a short while and he paid the price. He lost you. Now he wants you back.'

'I don't want him.' Her voice trembled but she couldn't stop it. 'I want you. I love you.'

He shook his head, a slow smile creeping across his face. 'I don't know what I've done to deserve that, to deserve you, but if you can be the woman crazy enough to fall for the bad-tempered computer nerd, I can be the guy stupid enough to fall for the totally-out-of-his-league CEO.' He drew in a shaky breath, his eyes searching hers. 'I love you, too.'

She stared back, her heart bouncing around like a crazy thing, almost too scared to believe him. 'You don't have to say it back if you aren't sure. I'd rather you didn't, in fact, because false hope is the cruellest hope—'

'Since when did I ever say anything I didn't mean?' he interrupted as his mouth found hers. 'I love you.' He repeated the words again and again, interrupting them only to ply her with searing hot kisses.

Yet beneath the pleasure, Damien's words wouldn't stop haunting her. 'But will you still,' she breathed, 'when the shine wears off? Will you still love me when you start to feel like my underling?'

The breath from his laughter fluttered across her face. 'I am your underling. And it's not stopped me so far.' His gaze snagged hers, eyes dark and intense. 'My ego isn't huge. I'm happy to live in your shadow. What I hated was thinking you were ashamed of being with me.'

'Ashamed? God, no.' She felt sick, just thinking about it, thinking how he must have tortured himself. 'The desire for secrecy was never about that. You have to believe me.'

His smile touched his eyes. 'You're out here, snogging me in public. I believe you.' And as if to prove his point, he bent to kiss her again.

It wasn't long before her skin felt too hot, her clothes too tight. With a final rough curse, he eased away, his breathing ragged. 'Any chance you've reserved a room here?'

She barked out a laugh. 'As it happens, yes.'

His eyes lit up. 'Remind me to tell you later how in awe I am of your long-term planning.' As her hormones struggled to settle he tugged on her arm. 'Make that a lot later. After I've shown you how much I love you at least half a dozen times.'

Dimly she became aware of him pulling her back inside. To the hotel. Where ... she ground to a halt. 'We can't. Not yet. The party. Oh shit.' The man was making her lose her mind. 'We have to go back to it.'

He smiled, a full-on sensual smile clearly designed to leave her in a puddle of lust. 'You sure about that?' His lips teased, his hips pressing seductively against her.

Through the fog of arousal she remembered the text she'd received just before she came out. 'Ah, Ryan, we need to stop.'

Breathing heavily, she took a step back. 'Remember where we left off, please God remember, but for now we have a party to get back to.'

He sighed, giving her a rueful smile as he adjusted his trousers. 'It had better be worth it.'

They walked back inside, his hand holding hers, and Sam felt a flutter of nerves. Would it be worth it? Would he be pleased? She thought yes, hoped yes, but his prickly pride made it hard to predict.

Taking a deep breath, she strode through the door he held open for her.

The moment he stepped inside, Ryan lurched to a stop. 'Bloody hell.'

Maggie, looking wonderful in a simple pink dress that added colour to her cheeks, grinned at her son before planting a smacker of a kiss on his cheek. 'Is that any way to greet your mother?'

'And your sister?'

Erin, stunning in a long black dress that highlighted her slender figure, hugged Ryan, winking at Sam over his shoulder.

Ryan's gaze bounced from his mum to his sister to Sam. 'I don't understand.'

'It's quite simple,' Sam replied, her stomach still squirming. 'This party is a celebration for employees and their families.'

'We caught the train down.' Maggie smiled gently at her son. 'A posh black car was waiting to bring us here.'

'You should see our room,' Erin interjected. 'It's sick. Two enormous beds, a shower you can walk right into, with so many shower heads it was like having a stand-up massage.'

'I can't believe you're both here.' Ryan looked dazed, but ... not unhappy? His gaze rested on Sam. 'That you arranged this.'

Was there an unspoken follow up ... *That you paid for this*. Or was she being ridiculously sensitive? 'I can't believe you got this app ready in less than two months, when originally I gave you an impossible deadline of three.' She looked him dead in the eye and repeated words he'd said to her, earlier. 'You deserve this, your mum and Erin deserve this. I'll catch up with you later.'

She was about to move away when his hands reached for her waist. 'Mum, Erin, you might want to look away for a minute.' As she heard his mum laugh, and Erin make gagging noises, Ryan's mouth landed on hers for a long, seductive, bone-melting kiss. 'Thanks,' he said gruffly. 'For thinking of them, bringing them here, for what you said to me outside ... for everything.'

Relief mixed with delight, threatening to bubble over. 'Are you getting mushy on me, Black?'

He let out a bark of laughter. 'Bugger off, boss lady.' But his smile told her he couldn't wait for later. And his eyes, they told her he loved her.

Ryan spent two hours catching up with his mum and sister. He watched with amusement as Erin stuffed her face with the fancy finger food, giggling over everything Lucas said. Turns out teenage girls found him legit hilarious. Go figure. And he watched with pride while his mum drank sparkling water and chatted to everyone who walked by. There was a long road ahead, but so far she'd kept to her hospital promise and stayed off the booze.

Much as he loved having them both here though, he couldn't wait for the party to end.

As if she read his thoughts, Sam caught his eye from the other side of the room and smiled. Full of promise, of love, it settled over him like the softest of blankets. She *knew* him. He hoped she hadn't seen the best of him yet, but she'd certainly seen the worst. Here she was though, willing to trust him with her heart.

He wasn't just going to see her tonight, he was going to see her for days and nights to come. His future was going to have her in it.

How frigging unbelievable was that?

THE END

Acknowledgements

I love writing, but I have loved, loved, loved writing this book. Why? Because the idea was born not from me, sitting in isolation at my desk, but from a discussion with my fabulous editor, Charlotte Ledger. It's the first time I've written a book with such inspiring, enthusiastic input right from the start and when it came down to writing it, I had such a clear vision of the journey Ryan and Sam would take. Thank you so much, Charlotte, and roll on the next book.

I didn't have such a clear vision of the actual app development process. At all. My background is pharmacy, my experience is related to the pharmaceutical industry. For what I knew about app development, even the back of a postage stamp held too much space.

So a big thank you to my 'app guru' Jack Cookson for navigating through the choppy waters of technical fiction and making sure it wasn't too crazy.

As for the idea for the app itself, for that I have to thank the men in my life; my husband Andrew, and my sons, Harry and Ben. It was through discussions around the dinner table that the idea of the Privacy app was born. Eventually. After many wacky and utterly ridiculous ideas were shot down.

I'd also like to thank members of the writing community, the authors and bloggers, who are always so supportive. In the case of this book, a very special thanks to a very special author. Jules Wake, this book would not have happened without you. When my head was down, you brought it back up. Thank you so, so much.

Finally a shout out to friends and family who've helped me not just with *The New Guy* but with every book I've written. To David, Jayne, Anne and Keith, Shelley, Kath, Karley, Kirsty, Charlotte, Sonia, Gill and Jane to name but a few.

And a big thank you kiss to my lovely mum, who won't have a clue what an app is, but who'll read the book anyway, because I wrote it.

Most importantly of all, thank *you* for buying and reading *The New Guy*. I hope you had as much fun reading it as I had writing it.